Crossin

Also available in Indigo

Naked Graffiti
Love is Strange
edited by Richard Glyn Jones

Crossing the Border

Tales of Erotic Ambiguity

Edited by
Lisa Tuttle

INDIGO

First published in Great Britain 1998
as an Indigo paperback original

Indigo is an imprint of the Cassell Group
Wellington House, 125 Strand, London WC2R OBB

© 1998 Lisa Tuttle

The right of Lisa Tuttle to be identified as author
of this work has been asserted by her in accordance with
the Copyright, Designs and Patents Act, 1988.

A catalogue record for this book is
available from the British Library.

ISBN 0 575 40117 6

The acknowledgements on pages 379–382
represent an extension of the copyright page

Photoset by SetSystems Ltd, Saffron Walden, Essex
Printed and bound in Great Britain by
Guernsey Press Co Ltd, Guernsey, Channel Isles

98 99   10 9 8 7 6 5 4 3 2 1

For Colin

Contents

Introduction

Long ago, when Tiresias was a young man, he came upon two large serpents intertwined, and struck them with his staff, killing the female. At that moment he became a woman, and continued to Thebes, where she became a celebrated sacred prostitute. Seven years later, she happened upon two intertwined serpents at the same spot, struck them again, and was changed back into a man. Years later, Tiresias was summoned to settle an argument between Zeus and Hera over which sex received greatest pleasure from the act of love. The reply from the prophet who had been both female and male was that men experienced only one-tenth of the pleasure that women knew. For this reply, Hera struck him blind, but Zeus rewarded him with second sight.

Tiresias featured in other Greek and Roman tales as a wise old prophet, and his wisdom unquestionably came from his unique perspective. He'd crossed the border between the sexes, twice, had lived both as man and woman: naturally, he knew everything that mattered.

INTRODUCTION

In Tim Parks's novel *Europa* the male narrator expresses his wish to be a woman 'for a day or a week' and is well aware that this is not some bizarre kink in his personal psyche, but the reflection of a universal desire, 'a yearning to do and to be and to have everything'.

From the moment we're born (if not before) each one of us is tagged as either male or female. And on those rare occasions where the shape of the visible sex organs means there is some doubt, the baby is never allowed (unlike the royal hermaphrodite in Stella Duffy's *Singling Out the Couples*) to be 'a bouncing baby Both', but is pushed, through surgery or naming, into one camp or the other. Boy or Girl. Pink or Blue. It's a club where membership is for life and decided by anatomy.

Yet throughout history, in most cultures, there have always been individuals who have managed to rebel against their original gender assignment – although only if they have the appearance, skill and luck to 'pass' as a member of the other gender. We haven't yet reached the future some science fiction writers have imagined, in which sex-change operations are easy and painless enough to be indulged in on a temporary basis – 'just to see what it's like' – but even so there are individuals like the modern-day Tiresias who returned to America's *Phil Donahue Show* one day in 1992 to tell an avid audience what it was like to be born female, have an operation to become a man, have another operation to become a woman again, only to return to being a man again. Maybe neither male nor female was exactly the right fit . . . But, as yet, these are the only choices, and, despite author/performer Kate

Bornstein's challenge in *Gender Outlaw* to resist the binary and try to conceive of gender as a whole spectrum of possibilities, most people seem to accept the 'either/or' set-up, and if they chafe against the restrictions of always being only one, fantasy and fiction can offer a temporary escape.

Writers have always been able to explore life from the perspective of 'the other' – and so have readers, and viewers. Even work aimed quite obviously at heterosexual men isn't necessarily experienced, even by the target audience, through a simple identification with the male protagonist.

In *Vice Versa: Bisexuality and the Eroticism of Everyday Life* Marjorie Garber asks, in connection with the myth of Tiresias, if the 'erotic pleasure of bisexuality' is not, in part, 'about *being the other*, whether through explicit role-playing, memory, fantasy, or the erotic effect of transgression?'

There is, I think, an erotic *frisson* in the very fact of sexual ambiguity. It can be both frightening and arousing. Not knowing whether someone is male or female is disturbing to most people. Sometimes the response is rage – the homophobic panic which makes some men respond with violence to any perceived threat to their own heterosexual identity. Yet if they aren't responding to their own, forbidden desire for the effeminate male or the mannish female they're bashing, then what is the threat? The popularity of a film such as *The Crying Game* or a musical like *Miss Saigon*, both of which turn upon the passion felt by a supposedly heterosexual man for another man whom he mistakenly believes to be a woman, as well as the widespread acceptance of cross-dressing entertainers, suggests that a lot of people are attracted to a sexuality which crosses the borders and questions the old-fashioned notion that male and female are opposite and exclusive categories.

Jeanette Winterson's refusal to specify whether the narrator of *Written on the Body* is female or male increases that novel's erotic power. Virginia Woolf's *Orlando* has long been popular for his/her slippery sexuality; Orlando's creator was a married woman who had a passionate affair with another married woman who liked to dress up as a young man she called 'Julian'. Where once all male cross-dressers were assumed to be drag queens, now they can be all-American football players expressing their feminine side. Wearing a dress and make-up has made Eddie Izzard more rather than less attractive to the women in his audiences.

With the arrival of virtual reality and meetings in cyber-space have come new possibilities for sexual role-playing and exploring the meaning of gender. Without any physical, visual clues to give you away, changing identities has never been easier. As Sherry Turkle writes in her fascinating sociological study, *Life on the Screen: Identity in the Age of the Internet*, 'When we step through the screen into virtual communities, we reconstruct our identities on the other side of the looking glass.' Virtual gender-swapping is commonplace. But although it's easy to do – a mere matter of typing in a verbal description can transform an obese, sixty-three-year-old heterosexual male into a slim, athletic, eighteen-year-old lesbian – the results can be extremely complicated, resulting not only in hot, on-screen sex, but in profound psychological changes,

INTRODUCTION

marital breakdowns, shock-horror meetings in real life, and
expensive law-suits.

The impulse behind this anthology was to explore the
eroticism of sexual ambiguity and fantasies of being both, and
also of going beyond the binary into a realm where gender is
not either/or, but fluid and multiple, with shifting borders.
My aim was to gather together stories which would examine
the experience of a modern Tiresias, reconsider androgyny,
play with notions of masquerade and dressing up, with gen-
der-bending and gender-morphing, with sexual ambiguity
both deliberate and unexpected.

Originally I had intended *Crossing the Border* to be a
showcase for brand new stories, with a sprinkling of favourite
reprints, but, inevitably, some of the writers I asked were too
busy with other work, and suggested previously published
work I could use. Perhaps appropriately, *Crossing the Border*
crosses the border between reprint and original anthologies,
being neither entirely original nor entirely reprint, neither
male nor female. The stories themselves range widely, from
the nearly factual ('Enough Rope' and 'James Miranda Barry')
to the virtually real ('Pinkland' and 'The Talent for Virtuality'),
from contemporary Britain ('Nude on the Moon', 'Failing to
Fall', 'The New Girlfriend') and America ('The Sweet Reward',
'Jack', 'What's Normal?') to fantastic futures ('Hyena Winter',
'Omnisexual'), from a Portugal of the mind ('The Secret
Mirror') to ancient Greece ('Hermaphrodite'), through the
looking glass ('Reflections') and into the strangest recesses of
the human mind. Somewhere among all of these dreams and

13

possibilities you may find some echo, shadow or reflection of
your own ambiguous desires.

Lisa Tuttle
Argyll
April 1998

POPPY Z BRITE

Poppy Z Brite was born in 1967 in New Orleans. The publication of her first novel, *Lost Souls*, in 1992 met with both critical and popular acclaim; her disturbing, homoerotic take on vampirism, violence, lust and end-of-the-century decadence struck a chord with the fears and fantasies of many. Her other books include the novels *Drawing Blood* and *Exquisite Corpse*, a short story collection and a biography of Courtney Love. She describes 'Enough Rope' as 'a sort of gender autobiography ... it's not exactly a piece of fiction, but it's not exactly *not*, either, if that makes any sense at all.'

Enough Rope
(with apologies to Mr Rabelais and Mrs Parker)

Snapshot, one hour old: barely out of the womb, I am flatfaced and red, seven pounds six ounces, topped with a great shock of jet-black hair. I am brought in with great fanfare.

My mother says, 'Is she OK?'

My father says, 'You got your girl.'

*

15

Snapshot, 3 years old: I'm sitting at the kitchen table eating vanilla ice-cream. Today or very recently, in some academic fashion, I have learned about the rudimentary design and function of the human penis. I can't stop pondering the image I have of it, pink and round like some strange cheese, leaking big fantasy tadpoles. It attracts me and disturbs me. My ice-cream is melting in the heat of a New Orleans summer afternoon. I imagine sperm swimming in it and push the bowl away half-finished. But after a few minutes, I cautiously start eating again.

For several years of my life, I wanted people to believe I was something that I was obviously, to all appearances, not: a big, butch gay man.

People would hear that and expect me to show up looking like a leather dyke, but that wasn't how it worked. I didn't even try to look male. Since I am barely five feet tall in socks, with a baby-soft complexion and a big wide ass, there never seemed to be much point. I felt male enough that I didn't have to look it.

In 1993 I moved into the heart of the French Quarter, one of the most physically judgmental gay communities on earth, and grew depressed because I couldn't go out at night and fuck greased boy-ass in some back room. I mourned the fact that when I walked down Bourbon Street, no one saw the swaggering leather daddy inside me.

My sexual dysphoria caused me to take stupid risks with my own health – physical and emotional – and that of my lifetime companion, C. The urge to be placed in context nearly killed me. The herd instinct, deeply buried but still present in my rebel heart, caused me to expose and embarrass myself in hopes of finding a peer group that didn't exist. And all for what? To arrive at the 'conclusion' (this is a relative term) that I don't know what the hell I am – gender-wise, preference-wise, any-kind-of-label-wise.

Funny thing is, I've calmed down a lot since I came to that conclusion.

Snapshot, 5 years old: We live in a duplex in New Orleans East, a neighbourhood that will later become a burned-out shooting gallery, but in 1972 is a prefab-gentrified oil-boom suburb. The family on the other side has a little boy just my age named David. The first time I saw him, he was peeing in the driveway and my grandmother yelled at him, but now we play together almost every day. David's father is a big pumped-up guy (I picture him as looking like Marlon Brando in *A Streetcar Named Desire*, though this is probably inaccurate) who often whips his son's bare ass with a leather belt. One day David is about to get a whipping and I follow them to the bedroom and no one stops me.

The yelling, the crying, the snap of leather on skin that must have ensued – all these are hazy. What is crystal clear is the hard little knot of David's cock and balls, hairlessly exposed as he squirmed beneath the cracking leather, and the shock of recognition that ran through me at the sight.

(Recognition? How do you mean, recognition?)

I mean, *I want that.*

(You wanted dick at age five?)

17

I didn't want it *in* me, I wanted it *on* me.

(*On* you???)

Attached to me. You know at the end of that Bongwater song, 'Nick Cave Dolls', where Ann Magnusson whines, 'I *waa-aaa-aant* one'? No? Well, anyway, that's just how I felt.

The most cringe-inducing artifacts of my dysphoria are the interviews I gave on my first trip to London. My British publisher had flown me over to promote a novel, so in addition to being dazzled and distracted, I had a very swollen head.

The journalists, for their part, all wanted to talk about sex. Why had I, a young female of dubious morality but favourable aspect, written a raunchy book full of gay male characters?

'Biologically I am a woman writer,' I blathered happily to the *Independent*, 'but it's never the way I've thought of myself. Ever since I was old enough to know what gay men were, I've considered myself a gay man that happens to have been born in a female body, and that's the perspective I'm coming from.' Not content to leave it there, I twittered on, 'I have no off-limits subjects. You can print anything I say . . . I live with two boyfriends. They are both bisexual and we have a three-way relationship.'

(This was a particularly short-lived and ill-advised phase. One of these 'bisexuals' was my long-suffering companion, C, with whom I am now monogamous. The other was a beautiful, essentially gay Canadian slaveboy whose IQ may have been greater than his penis size, but not by much. My IQ wasn't much higher, at least when Slaveboy and his penis were around: at one point I actually married him so that I would be able to import him more easily.)

I was only too happy to explain it all in London. Over and over. And over. The satirical magazine *Private Eye* later awarded me a spot in 'Pseuds' Corner' for my '5,233,677th assertion that [I was] a gay man in a female body', or something to that effect.

And the thing is, it was all true, or so I genuinely believed. I *was* a fag inside. That fag is still inside me. What's embarrassing is the naiveté with which I believed readers would take my explanations at face value. 'Oh, she's really a gay man! That explains everything!'

I acted out my fantasies by having unsafe sex with an array of beautiful bisexual boys, all much younger than me, lean and pierced and cheerfully voracious. The last person I'd had an affair with was a short, bald, old writer, and *everybody* knew about that one, so I was thrilled to advertise the fact that I was now snagging these sweet young things and tossing them away like Kleenex. I thought I was such a fucking stud.

C stood patiently by, the least self-conscious person in the world, not giving a damn that everyone thought he was a pussy-whipped patsy, just waiting for me to grow up. I'd been drinking three-dollars-a-bottle wine and smashing windows with my shoes when he met me, so he knew I still had a ways to go.

Snapshot, age 7: My parents are newly divorced. My mother actually made the decision to move to North Carolina, and I won't learn the details of my father's infidelities until much later, but my perception at this time is that he deserted us and sent us to live far away. I stay after school with a family whose nasty little boy (another David) teaches me bad words (and sometimes inaccurate ones: for two years I thought 'bogus' was a slang term for penis). None of these seem to phase my mother until one night I ask what 'fuck' means. She tells me in a very serious voice never to say that word again. She explains that it should be a beautiful word but has been turned into an ugly one. It seems to me that she is almost crying. I am engulfed by the deep, uncomprehending embarrassment only a child can know. I never say 'fuck' to my mother on purpose again.

Why did I insist upon being a man? Why not identify myself as a strong, gay-friendly woman and leave it at that?

My only explanation, inadequate as usual, was that I'd just never felt like a woman.

Well, what is 'a woman' supposed to feel like? Didn't this imply that I was stereotyping women, lumping them into an inferior porridge from which I stood apart?

All I could say was that some people appear to identify strongly with their born gender, and I wasn't one of them. I didn't 'enjoy being a girl'. Nor was I a tomboy; I was the kid forging notes to excuse myself from gym class, reading my library book on the sidelines while the other little savages fought over some ridiculous ball. And the first two albums I ever fell in love with – at age three – were the soundtracks from two Broadway shows, *Camelot* and *Man of La Mancha*.

Looking back, it seemed obvious that I'd been a little queen right from the start.

My earliest awareness of homosexuality was a TV farce called *Three's Company*. The male character pretended to be gay so he could shack up with two female roommates, and of course this involved much pursing of lips, flapping of wrists, and mincing around in the girls' lingerie – preferably in front of the landlord, whose face would crumple into an expression of disgust so visceral that it needed no explaining. The message was clear: this was something you didn't want to be.

So why did I watch the show each week, my eyes fixed on John Ritter's parody of camp? My ten-year-old heart was simultaneously stabbed by the show's offhand cruelty and buoyed by the affirmation that an option other than boy-girl did exist. But why did I live ten years without knowing that, and why did it take a piece of trash like *Three's Company* to show me? My parents were not homophobic and never prevented me from reading anything I wanted to, but evidence of homosexuality was absent from my world and I suppose they never thought to mention it – just as they never thought to question whether I was anything other than the girlbaby they'd wanted.

This is not a criticism. Why should they have questioned such an obvious fact?

Snapshot, age 13: Caught by other kids reading a book about gay and lesbian history on the schoolbus. They already know I'm a geek. Now I get to be a gay one. A living, mouth-breathing teenage hell ensues for the next four years. Saying 'I don't consider that an insult' does no good at all; explaining 'I'm not a lesbian, I'm a fag' does even less. It will culminate in my senior year with me cutting my arm and shedding my (presumably AIDS-infected) blood to dissuade a football player from attacking me.

Sixteen years later, I read a critique of my latest novel in which the androgynously named Kim Newman declares my fiction and my sexuality invalid because I didn't suffer while growing up like real gay people did. Fuck you, Kim, I stood up and *asked* for my abuse.

I was completely unprepared for the people who thought my sexuality was some kind of promotional gimmick, but I kidded myself that I was prepared for the ones who, like Ms/ Mr Newman, simply found it annoying, offensive or incomprehensible. I thought I was ready to be called a 'fag hag' with 'penis envy', but I wasn't.

I had no defence against these terms. I could go on all I liked about how I thought of 'fag hags' as women who sought to sleep with and 'convert' gay men and I never did that; I could more accurately call my penile longings anything from 'worship' to 'God-given right' than 'envy'. But nobody much understood the difference, and the more I tried to explain it, the less sure I was that I understood it either.

All I'd really wanted was for my readers, particularly my gay readers, to have a better shot at understanding why I wrote the things I did. With a few exceptions, though, the gay press ignored me. After all, I was a 'horror writer', not a 'gay writer'. Those labels again.

Snapshot, 27 years old: Slaveboy is always begging me to tie his hands and feet, drip hot candle wax on him, stick things up his butt, beat him. Our relationship has deteriorated, and the more he wants this kind of treatment, the more boring it is to give it to him.

One night, though, he's pissing me off about some trivial thing, and instead of running him through the verbal shredder like I usually would, I sling him across the bed, grab a heavy cardboard mailing tube, and give him a good, long, thorough whacking. We fuck and he leaves.

I don't hear from him for days. Finally a mutual friend informs me that Slaveboy is mad because I hit him. Last week he was mad because I *didn't* hit him. I realize that this confused creature is the only person who has ever really believed I am a man.

In 1996, I was asked to write for an anthology called *Dick For A Day*. The premise: what various woman writers, artists, and media mavins would do if they had a . . . well, read the title. My little piece is reprinted here in its entirety. I still think this is the least pretentious and most honest explanation I ever managed of a fundamentally inexplicable matter.

In my dreams, I have a dick. Not in all of them, only in the good ones. Not just for a day, but for always.

The first time I dreamed of having a dick, I was seven. I was standing in the bathroom wearing a pair of big white boxer shorts, and attached to my body was a new organ filled with wonderful sensation. The sensuality of the dream was marred only slightly by the fact that I was Tom Bosley of *Happy Days*.

I've always known I was queer, but saying 'I'm not a lesbian, I'm a gay man in a female body' doesn't help matters a great deal in high school, so I stayed home nights dreaming, and eventually writing, about the torrid sex lives of gay boys. In 1995, Kate Bornstein's book *Gender Outlaw* finally clued me in to the liberating term 'non-operative transsexual'.

A dick for a day? I would spend the day worshipping it, as dick possessers tend to do, and letting it do the thinking, as dicks will. I would give it over to the mouths and hands and assholes of as many tantalizing men as I could get my hands on. I would be the worst nelly slut you ever saw. And, for once in my life, I would mourn the coming of night.

Yes, knowing I was a 'non-operative transsexual' was liberating – for about a month. This happy complacency was shattered by a decidedly *operative* transsexal who hadn't had her surgery yet but was still as much woman as anyone I'd ever met, a big sleek predator, bloody of tooth and claw. She was the kind of person who, given the technology to work with, wouldn't just become a *girl*; she'd become a *lioness*.

Symmetrically enough, we became intimate after I'd rescued

her from the clutches of my short, bald, old ex-lover, who wanted her to breathe life into his flagging career with a collaboration. She was a predator, yes, but only if you were stupid enough to leave her no alternative. He hadn't gotten that stupid yet, though he was working on it.

Warning her away from such potentially painful sleaze made me feel protective. She let me be her champion, even started calling me 'sir'. For the first time in my life, I thought I might get to say, 'Leave my girlfriend alone or I'll kick your ass.' But Mr Ex never bothered her again. And she was so smart and beautiful and exotic . . .

Around this time, strangely enough, my sexual self-perception just sort of imploded. I'd finally figured out what I was, a male, a fag. I was a man on the inside, and I liked men who were men on the outside. I'd gone public with it out of naiveté and a desire to illuminate my work for those who cared. I'd weathered the scorn. I'd jettisoned Slaveboy. Everybody who knew me at all knew I was a slightly misogynistic queen.

Now I had a girlfriend with a dick, and though I loved her dearly, it was all too much. Lesser men, I say in my own defence, might have crumbled long before.

I apologized to my lioness, who handled my confusion with a grace born of long experience. I stopped sleeping with everyone but C, and I renounced all labels.

Of course, the previously uninterested gay press discovered me at once. I'd just managed to have a novel rejected by both my American and English publishers on the grounds of its being 'too extreme, a bloodbath without justification'. (For the record: most of the characters in this novel were HIV-positive, and when I started writing it, I'd never had an AIDS test. I felt utterly incapable of having one until I finished two years later. I was certain that my test would be positive. It wasn't.) When the book was picked up by new publishers, I entered one of my cycles of notoriety.

'You've said you're a gay man trapped in a woman's body,' these new interviewers would begin.

'Not *trapped*,' I'd say, 'I never used the word *trapped*, it was put in my mouth mistakenly.' And maybe this was true, I think it was true; I'd *felt* trapped, sometimes, but I'd never wanted the readers to know how uncomfortable I could be in my own body.

'This whole thing has been so widely misinterpreted,' I'd say.

'I like the word "queer" because it fits those of us who don't fit so easily into the other categories,' I'd say.

'I've decided the Z isn't a middle initial, it's a chromosome,' I'd say.

'I don't know what the hell I am anymore,' I'd say, over and over, until finally there was nothing else left to say.

Roll of snapshots, one month shy of 30: One day recently, just because I wanted to, I cut my hair to about a quarter-inch long. It's grown out some now, but it's still shorter than I've ever had it before. I bought myself a pair of diamond stud earrings the last time I was in Amsterdam, just because I wanted them, and I don't wear much other jewellery any more. Now that I've stopped insisting on being a boy, I probably look more like one than I used to.

C and I take a visiting friend to see one of New Orleans' famous cemeteries. As we cut through the projects, a young man on a streetcorner spies my shorn head and hollers, 'Hey, white boy!' I grin, pure joy, but I no longer kid myself that it could happen in the French Quarter.

Because I want to, and because it's been a lean year, I do photo shoots for two porn magazines. *Rage*, a Larry Flynt venture, has me fingering my pussy in the graveyard. *Blue Blood*, a Gothic sex rag, has me wearing a big black strap-on dildo. In several shots, I am threatening my manhood with one of C's butcher knives.

You can probably guess which of these shoots I prefer.

The phone rings. It's my best girlfriend, the lioness. In the course of our conversation, she asks whether I enjoy the work of another writer. 'He doesn't really yank my crank,' I hear myself saying.

I think it'll always be there, that phantom crank I allude to without thinking twice. I wouldn't wish otherwise. But I don't have to haul it out nearly as much as I used to.

GRAHAM JOYCE

When people meet on the Internet, bodies are immaterial – you are whatever you say you are. And it shouldn't matter what two consenting whatevers get up to in virtual reality, but the hotter a love affair is in virtuality, the more determined the lovers become to translate their passion into flesh. Psyche had the perfect marriage, but her husband would only come to her in the dark. He warned her he would have to leave if she ever saw him, but she went and lit a candle anyway.

Graham Joyce is the author of a number of highly regarded psychological dark fantasies including *Dreamside, Dark Sister, Requiem* and *The Tooth Fairy* (these last three winners of the 1997 August Derleth Award) and most recently *The Stormwatcher*.

Pinkland

The two had been ethereal lovers for almost six months before Nat admitted to Sammy she was a woman. Sammy had to go out of the room just to, well, fan the face, draw breath, squat down and mull over the irony of it. When Sammy got it together to squeeze an inflating skull back into the room Nat was still waiting for some kind of a response. Winking, as it were.

>Still want to meet?< Nat was asking.

Hair on fire, fingers atremble, Sammy typed >Yes, of course I'll meet you. Why wouldn't I?<

A woman! A *woman*! Sammy knew some of the dangers involved in conducting a relationship on the Net. Truthfulness was the first casualty in any sustained campaign. You meet someone in a chat room, establish a few details and move breezily on to other things. Nat (Natalie? Nathaniel?) had simply typed in abbreviated style: *male, 31, single* in answer to early questions. One always predicts, suspects and occasionally encourages dissembling along the way – hell, thought Sammy, that's what modern communication is all about isn't it? – but after six months of spinning out a serious electronic mating game Sammy felt comfortable in the knowledge of who and what was vibrating the other end of the line.

Wrongo! Double-double wrongo!

What the hell had Nat been playing at? All that wasted time webflirting and chatting about music, yeh check it out; and films, catch this, catch that; and what's your favourite drink, say daiquiri to conjure enigma. But Nat had made Sammy laugh out loud when he – drat, she – had said *pre-coital cocoa*. This was all long before their first nervous, faltering Internet kiss.

According to Nat, Sammy was a natural. A linguist.

>A cunning linguist you be< Nat typed.

>Slippery slidey tongue< Sammy tapped back. >Moist, hot, furry, slidey, slightly saline, semen-bearing . . .<

>Stop stop stop!< Nat replied that first time, >You're making me hot, and I haven't been hot in . . .< The cursor faltered, winking. >. . . in ages<

And then the new ages, endless hours logged on, constructing their own Website home together, dubbed Pinkland; carefully choosing the decor, *nouveau* naturally, Nat; filling it with favourite books, nothing post-modern, also Nat; installing works of art, anything abstract, Sammy. Building a life together, all while Sammy squirmed, typed, and double-entendrered towards getting Nat naked, before finally abandoning broad hints altogether:

>Nude. Naked. Stripped. Buff. In the skin. Peeled. Flensed to the pink<

Which, after all was what an Internet relationship was all about. Flesh. It became conditional upon creating Pinkland that clothes should be discarded at the virtual door, consigned to a decorously described heap. Sammy, at least, was always faithfully nude at the keyboard.

Then without preamble one day Nat produced the silver handcuffs.

>See how they wink in the indigo light? Slip your hands behind your back, darling. That's good. Don't you love that icy breath of cold, cold steel, the intimate clink and click of chain and catch? Now, don't squeal. I'm going to fuck you savagely from behind<

And Nat had done exactly that. In retrospect, and now that Nat had confessed to being a woman, Sammy failed to see what pleasure that afforded, and felt abused by the fact that Nat couldn't do it in *restricted* time. (Sammy and Nat never referred to *real* time. Was not time on the Net real? Was not their relationship between real people? Not as if, they both agreed, the Net was a dream or anything.)

But now Sammy had agreed to meet Nat to confront her at the Orbit Café in South Kensington. Sammy wanted to gloat, to study minutely Nat's response. Natalie, you see, having made her own confession, still thought Sammy was a man.

Sammy certainly didn't go along to denounce her or anything. They had lied to each other, that was all it amounted to. No one had any right to be furious. Or aggrieved. Or to feel cheated. Or anything.

Favouring a feminine, clinging satin skirt and wearing a nimbus of flowery perfume, Sammy deliberately arrived half an hour early, taking up position. It was a dead-hour zone. The place glowed with amber light and the smoky loneliness of mid-afternoon. A few couples leaned together and two single men sat alone, one at the bar and one at a shadowy table. Sammy was already having second thoughts.

Supposedly a drinker of Brandy Alexanders, Sammy hadn't got a clue what they tasted like, didn't drink alcohol as a rule, and so ordered a cola. Three quarters of an hour later Nat still hadn't showed up. Sammy began to nurse suspicions about the two single men. Maybe Nat had lied, was a man after all, had got there in advance, to get the drop.

Sammy took a deep breath and approached the man at the bar. >Are you drinking daiquiri?<

>What does it look like?<

Sammy wouldn't know a daiquiri if it squirted from a nipple, but it was exactly the evasive answer Nat might give.

>Looks like you got here before me< Sammy gave the lips a polish with an extraordinarily versatile tongue, knowing that drove Nat wild.

>Wanna fuck?<

Only Nat would be so upfront. Sammy knew it was him. >Can I finish my drink first?< It was important in this game to appear *cool*. Something Nat and Sammy had fallen into from the beginning, out-cooling each other, but like the sugar-frost cool of the rim of a cocktail glass. Sammy said nothing concerning Nat's lie about being a woman, and Nat said nothing about the sudden discovery that Sammy was, in truth, a woman. Weird but exciting. Neither alluded to the fact that they'd known each other for six months on the Net. They were playing the *strangers* game: you crack, you lose.

Drinks finished, Nat took Sammy back to a shabby one-room bedsit. Nothing like the penthouse suite overlooking the Thames he'd often described when they set up Pinkland. Sammy was about to protest before being bundled, quite roughly, against the wall.

Sammy took a deep breath of him, a gulp, almost a lick. He smelled good, earthy, natural. No resistance was offered as Nat pushed up Sammy's vest, slaking himself on the small, boyish breasts. Sammy's nipples hardened instantly at the lashing of his tongue. Soft noises of encouragement seemed to make him rabid with excitement. He pulled up Sammy's skirt, exposing a smooth midriff and the fur purse. Whenever they'd had Internet sex Sammy had never worn underwear but Nat seemed slightly surprised this time. Sammy felt his fingers probing, slithering inside, deep, up to the third knuckle. Then Nat crumpled to his knees, pushing his tongue where his fingers had been, swaying slightly as if made dizzy by the brimstone-and-honey odour of sex.

Because the air was seeded, streaming, drenched with genital perfume. They had irresponsible and delirious unprotected sex, though Sammy complained when, losing control and with fingers tangled in sweat-matted hair, Nat inadvertently pushed Sammy's head against the wall as he ejaculated. >Easy, Nat< Sammy said. >Easy<

He flickered as he recovered his breath. As soon as he was able to speak, he said >Who the fuck is Nat?<

Sammy hurried back to the Orbit Café. It was beginning to fill up, but by now there wasn't a single person, male or female, sitting alone. There was nothing to do but hang around for a while, feeling naive, humiliated, and furious with Nat.

Next time they were online together, Sammy gave him (or her, since now it wasn't possible to trust a single word Nat said) hell. >You could at least have left a message, to say you weren't coming<

>I'm sorry. Something came up. I couldn't make it.<

>You put me at risk!<

>Why? What happened?<

>Nothing happened. Forget it<

>Are you sure nothing happened?<

>I said forget it<

>I promise I'll be there next time<

>Next time? There isn't going to be a next time. Listen, Nat, after what happened to me I'm never going to trust you again. Final<

But that was all talk. Sammy didn't want it to end. What Nat got from the relationship was a mystery; but Sammy got insight, Sammy got experience, and most of all Sammy got *language*, the exotic kind that squished on the tongue like choux pastry or stung like liquorice.

Nat was endlessly critical of the shortcomings of the English language. >I don't know how we're expected to be erotic with these shoddy goods. I mean how erotic can a language be when there's no word for the most tender and erogenous part of the leg? Or for the natural genital perfume of a clean woman? I don't know why I bother<

But bother Nat did, and Sammy learned that the Germans had a word, *kniekehle*, for that fold at the back of the knee, the erotic cleft to which Nat referred; and the French too were unafraid, in nominating the *cassolette* he so delighted in. And it was when Nat started talking dirty, foreign dirty, angelic dirty, that Sammy knew they were about to have Internet sex.

What Sammy truly appreciated was Nat's sensitivity, a knowledge of when tenderness was required and when rough handling might be in order. Sammy was mightily impressed by this verbal dexterity, and Nat's hoochy-coo was like a sexy English lesson, demonstrating a virtuoso's ability to switch smoothly, despite his complaints about the language's short-comings, between the polysyllabic caresses of the Romance-root and the good old-fashioned hard-thrust Anglo-Saxon.

Nat was the perfect Internet lover. One hand on the keyboard, the other dipped at the thigh, it never took long for Sammy to come. Oddly, it was always the keyboard fingers Sammy sniffed for residual fuck after the event.

For Sammy, the imagined scent of Nat lingered there for hours. There was none of this so-called post-coital *tristesse* after Internet sex. Just the longing. And a back-brain howling, like the wind moaning through circuits girdling the planet.

So of course Sammy agreed to meet Nat again, though flatly refusing to return to the Orbit Café, certain that the rough lover was there even at that moment, laughing, regaling the waiters and customers, making a bonfire of the needs of the naive and the desperate.

Nat, of course, had indeed been joking around, and was a man after all. They met in a hotel lobby this time. Sammy, to get revenge, declared manhood. Nat was easy to identify because he kept approaching other men.

It was a laugh to see him hitting on passing strangers. >Are you Sammy?<

>No. Nope. Noedy. No sir. And no sireeee<

Sammy's smirk was a mile wide. Nat just wasn't looking for a woman.

Finally Sammy tipped the wink. Trying to stay cool, Nat merely levitated an eyebrow. After six months on the Net, the joke was on him. Sammy enfolded long, slender arms about him, inhaling the scent of him.

>You smell good,< Sammy said. >Just like I knew you would<

>How do I smell?<

>Sugar almonds; lychees; the wet earth. In fact you smell just like the taste of your come< (It was what the rough lover from the Orbit Café had said: his words exactly.)

>Very poetic. Want to go to a room somewhere?<

>No. I want to do it right here< It was true. That's what Sammy wanted, still slightly sore from that recent experience, but aching for excess and still fixed on exacting some revenge. Making his zip rasp and hooking his trousers down around his ankles, in one deft move Sammy had a hand inside Nat's boxer shorts. Not until Sammy's mouth was clamped around Nat's fattening cock did either of them notice the conversation in the lobby around them had gone completely dead.

>Can't we go to a room?< Nat wailed.

>Why bother?<

>I can't do this< Nat said.

>Just relax<

>It's too weird. I'm going< And logged off. Leaving Sammy's knees indenting the virtual carpet, as it were, sucking on air and mouthing noises to a lobby full of blasé onlookers, quite accustomed to acts of public sex. Realizing Nat had withdrawn, Sammy hurriedly logged off too, and shut down the computer.

It was days before Sammy spoke to Nat again, having twice now been left in embarrassing and faintly ridiculous situations. Trust was at an ebb. Sammy sat contemplating Pinkland, reviewing all of the books and the music and the artwork built up there, thinking about destroying it all with a key-stroke, when Nat appeared in an Instant-Message Box.

>I've had it with you< typed Sammy.

>Why? You in Pinkland?<

>Yes. You don't take this relationship seriously<

>I'll call it up. How can you say that? We've been together for over six months now. We've got a good thing going haven't we?< Then he typed >g<, which in Net communication means grin, and that absolutely *sickened* Sammy.

>You don't turn up when we arrange to meet. You log off when we're in the middle of something. Why don't we just forget it?<

>Sometimes, Sammy, I think you take things too seriously. It's only a game<

>IT'S NOT A FUCKING GAME!< Typing this in capitals, even though it was considered bad form to shout on the Internet. Sammy *wanted* to shout. To scream. Instead, Sammy started deleting music they'd carefully downloaded to their room in Pinkland. The Pet Shop Boys. Deleted. Tom Jones. Deleted. The Monkees. Deleted.

>What are you doing?<

>What does it look like? I'm ending it. If it's all just a fucking game I can't win then I'm hooking over the chessboard<

It was their first real Internet fight. Then, after a while, Nat started cooing, and finally he said *kniekehle*, and incredibly he got Sammy to agree to do it all over again; though Sammy did exact a promise that The Monkees would stay deleted. After all it was Sammy's favourite Internet sex game, keeping Nat guessing over the current gender. Many times they'd agreed to meet up outside the safety and exclusivity of the Instant Message or the private Chat Room, on some pre-selected Internet site where other Net users of any stripe were at large, and to behave as though they were meeting for the very first time.

The point of this game was to preserve the excitement of novelty. Although they'd known each other on the Web for six months, they could still surprise each other this way. They could, and often did pretend to be someone of the opposite sex. Both of them.

Deep down, Sammy suspected Nat of being a woman.

Sammy had tried, over the last couple of weeks, to look for deep clues. Little mistakes, insensitivities, gaps in knowledge, things a woman should know, things a man shouldn't. But the Net allowed for such a range of improvisation that one's persona could easily become subsumed by the alter-ego. There was always, and in everyone, a shadow just aching to come out and play, to don the leather trousers or the frilly frock, to taste the whip, to pop the amyl, bind the chord, lick the cream, crush the fruit, sting the skin and to stretch the neck right up to the hissing wind of mortality's scythe.

Sammy's preference was for coming on as a man, set upon by a small crowd of rampant women, stripped and molested and then re-clothed in somewhat tarty women's gear before they began a systematic programme of mild abuse, leaving Sammy aching, and sore, and spent.

Even on the Net this fantasy was difficult to deliver.

But then Nat shocked Sammy. >I'm not talking about meeting on the Net anymore<

>Anytime, anyplace< Sammy said, pretending not to have grasped the significance of what Nat now proposed. A meeting in *real* real life. Beyond cyberspace was another country.

>Stop it!< Nat said sharply. >Stop making out you don't know what I'm talking about. Things have come to a head, as you knew they would. That's what all this pouting and complaining is all about. If you want this to be a real relationship – and I mean a corporeal, physical, off-line thing, a caring relationship where yes means yes and no means no, where people have flu and sour breath in the mornings and where we have to endure each other's black moods and we do all that 'cos we genuinely love each other – then we have to meet. Engage. We have to press flesh, Sammy. Press flesh<

Love? thought Sammy. Who said anything about love? This was getting weird. There was a hierarchy of steps to be taken before making the thing corporeal. A file transfer here and there; a telephone call; an exchange of the kind of mail which requires a postman to come whistling up the path; a trading of photographs; gifts even. Love wasn't something you just downloaded.

But Nat hadn't finished. >Just be clear I'm not talking about faking it all over again and again and again. I've been thinking about this for a while. I don't know what happens to you when we go offline, but me, I'm left alone, trying to guess whether it really is just a game. Totally alone. Longing for you. And if you've felt me retreating lately, that's why. So there it is<

Long pause while Sammy's cursor blinked, waiting for a response >Can't we keep things as they are? We've got a good thing going haven't we?< Sammy typed those words fully aware of how weakly they echoed Nat's earlier remarks. Even in typescript it was possible to make words curve, wail. >Can't we just stay in Pinkland? Aren't you happy here?<

>Do whatever you want with Pinkland. But on your own. If we don't meet, we don't no more greet. That's it. That's what it means to me<

Nat would brook no argument, and since they both lived in London there were no practical constraints. He proposed that they flesh-rendezvous the following Saturday in a bar just off Soho which he said was quiet, where he sometimes went alone. He said he'd be there whether Sammy showed or not. >Now I'm logging off. The choice is yours. Forever Sammy<

>But how will I find this place?<

>Got a tongue in your head haven't you? Lingual aren't you?< A sneer in the words made Sammy afraid.

>Wait, wait, how will I know you?<

>You'll know me<

>I don't even know if you're a man or a woman!<

Pause. >You'll know me<

Sammy agonized about going. They'd played this game too many times on the Net, with dire consequences, for it to be merely intriguing.

The journey in on the tube was awful. Sammy's pulse rate rose and fell with the approach and departure of the underground trains. On the Internet it was always possible to touch a button and scuttle away. Real life has no keypad. Throat dry, hands trembling, Sammy kept asking what was to be gained from doing this. But the answer was the same every time. Sammy didn't want to lose Nat. The thought of life without him was worse than the thought of meeting him.

Not only was Nat Sammy's demon lover, Nat was number one best friend. Nat was the only person who could make Sammy fall from a stool laughing, whenever at the keyboard. Sammy had never met anyone half so witty or funny. Presented with a problem, Nat always had something for Sammy. When Sammy's dad died just five weeks into the relationship, and Mother was useless and remote, Nat was the one who brought Sammy through it, weeping at the keyboard sometimes; and Sammy suspected he was weeping at his end of things, too. Nat was the only person in this world who treated Sammy as an adult, with respect, with recognition, with responsibility.

On reaching the nominated bar Sammy dithered outside for a while, trying but failing to peer through the semi-frosted glass; finally stiffening the sinews and finding the courage to enter. It was dark inside, with a double row of tables lit by soft amber light. A candle burned at each table.

An irritating couple, hopelessly in love, sat holding hands in the corner. Apart from a barman crunching an ice-machine behind the bar, there was only one other person, deep in the gloomy recesses of the bar. Sammy knew instantly it was Nat.

Nat looked up at Sammy, and exhaled a rich blue plume of cigarette smoke. Betraying no sign of recognition, Sammy marched up to the bar and ordered a daiquiri. The barman turned slowly and winched a single eyebrow very high.

GRAHAM JOYCE

Sammy tried to outstare him. The barman notched his eyebrow a fraction higher still. Sammy coloured and muttered
something about accepting a Coke.

Taking the Coke and sitting at an empty table, Sammy tried
to take a drink, the glass colliding with teeth. Nat gathered up
cigarettes, lighter, drink and handbag, clearly preparing to
come over. For Sammy, everything went slow-mo.

Nat was very tall. Sammy simultaneously marvelled at and
was horrified by the extraordinary length of Nat's legs. The
calf-muscles were too large. They were exaggerated by stiletto
heels and an excessively short skirt. Even under the light
Sammy could see that Nat wore too much make-up.

When Nat slid into an adjacent seat, Sammy felt suffocated
by the scent of cheap perfume. Sammy looked round wildly
for that keypad, that escape button. But on this occasion there
was no way out. Nat lit another cigarette, offering one for
Sammy to decline before extending a hand that wanted shaking. Sammy accepted the hand. It was very large with promi-
nent blue veins, highly manicured and with brightly polished
fingernails.

'Sammy.'

Sammy nodded an answer. Nat's voice was rather husky.

'Does your mother know you're out?'

'She thinks I'm at a friend's.'

'Thought you hadn't got any friends.'

'I invented one.'

'You sure did.' Nat let out a sigh and a lungful of smoke
altogether, on which cloud Sammy heard Nat float the word
Christ. Then, 'I'm surprised they even let you in here. If I'd

42

known I'd have arranged to meet you at a milk bar or something. Did you qualify for half-fare on the train?'

'Sorry.'

'I suppose that's it, then. Over before it's begun.' Nat whisked a compact mirror from his handbag, smoothed an eyebrow and plucked at something in the corner of his eye.

'Is that a wig? You're a—'

'Don't!' Nat said sharply. Then more gently, 'It's only words. And I can be anything I want.'

Sammy saw the light from the candle starbursting in Nat's eye. 'Are you upset?'

'Upset? Listen, kiddiwinks, I've been upset by the best of them. It takes more than a fucking teenybopper to get me upset.'

'Shall I go?'

'Yes. Run along. Run along for Christ's sake.'

Sammy got up from his seat. He tried to offer a handshake but Nat wasn't having any of it. He wouldn't even make eye-contact. In the end Sammy got out very quickly. In fact he didn't even finish his extremely expensive Coke.

The ride back was a nightmare. Sammy spent the entire journey from Leicester Square to Hounslow with his ears between his knees and the palms of his hands pressed against his flaming cheeks. The other passengers just thought he was a sick boy.

Sammy knew what he had lost. He also felt he had let himself down in a way quite mysterious. Because at the same time he knew it was hopeless. He had, during this brief encounter, stolen a glance at Nat's *kniekehle*. The blue vein in

43

the fold at the back of the knee had pulsated in a manner quite threatening. It was not at all erotic. Indeed it made him feel slightly queasy. The thought, too, of Nat's *cassolette* made him want to faint away.

Some days later he resolved to try to find a new partner, and not on the Net either. But real life wasn't the same. It wasn't possible to converse in the same way. He discovered, with a girl his own age, that ordinary relationships often consisted of spending large blocks of time together saying nothing; whereas on the Net the convention was always to be saying *something*. Even if it amounted to nothing.

Some nights he cruised the chat rooms back on the Net, hoping to stumble across Nat. He suspected Nat had given up, or was going under a different screen name. Once or twice he thought Nat was there, hiding behind a new persona, toying with him. But if it was the case, Nat never let on. After a while Sammy simply let go and stopped looking. But he always knew that he'd been tested, right at the confluence of technology and the flesh, and he'd failed.

Some nights Sammy dreamed of ghosts on the Net, but on waking the dreams made no sense. There are no ghosts of ghosts, he thought. He often considered going to Pinkland and deleting all the music and the pictures and the books. But he never did, even though it hurt him to think of Pinkland unvisited, untenanted, and echoing strangely on the Net forever.

ANGELA CARTER

The late, great Angela Carter (1940–1992) wrote frequently about sex and gender, usually in the Gothic tradition, utilizing a strong fantasy element which she called the 'social realism of the unconscious'. *The Passion of New Eve* examines the construction of gender through a romance between a transvestite and a transsexual, and both *Nights at the Circus* and the short stories in *The Bloody Chamber* celebrate women's fantasies and desires. She recognized that these desires can be both masochistic and dangerous while still being pleasurable, and also wrote *The Sadean Woman*, a critical/philosophical look at women, power and sex. 'Reflections' is taken from *Fireworks: Nine Profane Pieces*, which was Angela Carter's first published collection of short stories.

Reflections

I was walking in a wood one late spring day of skimming cloud and shower-tarnished sunshine, the sky a lucid if intermittent blue – cool, bright, tremulous weather. A *coloratura* blackbird perched on a bough curded with greenish mayblossom let fall a flawed chain of audible pearl; I was alone in the spring-enchanted wood. I slashed the taller grasses with my stick and now and then surprised some woodland creature, rat or rabbit, that fled away from me through long grass where little daisies and spindly branches of buttercups were secreted among gleaming stems still moist at the roots from last night's rain that had washed and refreshed the entire wood, had dowered it the poignant transparency, the unique, inconsolable quality of rainy countries, as if all was glimpsed through tears.

The crisp air was perfumed with wet grass and fresh earth. The year was swinging on the numinous hinges of the solstice but I was ingenuous and sensed no imminence in the magic silence of the rustling wood.

Then I heard a young girl singing. Her voice performed a trajectory of sound far more ornate than that of the blackbird, who ceased at once to sing when he heard it for he could not compete with the richly crimson sinuosity of a voice that pierced the senses of the listener like an arrow in a dream. She sang; and her words thrilled through me, for they seemed filled with a meaning that had no relation to meaning as I understood it.

'Under the leaves,' she sang, 'and the leaves of life—' Then, in mid-flight, the song ceased and left me dazzled. My attention abstracted from my surroundings, all at once my foot turned on an object hidden in the grass and I tumbled to the ground. Though I fell on the soft, wet grass, I was shaken and winded. I forgot that luring music. Cursing my obstacle, I searched among the pale, earth-stained rootlets to find it and my fingers closed on, of all things, a shell. A shell so far from the sea! When I tried to grasp it in order to pick it up and examine it the better, I found the act unexpectedly difficult and my determination to lift it quickened although, at the same time, I felt a shiver of fear for it was so very, very heavy and its contours so chill that a shock like cold electricity darted up my arm from the shell, into my heart. I was seized with the most intense disquiet; I was mystified by the shell.

I thought it must be a shell from a tropic ocean, since it was far larger and more elaborately whorled than the shells I'd found on the shores of the Atlantic. There was some indefinable strangeness in its shape I could not immediately define. It glimmered through the grass like a cone of trapped moonlight although it was so very cold and so heavy it seemed to me it might contain all the distilled heaviness of gravity itself within it. I grew very much afraid of the shell; I think I sobbed. Yet I was so determined to wrench it from the ground that I clenched my muscles and gritted my teeth and tugged and heaved. Up it came, at last, and I rolled over backwards when it freed itself. But now I held the prize in my hands, and I was, for the moment, satisfied.

When I looked at the shell more closely, I saw the nature of the teasing difference that had struck me when I first set eyes on it. The whorls of the shell went the wrong way. The spirals were reversed. It looked like the mirror image of a shell, and so it should not have been able to exist outside a mirror; in this world, it could not exist outside a mirror. But, all the same, I held it.

The shell was the size of my cupped hands and cold and heavy as death.

In spite of its fabulous weight, I decided to carry it through the wood for I thought I would take it to the little museum in the near-by town where they would inspect it and test it and tell me what it might be and how it could have arrived where I found it. But as I staggered along with it in my arms, it exerted such a pull downwards on me that, several times, I nearly fell to my knees, as if the shell were determined to drag me, not down to the earth but into the earth itself. And then, to complete my confusion, I heard that witching voice again.

'Under the leaves—'

But, this time, when a gasp stopped the song, the voice changed at once to the imperative.

'Sick 'im!' she urged. 'Sick 'im!'

Before I had a chance to do more than glance in the direction of the voice, a bullet whirred over my head and buried itself in the trunk of an elm tree, releasing from their nests in the upward branches a whirring hurricane of crows. An enormous black dog bounded towards me from the undergrowth so suddenly I saw no more than his yawning scarlet maw and lolling tongue before I went down on my face beneath him. The fright nearly bereft me of my senses. The dog slavered wetly over me and, the next thing I knew, a hand seized my shoulder and roughly turned me over.

She had called the dog away and now it sat on its haunches, panting, watching me with a quick, red eye. It was black as coal, some kind of lurcher, with balls the size of grapefruit. Both the dog and the girl glanced at me without charity. She wore blue jeans and boots, a wide, vindictively buckled leather belt and a green sweater. Her tangled brown hair hung about her shoulders in a calculated disorder that was not wild. Her dark eyebrows were perfectly straight and gave her stern face a gravity as awful as that of the shell I held in my hand. Her blue eyes, the kind the Irish say have been put in with a sooty finger, held no comfort nor concern for me for they were the eyes that justice would have if she were not blind. She carried a sporting rifle slung across her shoulder and I knew at once this rifle had fired the shot. She might have been the game-keeper's daughter but, no, she was too proud; she was a savage and severe wood-ranger.

Why I do not know, but every impulse told me to conceal my shell and I hugged it close to me, as if my life depended on keeping it, although it was so heavy and began to throb with a wild palpitation so that it seemed the shell had disordered my own heart, or else had become my own disordered heart. But my brusque captress poked at my hands with the barrel of her rifle so roughly my bruised fingers let the shell fall. She bent forward so that her necromantic hair brushed my face and picked up the shell with amazing ease.

She examined it for a moment and then, without a word or sign to me, tossed it to her lurcher, who seized it in his mouth ready to carry it for her. The dog began to wag his tail. The rhythmic swishing of his tail upon the grass was now the only sound in the clearing. Even the trees had ceased to murmur, as though a holy terror hushed them.

She gestured me to my feet, and when I was upright, she thrust the mouth of the gun in the small of my back and marched me through the wood at gunpoint, striding along behind me while the dog padded beside her with the shell in his mouth. All this took place in unadulterated silence, but for the raucous panting of the dog. The cabbage white butterflies flickered upon the still air as if nothing whatsoever were out of the ordinary, while delicious-looking apricot and violet coloured clouds continued to chase one another across the sun according to the indifferent logic of the upper heavens, for the clouds were moved by a fierce wind that blew so high above the wood everything around me was as tranquil as water trapped in a lock, and mocked the inward perturbation that shook me.

Soon we reached an overgrown path that took us to a gate set in a garden wall where there was an old-fashioned bell-pull and, dangling above it, a bell stained with moss and rust. The girl with the rifle rang this bell before she opened the gate as if to warn whoever was at home that visitors were arriving. The gate led into a graceful and dilapidated walled garden full of the herbaceous splendours of early summer, hollyhocks, wallflowers, roses. There was a mossed sundial and a little stone statue of a nude youth stretching his arms up out of a cuirass of ivy. But, though the bees hummed among the flower-bells, the grass was as long as it had been in the wood and just as full of buttercups and daisies. Dandelions expired in airy seed-heads in the flower beds; ragged robin and ground elder conspired to oust the perennials from the borders and a bright sadness of neglect touched everything as though with dust, just as it did the ancient brick house, almost covered with creepers, that slept within the garden, an ancient, tumbledown place with a look of oracular blindness in windows that were stopped up with vines and flowers. The roof was lichened quite over, so that it seemed upholstered in sleek, green fur. Yet there was no peace in the dishevelled loveliness of the place; the very plants that grew there seemed tensed in a curious expectancy, as though the garden were a waiting-room. There was a short, crumbling flight of steps that led to a weathered front door, ajar like the door of a witch's house.

Before the door, I involuntarily halted; a dreadful vertigo seized me, as if I stood on the edge of an abyss. My heart had been thumping far too hard and far too fast since I had picked up the shell and now it seemed about to burst from too much strain. Faintness and terror of death swept over me; but the girl prodded me cruelly in the buttocks with her rifle so I was forcibly marched into a country-house hall with dark stained floorboards, a Persian carpet and a Jacobean oak chest with an antique bowl on it, all complete yet all as if untouched for years, for decades. A maze of dust danced in the beam of sunshine that disturbed the choked indoors air when we broke into it. Every corner was softened by cobwebs while the industrious spiders had wound filaments of geometric lace this way and that between the crumbling furniture. A sweet, rank smell of damp and decay filled the house; it was cold, inside, and dark. The door swung to behind us but did not close and we went up a staircase of worm-eaten oak, I first, she after and then the dog, whose claws clattered on the bare wood.

At first I thought the spiders had cast their nets on both

sides of the stair but then I saw the workmanship that wound down the inner side of the staircase was not that of the spiders for, though it was the same colour, this web had a determinate pattern that resembled nothing so much as openwork knitting, the kind of feather-like, floating stuff from which they make courtesans' bedjackets. This knitting was part of an interminable muffler that, as I watched it, crept, with vegetable slowness, little by little downstairs towards the hall. Yard upon yard of the muffler was coiled up in airy folds on the landing and there I could hear the clack, clack, clack of a pair of knitting needles ticking away monotonously near at hand. The muffler came out of a door that, like the front door, stood a little open; it edged through the gap like a tenuous serpent.

My captress motioned me aside with the muzzle of her rifle and knocked firmly on the door.

Inside the room, someone coughed dryly, then invited us: 'Come in.'

It was a soft, rustling, unemphatic, almost uninflected, faded, faintly perfumed voice, like very old lace handkerchiefs put away long ago in a drawer with pot-pourri and forgotten.

My captress thrust me through the door before her; when I was close to her, my nostrils quivered at the vicious odour of her skin. It was a large room, part drawing-room, part bedroom, for the being who lived in it was crippled. She, he, it – whoever, whatever my host or hostess may have been – lay in an old-fashioned wicker bathchair beside a cracked marble fireplace bossed with swags and cupids. Her white hands finished in fingers so indecently long, so white and so translucent they raised lewd thoughts of candles and feminine self-

gratification; those tapering fingers were the source of the
bewildering muffler, for they held two bone needles and never
ceased to move.

The volatile stitchery they produced occupied all the car-
petless area of the floor and, in places, was piled up as high
as the crippled knees of its maker. There was yards and yards
of it in the room, perhaps even miles and miles of it, and I
stepped through and across it very carefully, nudging it out of
the way with my toes, to arrive where the girl directed me
with her gun, in the position of a suppliant before the
bathchair. The crippled being who lay in it had the most regal
cast of chin and mouth imaginable and the proud, sad air of
the king of a rainy country. One of her profiles was that of a
beautiful woman, the other that of a beautiful man. It is a
defect in our language there is no term of reference for these
indeterminate and undefinable beings; but, although she
acknowledged no gender, I will call her 'she' because she had
put on a female garment, a loose négligé of spider-coloured
lace, unless she, like the spiders, spun and wove her own
thread and so had become clothed, for her shadowy hair was
also the colour of the stuff she knitted and so evanescent in
texture it seemed to move of its own accord on the air around
her. Her eyelids and the cavernous sockets of her eyes were
thickly stuck with silver sequins that glittered in the strange,
subaqueous, drowned, drowning light that suffused the room,
a light filtered through windows caked with grime and half
covered by creeper, clairvoyant light reflected, with an
enhanced strangeness, by the immense mirror in a chipped
gilt frame hanging on the wall opposite the fireplace; it seemed

the mirror, like the moon, was itself endowed with the light it gave back to us.

With a touching fidelity, the mirror duplicated the room and all it contained, the fireplace, the walls covered with a stained white paper stippled with fronds of greenery, every piece of neglected ormolu furniture. How pleased I was to see my experiences had not changed me! though my old tweed suit was stained with grass, my stick gone – left behind where I had dropped it in the wood. And so much dirt on my face. But I looked as if I were reflected in a forest pool rather than by silvered glass for the surface of the mirror looked like the surface of motionless water, or of mercury, as though it were a solid mass of liquid kept in place by some inversion of gravity that reminded me of the ghastly weight of the shell that now dropped at the androgyne's feet from the dog's mouth. She never stopped knitting for one moment as she nudged it with a beautiful toe painted with a rime of silver; woe gave her a purely female face.

'Only one little stitch! And I only dropped one little stitch!' she mourned. And she bowed her head over her work in an ecstasy of regret.

'At least it wasn't out long,' said the girl. Her voice had a clanging resonance; mercy was a minor key that would never modify its martial music. '*He* found it!'

She gestured towards me with her gun. The androgyne directed upon me a pair of vague, too-large, stagnant eyes that did not shine.

'Do you know where this shell comes from?' she asked me with a grave courtesy.

54

I shook my head.

'It comes from the Sea of Fertility. Do you know where *that* is?'

'On the surface of the moon,' I answered. My voice sounded coarse and rough to me.

'Ah,' she said, 'the moon, the source of polarized light. Yes and no to your reply. It is an equivalence. The sea of fertility is a reversed system, since everything there is as dead as this shell.'

'He found it in the wood,' said the girl.

'Put it back where it belongs, Anna,' said the androgyne, who possessed a frail yet absolute air of authority. 'Before any harm is done.'

The girl bent and picked up the shell. She scrutinized the mirror and took aim at some spot within it that seemed to her a logical target for the shell. I saw her raise her arm to throw the shell into the mirror and I saw her mirrored arm raise the shell to throw it outside the mirror. Then she threw the duplicated shell. There was no sound in the room but the click of the knitting needles when she threw the shell into the mirror while her reflection threw the shell out of the mirror. The shell, when it met its own reflection, disappeared immediately.

The androgyne sighed with satisfaction.

'The name of my niece is Anna,' she said to me, 'because she can go both ways. As, indeed, I can myself, though I am not a simple palindrome.'

She gave me an enigmatic smile and moved her shoulders so that the lace négligé she wore fell back from her soft, pale breasts that were, each one, tipped by nipples of deep, dark pink, with the whorled crenellations of raspberries, and then she shifted her loins a little to display, savage and barbaric in their rude, red-purple repose, the phallic insignia of maleness.

'She can,' said Anna, 'go both ways, although she cannot move at all. So her power is an exact equivalent of her impotence, since both are absolute.'

But her aunt looked down at her soft weapon and said gently: 'Not, my darling, *absolutely* absolute. Potency, impotence *in potentia*, hence relative. Only the intermediary, since indeterminate.'

With that, she caressed her naked breasts with a stunted gesture of her forearms; she could not move her arms freely because she did not stop knitting. They looked at one another and laughed. Their laughter drove icicles of fear into my brain and I did not know which way to turn.

'You see, we must do away with you,' said the androgyne. 'You know too much.'

Panic broke over me like a wave. I plunged across the room towards the door, careless of Anna's gun in my attempted flight. But my feet were snared by the knitting and once again I plunged downwards but this time my fall half stunned me. I lay dazed while their renewed laughter darted cruelly about the room.

'Oh,' said Anna, 'but we shan't kill you. We shall send you through the mirror. We shall send you where the shell went, since that is where you belong, now.'

'But the shell vanished,' I said.

'No,' replied the androgyne. 'It did not vanish in reality. That shell had no business in this world. I dropped a stitch, this morning; only one little stitch . . . and that confounded shell slipped through the hole the dropped stitch made, because those shells are all so very, very heavy, you see. When it met its reflection, it returned to its proper place. It cannot come back, now; and neither will you, after we have sent you through the mirror.'

Her voice was so very gentle, yet she offered me a perpetual estrangement. I let out a cry. Anna turned to her aunt and placed her hand on her genitalia, so that the cock sprang up. It was of redoubtable size.

'Oh, auntie, don't scare him!' she said.

Then they tittered, the weird harpies, so that I was quite beside myself with fear and bewilderment.

'It is a system of equivalences,' said the androgyne. 'She carries the gun, you see; and I, too.'

She displayed her towering erection with the air of a demonstrator in a laboratory.

'In my intermediary and cohesive logic, the equivalences reside beyond symbolism. The gun and the phallus are similar in their connection with life – that is, one gives it; and the other takes it away, so that both, in essence, are similar in that the negation freshly states the affirmed proposition.'

I was more bewildered than ever.

'But do all the men in the mirror world have guns between their thighs?'

Anna exclaimed with irritation at my simplicity.

'That's no more likely than that I could impregnate you with this—' she said, pointing her gun at me, 'here or in any other world.'

'Embrace yourself in the mirror,' said the androgyne, knitting, knitting, knitting away. 'You must go, now. Now!'

Anna maintained her menace; there was nothing for it but to do as they bid. I went to the mirror and examined myself in its depths. A faint ripple ran over its surface; but when I touched it with my fingers, the surface was just as smooth and hard as it should have been. I saw that my reflection was cut off at the thighs by the gilt frame and Anna said: 'Climb on a stool! Who'd want you truncated, here or there?'

She grinned in an appalling fashion and slipped back the safety catch on her rifle. So I pulled a little, cane-seated, gilt-backed chair to the mirror and clambered up. I gazed at myself in the mirror; there I was, complete from head to toe, and there they were, behind me, the androgyne weaving her ethereal coils and the armed young girl, who, now that she could kill me with one little flick of her finger, looked as beautiful as a Roman soldier plundering a North African city, with her rapist's eyes and her perfume of murder.

'Kiss yourself,' commanded the androgyne in a swooning voice. 'Kiss yourself in the mirror, the symbolic matrix of this and that, hither and thither, outside and inside.'

Then I saw, even if I could no longer be astonished, that though she knitted in both the room and the mirror, there was, within the room, no ball of wool at all; her yarn emanated from inside the mirror and the ball of wool existed only in the medium of reflection. But I did not have time to wonder at this marvel for the rank stench of Anna's excitement filled the room and her hand trembled. Out of rage and desperation, I advanced my own lips to meet the familiar yet unknown lips that advanced towards mine in the silent world of the glass.

I thought these lips would be cold and lifeless; that I would touch them but they could not touch me. Yet, when the twinned lips met, they cleaved, for these mirrored lips of mine were warm and throbbed. This mouth was wet and contained a tongue, and teeth. It was too much for me. The profound sensuality of this unexpected caress crisped the roots of my sex and my eyes involuntarily closed whilst my arms clasped my own tweed shoulders. The pleasure of the embrace was intense; I swooned beneath it.

When my eyes opened, I had become my own reflection. I had passed through the mirror and now I stood on a little cane-seated, gilt-backed chair with my mouth pressed to an impervious surface of glass I had misted with my own breath and moistened with my own saliva.

Anna cried: 'Hurrah!' She dropped her rifle and clapped her hands while her aunt, continuing, all the time, to knit, gave me a peculiarly sultry smile.

'So,' she said. 'Welcome. This room is the half-way house between here and there, between this and that, because, you understand, I am so ambiguous. Stay in the field of force of the mirror for a while, until you are used to everything.'

The first thing that struck me was, the light was black. My eyes took a little time to grow accustomed to this absolute darkness for, though the delicate apparatus of cornea and aqueous humour and crystalline lens and vitreous body and

optic nerve and retina had all been reversed when I gave birth
to my mirror self through the mediation of the looking-glass,
yet my sensibility remained as it had been. So at first, through
the glass, I saw darkly and all was confusion but for their
faces, which were irradiated by familiarity. But, when the
inside of my head could process the information my topsy-
turvy senses retrieved for me, then my other or anti-eyes
apprehended a world of phosphorescent colour etched as with
needles of variegated fire on a dimensionless opacity. The
world was the same; yet absolutely altered. How can I describe
it . . . almost as if this room was the colour negative of the
other room. Unless – for how could I ever be certain which
was the primary world and which the secondary – the other
room, the other house, the other wood that I saw, transposed
yet still peeping through the window in the other mirror – all
that had been the colour negative of the room in which I now
stood, where the exhalations of my breath were the same as
the inhalations of my mirror-anti-twin who turned away from
me as I turned away from him, into the distorted, or else
really real, world of the mirror room, which, since it existed
in this mirror in this room beyond the mirror, reflected all of
this room's ambiguities and was no longer the room I had left.
That endless muffler or web wound round the room, still, but
now it wound round contrariwise and Anna's aunt was knitting from left to right, instead of from right to left with hands,
I realized, had they wished, could have pulled a right-hand
glove over the left hand and vice versa, since she was truly
ambidexterous.

But when I looked at Anna, I saw she was exactly the same

as she had been on the other side of the mirror and knew her face for one of those rare faces that possess an absolute symmetry, each feature the exact equivalent of the other, so one of her profiles could serve as the template for both. Her skull was like a proposition in geometry. Irreducible as stone, finite as a syllogism, she was always indistinguishable from herself whichever way she went.

But the imperturbably knitting androgyne had turned its face contrariwise. One half of its face was always masculine and the other, no matter what, was feminine; yet these had been changed about, so that all the balances of the planes of the face and the lines of the brow were the opposite of what they had been before, although one half of the face was still feminine and the other masculine. Nevertheless, the quality of the difference made it seem that this altered yet similar face was the combination of the reflection of the female side of the face and the masculine side of the face that *did not appear* in the face I had seen beyond the mirror; the effect was as of the reflection of a reflection, like an example of perpetual regression, the perfect, self-sufficient nirvana of the hermaphrodite. She was Tiresias, capable of prophetic projection, whichever side of the mirror she chose to offer herself to my sight upon; and she went on knitting and knitting and knitting, with an infernal suburban complacency.

When I turned from the mirror, Anna was holding out her right or left hand towards me but, although I felt sure I was walking towards her and lifted up my legs and set them down again with the utmost determination, Anna receded further and further away from me. Niece and aunt emitted a titter

61

and I guessed that, in order to come to Anna, I must go away from her. Therefore I stepped sturdily backwards and, in less than a second, her hard, thin, sunburned hand grasped mine.

The touch of her hand filled me with a wild loneliness.

With her other hand, she opened the door. I was terribly afraid of that door, for the room that contained the mirror was all that I knew, and therefore my only safety, in this unknown world that Anna, who now smiled inscrutably at me, negotiated as skilfully as if she herself, the solstice in person, went on curious hinges between this place and that place unlike her aunt, who, since she was crippled, could not move unless her condition of permanent stasis meant she was moving too fast for me to see, with a speed the inertia of the eye registered as immobility.

But, when the door creaked open on everyday, iron hinges that had never been oiled in this world or any other world, I saw only the staircase up which Anna had led me, down which she would now lead me, and the muffler that still curled down to the hall. The air was dank, just as it had been. Only, all the alignments of the stairwell had just been subtly altered and the light was composed of a reversed spectrum.

The webs of the spiders presented structures of white fire so minutely altered from those I had passed on my way upstairs that only memory made me apprehend how their geometrical engineering had all been executed backwards. So we passed under the spectral arch they had prepared for us and out into the open air that did not refresh my bewildered brain, for it was as solid as water, dense and compact, of an impermeable substance that transmitted neither sound nor odour. To move through this liquid silence demanded the utmost exertion of physical energy and intellectual concentration, for gravity, beyond the mirror, was not a property of the ground but of the atmosphere. Then Anna, who understood the physical laws of this world, exerted a negative pressure upon me by some willed absence of impulse and to my amazement I now moved as if propelled sharply from behind along the path to the gate, past flowers that distilled inexpressible colours from the black sky above us, colours whose names only exist in an inverted language you could never understand if I were to speak it. But the colours were virtually independent of the forms of the plants. Haloes of incandescence, they had arbitrarily settled about spread umbrellas of petals as thin yet as hard as the shoulder blade of a rabbit, for the flesh of the flowers was calcified and lifeless; no plant was sentient in this coral garden. All had suffered a dead sea-change.

And the black sky possessed no dimension of distance, nor gave none; it did not arch above us but looked as if it were pasted behind the flat outlines of the half-ruinous house that now lay behind us, a shipwreck bearing a marvellous freight, the female man or virile woman clicking away at her needles in a visible silence. A visible silence, yes; for the dense fluidity of the atmosphere did not transmit sound to me as sound, but, instead, as irregular kinetic abstractions etched upon its interior, so that, once in the new wood, a sinister, mineral, realm of undiminishable darkness, to listen to the blackbird was to watch a moving point inside a block of deliquescent glass. I saw these sounds because my eyes took in a different

63

light than the light that shone on my breast when my heart beat on the other side of it, although the wood through whose now lateral gravity Anna negotiated me was the same wood in which I had been walking when I first heard her sing. And I cannot tell you, since there is no language in this world to do so, how strange the antithetical wood and sweet June day were, for both had become the systematic negation of its others.

Anna, in some reversed fashion, must still have been menacing me with her gun, since it was her impulse that moved me; on we went, just as we had come – but Anna, now, went before me, with the muzzle of her gun pressed in the belly of nothingness, and the dog, her familiar, this time in the van. And this dog was white as snow and its balls were gone; on this side of the mirror, all dogs were bitches and vice versa.

I saw wild garlic and ground elder and the buttercups and daisies in the fossilized undergrowth now rendered in vivacious yet unnamable colours, as immobile arabesques without depth. But the sweetness of the wild roses rang in my ears like a peal of windbells for the vibrations of the perfumes echoed on my eardrums like the pulse of my own blood since, though they had become a kind of sound, they could not carry in the same way that sound did. I could not, for the life of me, make up my mind which world was which for I understood this world was coexistent in time and space with the other wood – was, as it were, the polarization of that other wood, although it was in no way similar to the reflection the other wood, or this wood, might have made in a mirror.

The more my eyes grew accustomed to the dark, the less in common did the petrified flora seem to have with anything I knew. I perceived all had been starkly invaded with, yes, shells, enormous shells, giant and uninhabited shells, so we might have been walking in the ruins of a marine city; the cool, pale colouring of those huge shells now glowed with a ghostly otherness and they were piled and heaped upon one another to parody the landscape of the woodland, unless the trees parodied them; all were whorled the wrong way round, all had that deathly weight, the supernatural resonance of the shell which seduced me and Anna told me in a soundless language I understood immediately that the transfigured wood, fertile now, only of metamorphoses, was – for how could it be anything else – the Sea of Fertility. The odour of her violence deafened me.

Then, once again, she began to sing; I saw the mute, dark, fire burning like Valhalla in *Götterdämmerung*. She sang a funeral pyre, the swan's song, death itself, and, with a brusque motion of her gun, she forced me forward on my knees while the dog stood over me as she tore open my clothes. The serenade smouldered all around us and I was so much at the mercy of the weight of the air, which pressed down on me like a coffin lid, and of the viscosity of the atmosphere, that I could do nothing to defend myself, even if I had known how, and soon she had me, poor, forked thing, stretched out upon a bank of shells with my trousers round my knees. She smiled but I could not tell what the smile meant; on this side of the mirror, a smile was no clue whatsoever to intention or to feeling and I did not think she meant to do me a good deed as she unbuckled her uncouth leather belt and stepped out of her jeans.

Parting the air with the knives of her arms, she precipitated herself upon me like a quoit on a peg. I screamed; the notes of my scream rose up on the air like ping-pong balls on a jet of water at a fun-fair. She raped me; perhaps her gun, in this system, gave her the power to do so.

I shouted and swore but the shell grotto in which she ravished me did not reverberate and I only emitted gobs of light. Her rape, her violation of me, caused me atrocious physical and mental pain. My being leaked away from me under the visitation of her aggressive flesh. My self grew less in agony under the piston thrust of her slender loins, as if she were a hammer and were forging me into some other substance than flesh and spirit. I knew the dreadful pleasure of abandonment; she had lit my funeral pyre and now would kill me. I felt such outrage I beat in the air behind my head with my helpless fists as she pumped away indefatigably at my sex, and to my surprise, I saw her face cloud and bruises appear on it, although my hands were nowhere near her. She was a brave girl; she only fucked the harder, for she was intransigent and now resembled the Seljuk Turks sacking Constantinople. I knew there was no hope for me if I did not act immediately.

Her gun lay propped against the shells beside us. I reached the other way and seized it. I shot at the black sky while she straddled me. The bullet pierced a neat, round, empty hole in the flat vault of the heavens but no light, no sound, leaked through; I had made a hole without quality but Anna let out a ripping shriek that sent a jagged scar across the surface of the wood. She tumbled backwards and twitched a little. The dog growled at me, a terrible sight, and leaped at my throat but I quickly shot her, also, in this negative way and, now free, there remained only the problem of the return to the mirror, the return to the right-hand side of the world. But I kept tight hold of the gun, by grasping it loosely, because of the guardian of the mirror.

To return to the house, I struck out from the shell grotto where Anna lay, in the opposite direction from the one we had come from. I must have fallen into a mirror elision of reflected time, or else I stumbled upon a physical law I could not have guessed at, for the wood dissolved, as if the blood that leaked from Anna's groin was a solvent for its petrified substance, and now I found myself back at the crumbling gate before her juices were dry on my cock. I paused to do up my flies before I made my way to the door; I used my arms like scissors to snip through the thickness of the atmosphere, for it grew, moment by moment, less liquid and more impalpable. I did not ring the bell, so great was my outrage, so vivid my sense of having been the plaything of these mythic and monstrous beings.

The knitting curled down the stairs, just as I expected, and, in another moment, I saw, on a staccato stave, the sound of the needles.

She, he, it, Tiresias, though she knitted on remorselessly, was keening over a whole dropped row of stitches, trying to repair the damage as best she could. Her keening filled the room with a Walpurgisnacht of crazy shapes and, when she

67

saw I was alone, she flung back her head and howled. In that decompression chamber between here and there, I heard a voice as clear as crystal describe a wordless song of accusation.

'Oh, my Anna, what have you done with my Anna?'

'I shot her,' I cried. 'With her own weapon.'

'A rape! She's raped!' screamed the androgyne as I dragged the gilt chair to the mirror and clambered up on it. In the silvered depths before me, I saw the new face of a murderer I had put on behind the mirror.

The androgyne, still knitting, kicked with her bare heels upon the floor to drive her bathchair over the wreathing muffler towards me, in order to attack me. The bathchair cannoned into the chair on which I stood and she rose up in it as far as she could and began to beat me with her tender fists. But, because she did not stop knitting, she offered no resistance when I brought my ham-hand crashing down on her working face. I broke her nose; bright blood sprang out. I turned to the mirror as she screamed and dropped her knitting.

She dropped her knitting as I crashed through the glass
through the glass, glass splintered round me driving
unmercifully into my face
through the glass, glass splintered
through the glass –
half through.

Then the glass gathered itself together like a skilful whore and expelled me. The glass rejected me; it sealed itself again into nothing but mysterious, reflective opacity. It became a mirror and it was impregnable.

Balked, I stumbled back. In Tiresias' bed-sitting room, there was the most profound silence, and nothing moved; the flow of time might have stopped. Tiresias held her empty hands to her face that was now irretrievably changed; each one snapped clean in two, her knitting needles lay on the floor. Then she sobbed and flung out her arms in a wild, helpless gesture. Blood and tears splashed down on her robe, but in a baleful, hopeless way she began to laugh, although time must have started again and now moved with such destructive speed that, before my eyes, that ageless being withered – a quick frost touched her. Wrinkles sprang out on her pale forehead while her hair fell from her head in great armfuls and her négligé turned brown and crumbled away, to reveal all the flesh that sagged from the bone as I watched it. She was the ruins of time. She grasped her throat and choked. Perhaps she was dying. The muffler was blowing away like dead leaves in a wind that sprang up from nowhere and raced through the room, although the windows stayed shut tight. But Tiresias spoke to me; she spoke to me once again.

'The umbilical cord is cut,' she said. 'The thread is broken. Did you not realize who I was? That I was the synthesis in person? For I could go any way the world goes and so I was knitting the thesis and the antithesis together, this world and that world. Over the leaves and under the leaves. Cohesion gone. Ah!'

Down she tumbled, the bald old crone, upon a pile of wisps of unravelled grey wool as the ormolu furniture split apart and the paper unfurled from the wall. But I was arrogant; I was undefeated. Had I not killed her? Proud as a man, I once again advanced to meet my image in the mirror. Full of self-confidence, I held out my hands to embrace my self, my antiself, my self not-self, my assassin, my death, the world's death.

PAUL MAGRS

Paul Magrs was born in 1969 in County Durham and currently teaches creative writing and English literature at the University of East Anglia. He's the author of three novels, *Marked for Life, Does it Show?* and *Could it Be Magic?* and a short story collection, *Playing Out*. The characters in 'Nude on the Moon' will be recognized with pleasure by anyone who has read *Does it Show?*; those who haven't may want to seek out that funny and touching novel to find out what happened *before* the following events.

Nude on the Moon

Liz was the perfect passenger. She never drove, though once she could. She left it all to Cliff and made no suggestions, no criticisms. When he passed her the map, the day they came to the mountains, she looked at it and it was a different language. He was expecting her to tease out their route, but she looked blank. Liz didn't care.

Just go, she said, drive north.

This was two months after leaving home. They still had no

aim but getting away. Liz concentrated on not looking back, passing the mints, lighting the cigarettes, and turning the tape over. 'Forty one,' she thought, 'and still running away from home.'

In a car park between mountains she took advantage of the pause to touch up her make-up. Dabbing grey on to her eyelids in the rearview mirror, she caught sight of the valley they had driven through. It was like she could see all the way back to Aycliffe, the yellow council house and the teenage daughter she had left behind.

She saw her lover Cliff at the edge of the car park, pitching stones into a crevasse. His black hair whipping about in the wind, his shirt sleeves rolled. She hoped no one was down there. Sometimes he was heedless. It was he who had begged her to come away like this. Over dinner in the Around-the-World restaurant under the translucent dome of the Metro Centre, she had at first laughed in his face. 'I can't run away with a bus driver!'

'Why not?'

'I've a child to look after!'

'She's seventeen. She'll look after herself.' He reached across the table and grasped her hands in his. She felt his legs nudging aside the heaped carrier bags under the table. His knees pressed into hers. 'I need you to come away with me,' said the bus driver earnestly, and he was so ridiculous Liz had to give in. She was tempted to see if she really could just walk away from her life. And here she was. Up a mountain in January, with mist all around the same dove grey as her eyeshadow.

But look at Cliff there. He had stolen a bus for her. The bus he usually drove in pointless, intricate loops around Aycliffe and Darlington. One day in November he'd shook both himself and his lover free.

I didn't ask him if this was the highest we'd been up. I thought it must have been. He pointed out the moon, how we could see it coming up in the east and I said this was the blackest I had ever seen the sky. Look at the lochs, he said. We'd driven this long way especially to see them and now it was too dark. They had even smaller islands afloat on them, just tussocks of grass clumped in their middles. I said, they look like bowls of stew and dumplings, that's what they look like in the night. Cliff didn't laugh. I think he's a real country boy at heart. He comes from Yorkshire and takes nature very seriously. Me and nature . . . I can take it or leave it. Coming over the glens I just wanted to sleep. You can only look at the yellow moon for so long.

Beside a black cut-out of a perfectly triangular mountain we found a hotel. Cliff had been here before, when he skied. He's sporty, too. I can't abide anything sporty. This would do us for the night, he said. We could have a proper dinner in the bar. I pulled a face, knowing this meant scampi in a basket with the locals. Probably karaoke. We could take the bridal suite, he added, as we got out of the car. It's right above the bar and quite sumptuous. Bridal suite indeed. As we hurried into the porch of the hotel, I said, don't push it, sunshine.

But I like him sorting things out like this. Though I feel old enough to be his mother, Cliff's taken charge of everything: this trip, my life. Funny I let him.

The foyer was empty and smelled musty. Stuffed otters. They had those glass cases on the walls, the ones everyone's got up these days, full of dried flowers, fruit and shells. They do them in Ikea. Before I ran away I was thinking of getting some for our hallway, and putting things in them.

Dinner last night was in the car, watching mist come over the sea, or a loch or something. I don't know what it was, or how open to the sea we were. I've lost all sense of direction.

We got ourselves a takeaway from the only Indian in Oban. Cliff's been flash with his money. 'I'll get this,' he always says. Buying this old car in Kendal for cash. And we're eating out every night. This place wasn't cheap. A restaurant with two tables. Two very young couples having an anniversary. 'This must be a busy night,' Cliff whispered.

Waiting for our food we crossed the main street and walked into the waterlogged grass that fronted the town and met the sea. I was in my heels and soon I was sinking. Mud smarmed between my toes. Cliff laughed at me and I was yelling. I only had about three pairs of tights with me. Back on the road, three or four lads were laughing too, as we traipsed back from the quagmire. That must be all the youth round here had to do, I thought. Stand along the roadside, looking for strangers. It was worse than Aycliffe. 'What are you lot staring at?' I cackled as we went back to the Indian. They looked at each other like I was foreign.

I was so hungry by then, I didn't care about mucky feet. I'd make Cliff clean my shoes later. It was his fault.

We got the food and drove off to a picturesque spot across the bay, as twilight came on. We're always seeing sights in the dark.

I used his book of maps as a table mat. That caused a row later. It was too dim in the car to tell, but the brown grease from my Rogan Josh was spilling slowly over a lip in the tin foil tray. It bled into maps, page after page, orange and blotting out the north worst of all. But it was a tricky business eating with a plastic spoon and still managing to appreciate the view. The tinsel of the towns across the bay. Lit-up bed and breakfasts. It was like I had to admire everything Cliff stopped the car to look at. He had his camera with him. He would always say, come on, Liz. Let's get you in, standing next to this view. As if when he had a whole film with me on, it proved we were together. When he finished a roll he went to the first Boots we saw and got it printed in an hour. Me after me after me, in breathtaking locations.

'But I'm not dressed,' I would say each time, unklunking and unclicking my seatbelt.

'Oh, you are,' he'd assure me, testing the light.

And of course I always *was* dressed for my photo. I always am.

So they look taken aback when I walk in the hotel bar on the moors. I make an entrance; gold head to foot and shining. That's when I'm at my happiest, when I'm at my least reluctant to face the public. Roped in theatrical jewellery, with golden-heeled slippers and I'm ... sheathed, I suppose is the word for it, throat to ankle in gold lamé. Out to dinner in a dress I shouldn't be able to sit down in.

I perch half-on, half-off a red barstool. I light black Sobranies for Cliff and myself as he orders our vodkas. The regulars go back to their darts, the other barman to his cable and satellite magazine.

Cliff tells me it's all right; they don't just do meals in a basket. We can go through and have dinner properly. Sometimes he talks to me like I'm Princess Anne.

In the bridal suite above the hotel barroom. Burgundy flock wallpaper and a baby chandelier. 'Like being in a western,' said Liz, twisting her back so he could find the zipper. 'Like *Destry Rides Again*.' She imagined herself all corseted up with a feather boa laid across her shoulders.

He lifted strands of hair away from her neck. Nowadays Cliff didn't say much when they went to bed. At first he had been chatty, almost hearty, and Liz wondered if that was because he thought she liked that. He was naturally quieter than her. In the car he didn't mind if the conversation died down. He could absorb himself in driving, which he loved. She became aware of how he changed gears, how he popped on different lights in the dark. Everything with great deliberation. Nothing was erratic about Cliff.

Down came her zip with a purr, unsealing the hard shiny fabric of her dress. She tried not to say anything else. Cliff's easy quiet made her tire of the sound of her own voice. That was a new thing for her. Now all she said was, 'Here,' and turned to undo his shirt. She felt the dark hair on the back of her hand and she grew hard just from that.

He kissed at her neck and then her mouth with hard, bunched, silly kisses. Again and again, like eating soft fruit. He made her laugh and tell him to stop. 'Kiss me properly!'

'This *is* proper!' he said and started pecking at her again. 'You're making me all self-conscious now.'

'*You* self-conscious!' she smiled, because he was the most easy-going man she knew. At garages when he went to pay for petrol, he'd go loping in, holding the door open for anyone who wanted past. She would watch him talking with the girl serving, laughing about nothing. He behaved as if he didn't mind about giving himself away.

When he came back out to the car with Coke and mints and a tub of Häagen Dazs from the garage freezer, he'd still have a cigarette clamped between his teeth. No one told him to put it out. It was as if, because he wasn't concerned, no one else was.

'You worry too much,' he told her. 'You'll get ulcers.'

'Ulcers!' she said. Then she thought about her stomach lined with pale white dots. Like sequins on the inside for a change.

Let's see where this goes. Why is it some people get all excited? They see a turn-off like this and away they go. Ferreting off into the wide blue yonder.

Liz couldn't give a bugger. She was never much of an explorer. Stick me on the straight and narrow, she says, and I'll not wander far. I like to know what's what. A simple, prosaic soul; that's what she wants to be. Straight up and down.

'Oh, don't be sarcastic.'

'I'm not,' laughs Cliff, and he isn't. He thinks it's funny Liz like to think herself so normal. It tickles him.

He sees this turn-off which seems to lead nowhere. He wants them to chase up this road into a valley full of 'sharp crests and blind summits'.

'Sums up my bloody life,' Liz tuts as they set off, with Cliff peeping his horn when they come upon each blind summit. It's an eerie punctuation to their ride. Eleven miles into the middle of nowhere and then the road simply stops, as if the planner's ink ran out, beside a lake the colour of old pennies.

As they get out of the car, Cliff says, 'That mountain looks like two buttocks.' He's always seeing shapes in things. Liz puts it down to him growing up on the Yorkshire moors, starved of diversions, bless him. She looks at this mountain.

'Honestly, you're arse-mad, you are,' and she snorts with laughter. He thinks she looks like a horse. She looks round and sees only a dilapidated boat house right at the water's edge. 'This is what you've brought me all these miles to see? A burned out little house?'

'I thought there might have been more here,' he says, and tramps off through the broken shale and granite, looking for somewhere to pee. 'You never know what's there if you don't look.'

To Liz the boat house looks like where a maniac would drive with a transit van full of prisoners. His victims would be found butchered up months later. It's a landscape made for maniacs, this.

All the places get to be the same in the end. One night, when they had set themselves a hundred miles to travel before they slept, Liz said, 'Look for a phone.' She wanted to call her daughter. Sometimes she would get impulsive like that.

They stopped in a village and Liz bundled out, into the phone box. Cliff sat watching her as she talked in that column of light. She was squinting at the houselights opposite, the pub lights, the closed shops. Liz was thinking: people live here; a place I might never come to again. These are people I will never meet. It made her feel perplexed, that she could dash through like this and use their phone, even if it was a public box.

In bed last night a similar thought had struck her. She mulled over all the beds where she'd fucked with Cliff just once. It seemed cavalier of them. It made her feel they were trying very hard to keep the novelty up, under bedspread after bedspread and never the same one twice.

On the phone that night Liz's daughter sounded non-plussed. Nothing had changed at home. 'She can be ever so surly,' Liz sighed as they drove and left the village behind.

Cliff knew better than to add anything. He twizzled the radio on to a station with a request show for ninety-year-olds. Organ music from the 1920s. 'The Sun Has Got His Hat On'. After a while they sang along.

*

It was one morning when they left another of their bed and breakfasts that Liz said you could soon sicken of not having your own place.

'You can't exactly rest your bones in someone else's house. Not properly. I'm always on my guard.'

Cliff was manoeuvring the car down the sharp zigzag back to the main road. He snapped, 'When are you *not* on your guard?'

She pursed her lips, deciding not to tell him about this morning. He thought it was odd that the woman from the b. & b. let them see themselves out. When she told them to just leave the cheque on the breakfast table he marvelled at her trust.

The b. & b. woman had said, 'I must dash. I've got a dressmaking class starting at ten. I'm so silly I forgot!' She hurried out in a flap and Liz and Cliff listened to her engine revving in the driveway. They stared at the table. Cliff said, 'I hope I haven't blocked her in the driveway.' But he hadn't, and they watched her car hare across the bay.

Who has a dress-making class at ten o'clock in the morning? Liz thought. But she didn't say anything.

They had found the bungalow in the dark last night. It had a fine, wide picture window overlooking the bay, and they could see the woman sitting at her desk, under a green-shaded lamp. She was doing her accounts in a houndstooth jacket and a white blouse with ruffled collar. All the bungalows here did b. & b., Cliff said. When summer came they cleaned up with passing trade. That's what we are, thought Liz gloomily, just passing trade.

Several years back Cliff had lived on this peninsula, doing manual work on somebody's estate. 'It's such a close-knit community, with everyone looking out for each other. I wonder if they recognize me still!' So far no one had. It amazed Liz that he wanted so much to be recognized here: in the petrol station, the post office and by this b. & b. woman. When at home, in Aycliffe, everyone knew Cliff by sight, because of his being on the buses. He had gained the easy appreciation of all the women Liz knew. She bet they still talked about him even now. What was so special about the people here?

When this woman let them into her bungalow – and it wasn't *that* special inside – Liz felt condescended to. Her hackles went straight up. The b. & b. woman looked her up and down, as if she thought she was too dressed up for a car journey. Liz felt like a mad woman, or someone kidnapped.

'I've a double room, or a room with twin beds.'

'Double,' said Cliff with a smile as Liz made her way to the door marked 'bathroom'.

The b. & b. woman called after her: 'We turn the "occupied" sign over on the door when we use the bathroom. That way we *know*. And when we leave we open the window for the condensation. All right?'

Liz smiled and slammed the door after her.

Cliff put all their bags in the double room. The bed was very high up. He was sitting on it when Liz came back. 'All right?'

She rolled her eyes. He went into the living room, to be sociable.

Liz looked at a shelf of books by the bed. Everything Dick Francis had ever written and seven years of the *Reader's Digest*. She picked one out and sat down on the two laid-out towels, pink and blue. *On Top of a Glacier*. She should be getting out her night things. She could hear Cliff mumbling away, asking about people here. The b. & b. woman recognized him at last. She said how last year had been bad for deaths. The weather came in and picked the oldies off. Someone's twins had been in a road accident. The roads were atrocious. One of the twins had died and Cliff said that's the one he'd been friendly with.

Liz changed into a black dress. Nothing too showy. She went through.

'Will you have some tea or whisky before you go?'

Cliff was saying they'd go for a drink down in the village, so he could show Liz where he'd hung out for a year.

The b. & b. woman added, 'I don't always drink whisky by myself, you know.' She tilted her wine glass, full to the brim with gold. 'Only when I'm doing my accounts.' She chuckled.

'Ha!' laughed Cliff, over-eager, and Liz shot him a glance.

In the car Cliff said, 'She didn't remember me at all.' He waved vaguely at the picture window.

'Should she?'

'She used to come and cook for the old bag I was working for. I remember being in the kitchen once and she was being made to cook lobster "the correct way". She was bullied into it.'

They got on to the main road. Liz didn't want to go for a

drink, but anything to get out of the b. & b. 'What was the correct way?'

'Cut it in half lengthways, while it's still alive. Rubber bands around its pincers, or it'll have your fingers off. Then shove the two halves under the grill while it's still twitching. The old bag insisted and her from the b. & b. did it.'

All the way to the village in the dark – another pub I'll never go to! Someone else's local – Liz thought about Cliff watching the b. & b. woman gritting her teeth and splitting a lobster into neat halves, the knife grinding down on the wet shell.

She slept badly, even though the air was so healthy. Even though everyone round here said how it was gloriously peaceful. She lay awake and watched Cliff, who always went off like a light. Liz didn't even have anything to read.

They hadn't made love tonight. She didn't know which room the b. & b. woman slept in or how close within hearing range it was. Liz knew she and Cliff were noisy. 'What does it matter?' he complained. 'We're paying her thirty quid!'

Liz tutted. In the middle of the night she had to go to the loo. Cliff stirred. 'You know me,' she said. 'My bladder holds as much as a dessert spoon.' When she climbed off the too-high bed she couldn't be bothered searching in the bags for her kimono, or anything else to cover herself. Let the dark be enough. So she crept into the hallway in a pair of pants.

She stood a moment, readjusting to the moonlight. There was a noticeboard with a map of the whole area, plastic pockets full of leaflets to do with walks and nature. Fancy someone putting all this stuff up in their own house. It was to be helpful, but Liz thought it was weird. Like playing at schools. A thermometer thing on a card was pinned to the map; a universal scale reader, whatever that was. You were meant to take it out of the plastic, read your scales, and put it back. Everything on the noticeboard looked like it had rules attached.

Liz opened the bathroom door.

There sat the b. & b. woman, on the toilet, in her slippers with her nightie pulled up round her midriff. She was holding the *Reader's Digest* at arm's length.

Liz jumped back, shocked. But the b. & b. woman looked more shocked. She stared.

Liz without her wig. And in nothing but her pants.

At first the b. & b. woman simply didn't recognize her house-guest. She saw a nude intruder. A skinny little man in black clingy pants. Not a stitch of hair on his pale body.

Then their eyes locked and the b. & b. woman knew she was looking at Liz.

They both heard the distinct plop as the b. & b. woman finished her nocturnal business. Liz slammed the door and hurried back to the room, her heart playing merry hell. As she flung herself under the heavy duvet, all she could think was: that woman didn't keep by her own rules. The 'occupied' sign wasn't turned round.

So the next day the b. & b. woman ran off to her dressmaking class. She couldn't face me, Liz thought, with a peculiar satisfaction.

She made herself up carefully at the old-fashioned dressing table. Crotcheted antimacassars stood under everything, protecting the wood.

When she sat down to breakfast everything was out and ready. Liz ate some new kind of bran. Hard little brown balls. She ate sausages with mustard from Arran. Cliff had black pudding and she imagined kissing him later, pretending he hadn't had sticky pig's blood on his teeth. She kept eating, suddenly hungry.

'Get your money's worth,' said Cliff, smiling.

Everything was laid out properly. Milk in a jug, even salt in a dish, with a tiny silver spoon. 'What's this?'

He sighed. 'I can't believe you've never seen a salt spoon before.'

'A salt spoon,' she muttered derisively and popped it into her pocket. 'I want to go now,' she said and stood up. She looked around. 'Fancy sharing your home with strangers.'

The b. & b. woman had explained she'd take just about anyone in. She wasn't prejudiced, though she'd had some bother with Italians. They shouted from room to room and the walls here were paper thin.

Liz said, 'The next time I live somewhere that's my own, I won't let *any* strangers in. It'll just be for me and who I want.'

'What's the matter with you?' Cliff said.

Liz shrugged. 'Sometimes I feel like private property.'

It was where they had their first proper row; some sort of National Park, crammed with wonders. It wasn't quite in public, but close enough. There were other couples wandering around the shaded, composty paths, and they all looked like National Trusty, nature-loving couples, all in walking boots, with leaflets open and pointing at things. Liz was embarrassed to be heard shouting by them.

'We didn't pay the two pound to get in,' was how it started, Liz looking back at the people on the trail behind them. They were slotting coins into a perspex box on the gate.

Cliff tutted. 'I'm not paying to walk round some old garden.'

'It's a done-up garden,' said Liz, sounding sullen even to herself. Small ponds were cut into the lawn, kidney-shaped and swarming with livid orange, shoe-sized fish. 'You'd complain if someone climbed on your bus and didn't pay.'

'That's different.'

'I don't see why.'

He grunted and they headed for the trees. 'Anyway,' he said. 'Scotland's different. In Scotland you have the right to walk anywhere. It's not the same as England. No one can tell you to get off their land.'

'I didn't know that.'

'They think it should all be public.'

'Well,' said Liz.

In the woods it smelled damp. It smelled like something left in a fridge to go off. They left the path – oh, foolishly! Liz warned herself, thinking of Red Riding Hood – and Cliff went striding ahead. The mossy ground, springy and treacherous, made Liz's heart sink as, once more, her shoes got filthied up. 'You keep dragging me out to terrible places!' she muttered. She watched his back as he wove and ducked through the trees. His beautiful back incensed her. 'I mean, what are we doing here? Looking at trees!'

'I like looking at trees,' he said.

They came to the edge of the woods, where the ground dropped away and there was the sea, suddenly. Cliff was kicking at the vast, upturned roots of a fallen tree. They were ripped apart, as if in a terrible storm. Broken shards of bark and blackened wood stood up in nasty spikes.

'This looks like lightning,' said Liz with a shudder.

He shook his head. 'Just frost.' He pointed to clearly cracked-open rocks tangled in roots thick as his arm. 'Water in cracks in the rocks freezes and the whole thing bursts open.'

'You always know everything,' she said, turning away. 'You can be too practical you know. It gets on people's nerves. I still say it was lightning.'

'Well, you would.'

She raised an eyebrow. There was a bench so you could watch the sea. Liz swished over to it, and Cliff followed.

'Didn't you tell me some story about you being struck by lightning once?' he asked.

Liz eyed him.

'I remember,' he said, sitting beside her. 'You said you were holding your Penny at the time. She was a baby and you were outside—'

'In a car park,' Liz prompted.

'—in a car park, and lightning struck you . . . and that's why you turned into a woman!' He sat back on the metal bench, stretching out his legs with a chuckle.

Liz had gone red, but her voice was very cold. 'You're simplifying that just a bit.'

Cliff laughed. 'You make things sound so sensational. It's ridiculous.' He shook his head. He realized what he thought Liz was like: a comic book superhero. Each superhero had an origin story that they flashbacked to, telling you how they ended up like that. The She Hulk was bathed in green radiation. Spider Woman was bitten by a radioactive spider. Liz got struck by lightning. What did she become? *Woman* Woman.

'What's ridiculous about it?' Liz was shrill suddenly.

He sighed. 'Lightning can't give you ideas about a thing like that! You just made it up! You make everything up!' He stood up. 'You know what I think?' He was baiting her now.

Liz saw one of the couples with proper leaflets and boots coming through the gap in the trees, and she shushed Cliff. The intruders looked mortified at disturbing the row and they backed carefully away.

'What do you think?' she asked through gritted teeth.

'You can't face the truth of any of it. You make up all these stories, just to cover the fact of your own decisions.'

'Oh, really?'

'You can't face it, so you dress it up like fate, like everything changed in a flash of light.'

'Cliff,' she said. 'You understand nothing.'

'I understand that you think you're the Queen of bloody Sheba, and the laws of the universe run different for you.'

They both fell quiet at this. Liz was shocked by his bitterness.

'Have I been getting on your nerves?' she asked.

Cliff glowered. 'All you go on about is leaving Newton Aycliffe behind, about how I've taken you away from everything that's yours.' He sighed. 'You make me feel like I've dragged you off and made you a rubbish bargain.'

'Cliff,' she said. 'It's been wonderful, this trip. I've loved it. It's just not . . .'

'It's not real life, is it?'

When they walked back through the park they started to notice the brighter flowers that hung from some of the trees, looking tagged on like Christmas decorations. Amazing this far north, this time of year. Obviously a well-cared-for garden. Liz dropped some change in the box as they left.

In the car Cliff said, 'Do you want me to take you home?'

She stared at the windscreen as it started to rain. 'Don't know, Cliff.' She pulled a face into her mirror. 'I don't think so.'

I tried to tell him I needed a routine. It does me no good not knowing what's coming next. That sense that you are free to do anything depresses me. Because in the end anything *that* free has to be boring. Life made up minute-by-minute makes me sad. It's like being old or mad or with nothing to do. Cliff never agreed. Cliff with nothing to do was like a child.

My Aycliffe routines. I loved them even though I didn't know it. How's about that for a sad, small life? But it's only when I'm stranded in the mountains, looking at bigger skies than I've ever seen, that I start to appreciate . . . I don't know. Getting the Road Ranger to the town centre. The tantalizing

Cliff taking my money, punching my ticket. Belting round the supermarket, filling a trolley. Fresh bread and sausage rolls from the bakers. Picking up shiny magazines in Stevens. Sitting in the Copper Kettle and gassing with whoever I see there. Swanking through the precinct and knowing that I – more than anyone there – am looking drop dead.

Here there's no one to see me but Cliff and is it awful to say this? He looks less tantalizing driving a car than his bus, when it was scandalous to talk too much with him. The sign by his head warned his passengers not to address him when he was driving. So we stared at the sunburned nape of his neck, his dark curls sweated down on the skin.

I've got him and don't know what to do with him.

He pointed out that it could be the countryside that was getting her down. 'You're not one for open spaces.'

He took them to Glasgow, where the rain kept up and the turn-offs into town confounded them. The middle of the city was like being in canyons. They parked and hunted the car boot for an umbrella.

'Full of holes,' Cliff muttered and chucked it. They went by the town hall. Elkie Brooks was on posters outside.

'Pearl's a singer . . .' said Liz reflectively.

'We could go and see her if you liked,' Cliff said.

They found a bar instead.

Whenever Cliff comes to a city he wants to know about the gay scene. It's funny, but I can never be bothered, really. It's the same old thing wherever you go. Smell of poppers, dance music, old fellas sitting round. It's not something I'm used to, but Cliff likes it and so I go.

This bar we're in, Friday teatime, is like a barn inside and filling up already. I'm forty-one and sitting in a bar where the only words in the song they're playing that I can make out are, 'Tie me up'. If I wasn't in a frock, would I look like the other, older men here?

Cliff's theory about me and gay bars. If he believed in it, he wouldn't bring me to another one, but he does anyway. He says they are the places I look less real. Is it because of strobe lighting? My make-up looks put on with a shovel. Once he said I had this mask on. When he said it my face could barely move. My eyes felt like holes cut into an egg shell. My clothes feel over-dressy, but that's not me trying to look smart, me trying to outshine. It's me sending up the idea of wearing women's clothes. That's what it looks like when you put me here. That's what, I think, Cliff's trying to say. Here, everyone can tell I'm a man.

No one has to look twice. Of course I'm going to hate a place like that. The scene unwomans me.

The room this time is small. When they open the window for more air the noise of the rain is too fierce. It bounces off the glass and soaks into the golden, velvety curtains.

Liz lies her slimmer, paler body over her lover's and wriggles herself as if into him. His cool knees press against her sides and how secure she feels. Her palms rest flat on his stomach. So hard, like a carapace, like the red, cooked shell of a lobster. Imagine sliding your lover under the grill.

And what else did he say – that expert – about cooking a lobster?

She stirs, wondering what to do with him next. Their eyes lock over his body and they pause. Seconds creep by.

He said you have to keep their claws still with elastic bands, or they'll cut you to ribbons. They'll nip your vitals off. And here is Cliff, flat on the mattress, trussed up with the belts from both their dressing gowns. His wrists are bound and lashed to the door handle of the en suite bathroom. How he loves to be beyond control like this.

Liz looks him over, gives the smooth, rosy skin of his rib cage a cautious lick. She savours the bouquet of their mingled smells and pulls both their cocks together in one hand.

She's almost delirious with tiredness because once again they've been awake most of the night. In hotel rooms and b. & b.'s they've taken to watching late movies, one after another. Tonight in this fuggy Glasgow hotel room they've seen *Queen Christina*. Garbo dressing in a velvet Robin Hood suit in snowy old Russia, being a pretend boy to woo a Spanish nobleman. Playing Cesario to his perplexed – until he sees her breasts – Orsino.

As they make love Liz thinks about the film. She looks far away. Cliff has noticed that this is what she's like, in the seconds before she comes. When she does, her sperm shoots past him, falls on to the pillow case with a loud crackle in his ear. Cliff comes at the exact same moment she does. He always does. Somehow, like spies, they've managed to get themselves synchronized.

He lies quiet and waits for Liz either to untie him or wipe

him off. He feels covered, as if someone has painted him with the stuff. Jackson Pollocked, he rests with Liz's slight weight keeping him down. He stares at her thin chest and torso. The plump nipples and the odd swelling of her pectorals, almost like an adolescent girl. As if Liz's gender is changing course through sheer force of will. He knows she is off the hormone treatment. Liz stares down at him, with one fingertip smearing sperm into his hairy stomach, like Nivea.

I dream sometimes when I have sex, she thinks. That's not to say I get bored and make things up to pass the time. Nor does it mean I've fallen asleep and these are real dreams. And I don't exactly mean those all-too-brief flashes of utopian insight you might get on the way to coming with someone. I don't exactly mean that, but it's similar. It's just funny, what goes round your head when you're making love.

I saw Cliff in red and gold soldier's braid, in a horrid woodland, banging on a tree under which he knew a witch lived. She had a home tiled in black and white, well below the stinking forest floor, its roof tangled in tree roots. She showed Cliff the three dogs guarding the three pots of treasure – gold, silver and copper. And the dogs had eyes in ascending sizes; eyes the size of dinner plates, of cartwheels, of round towers. I thought, how does she fit such vastly-eyed hounds in her underground home?

As Cliff thought about stealing the treasure and winding up with the beautiful princess – which was me, of course – I was coming to the realization that it was *The Tinder Box*, the story I was thinking of.

Cliff took both of us in his hands to make us come; speeding up, making the red tender flesh inside the skin appear, then disappear. Now you see it, now you don't

I saw the nude princess strapped to the back of the dog with the biggest eyes. Baying at the yellow moon, he pelted through the streets of the city; obeying the soldier, his new master. And no one from the princess's family ever saw her, or could find her again.

That was the dream I was going over.

Cliff says that, during sex, all he ever thinks about is whether he's doing it right. He says he can't stop it. And there's me supposing he's all easy and unselfconscious. He tells me how he thinks over what we're doing. Afterwards he narrates it all back to me. I think it's just an excuse to talk dirty to me.

Bless him.

It rained the whole time they were in Glasgow.

They went to the Versace shop and made each other try things on. Liz always found herself marvelling at Cliff's perfect shape. She liked to show off for him. She marched him into their poky, minimalist dressing rooms, and out again, in a variety of improbable outfits. Clothes just hang off him, she thought. He looks so nonplussed.

A display dummy fell and almost crushed somebody's child while they were there. The mother was off chatting to her friend and, before she knew it, the kid had pulled this metal thing down on himself. Liz managed to pull him away just in time.

The woman looked a bit spacey as she thanked Liz, then Cliff, then Liz again, and she pulled her toddler to her. Cliff dragged Liz out into the street before she gave the woman a piece of her mind.

'Careless people like that,' Liz ranted, 'shouldn't be allowed to have kids.'

He looked glum. 'I'm careless.'

In another gay bar for lunch – Cliff was finding them everywhere – they were playing Karen Carpenter's long-lost solo LP.

'She should have sung a song with Elvis,' Cliff said.

'That would have been something.' Liz looked round. The bar was dark and full of flashing games machines. Karen Carpenter's voice made Liz feel sad, and vaguely guilty for being hungry and looking through the menu. She was pleased Karen managed a year away from her drippy brother for her own music. At least she had that time away.

'Just think,' said Cliff. 'As Elvis was getting fatter and fatter, Karen Carpenter was getting thinner and thinner.'

'Maybe he was eating her.'

'That's horrible!'

'I wish I hadn't thought of that.' She shook her head to clear it. 'Look, can we go to a *normal* bar once in a while?'

'What's wrong with this?'

She sighed. 'It's like the Cantina scene in *Stars Wars before* they tarted it up.'

'I thought we were escaping from the straight world.'

'Well, that's ridiculous. That's like saying we're escaping into the universe of anti-matter. Life's not like that.'

He had *BOYZ* magazine open on the table. It showed a map dotted with all the queer hotspots. It was an alternative Britain. When they re-entered England tomorrow, as they planned to, it would be according to this map. Heading down the west coast; to Blackpool, then across to Manchester. You could plan your life and never go near the straight world again. Suddenly Liz felt queasy.

'Everything's about having a good time,' she said thoughtfully.

'Yeah?'

'I mean, it's what we used to call the nite life. Everything on this map is about the nite life.'

'Don't sound so disapproving,' he said. '*We* met in a seedy nightclub, remember.'

'I know, and I wouldn't be without it, but . . . you can't make a whole life out of the things you do at night!' She burst out with this too loudly and the people at the next table looked up.

Then their food came and the next thing was that Liz had a headache because of the dim lights. It could have been any time of the day or night in lighting like that, which is flattering to the over-forties, but it always killed Liz's eyes.

They set off the next morning. The weather was lifting.

Cliff said, 'Anyway, when we get back to England it won't all be fun and games. We need money. I'll have to get some work.'

'Doing what?'

'Some kind of labouring thing, I suppose.'

She watched the countryside flash by. They were heading to some gay b. & b. in Penrith he'd read about.

'I don't know where all the money's gone,' he said. 'We've just been chucking it away.'

'Yes,' she said. Talk of money always filled Liz with dread. Being asked what she did with money was like being asked what she did with time. They both just vanished. That's how life went by. Best not keep count. She'd never balanced a cheque book or kept a diary in her life.

'You're very quiet,' Cliff said.

'I was just thinking, I never have anything to show for what I spend.'

He laughed. 'That just means you've had a good time. You've blown it all.'

She smiled.

'People are jealous of people like you,' he added. 'You don't worry about blowing it.'

'Everything vanishes,' she said.

When we leave Scotland, more pictures at the border.

A twelve-foot column of rock on a hill marks the change, with the names of the countries it divides chiselled either side. Cliff wants to photo me pointing at the names. This is where we've been.

A woman with an accent you can't pin down is boiling hot dogs and pouring cups of tea in a caravan. She's got a plastic headscarf on, keeping down her wispy hair, because the wind manages to reach right into her van.

We are about to be served when from behind us a little old man shouts out that he wants two bacon sandwiches, but he's not queueing in the cold. He'll wait in his car with his little old wife. Then he sees he's pushed in on us.

'Sorry, honey,' he shouts to me across the car park. 'Ladies first.'

CECILIA TAN

Cecilia Tan is the author of *Black Feathers: Erotic Dreams* and *The Velderet*. Her stories have appeared in *Best American Erotica 1996* and 1998, *Best Lesbian Erotica 1997* and in many other anthologies and magazines. She also edits anthologies of erotic science fiction and fantasy for Circlet Press in Cambridge, Massachusetts.

'Juno,' she says, is 'something of a period piece, as it takes place in the 1980s prior to militant gay activism and high profile gay media.' However, the situation it describes is timeless, like the incomprehensible workings of the laws of attraction.

Juno

Jean-Michel rolls over in bed. The manoeuvre must be done with care, as the bed is so narrow he has fallen out more than once. Jean-Michel yawns and stretches, as best he can, feeling languid and warm. His partner has long since gone, but he basks in the afterglow, brushing the hairs on his stomach with his fingertips while he remembers the evening in greater detail. He picks up the red telephone by his head and dials his sister.

'Hello?'

'*Bonjour.*'

'Mee-shay,' she says. 'I am just on my way out. How are you?'

'Fine. I am still in bed.'

'Lazy. You had a date last night, didn't you?'

He smiles, pressing his hand against his stomach. 'Let me tell you about it. I met her in the hospital.'

'Did you get the bandages off your foot?'

'Yes, yes, the cast is off. Now be quiet and let me tell.' He closes his eyes, draws a deep breath, and speaks. 'Her skin was white as pearl, white but with a glow underneath, and her hair was black like the feathers of a raven. She spoke so quietly to me, and touched me so gently, I just knew I had to bring her home with me.'

'She was your nurse?'

'Yes. She took to me like a fish to the sea, drinking me in. She slept here last night. I am exhausted!' Jean-Michel rolls over with the telephone, hugging the dark blue sheets.

'You are a liar. Tell me what was *his* name, really.'

He replies 'Sherrie,' but the pause has been long enough that Amanda knows it is a bluff.

'Why do you even bother to lie to me, Mee-shay? You do not delude me. You delude yourself.' She moves the phone from one ear to the other. 'You listen to me. Mother would turn over in her grave if she could see you, now. I kept your secret only because I thought the news would kill her . . .'

Jean-Michel puts the pillow over his head, reducing Amanda's voice to a tinny squeak. When he hears a moment of silence he sits up and talks to the receiver. 'Tell me why we came to this country.'

'You are an idiot. I have to go to meet a client, now. You go back to your fantasies and—' Before she can say more, Jean-Michel has hung up.

He stands up in the narrow space between his bed and desk. The desk has had many coats of paint in its lifetime, the latest one white, the colour of paper. A late-model Selectric typewriter sits next to a plastic cup full of pens and pencils and other elongated objects which have found a home there – markers, crayons, chopsticks, things of unknown use and origin. When Jean-Michel touches the wall above the desk with his hand, he can reach the wall the bed is against with his good foot. From the wardrobe next to the desk he takes a robe and hobbles to the kitchen to make some tea.

He picks up the sturdy cane they gave him at the hospital. Just two or three weeks with the cane, they said, and you should be walking fine again. He smiles into the mirror, leaning on the cane with his head at a rakish angle. The ankle is still stiff from the injury and the time spent in plaster, but the cane looks good. He has put on loose, canvas pants and a white shirt with long sleeves. He twirls the cane. He lunges with it. He glances to see if it is raining and decides to take the cane for a spin.

He browses though the racks at the large newsstand on the corner. Many people are standing in the aisles, reading science magazines, literary journals, comic books, newspapers from faraway places. While he appreciates the owner's leniency, it makes it difficult to see the racks. He looks for *Advocate Men*. He has never read it before; he has never dared to buy it. But it is time to look for new markets to write for, and he justifies his decision to buy it that way. He spots one copy on the rack one aisle over.

From between two overcoats, a small, plain hand reaches for the only copy there. Curious, he traces the arm back to the face. At first, he thinks it is a boy, with short black hair, coarse like an Oriental's and cut bluntly. But as the rest of the body steps between the businessmen, Jean-Michel knows it is a girl. A woman, rather, wearing oversize canvas pants like his and an open suit jacket. He wonders if she is a student at New York University. She catches him looking at her, then, and winks.

She starts toward him. He notices she is also carrying the *Village Voice*, and another magazine under it. 'Did you want this?' she says, holding up the magazine with a beefy, bare-chested blond leering from its cover. He cannot answer. He is too conscious of the people filling the aisle, of the man at the cash register looking down over him, of the volume of her voice.

As she comes closer it softens. 'If you really want it I'll give it to you.' She smirks. 'But if you are just interested in the pictures, *Playgirl* is much better this month.'

He opens his mouth but still hasn't thought of something to say. He can't. She laughs. 'Don't be embarrassed. I'll buy it for you if you want.'

'No, that's all right.' He eyes the door. 'I'm a writer and I was curious—'

'OK, OK, I won't hassle you about it. I can always borrow a copy.' She jerks her head toward the high counter where a clerk is perched looking for shoplifters. Magazines in hand, she works her way through the crowd and Jean-Michel follows. Her eyes barely see over the tall countertop when she is on tip-toe. She must be just over five feet tall, he thinks. She pays for all of the magazines, takes them in a bag and then beckons for him to come outside.

'Here you go.' She takes her purchases from the bag and hands it to him with *Advocate Men* inside. She pats the bag. 'Since you are still sensitive about that sort of thing . . .'

'Thank you.' He cannot take his eyes away from hers. She has an uncanny stare. 'How much do I owe you?'

'Oh, don't worry about it.' She makes a loose-wristed motion. 'But if you really feel indebted you could take me to lunch.'

Her smile is open and friendly. Intrigued, he nods. 'Very well, lunch it is. What do you eat?'

'Anything. What is your name?'

'Jean-Michel.'

'That is very beautiful.' She falls silent a moment before speaking again. 'I am Juno.' She offers him her arm, and they walk in search of lunch, a bit slowly because of the cane.

Juno takes him to a place called Phebe's in the East Village, where she seems to know all of the waitresses and waiters. 'Quite a few of them are gay, you know,' she says, sipping a straight club soda through a stir-stick.

'That's very interesting.' He cannot figure what she is driving at.

She crosses over to his side of the table and they look at the magazines together. He has never seen the inside of a *Playgirl* before. Where do they find all these dark-skinned men with blue eyes? Jean-Michel wonders aloud. She points out that they could be coloured contact lenses.

'But it's nice to fantasize, isn't it?'

'Yes.' Briefly he wonders what Amanda would say if she saw him lunching with a woman and poring over glossy photos of naked men. Juno picks out Mr March as her favourite. He can feel the strain of an erection stirring in his groin.

Juno tells him about her friends. The waitress who serves them is named Judy, and she is also a poet. She helps out at the WOW café, a performance space for women just around the corner. The bartender's name is Russell, but he is engaged to another man, Juno says, so Jean-Michel shouldn't even think about him. He has to laugh. She says the things that he will not. She asks him very few questions, almost, he thinks, as if she already knew all about him.

'When I was a child,' she says, 'my mother used to put a *pink* bow in my hair and take me for walks in the park. And people would bend down to the stroller and say "oh, what a cute little boy!" As an infant, of course, I didn't notice it much. Later I grew to like it. I always kept my hair short, since it would mat into terrible knots and I would scream and scream while my mom tried to brush them out. Ugh, thank God for creme rinse!'

She has him smiling and laughing all through the meal.

'Men's clothes fit me better, too. Except for shoes, of course. If it weren't for my feet, I'd say I would have made a pretty good boy. Eh?'

He nods.

She cocks her head. 'Jean-Michel, do you think I would have been a good-looking boy?'

'You would have been a very sexy boy, Juno.'

She smiles, quiet for a moment. Then, she sits back, and smirks. 'I bet Mr March is gay.' Before he knows it, the subject has changed. She smooths his light-brown waves of hair with her small hand. In the front there are streaks of blond from the sun. She tugs lightly on his forelock and it covers his left eye. 'Have you always had your hair this way?'

'I have been letting it grow since we came to America.'

'We?' For a moment her eyes are guarded.

'My sister and I. We came a few months ago. She is living uptown with her American fiancé.' He feels gooseflesh as she moves her hand up the nape of his neck, combing the hair out of his collar with her fingertips.

'If you want to get it cut, I can recommend some places to you.' Her voice is the quietest it has been all afternoon. 'Or, I can do it myself.' He cannot take his eyes away from hers. He is frozen. He wants to protest, but can't help but think he must be imagining this come on. He tries to think back to when it began, to prove to himself it is just his imagination. But it is hard to think of anything other than the wad of flesh in his canvas pants and the round face of a boy in front of him.

*

'So, how did you hurt your foot?' She is spooning gourmet ice-cream into her mouth, pausing only to chew the almonds.

He chuckles. 'Moving into my apartment. There is a step which is higher than the others, and I tripped on it and fell down the stairs. That was before the elevator was fixed.' He points east with the cane. 'The cast was just removed yesterday over at Beth-Israel.' From where they are seated in the park, the round shape of the hospital building is not visible.

Juno shoos away pigeons with her foot. 'Does it hurt?'

'No. It would if I twisted it, though.'

A smirk lifts her cheeks. 'Want to go uptown, then?'

Jean-Michel thinks for a moment. 'Where, uptown?'

'Anywhere!'

She takes him first to Thirty-fourth Street on the subway. She speaks Spanish to the vendors selling toy birds, sunglasses, hats. She buys a cabbie hat. She shows him the vast outside of Macy's and swears she has never bought anything in it. She puts a token in his hand and they ride the bus further up, to Trump Towers, where pieces of chocolate are sold for more than the price of their entire lunch. He offers to buy some for her, but she insists that the chocolate is better at another place she knows, and cheaper, too. She talks a carriage driver she knows into taking them through Central Park.

After dark, they take the bus back down to the East Village. Jean-Michel has some trouble manoeuvring with the cane at first, trying to hang on to a pole and it at the same time, but a few blocks later more seats become free and he sits. Juno is silent in the bus, not meeting the eyes of the other passengers.

Jean-Michel worries a bit. In the hours he has known her, she has never been so quiet or withdrawn. He follows her off the bus at St Mark's Place and walks with her a block east before speaking. 'Juno? Do you feel all right?'

She stops walking, faces him. 'I don't know what to do.'

'What do you mean?'

She chews her bottom lip. 'I—' She looks around the street.

'Do you want to go home? Do you want to tell me something?'

'Yes. Yes, please.' She jerks her chin forward, indicating he should lead the way.

He walks her to his apartment. They ride the cage elevator in silence. He wishes he had a secondhand sofa to sit her on, but there is no furniture yet but his bed and his desk. He puts her at the edge of the bed and leans the cane and himself against the desk gently, as if to make a loud sound might frighten her away. 'Please tell me what's wrong.'

She looks at him. He feels her appraisal of his figure, her eyes lingering over his hips, his hands, his chest, before she looks into his eyes. 'Jean-Michel,' she begins. 'I'm confused. I'm mixed up. I don't know what I want.'

He waits for her to say more, encouraging her by squatting down in front of her. His ankle makes a small sound, but holds.

'You are a very nice person,' she says. 'You could be my friend.'

'I am your friend.' He cannot figure what she is driving at.

'Yes, you are my friend. I am your friend, too.' She reaches with both hands toward him. She holds his head behind his ears. 'But—' She drops her hands and closes her eyes.

Jean-Michel thinks of the restaurant and feels something in the pit of his stomach move, a dull throbbing down below. 'Juno,' he says, hoping she will open her eyes again, 'I have been with women before in my life. I think you are very . . .'

She stiffens, clenching her eyes. 'No. You don't understand.'

'Are you afraid that if I love you, that I will not like you?' The palms of his hands grow hot and he wants to touch her.

'Yes. And no.' She fixes her gaze in the middle of his chest. 'I want to be friends. That's true.' She lets out another slow breath. 'And I want you.' Another breath. 'But I want you to . . .' She whispers the rest and he cannot hear it. She rolls over on to her side, the bed creaking as she moves.

'Juno?' He moves to the floor to sit by her head. He grasps her hand. 'Tell me?'

She pulls his ear to her mouth. 'I want to be your boy.' Unable to move, she does not let go.

Her fear paralyses him for only a moment. Then he kisses her ear, wets it with his tongue. She begins to uncurl, peers at him, questioning.

'And I thought I had a difficult time, sometimes,' he says, smoothing her hair back from her face. He sits back on his heels and his erection shifts.

She moves on to the floor next to him, straightens the flannel hat on her head. 'Do you want me?'

He pauses for a moment, while some overly sensible part of his brain tries to stop him on principle. 'Yes.' He touches her lips with his fingers. 'Don't be ashamed. I'm not.' I am not, he tells himself. He tastes the back of her neck and the desire to throw her down on her stomach grows.

'Don't be afraid to hurt me,' she whispers.

He reaches around her waist from behind and slips the wide pants off her narrow hips. He holds her close and feels her heart beating like a hummingbird's. 'Come here.' The jacket and shirt slip off, too, and he tosses them with his own shirt up on to the bed. The skin of her back is smooth as he runs his hands down from her shoulders to her buttocks. 'Relax. Relax.' Her back, her narrow, fine back reminds him of Jean-Pierre, when they were both fourteen and summered together with their families. He tells her so with a whisper into her ear. 'He had hair like yours, black and feathery, and his grandmama would never let him out into the sun, so we spent hours and hours in the attic of her summer house . . .' He presses her against the carpet in the small space between the bed and the desk and the hat falls away. As he presses his bare skin to hers, he kneads her shoulders. The tip of his penis has pushed out of his waistband.

'We would sit in the attic and make ourselves hard. And I would always let him when he would want to come inside me.' He runs his hands down that back again, holding her hips. She lets out a small gasp. 'But when it would be my turn to come into him, he would sometimes get scared.' He strokes her hairless buttocks. 'And I would whisper to him, "Jean-Pierre, Jean-Pierre, do not be afraid. It is only fair that you do your manly duty." She shivers, when she feels his naked legs against hers. 'And though he would moan and whimper, he would never fight me.'

109

A terrific shudder wracks her small body as she anticipates his entry. 'Don't wait,' she whispers. Her voice is low and hoarse. 'Take me.'

He wonders if there is another woman like this in the world, with a lonely boy trapped inside. 'As you give yourself to me,' he says, and pushes against her tailbone. The tip is becoming slick and he spits into his hand and helps it along. He spreads her buttocks and uses the tip of his tongue to moisten the way. And then he presses the head against the tightness there, and presses, holding her firm by the hips, and presses, until the flesh begins to give, and he nearly falls forward into her.

She claws at the carpet and opens her mouth but makes no sound.

'Oui, my darling boy,' he says, his voice coming rough through his own fast breaths, as he feels like his whole body is sinking as he penetrates her, 'oui, my sweet one.' He moves his grip to her shoulders as he moves in and out of her. 'Jean-Pierre always said that it hurt, but I suspect that he liked it that way best.'

'I am sure,' she gasps a bit as she speaks, 'that he did.' She presses her face to the carpet and closes her eyes, but not too tight. As his rhythm builds she twitches a bit, and seems lost in it.

He is beginning to lose himself, too. It is only when his ankle begins to throb that he thinks perhaps he must end this. 'Jean-Pierre,' he whispers, 'Jean-Pierre, do you remember how you used to make it so tight . . .?'

'I do.'

And then there is nothing to hold him back from a final frenzied set of thrusts. He spends himself with a guttural cry as he presses his cheek to the smoothness of her back.

A minute or so later, he helps her into the bed and they lie together soaking up each other's sweat. 'What else can I do for you?' he asks, trying to think of an adequate way to reciprocate.

'Nothing,' she murmurs, a wide, satisfied smile on her face. 'I'm full.'

'Amanda?' He presses the receiver to his ear with his shoulder.

'Yes, Miche' is that you? How are you?'

'I'm fine. I met someone I think you would like to meet.'

Amanda snorts. 'Don't tell me, let me guess. She has black hair and fair skin.'

'You are right so far.'

'Come, now, Jean-Michel, when are you going to get tired of—'

'Her name is Juno. She is right here.' She puts her hand over her mouth, trying to keep from laughing aloud. Jean-Michel continues. 'Would you like to know more about her?'

'Yes, yes, for the sake of your future as a romance novel writer. Tell me about this ravishing beauty.'

He looks her over with a critical eye. 'Well, first of all, she is very short. Five feet and five inches. And she wears no make-up. Her bright eyes and smiling lips need none. On her hands are no rings, just short, round, trimmed nails, and smooth skin. As you said before, her hair is black, and is shorter than mine.'

111

'Delightful.' Amanda applauds. 'So, this is your ideal lover? She sounds like a boy.'

'Thank you,' says Juno into the receiver, ready to burst from contained laughter. 'Let's do lunch sometime.' That sets him to laughing, and together they hang up the phone.

FAY WELDON

Fay Weldon's first novel, *The Fat Woman's Joke*, published in 1967, was one of the first, prescient books to catch the mood of an emerging feminist consciousness. She has gone on to write many more novels, plays and short stories, many offering a polemical commentary on the relations between men and women. Her best-known novels include *Praxis*, *Puffball*, *The Lives and Loves of a She-Devil*, *The Cloning of Johanna May*, *Affliction* and *Splitting*.

What's normal? Stay out of the hands of psychiatrists and/or the law and you can work it out for yourself. Otherwise, you may find it necessary to spend your life playing a role defined by musty old rule-books.

Down the Clinical Disco

You never know where you'll meet your own true love. I met mine down the clinical disco. That's him over there, the thin guy with the jeans, the navy jumper and the red woolly cap. He looks pretty much like anyone else, don't you think? That's hard work on his part, not to mention mine, but we got there in the end. Do you want a drink? Gin? Tonic? Fine. I'll just have an orange juice. I don't drink. Got to be careful. You never know who's watching. They're everywhere. Sorry, forget I said that. Even a joke can be paranoia. Do you like my hair? That's a golden gloss rinse. Not my style really: I have this scar down my cheek: see, if I turn to the light? A good short crop is what suits me best, always has been: I suppose I've got what you'd call a strong face. Oops, sorry, dear, didn't mean to spill your gin; it's the heels. I do my best but I can never quite manage stilettos. But it's an ill wind; anyone watching would think I'm ever so slightly tipsy, and that's normal, isn't it. It is not absolutely A-okay not to drink alcohol. On the obsessive side. *Darling, of course there are people watching.*

Let me tell you about the clinical disco while Eddie finishes his game of darts. He hates darts but darts are what men do in pubs, okay? The clinical disco is what they have once a month at Broadmoor. (Yes, that place. Broadmoor. The secure hospital for the criminally insane.) You didn't know they had women there? They do. One woman to every nine men. They often don't look all that like women when they go in but they sure as hell look like them when (and if, if, if, if, if, if) they go out.

How did I get to be in there? You really want to know? I'd been having this crummy time at home and this crummy time at work. I was pregnant and married to this guy I loved, God knows why, in retrospect, but I did, only he fancied my

114

mother, and he got her pregnant too – while I was out at work – did you know women can get pregnant at fifty? He didn't, she didn't, I didn't – but she was! My mum said he only married me to be near her anyway and I was the one who ought to have an abortion. So I did. It went wrong and messed me up inside, so I couldn't have babies, and my mum said what did it matter, I was a lesbian anyway, just look at me. I got the scar in a road accident, in case you're wondering. And I thought what the hell, who wants a man, who wants a mother, and walked out on them. And I was working at the Royal Opera House for this man who was a real pain, and you know how these places get: the dramas and the rows and the overwork and the underpay and the show must go on though you're dropping dead. Dropping dead babies. No, I'm not crying. What do you think I am, a depressive? I'm as normal as the next person.

What I did was set fire to the office. Just an impulse. I was having these terrible pains and he made me work late. He said it was my fault Der Rosenkavalier's wig didn't fit: he said I'd made his opera house a laughing stock: the wig slipped and the *New York Times* noticed and jeered. But it wasn't my fault about the wig: wardrobe had put the message through to props, not administration. And I sat in front of the VDU – the union is against them: they cause infertility in women but what employer's going to worry about a thing like that – they'd prefer everyone childless any day – and thought about my husband and my mum, five months pregnant, and lit a cigarette. I'd given up smoking for a whole year but this business at home had made me start again. Have you ever had an abortion at five months? No? Not many have.

How's your drink? How's Eddie getting on with the darts? Started another game? That's A-okay, that's fine by me, that's normal.

So what were we saying, Linda? Oh yes, arson. That's what they called it. I just moved my cigarette lighter under the curtains and they went up, whoosh, and they caught some kind of soundproof ceiling infill they use these days instead of plaster. Up it all went. Whoosh again. Four hundred pounds' worth of damage. Or so they said. If you ask me, they were glad of the excuse to redecorate.

Like a fool, instead of lying and just saying it was an accident, I said I'd done it on purpose, I was glad I had, opera was a waste of public funds, and working late was a waste of my life. That was before I got to court. The solicitor laddie warned me off. He said arson was no laughing matter, they came down very hard on arson. I thought a fine, perhaps: he said no, prison. Years not months.

You know my mum didn't even come to the hearing? She had a baby girl. I thought there might be something wrong with it, my mum being so old, but there wasn't. Perhaps the father being so young made up for it.

*

There was a barrister chappie. He said look you've been upset, you are upset, all this business at home. The thing for you to do is plead insane; we'll get you sent to Broadmoor, it's the best place in the country for psychiatric care, they'll have you right in the head in no time. Otherwise it's Holloway, and that's all strip cells and major tranquillizers, and not so much of a short sharp shock as a long sharp shock. Years, it could be, arson.

So that's what I did, I pleaded insane, and got an indefinite sentence, which meant into Broadmoor until such time as I was cured and safe to be let out into the world again. I never was unsafe. You know what one of those famous opera singers said when she heard what I'd done? 'Good for Philly,' she said. 'Best thing that could possibly happen: the whole place razed to the ground.' Only of course it wasn't razed to the ground, there was just one room already in need of redecoration slightly blackened. When did I realize I'd made a mistake? The minute I saw Broadmoor: a great black pile: the second I got into this reception room. There were three women nurses in there, standing around a bath of hot water; great hefty women, and male nurses too, and they were talking and laughing. Well, not exactly laughing, but an Inside equivalent; a sort of heavy grunting ha-ha-ha they manage, halfway between sex and hate. They didn't even look at me as I came in. I was terrified, you can imagine. One of them said 'strip' over her shoulder and I just stood there not believing it. So she barked 'strip' again, so I took off a cardigan and my shoes, and then one of them just ripped everything off me and pushed my legs apart and yanked out a Tampax – sorry about this, Linda – and threw it in a bin and dunked me in the bath without even seeing me. Do you know what's worse than being naked and seen by strangers, including men strangers? It's being naked and unseen, because you don't even count as a woman. Why men? In case the women patients are uncontrollable. The bath was dirty. So were the nurses. I asked for a sanitary towel but no one replied. I don't know if they were being cruel: I don't think they thought that what came out of my mouth were words. Well I was mad, wasn't I? That's why I was there. I was mad because I was a patient, I was wicked because I was a prisoner: they were sane because they were nurses and good because they could go home after work.

Linda, is that guy over there in the suit watching? No? You're sure?

They didn't go far, mind you, most of them. They lived, breathed, slept The Hospital. Whole families of nurses live in houses at the foot of the great Broadmoor wall. They intermarry. Complain about one and you find you're talking to the cousin, aunt, lover or best friend of the complainee. You learn to shut up: you learn to smile. I was a tea bag for the whole of one day and I never stopped smiling from dawn to dusk. That's right, I was a tea bag. Nurse Kelly put a wooden frame round my shoulders and hung a piece of gauze front and back and said 'You be a tea bag all day' so I was. How we all laughed. Why did he want me to be a tea bag? It was his little joke. They get bored, you see. They look to the patients for entertainment.

Treatment? Linda, I saw one psychiatrist six times and I was there three years. The men do better. They have rehabilitation programmes, ping-pong, carpentry and we all get videos. Only the men get to choose the video and they always choose blue films. They have to choose them to show they're normal, and the women have to choose not to see them to show the same. You have to be normal to get out. Sister in the ward fills in the report cards. She's the one who decides whether or not you're sane enough to go before the Parole Committee. The trouble is, she's not so sane herself. She's more institutionalized than the patients.

Eddie, come and join us! How was your game? You won? Better not do that too often. You don't want to be seen as an over-achiever. This is Linda, I'm telling her how we met. At the clinical disco. Shall we do a little dance, just the pair of us, in the middle of everything and everyone, just to celebrate being out? No, you're right, that would be just plain mad. Eddie and I love each other, Linda, we met at the clinical disco, down Broadmoor way. Who knows, the doctor may have been wrong about me not having babies; stranger things happen. My mum ran out on my ex, leaving him to look after the baby: he came to visit me in Broadmoor once and asked me to go back to him, but I wouldn't. Sister put me back for that: a proper woman wants to go back to her husband, even

119

though he's her little sister's father. And after he'd gone I cried. You must never cry in Broadmoor. It means you're depressed and that's the worst madness of all. The staff all love it in there, and think you're really crazy if you don't. I guess they get kind of offended if you cry. So it's on with the lipstick and smile, smile, smile, though everyone around you is ballooning with largactyl and barking like the dogs they think they are.

I tell you something, Linda, these places are mad-houses. Never, never plead the balance of your mind is disturbed in court: get a prison sentence and relax, and wait for time to pass and one day you'll be free. Once you're in a secure hospital, you may never get out at all, and they fill the women up with so many tranquillizers, you may never be fit to. The drugs give you brain damage. But I reckon I'm all right; my hands tremble a bit, and my mouth twitches sometimes, but it's not too bad. And I'm still *me*, aren't I. Eddie's fine – they don't give men so much, sometimes none at all. Only you never know what's in the tea. But you can't be seen not drinking it, because that's paranoia.

Eddie says I should sue the barrister, with his fine talk of therapy and treatment in Broadmoor, but I reckon I won't. Once you've been in you're never safe. They can pop you back inside if you cause any trouble at all, and they're the ones who decide what trouble is. So we keep our mouths shut and our noses clean, we ex-inmates of Broadmoor.

*

Are you sure that man's not watching? Is there something wrong with us? Eddie? You're not wearing your earring, are you? Turn your head. No, that's all right. We look just like everyone else. Don't we? Is my lipstick smudged? Christ, I hate wearing it. It makes my eyes look small.

At the clinical disco! They hold them at Broadmoor every month. Lots of the men in there are sex offenders, rapists, mass murderers, torturers, child abusers, flashers. The staff like to see how they're getting on, how they react to the opposite sex, and on the morning of the disco Sister turns up and says 'you go' and 'you' and 'you' and of course you can't say no, no matter how scared you are. Because you're supposed to want to dance. And the male staff gee up the men – hey, look at those titties! Wouldn't you like to look up *that* skirt – and stand by looking forward to the trouble, a bit of living porno, better than a blue film any day. And they gee up the women too: wow, there's a handsome hunk of male: and you have to act interested, because that's normal: if they think you're a lezzie you never get out. And the men have to act interested, but not too interested. Eddie and I met at the clinical disco, acting just gently interested. Eddie felt up my titties, and I rubbed myself against him and the staff watched and all of a sudden he said 'Hey, I mean really,' and I said 'Hi,' and he said 'Sorry about this, keep smiling,' and I said, 'Ditto, what are you in for?' and he said 'I got a job as a woman teacher. Six little girls framed me. But I love teaching, not little girls. There was just no job for a man,' and I believed him: nobody else ever had. And I told him about my mum and my ex, and he seemed to understand. Didn't you, Eddie! That's love, you see. Love at first sight. You're just on the other person's side, and if you can find someone else like that about you, everything falls into place. We were both out in three months. It didn't matter for once if I wore lipstick, it didn't matter to him if he had to watch blue films: you stop thinking that acting sane is driving you mad: you don't have not to cry because you stop wanting to cry: the barking and howling and screeching stop worrying you; I guess when you're in love you're just happy so they have to turn you out; because your being happy shows them up. If you're happy, what does sane or insane mean, what are their lives all about? They can't bear to see it.

Linda, it's been great meeting you. Eddie and I are off home now. I've talked too much. Sorry. When we're our side of our front door I scrub off the make-up and get into jeans and he gets into drag, and we're ourselves, and we just hope no one comes knocking on the door to say, hey that's not normal, back to Broadmoor, but I reckon love's a talisman. If we hold on to that we'll be okay.

MARY FLANAGAN

Mary Flanagan was born and educated in the United States but has lived in London for many years. Her first book, a collection of short stories called *Bad Girls*, came out to much acclaim in 1984, followed by the novels *Trust* and *Rose Reason* and another collection, *The Blue Woman*. Her most recent novel, *Adele*, is an erotically charged thriller concerning the discovery, by present-day academics, of the history of a mysterious French prostitute imprisoned and examined by an English doctor pursuing his research into human sexuality in Paris in the 1930s.

Definition of what was 'normal' in human sexuality could be pronounced on with far more authority by doctors in the 1930s than most would dare today. For many of us, as for the characters in the following story, 'normal' is a moveable feast . . . although there *are* limits!

What's Normal?

Remember me in 1982? Remember how restless and antsy I was, running back and forth to Europe and getting on and off planes with a passport and no plans? Spreading myself across the planet like it was toast and I was raspberry jam. Six different apartments I lived in that year, or maybe that was '83. Plus no money and no regular job in that dawn of the new age of big-time spenders. Didn't own a television or CDs or a video or a personal computer. Didn't *own*, period. Well I guess you remember all right. I wanted an anarchistic existence, a chequered career, and boy that's what I got. Didn't even have to try very hard.

Anyway, let's forget about me. I'm only reminding you of that louche chapter to stress the contrast with my present situation. I mean I'm settled, right? Got a job, got my own apartment, got a patio with pots, got a clematis whose name I can't remember, but it's pretty impressive, don't you think? Yeah, I'm glad I changed my lifestyle. What might have happened if I hadn't. I mean the way things are now I'd be on the streets, right, living in a refrigerator crate if I was lucky. And who'd help me besides Saul? Well of course you, darling. But who else?

So, things have changed. QED. Listen, don't get impatient. It's important to sort of review all this before I tell you about Saul. You have to appreciate the dichotomy: what I was, what I am; what he was, what he is. The details are important (I've learned *that*, at least) if you don't want to be lost in abstractions all your life.

Well Gail was no abstraction, though in the beginning I thought she might be a figment of Saul's deviant imagination. It took her a while to like materialize. It also took Saul a while to tell me about her and how everything that went wrong with his life back then was down to women and to Gail and VJ in particular. Maybe he didn't want to tell me because we'd had a scene once and were possibly about to replay it, though I had misgivings. I mean Saul's a lovely guy, really lovely, and a good friend and everything, but when I saw him in September '82 I kept thinking don't trust him, don't believe him. He's your dear old friend, but something is *seriously* wrong.

Well it was. When I heard he'd left California and moved back to Manhattan which, as you know, he hated with a passion, and then that he was living in one of those residential hotels on upper Broadway, I thought whoops! Has Saul hit the skids or what?

So when I was back in New York I thought better pay a call. At first I didn't notice anything very much. I mean he was still adorable – always was a dish, right? – tall and slender, very straight, like *excellent* posture, and that long black hair and brown eyes and cute little nose. And the mouth – *very* sensuous mouth. Only we met in a bar in Washington Square where it was so dark I could only recognize him because of the way his teeth shone like white neon light when he smiled, so I missed the signs.

We sat at the bar and hugged and kissed until the bartender got impatient and asked did we want anything. Well I did, but Saul didn't. Liquor is not his vice. Such a purist. I mean he *was*. I guess he still is only in a different way. I mean he's an extremist. All purists are. Anyway we held hands while I drank spritzers (New York was hot, like boiling, and most of the time I was dehydrated because I sweat so much, but it's actually very healthy, sweating) and he downed about two gallons of grapefruit juice.

So I'm stroking his fingers and they're elegant and brown,

only he bites his nails which is kind of a turn-off. Then I looked at his other hand and noticed it was shaking – no, trembling. Like a violin string, sort of *resonating*, do you know? I didn't say anything, but he saw that I saw and he looked at me for a nano-second right in the eye, only not wanting to, like someone begging don't ask, don't enquire. And naturally I didn't. I respect Saul too much to pry. Especially in his mind. Though it's a good mind, you gotta admit. Remember how smart he was when we were at college together, before he realized he was wasting his time on Marx and Maslow and dropped out to make money? And screw every woman he ever – but darling, you know about *that*.

Pretty soon it seemed appropriate so I said, 'Well my dear old friend, shall we go?'

And he squeezed my hand but sort of perfunctorily and said he had to go to the little boys' room first (funny that vulgar streak he has). And then he smiled and asked if I didn't want to make a similar trip to the women's. So I said OK and he winked at me like he does and slipped a packet of powder into my shorts.

It was quite nice stuff too, but when I met him back at the bar I could tell he'd taken a lot more than I had. He was orbital, believe me, and I thought well OK this'll be fun, and just at that minute he asked me where I was staying. I started to say 'with you' when I realized I wasn't.

'With Lucille and Turner. Only they're away and the loft's disgusting because the roaches are back, and Irwin down-stairs didn't come to empty the litter box like he promised, and the cat's shitting everywhere and there are maggots in its

Friskies, plus this deranged tortoise who keeps bumping into the wall.'

I think he got the message that I did not want to stay in the loft. Anyway, next thing I knew we were out on the street.

'I'll call you tomorrow,' he said.

And all of a sudden I was crying, struggling with all my might not to just *sob*. And I couldn't understand myself, why I was behaving like this, so uncool, when Saul was my friend and not someone I romantically loved who was rejecting me or anything. Maybe it was the stuff he gave me, because I hadn't taken any for a while, and in a flash I knew that he did all the time. I mean more than before and probably other things as well. But he pretends not to notice my tears and wants to know if I have a pen and I do, so he takes it and grabs my wrists and turns my arm white side up and writes his telephone number very neat and careful along the vein. Then I do the same.

I was still crying. I dreaded going back to Lucille and Turner's dump and I said so. Then Saul begins to plead disability: bad sinus troubles, which did not surprise me, but he whips out a nasal spray just to prove it, and does a massive inhale, and oh dear he's sick to his stomach as well and taking two different antihistamines etc, etc. 'OK,' I said, 'I read you.'

'Give me a hug, darlin'.' His eyes were pinned like little black bugs. And I did, and he felt so good and warm it seemed even worse having to spend the night alone. Wouldn't matter if I were taking a stretch limo to the Pierre, I'd feel the same.

*

Well, with the tortoise banging all night against the skirting board, and me lying rigid anticipating a massive cockroach attack, and the stink of the litter box, I don't have to tell you that I didn't sleep too well. And the air conditioner's like Concorde revving up. But at nine on the nose it's *brrriiinnnggg, brrriiinnngggg*, and big Saul calling just like he said he would. I told him about my bad night and he said, don't worry, go to sleep, come by around four and we can have high tea.

'You'll be back by then?' I asked.

'Honey, I never leave.'

'Guess last night was an exception.'

'Anything for you.'

Oh sure.

So maybe that explained the problem. Saul had become an agoraphobic. Well, suddenly I could sleep, which I did. At two I took a shower, fed Brucie the cat in a clean dish, had some waffles and an iced coffee at the Midnight Diner then took the MRT uptown.

The Warsaw Hotel is ten storeys high and covers nearly a quarter of a city block. Its stone probably used to be pinkish, but now it's rat brown like everything else. There was a big neon sign on the roof, and it must have had a short circuit because the second W kept flickering and fluttering like it had the DT's, not unlike many of the residents. The Warsaw has a certain rep.

At four thirty p.m. on Labor Day it is not a salubrious environment. For one thing the air conditioning is circa 1946, and it's like freezing only there's no ventilation. Plus everyone's smoking like crazy and this poison cloud hangs over the lobby like some secret nuclear installation in Siberia. I went to the desk to ask for Mr Kremen, and these two guys, white and black, in sweaters and jackets were playing vicious cards and watching the ball game at maximum volume so at first they didn't hear me. 'Mr Kremen?' I yelled.

'824C,' they yelled back without looking at me and went on slamming down cards. Saul must have been having a lot of visitors. Women and dealers, probably.

Well I was not wrong, because next to him on the bed – oh wait a minute, first I have to tell you about the door which had *five* locks. He kept the chain on the catch even when he saw it was me.

'Anyone out there?' he whispered. I checked the corridor which looked like the set of a Coen Brothers film.

'No.'

'Were you followed?'

'Come on, I'd have noticed.'

'OK.' He let me in.

He wore running pants and a black T-shirt and his feet were very brown with immaculate toenails that were so pretty I wanted to paint them.

The room was like an enormous vertical coffin. And after that house he'd had in Topanga Canyon. There was one big window that looked out on a brick wall about five feet away, but it didn't really matter because even if it'd been the Bay of Naples out there you couldn't have seen it, the glass was so filthy. And then a clothes closet where he'd hung a few items, mainly T-shirts with attacking aliens on them or SAS men wading through carnage with hand-held rocket launchers. And Saul was a *pacifist*. In the middle of the room was his fold-away bed which looked like it hadn't been folded for several years. The sheets were a tangled grey. It had obviously become Saul's living room and playpen, the limits of the known world and the most he could handle in his present condition. On it were music magazines, an old *New York Times*, tobacco shreds and discarded Rizla papers, three bottles of nasal spray, a couple of low-rent crime novels, a bag of Doritos, new and unopened, the remains of a submarine sandwich, two empty Pepsi tins and the remote control for a brand new 36″ television that stood at the end of the bed so that to cross the room you had to crawl over the mattress. The blankets were in a heap under the window. The bathroom was white (tiled with those little tesserae that are in every old building on the upper West Side, you know the ones) and badly needed an interview with Mr Clean. But the mirror over the sink was immaculate, just like Saul's state-of-the-art electric toothbrush.

'What do you pay for this dump?' He kissed me.

'Too much.'

He patted the crumpled sheets, an invitation to lie down with him, gently, so as not to spill the sugar bowl of cocaine or whatever it was next to his elbow. I kicked off my shoes and wriggled up against the deflated pillows. Saul is the perfect host.

I hadn't said anything yet about the noise. He was watching a video of *Cannonball Run* with the volume so loud that finally I put my hands over my ears and kept them there, making

Expressionist faces until he finally noticed that I was in agony
and turned it down.

'You like this stuff?'

'Yip.'

Well, this was 1982 when men were men.

He offered me a generous helping from the sugar bowl, but
I said I'd wait a while. I don't know why, but there's something
about that kind of desperate greed that offends even me. And
despite the sub, which he'd probably eaten within the past
hour, his eyes, I mean his whole *demeanour* had that hungry
look. Like Brutus, no, Cassius. ('*Yon*' Cassius, right.) Anyway
he helped himself, which he did every ten minutes or so and
played roulette with the remote, re-running the same scenes
of what I guess were supposed to be comic destruction.
Whenever – and it was like rare – we hit a patch of dialogue,
wham!, he'd fast forward to the next car chase (the movie's
mostly car chases and wrecks and near-miss accidents; it's
unbelievably infantile). We watched the same screaming
pedestrians – mainly middle-aged women with small dogs –
and smashed-up Chevrolets, that just kept on going whatever
the violence, and exploding gas tanks – forwards, backwards
and upside-down. But it wasn't like it gave him any pleasure.
I could tell, the way his lips were tense like two rubber bands
holding his teeth together. It was compulsive, see? He couldn't
control it any more.

The routine went like this: two snorts from a coke spoon,
collapse back on the pillows, press buttons till he found an
interesting collison, watch it with this kind of clenched
satisfaction, shoot a blast of nasal spray up each nostril, let

131

the film run on while he sort of relaxed and asked me over and over so how are you darling, who are you fucking, where have you been, have you seen Jules, Larry, Saundra, etc then, when I try to answer him, reach for the sugar bowl, offer me some, snort, press, rigidify, relax, address me, lose interest, inhale, press and so on. Christ, I thought, he's going to have a heart attack, and imagine what this room will be like full of frantic paramedics.

I was feeling so oppressed that finally I took a blow just to get nearer Saul's brain, which is a place I don't mind visiting though I certainly wouldn't want to live there. Well it worked, and suddenly we were actually talking, only both at once, like we were trying to save time by not stopping to listen. That room was a dialogue-free zone, I'm telling you. But pretty soon we calmed down, and I didn't even mind so much having to yell above the screech of tyres and the fake Hollywood Blue Grass. And Saul started to unclam and be less robotic, and we told each other all the things that had happened since we'd last met, and for a while he stopped looking like he wanted to eat the TV, no, to *be* the TV. Then suddenly he's all tense again.

'Did you hear that?' he asked.

'If you mean the deconstructing transmission, yes.'

'No, that bump. Where was it?'

'You're pretty sensitized for someone so blown away.'

'You didn't see anyone when you came in?'

'Give me a break, Saul.' I was starting to feel edgy myself and reached for the sugar bowl. I didn't wait to be asked. All

I wanted was to get back to that space we'd occupied two minutes ago.

'It must be that cretin upstairs.' And he dived across the bed and exhumed the phone from under the pile of blankets. He dialled and waited while it rang.

'Fuck off you crazy old bitch,' he said, all of a sudden dead calm, and put down the receiver like it was contaminated.

'Who was that?'

'That was Mrs Lamanna upstairs. She thinks the CIA's investigating her and that I'm an agent.'

'Are you?'

'She calls at three in the morning and says she knows we're bugging her room. Says she can feel the vibes through the walls and floor and that they're giving her cancer and she demands I pay the hospital bills. Then she starts moving all the furniture around looking for the hidden mike.'

'Oh cool.' A roach emerged from under the blankets and checked out the room. I threw a crime novel at it and it retreated to its nest. I was a Buddhist for a while, and I don't believe in killing defenceless creatures, but cockroaches I crunch without a pang. The phone rang and kept ringing. Saul picked it up.

'Lady,' he said, 'if you call me again you won't have to wait for the cancer, *I'll* kill you.' Bam went the receiver.

'How can you kill her if you never go out? Saul, why *don't* you ever go out?'

'I like it here.'

'Please be serious. You're a wreck, babes, and it isn't

just the drugs or Mrs Lamanna. Something's wrong with you, and it's getting on my nerves if you want to know, so can we discuss the matter openly like two old friends?'

'OK, OK, just let me—' He took another blow. The phone rang again.

'Mrs Lamanna?' I asked.

'Maybe, maybe not.'

'Why don't you take the phone off the hook?'

'She'll know I'm here.'

'But she knows already.'

I counted forty-eight rings.

'I see what you mean,' I said.

'You don't.' For the first time that day he looked at me. 'I've got this little problem, darling.'

'I'm getting the picture.'

'No you're not.' Then he actually turned down the volume on the TV. 'Not the big picture.' He gave me this rueful smile. God I wanted to hug him right then. And a lot more. But I kept my hands to myself.

He'd met Gail at a rock concert he was running in Denver. Not unusual. As you know, darling, he has a groupie at every gig. One-night stand, sleep until four p.m., then on to the next. But not this time, buster. The next week she turns up in Seattle, then San Francisco, then LA where she starts calling his house. *And* he's ex-directory, *and* he never gives his number to his passing fancies. So he changes the number and for a couple of weeks everything's copesettic like my big sister used to say. Until one day a blue jeep's parked at the end of his driveway and guess who's behind the wheel. Saul locks himself in the pantry.

So it starts all over again, only this time she's turning up at restaurants where he's wooing his squeeze of the week. Gail stands outside the window staring like some dement in a Munch painting. Or he's in the recording studio and then, 'Woman to see you. Claims she's got an appointment,' and Saul's out the window and down the fire escape. The telephone calls resume as well as the soap opera messages on the answering machine. 'Saul I have to see you. And you want to see me, I can feel it. You know it in your heart, Saul. Look at yourself. Be honest. Look into your heart. Don't be scared, Saul. Stop lying to yourself.' Some people just have no sense of irony.

So there he is, LA's only man, a plate of quivering jelly, and begging the police, of all people, to help him out. But they say sorry, pal, nothing we can do under the circumstances. Has she threatened you, injured you or yours, damaged your property? In that case forget it. And Saul says OK if she shoots me or my girlfriend or sets fire to my house or pours acid on my BMW you'll do something. Probably, they say.

So suddenly he's hoping for like assault and battery but satisfaction is not forthcoming. Then she disappears, gone, like he can't believe it. Two weeks, three, a month, five months, nothing. But celebrations are short-lived because he's losing his nice fat job, and VJ wants a new manager, *female* required, no men need apply. And now he's so paranoid he thinks maybe Gail has gotten to VJ. And this injustice is capped by the Inland Revenue catastrophe with which you and everyone else are familiar. (Well he never actually *said* to shut up about it.) Anyway, darling, the past is the past and Saul's money troubles are over, as you know. It was just one of those phases, we all have them, when your stars are like bastards and nothing is going anywhere but the abyss and you just have to be all Buddhist and relax and accept terminal depression for a while.

Which I have to say Saul did. Even if he took it too far and went masochistic. I mean coming back to New York and everything. Like he wanted to torture himself with a little bondage, tie himself up in his Jewish roots and give himself regular beatings.

Then wouldn't you know, just when he's hit the Ninth Circle, who's back on the scene but Gail. Either she's psychic or there's a mole in Saul's organization because how else could she get his room and telephone numbers at the Warsaw?

'Now is when you really need me, Saul. I haven't deserted you when you're broke and alone. Just speak to me Saul, and I can make it all right.' Same old garbage. Except now she's sitting outside his door for hours on end. Just waiting. Doesn't even read a magazine or smoke a joint. Just sits and waits like a dog tied up outside a Seven-Eleven.

And New York's finest are not exactly eager to assist him either. So Saul has to creep out like a crook whenever she's like quit the premises and sneak back with supplies. Then it's the TV and the sugar bowl and Mrs Lamanna. Hiding in the gloom like the cockroach under the blankets.

136

'Christ Saul,' was all I could say. I felt sorry for him, I really did, but still I had this nasty little satisfaction at the idea of worms turning. I took his hand and kissed it, but he still wouldn't look at me. That's right, Kremen, look away, look at the TV, look at Burt Reynolds breaking his cannonballs. Don't look at a real person, honey, and whatever you do, don't look at me.

We lay on the bed for a while, Saul with one arm around me and the other one free to press buttons and snort coke. (Something else must have been in it. I wasn't feeling so great.)

'Don't you have any other videos, Saul?' I pleaded.

'Yeah, I got *The Shining, Moonraker*—'

'Oh anything.' I gave up. Right then Steven King seemed like *Hiroshima Mon Amour*.

The phone rang. Three rings, stop, ring again. Obviously it was a signal, because he picked it up, sprawled on his nice flat stomach with his head hanging over the edge of the mattress, talking low, very low.

When he'd hung up he rolled over beside me. 'Sorry sweetie, my dealer's coming.'

Translation: please split.

'OK.' It didn't bother me; I was on to Saul's wavelength now. But I was amazed to see how much of the sugar bowl's contents had disappeared. There was still enough for three or four people of normal consumption. But then, what's normal?

He pulled me down on top of him. 'Come back at two this morning,' he said. And suddenly we were rolling around like

137

lust-crazed teenagers in the parental bed. Five minutes later we stopped. We were sweating, unzipped, unbuttoned, untied but technically still dressed.

He grinned up at me. 'See you at two.'

'Saul,' I said, 'you are a very sick boy.' And I needed my head examined.

You can imagine how carefully I opened the door while Saul hid in the bathroom. Something stirred beside me like an animal in its sleep. I slammed the door like fast. Saul was locked up and safe.

She was sitting on the stained carpet with her knees pulled up to her chest and next to her a floppy black bag that looked like a dead bat. I jumped.

'Tell Saul I have to see him,' she pleaded in a soft, flat voice.

'He doesn't want to see you, Gail,' I said, cool as possible under the circumstances. She didn't look very big all crumpled up like that with her dark hair falling across her face. She wore a loose suede jacket and black jeans and her legs were tucked up under the jacket so I couldn't see her feet too well, but it looked as if she was wearing a pair of funky sandals.

'Yes he does,' she said without emotion. 'He just doesn't realize it yet.'

She didn't seem at all jealous of anything I might be doing with Saul. I guess she was used to female visitors by now. Even Gail understood that someone as cute and elusive as Saul requires resignation on a cosmic scale. If ever a man was stamped 'To Be Avoided' . . .

'Maybe if you go away for a while he'll miss you.' I tried to be helpful.

'He's always missing me. That's why I'm here. He's a very troubled soul. And I understand him.'

I started to say listen, sister, how about you just give him a break when she looked at me with those wet brown eyes that seemed too used to sadness. Like sadness was the space she chose to inhabit. It made me go all prickly and impatient.

'Suit yourself but you really should lay off.' I walked away. I can't stand masochists. I mean life deals out enough punishment. Why go shopping for more?

Now I was in a really bad mood, and I'd forgotten the little packet Saul had given me to while away my empty hours. There I was on upper Broadway on a hot Saturday night without diversion, thrown back on my own shaky inner resources and marooned in a crowd of scuzz-balls for which the area is so justly famous. I was getting that bad feeling only New York can give you when things aren't exactly copesettic. The city takes every little nuance of emotion and magnifies it under its enormous microscope, so that whatever you are you're more of. Do you know?

I checked my wallet. I had $4.76 in change, so I went to the telephone booth and waited for this black guy to finish his very involved conversation. Ten minutes later he crashed out of the booth, leaving the receiver dangling.

'Does it work?' I called after him, but he was already out of sight. I stopped the receiver in mid-swing and put it to my ear. Finito. So I went back to the lobby of the Warsaw and rang my friend Muriel who I'd promised to call back three days ago.

'Hello, my dear. We were getting worried about you.' Muriel designs handbags. It's a sort of cottage industry. She was irritatingly happy just then because she had this lesbian lover – her first – and believed that now she'd extricated herself from sick relationships with men, a sick relationship with a woman would set the world to rights. So now it was 'we'.

I said I was between appointments and could I come over and take a shower and a nap and would they give me something to eat. Oh, and did she have any money to pay the taxi driver since I'd left all mine in Tribecca? And she seemed OK about that.

Muriel is crazy but sweet, except for her psychotic terrier who looked like a hairy rat and bit people's feet. However, her new friend about whom she'd been raving, like how marvellous and groovy and smart she was and how much I'd like her, was a complete harpy. Audrey was some kind of executive who wore suits to work. She was smart all right, I could tell, and very organized: set priorities, followed agendas, that kind of thing. And she was pretty successful in the plastics company she worked for. But she had absolutely no sense of humour. Like *none*. And Muriel's always been such a good giggle. Now she'd fallen under the spell of this *obersturmbahn-fuhrer* who, I quickly sussed, was running her life. Muriel does find it more relaxing to be told what to do. I suppose it is better for her to eat three meals a day and get up before noon and pick up her underwear and remember to wash her hands after going to the bathroom. It's not like I *object* to this, only she used to be a lot more fun.

Anyway it emerged pretty fast that I was broke, so they

took me to dinner at the Thai restaurant on First Avenue. Which, I have to say, was damned generous of Audrey. Especially under the circumstances, which were that she didn't like or trust me and regarded me as some kind of anarchist tart and a terrible influence on Muriel whose past she wanted to purge, that was clear. Maybe I shouldn't have been so candid about my lifestyle, I don't know, what can you do? Besides Muriel thought it was amusing and that I was a free spirit to be admired and envied.

You know me, I can't help it, it just comes out, and naturally I told them all about Saul and Gail and Saul and me and Saul's bad habits and the whole incredible scene at the Warsaw. Muriel was riveted. She lives out a lot of fantasies through me (correction: me and the terrier), but why should I mind? Muriel's harmless.

Unlike Audrey, whose eyes were narrowing to slits as I described the general depravity.

'Why do you let him treat you like that?' she interrupted, incensed.

'Like what?'

'Jump to do his bidding, come and go when he orders you to, respond to his every whim.'

I shrugged. 'It's interesting.' And interesting is more important than pride or shame or whatever she thought I had none of. Which was why, even though we were nearly the same age and she went to the gym and didn't smoke, she looked ten years older than me, so there.

Still, I didn't want to cause any aggro for Muriel, plus Audrey was paying so I toned it down after that and thanked

Audrey like *profusely* for the dinner. Then I had a shower but no nap. Crazy to think I could sleep, but I always believe that, in spite of my track record, I'll somehow do the sensible thing. At ten minutes to two I was whizzing through Central Park in a cab paid for by Audrey, the key to Muriel's apartment in my purse. 'Just come back whenever you want. We'll be here.' See what I mean? Muriel couldn't wait for the next instalment of my West Side romance.

I was hoping to see Gail before she saw me. Not that she was all that threatening, I just kind of needed the advantage, don't ask me why. Some instinctual, biological wariness, probably. Well the hallway was empty, thank God. Only I thought what if Saul isn't here either? And the same feeling came over me that I'd had outside by the telephone booth. And I wondered why I hadn't rung him from downstairs. What a jerk. Sometimes – don't ask me why, it's bananas I know – I'm compelled to hang on to my angst.

I put my face to the door. 'It's OK,' I said, 'the coast is clear.'

He opened the door, still on the chain, like he didn't trust her not to imitate my voice. Then he unhooked it.

'Hi darlin',' he said. And I walked into his arms.

Twelve hours later I was having coffee with Muriel who was up, dressed and doing the ironing, whereas normally she'd still be flapping around in fluffy slippers, a T-shirt and cotton underpants. Audrey's training programme was taking effect. The commandant had gone out for bagels, so Muriel and I had fifteen whole minutes to gossip while the terrier Ike tore around the apartment like they'd been putting amphetamine in his Puppy Chow.

'So what do you think of Audrey?' Christ. Why did she need me to love this sourpuss?

'I think there's nothing wrong with being focused as long as you're also blurred sometimes.'

'So she's not blurred enough.'

'It's just my opinion, Muriel.'

For someone so vague, she could be awfully literal. She was panting for the latest Warsaw episode. The night had gone pretty much like the one before, except that this time we made love. Well, we probably made love. I don't remember much except that it was brief. Otherwise there was a lot of heavy petting interrupted by the arrival of a pizza, then more coke snorting, fast forwarding and nasal spraying (yeah, I was into it too by now – and they say heroin's addictive). Plus two calls from Mrs Lamanna and again no sleep. So you can imagine I was a teense tense.

Plus I'd run into Gail in the Warsaw lobby. She looked fuzzy and distant but I knew right away it was her and that she was going to speak to me. I wanted to run but felt paralysed like in a dream where everything turns to foam rubber and there are no hard surfaces to push against. She was taller than I'd thought and quite slender. Her face was long and she could have been really attractive and exotic only there was something disproportionate about her bone structure.

'Why don't you leave Saul alone?' I wondered for a minute if she'd heard me or if I'd spoken at all.

'He hates you, you know,' I said casually.

Gail looked at me, very even and calm. Then she gave me this benign smile like she had limitless compassion for the unenlightened and put her hand on my arm. The hand felt heavy like an iron weight dragging on me, pulling me down, this huge force of gravity I wasn't strong enough to resist. I wrenched my arm away, pushed through the glass doors into the street and ran for the subway. I jumped on the first train. It was going uptown, so at the next stop I crossed the platform and went straight back to Muriel's. I was really pleased to see her. And to tell someone about this action adventure in which I was co-starring and which had only another night to run because I was leaving for Paris on Tuesday.

But I didn't tell her about my really strange experience, partly because Audrey came back and partly because it was the sort of thing I just didn't discuss with Muriel, especially in her new mode. I don't know what time it was, but I was lying in bed while Saul took a shower. He came into the room, dried himself and began sliding coathangers around in the closet, searching what was left of his wardrobe. (He really had abandoned everything, and he hadn't even been a Buddhist.) And you know I could not stop looking at him, his movements, the way he stood with his hip a little to one side like a Greek statue. I was stunned by his beautiful legs, his dark skin, his – oh I don't know, his *grace*, I guess, when all of a sudden I understood what I was doing. I was watching him the way a man watches a woman, with eyes that are really hands. I wanted to capture him with my eyes, force him to lie still while I did something to him, I wasn't sure what, my head was so messed up. If we'd been in an opera, I could have sung an aria just then, something reflective about lust and mortality and pain. It surprised me how you can analyse desire and even be intellectual about it; how there was a kind of philosophy of the body I hadn't known existed and suddenly I did, though maybe I'd never fully comprehend it. And I wondered whether it was better to know about it or just stay ignorant. It seemed to put a distance between me and Saul and I didn't want that. He was far enough away as it was. On his own planet. The Little Prince, for Christ's sake.

He must have read my thoughts because he smiled and came over to the bed and took my hand and kissed the palm. And I felt all this tenderness invade me, running from his hand into mine, sliding through me like velvet rivers in my veins. I didn't realize how tightly our hands were gripping until he let go to grab his remote and switch on the television. Saul's day was off and running.

Just as the bagels arrived the phone rang. It was Saul to say he was expecting his dealer, so I shouldn't come over until four. Did he need more of that stuff already, or was it different stuff? Whatever money he had left was obviously being spent on drugs, which was one of the reasons he lived the way he did. Minimum activity equals minimum expenditure. In a perverse way Gail was doing him a favour.

So I had a couple of hours to sleep but naturally I couldn't. I ate a bagel with cream cheese then lay down in the spare bedroom, my limbs twitching, my mind in a dance of romance – the tarantella, the funky chicken . . . I couldn't wait to get back to Saul and didn't think for a single minute about leaving New York on Tuesday. Life was in present tense mode, just how I like it. All these people I was supposed to see – old friends, family – and you know I just didn't bother. Saul made everything else seem like convent school.

By four thirty I was back with Aladdin in his cave. We watched nearly twelve hours of TV with the usual interruptions including sex and Mrs Lamanna rearranging the furniture. I'd never seen the late night strip shows and Saul was worried about this gap in my cultural perspective. He believed in being right up to the minute. Mustn't fall behind, he said, settle into any kind of *slot*. No comment, Saul.

We were watching a sixty-four-year-old grandmother from Flushing remove a Superwoman costume when the telephone rang. It went on ringing while this gay guy from White Plains talked non-stop about his tropical fish while gyrating in a rhinestone posing pouch. He was really funny and had a great ass, and I was thinking what a fantastic place New York was and maybe I should live here again. The problem was if I did, there wouldn't be any place left to go back to, do you see? Then I remembered Brucie. I hoped he was OK and promised myself to ring Irwin first thing in the morning.

We were having so much fun I hardly noticed the telephone. After about five minutes it stopped. (Probably Gail.) But this had no effect on Saul because he'd passed out. Yours truly continued to sit there giggling and munching my way through a packet of Doritos. At six thirty Saul was still comatose so I wrote him a billet-doux and left. Audrey would have gone to the office, so Muriel and I could have breakfast together then maybe I'd finally get some sleep while she worked on this handbag she was sewing in the shape of a panda. Oh yeah, and I'd definitely call Irwin.

I checked the hallway and closed the doors as quietly as I could with all those rattling chains. Except for the sound of a vacuum cleaner somewhere on an upper floor, everything was quiet. I waited for the elevator. The doors opened. Three or four night creatures were slouched against the walls, heading back to their holes, I guess. Then I flipped. They stepped aside and out walked Gail.

She wore her hair up with bangs, enormous dangling earrings and leather trousers. There were dark circles under her eyes.

'The bar's open,' she said in that low vacant voice you hear only on the West Coast. 'Let's go have a drink.'

I was feeling really fucked up and in no shape to deal with this confrontation. I'd run away again. Go home to Muriel. Even Audrey would be nice to see. I wanted like crazy to escape.

'Sure,' I answered and stepped into the elevator with the assorted freaks. See what I mean? I was always acting against my best interests. And it wasn't like I didn't recognize what they were. I was completely aware, as I slid into the booth opposite Gail, that a denouement was coming that I wasn't sure I wanted to be part of. Only like I said, it was all so interesting.

They wouldn't make us margaritas at that time of the morning, so we both ordered bourbon and sodas.

'I don't normally drink,' said Gail. 'But I really need this.'

'How come?'

'To give me courage.'

She seemed pretty brave already, if you accept that brave and crazy are close or even equivalent.

'You've got to help me with Saul.'

'Me?'

'I know you can.'

'My God you know everything – that he secretly needs you, that you're his destiny, and now that I'll do you this rather large favour even though Saul and I are—'

'You and Saul are friends.' Meaning insert 'just'.

'What makes you think that?' I was starting to get hostile. 'Oh pardon me. I forgot you're omniscient.'

She ignored my tone. 'He's denying his true self. That's why he's so unhappy.'

'Could be,' I conceded.

'You have to persuade him to see me.'

'You're nuts.'

'You'll do it.' She took a large swallow. 'I know you will. And it'll work.'

Her persistence impressed me. Through a haze of heinous chemicals and nasal spray and sex and bourbon and sleepless-ness, something was stirring in the back of my brain. A lazy sleepy notion about to yawn and stretch and get up and take a walk to my frontal lobes. My eyes were full of grit and I rubbed them, forgetting all about my turquoise mascara.

'Edie—'

'How do you know my name?'

'Saul told me.'

'Oh sure.'

'You're his friend.'

'You keep saying that.'

'So do this for him.'

'You mean do it for *you*.'

She sighed.

'Listen, Edie—' she began again.

'I don't want to help you. I don't want to talk to you. I don't want to see you. Get the picture?' I started to leave.

She placed her hand on mine to stop me, and I felt the same weight and strength I had the day before. The same sense of oppression. Or maybe it was the burden of knowledge. (*Is* there such an expression or did I just invent it?) I started to make a big theatrical gesture of removing the hand and placing it firmly back on the table. I picked it up and looked at it. I looked again, harder. Then I got the picture.

'OK so you fucked a guy. What's the big deal?'

'The big deal? He only sits outside my door day and night and won't stop calling me. I'm living like a recluse, sugar, in case you hadn't noticed.'

'Yeah. That's a drag.'

We were sitting naked and cross-legged on the bed with the bowl between us. The video was going but with the sound off. We had important matters to discuss.

'Besides, I don't like being tricked.'

'Well no one likes it. But then a woman might have done the same thing.'

'I know that.'

'Maybe you should try to like negotiate. Just try it. Have you ever tried?'

'Negotiate! What's to negotiate? I want that creep out of my life. Period.'

'Saul, I love you and everything, but really you are over-reacting. OK, your manhood's been threatened, I understand. But loosen up and maybe she'll leave you alone.'

'You don't know her.'

'Maybe you don't either. Maybe it's time to examine your own motivations, then you—'

He pressed the button and turned on the sound.

Well, well, the ladies' man had been laid. OK, I decided, he can't face it. I can't force him. I thought what a mystery my old friend Saul was and was it worth it trying to crack his case? Then it was time for all the *real* weirdos, those out there on the margins of the metropolis, to give us their views on drugs, gays, abortion, the president, UFO's and the health benefits of high colonics. So he switched to the TV and settled back for two hours of other people's dementia. I could understand the attraction of all this ranting and raving. He must have felt normal by comparison.

Finally he passed out. As usual I slipped towards the edge of sleep and hovered there. I still hadn't figured out how to work his remote. So I went into the bathroom and stuffed two wads of toilet paper in my ears and went back to bed. I spent the rest of the night with Saul in my arms and occasionally slipping off into unconsciousness.

I'll tell you something: I really wanted to be with Saul, but

I also saw that he'd gone some place I could never follow. Plus his lifestyle was making me ill. Around four a.m. I got up and dressed.

'Bye lover,' I whispered and kissed his forehead. 'See you when I see you.'

He tried to pull me back into bed without actually waking up. It was automatic, grabbing the nearest body in his dreams just like he did in life.

I stepped out into the hallway and there was Gail hunched next to the door in that suede jacket, her hair falling over her face. She looked up at me with those mournful eyes. Our Lady of Sorrows. Oh please. We didn't say anything, just stared at each other. I hitched up my shoulder bag and turned toward the elevator then stopped. Then you know what I did? I never told anyone this: I left the door open.

The apartment was completely silent when I got back. Even the terrier was asleep. I sat on the sofa and cried for a while, not howling or anything, just sort of enjoying the tears. My interesting romance with Saul had turned out the world's shortest affair. We'd return to being friends, I guessed. And that was OK, it really was, only I kept wondering what would have happened if I'd gone back to bed with him. Nothing, I guess. Well something was about to happen to *him*; in fact it was probably happening right then.

I stopped crying. I was hungry. Like ravenous. I opened the refrigerator and found some left-over broccoli quiche, an ossified triangle of brie and a piece of stale devil's food cake. I sat down at the table in the dark and ate every bit of them.

*

So it's nice out here, huh. On my minuscule south-facing patio. You know I was really lucky to find this place. My friends all said I'd never get a mortgage. But I did, thanks to Darren. You know everyone complains about the suburbs, but they're not nearly as boring as they make out. And from the mall to here's a pretty quick trip.

I saw Saul a couple of times. I called him as soon as I arrived in Paris, but there was no answer, and I started to worry that maybe there'd been some sort of affray. But that's not his scene, forget all those remarks about Mrs Lamanna. A couple of months later he called me and acted like nothing weird had happened at all. He was sweet but a little edgy. He's great, Saul, isn't he? A bad boy but a good man. I asked him about Gail, but he still didn't want to discuss her. 'Gail's gone,' was all he'd say. So I guess she found someone else to torture, or maybe they had the affair they should have had in the first place. I know it sounds funny, but I hope Gail's all right. Not every man's as non-violent as Saul. Although Lamanna might have driven him to homicide if he hadn't got out of the Warsaw a couple of months later and moved into one of those high-rises further up Columbus Avenue. And you know what? He got married. *Married*, it's true. To Shirley Baines, a little blond shiksa from Neptune, New Jersey. Boy. Now he lives in Westchester and sells insurance. Completely clean, he swears. And three kids.

Mmmmmmmm. Sure is nice out here. So tell me something. How did we ever get on to the subject of Saul Kremen anyway?

RUTH RENDELL

Ruth Rendell is a bestselling author as well known for her series of Inspector Wexford mysteries (*Road Rage* is the most recent in that series) as for her evocative explorations of psychological compulsions and Gothic melodrama in contemporary lives in books like *The Keys to the Street*. She also writes under the name Barbara Vine.

'Cross-dressing is a classic strategy of disappearance in detective fiction. The lady vanishes by turning into a man – or the man by turning into a woman,' writes Marjorie Garber in *Vested Interests* (1992) and it features as such in Ruth Rendell's *A Sleeping Life* (1978). In the story that follows neither reader nor characters are in any doubt as to the identity of the new girlfriend; the mystery here is not about gender, but the much darker subject of sex.

The New Girlfriend

'You know what we did last time?' he said.

She had waited for this for weeks. 'Yes?'

'I wondered if you'd like to do it again.'

She longed to but she didn't want to sound too keen. 'Why not?'

'How about Friday afternoon, then? I've got the day off and Angie always goes to her sister's on Friday.'

'Not *always*, David.' She giggled.

He also laughed a little. 'She will this week. Do you think we could use your car? Angie'll take ours.'

'Of course. I'll come for you about two, shall I?'

'I'll open the garage doors and you can drive straight in. Oh, and Chris, could you fix it to get back a bit later? I'd love it if we could have the whole evening together.'

'I'll try,' she said, and then, 'I'm sure I can fix it. I'll tell Graham I'm going out with my new girl friend.'

He said goodbye and that he would see her on Friday. Christine put the receiver back. She had almost given up expecting a call from him. But there must have been a grain of hope still, for she had never left the receiver off the way she used to.

The last time she had done that was on a Thursday three weeks before, the day she had gone round to Angie's and found David there alone. Christine had got into the habit of taking the phone off the hook during the middle part of the day to avoid getting calls for the Midland Bank. Her number and the Midland Bank's differed by only one digit. Most days she took the receiver off at nine-thirty and put it back at three-thirty. On Thursday afternoons she nearly always went round to see Angie and never bothered to phone first.

Christine knew Angie's husband quite well. If she stayed a bit later on Thursdays she saw him when he came home from work. Sometimes she and Graham and Angie and David went out together as a foursome. She knew that David, like Graham, was a salesman or sales executive, as Graham always described himself, and she guessed from her friend's lifestyle that David was rather more successful at it. She had never found him particularly attractive, for, although he was quite tall, he had something of a girlish look and very fair wavy hair.

Graham was a heavily built, very dark man with a swarthy skin. He had to shave twice a day. Christine had started going out with him when she was fifteen and they had got married on her eighteenth birthday. She had never really known any other men at all intimately and now if she ever found herself alone with a man she felt awkward and apprehensive. The truth was that she was afraid a man might make an advance to her and the thought of that frightened her very much. For a long while she carried a penknife in her handbag in case she should need to defend herself. One evening, after they had been out with a colleague of Graham's and had had a few drinks, she told Graham about this fear of hers.

He said she was silly but he seemed rather pleased.

'When you went off to talk to those people and I was left with John I felt like that. I felt terribly nervous. I didn't know how to talk to him.'

Graham roared with laughter. 'You don't mean you thought old John was going to make a pass at you in the middle of a crowded restaurant?'

'I don't know,' Christine said. 'I never know what they'll do.'

'So long as you're not afraid of what I'll do,' said Graham, beginning to kiss her, 'that's all that matters.' There was no point in telling him now, ten years too late, that she was afraid of what he did and always had been. Of course she had got used to it, she wasn't actually terrified, she was resigned and sometimes even quite cheerful about it. David was the only man she had ever been alone with when it felt all right.

The first time, that Thursday when Angie had gone to her sister's and hadn't been able to get through on the phone and tell Christine not to come, that time it had been fine. And afterwards she had felt happy and carefree, though what had happened with David took on the colouring of a dream next day. It wasn't really believable. Early on he had said: 'Will you tell Angie?'

'Not if you don't want me to.'

'I think it would upset her, Chris. It might even wreck our marriage. You see . . .' He had hesitated. 'You see, that was the first time I – I mean, anyone ever . . .' And he had looked into her eyes. 'Thank God it was you.'

The following Thursday she had gone round to see Angie as usual. In the meantime there had been no word from David. She stayed late in order to see him, beginning to feel a little sick with apprehension, her heart beating hard when he came in.

He looked quite different from how he had when she had found him sitting at the table reading, the radio on. He was wearing a grey flannel suit and a grey striped tie. When Angie went out of the room and for a minute she was alone with him, she felt a flicker of that old wariness that was the forerunner of her fear. He was getting her a drink. She looked up and met his eyes and it was all right again. He gave her a conspiratorial smile, laying a finger on his lips.

'I'll give you a ring,' he had whispered.

She had to wait two more weeks. During that time she went twice to Angie's and twice Angie came to her. She and Graham and Angie and David went out as a foursome and while Graham was fetching drinks and Angie was in the Ladies, David looked at her and smiled and lightly touched her foot with his foot under the table.

'I'll phone you. I haven't forgotten.'

It was a Wednesday when he finally did phone. Next day Christine told Graham she had made a new friend, a girl she had met at work. She would be going out somewhere with this new friend on Friday and she wouldn't be back till eleven. She was desperately afraid he would want the car – it was *his* car or his firm's – but it so happened he would be in the office that day and would go by train. Telling him these lies didn't make her feel guilty. It wasn't as if this were some sordid affair, it was quite different.

When Friday came she dressed with great care. Normally, to go round to Angie's, she would have worn jeans and a T-shirt with a sweater over it. That was what she had on the first time she found herself alone with David. She put on a skirt and blouse and her black velvet jacket. She took the heated rollers out of her hair and brushed it into curls down on her shoulders. There was never much money to spend on clothes. The mortgage on the house took up a third of what Graham earned and half what she earned at her part-time job. But she could run to a pair of sheer black tights to go with the highest heeled shoes she'd got, her black pumps.

The doors of Angie and David's garage were wide open and

their car was gone. Christine turned into their driveway, drove into the garage and closed the doors behind her. A door at the back of the garage led into the yard and garden. The kitchen door was unlocked as it had been that Thursday three weeks before and always was on Thursday afternoons. She opened the door and walked in.

'Is that you, Chris?'

The voice sounded very male. She needed to be reassured by the sight of him. She went into the hall as he came down the stairs.

'You look lovely,' he said.

'So do you.'

He was wearing a suit. It was of navy silk with a pattern of pink and white flowers. The skirt was very short, the jacket clinched into his waist with a wide navy patent belt. The long golden hair fell to his shoulders, he was heavily made-up and this time he had painted his fingernails. He looked far more beautiful than he had that first time.

Then, three weeks before, the sound of her entry drowned in loud music from the radio, she had come upon this girl sitting at the table reading *Vogue*. For a moment she had thought it must be David's sister. She had forgotten Angie had said David was an only child. The girl had long fair hair and was wearing a red summer dress with white spots on it, white sandals and around her neck a string of white beads. When Christine saw that it was not a girl but David himself she didn't know what to do.

He stared at her in silence and without moving and then he switched off the radio. Christine said the silliest and least relevant thing.

'What are you doing home at this time?'

That made him smile. 'I'd finished so I took the rest of the day off. I should have locked the back door. Now you're here you may as well sit down.'

She sat down. She couldn't take her eyes off him. He didn't look like a man dressed up as a girl, he looked like a girl and a much prettier one than she or Angie. 'Does Angie know?'

He shook his head.

'But why do you do it?' she burst out and she looked about the room, Angie's small, rather untidy living room, at the radio, the *Vogue* magazine. 'What do you get out of it?' Something came back to her from an article she had read. 'Did your mother dress you as a girl when you were little?'

'I don't know,' he said. 'Maybe. I don't remember. I don't want to *be* a girl. I just want to dress up as one sometimes.'

The first shock of it was past and she began to feel easier with him. It wasn't as if there was anything grotesque about the way he looked. The very last thing he reminded her of was one of those female impersonators. A curious thought came into her head, that it was *nicer*, somehow more civilized, to be a woman and that if only all men were more like women . . . That was silly, of course, it couldn't be.

'And it's enough for you just to dress up and be here on your own?'

He was silent for a moment. Then, 'Since you ask, what I'd

159

really like would be to go out like this and . . .' He paused, looking at her, 'and be seen by lots of people, that's what I'd like. I've never had the nerve for that.'

The bold idea expressed itself without her having to give it a moment's thought. She wanted to do it. She was beginning to tremble with excitement.

'Let's go out then, you and I. Let's go out now. I'll put my car in your garage and you can get into it so the people next door don't see and then we'll go somewhere. Let's do that, David, shall we?'

She wondered afterwards why she had enjoyed it so much. What had it been, after all, as far as anyone else knew but two girls walking on Hampstead Heath? If Angie had suggested that the two of them do it she would have thought it a poor way of spending the afternoon. But with David . . . She hadn't even minded that of the two of them he was infinitely the better dressed, taller, better-looking, more graceful. She didn't mind now as he came down the stairs and stood in front of her.

'Where shall we go?'

'Not the Heath this time,' he said. 'Let's go shopping.' He bought a blouse in one of the big stores. Christine went into the changing room with him when he tried it on. They walked about in Hyde Park. Later on they had dinner and Christine noted that they were the only two women in the restaurant dining together.

'I'm grateful to you,' David said. He put his hand over hers on the table.

'I enjoy it,' she said. 'It's so – crazy. I really love it. You'd better not do that, had you? There's a man over there giving us a funny look.'

'Women hold hands,' he said.

'Only *those* sort of women. David, we could do this every Friday you don't have to work.'

'Why not?' he said.

There was nothing to feel guilty about. She wasn't harming Angie and she wasn't being disloyal to Graham. All she was doing was going on innocent outings with another girl. Graham wasn't interested in her new friend, he didn't even ask her name. Christine came to long for Fridays, especially for the moment when she let herself into Angie's house and saw David coming down the stairs and for the moment when they stepped out of the car in some public place and the first eyes were turned on him. They went to Holland Park, they went to the zoo, to Kew Gardens. They went to the cinema and a man sitting next to David put his hand on his knee. David loved that, it was a triumph for him, but Christine whispered they must change their seats and they did.

When they parted at the end of an evening he kissed her gently on the lips. He smelt of Alliage or Je Reviens or Opium. During the afternoon they usually went out into one of the big stores and sprayed themselves out of the tester bottles.

Angie's mother lived in the north of England. When she had to convalesce after an operation Angie went up there to look after her. She expected to be away two weeks and the second weekend of her absence Graham had to go to Brussels with the sales manager.

'We could go away somewhere for the weekend,' David said.

'Graham's sure to phone,' Christine said.

'One night then. Just for the Saturday night. You can tell him you're going out with your new girl friend and you're going to be late.'

'All right.'

It worried her that she had no nice clothes to wear. David had a small but exquisite wardrobe of suits and dresses, shoes and scarves and beautiful underclothes. He kept them in a cupboard in his office to which only he had a key and he secreted items home and back again in his briefcase. Christine hated the idea of going away for the night in her grey flannel skirt and white silk blouse and that velvet jacket while David wore his Zandra Rhodes dress. In a burst of recklessness she spent all of two weeks wages' on a linen suit.

They went in David's car. He had made the arrangements and Christine had expected they would be going to a motel twenty miles outside London. She hadn't thought it would matter much to David where they went. But he surprised her by his choice of an hotel that was a three-hundred-year-old house on the Suffolk coast.

'If we're going to do it,' he said, 'we may as well do it in style.'

She felt very comfortable with him, very happy. She tried to imagine what it would have felt like going to spend a night in an hotel with a man, a lover. If the person sitting next to

her were dressed, not in a black and white printed silk dress
and scarlet jacket but in a man's suit with shirt and tie. If the
face it gave her so much pleasure to look at were not
powdered and rouged and mascara'd but rough and already
showing beard growth. She couldn't imagine it. Or, rather, she
could only think how in that case she would have jumped out
of the car at the first red traffic lights.

They had single rooms next door to each other. The rooms
were very small but Christine could see that a double might
have been awkward for David who must at some point –
though she didn't care to think of this – have to shave and
strip down to being what he really was.

He came in and sat on her bed while she unpacked her
nightdress and spare pair of shoes.

'This is fun, isn't it?'

She nodded, squinting into the mirror, working on her
eyelids with a little brush. David always did his eyes beauti-
fully. She turned round and smiled at him.

'Let's go down and have a drink.'

The dining room, the bar, the lounge were all low-ceilinged
timbered rooms with carved wood on the walls David said
was called linenfold panelling. There were old maps and
pictures of men hunting in gilt frames and copper bowls full
of roses. Long windows were thrown open on to a terrace.
The sun was still high in the sky and it was very warm. While
Christine sat on the terrace in the sunshine David went off to
get their drinks. When he came back to their table he had a
man with him, a thickset paunchy man of about forty who
was carrying a tray with four glasses on it.

'This is Ted,' David said.

'Delighted to meet you,' Ted said. 'I've asked my friend to join us. I hope you don't mind.'

She had to say she didn't. David looked at her and from his look she could tell he had deliberately picked Ted up.

'But why did you?' she said to him afterwards. 'Why did you want to? You told me you didn't really like it when that man put his hand on you in the cinema.'

'That was so physical. This is just a laugh. You don't suppose I'd let them touch me, do you?'

Ted and Peter had the next table to theirs at dinner. Christine was silent and standoffish but David flirted with them. Ted kept leaning across and whispering to him and David giggled and smiled. You could see he was enjoying himself tremendously. Christine knew they would ask her and David to go out with them after dinner and she began to be afraid. Suppose David got carried away by the excitement of it, the 'fun', and went off somewhere with Ted, leaving her and Peter alone together? Peter had a red face and a black moustache and beard and a wart with black hairs growing out of it on his left cheek. She and David were eating steak and the waiter had brought them sharp pointed steak knives. She hadn't used hers. The steak was very tender. When no one was looking she slipped the steak knife into her bag.

Ted and Peter were still drinking coffee and brandies when David got up quite abruptly and said, 'Coming?' to Christine.

'I suppose you've arranged to meet them later?' Christine said as soon as they were out of the dining room.

David looked at her. His scarlet-painted lips parted into a wide smile. He laughed.

'I turned them down.'

'Did you *really*?'

'I could tell you hated the idea. Besides, we want to be alone, don't we? I know I want to be alone with you.'

She nearly shouted his name so that everyone could hear, the relief was so great. She controlled herself but she was trembling. 'Of course I want to be alone with you,' she said.

She put her arm in his. It wasn't uncommon, after all, for girls to walk along with linked arms. Men turned to look at David and one of them whistled. She knew it must be David the whistle was directed at because he looked so beautiful with his long golden hair and high-heeled red sandals. They walked along the sea front, along the little low promenade. It was too warm even at eight-thirty to wear a coat. There were a lot of people about but not crowds for the place was too select to attract crowds. They walked to the end of the pier. They had a drink in the Ship Inn and another in the Fisherman's Arms. A man tried to pick David up in the Fisherman's Arms but this time he was cold and distant.

'I'd like to put my arm round you,' he said as they were walking back, 'but I suppose that wouldn't do, though it is dark.'

'Better not,' said Christine. She said suddenly, 'This has been the best evening of my life.'

He looked at her. 'You really mean that?'

She nodded. 'Absolutely the best.'

They came into the hotel. 'I'm going to get them to send us up a couple of drinks. To my room. Is that OK?'

She sat on the bed. David went into the bathroom. To do his face, she thought, maybe to shave before he let the man with the drinks see him. There was a knock at the door and a waiter came in with a tray on which were two long glasses of something or other with fruit and leaves floating in it, two pink table napkins, two olives on sticks and two peppermint creams wrapped up in green paper.

Christine tasted one of the drinks. She ate an olive. She opened her handbag and took out a mirror and a lipstick and painted her lips. David came out of the bathroom. He had taken off the golden wig and washed his face. He hadn't shaved, there was a pale stubble showing on his chin and cheeks. His legs and feet were bare and he was wearing a very masculine robe made of navy blue towelling. She tried to hide her disappointment.

'You've changed,' she said brightly.

He shrugged. 'There are limits.'

He raised his glass and she raised her glass and he said: 'To us!'

The beginnings of a feeling of panic came over her. Suddenly he was so evidently a man. She edged a little way along the mattress.

'I wish we had the whole weekend.'

She nodded nervously. She was aware her body had started a faint trembling. He had noticed it too. Sometimes before he had noticed how emotion made her tremble.

'Chris,' he said.

166

She sat passive and afraid.

'I'm not really like a woman, Chris. I just play at that sometimes for fun. You know that, don't you?' The hand that touched her smelt of nail varnish remover. There were hairs on the wrist she had never noticed before. 'I'm falling in love with you,' he said. 'And you feel the same, don't you?'

She couldn't speak. He took her by the shoulders. He brought his mouth up to hers and put his arms round her and began kissing her. His skin felt abrasive and a smell as male as Graham's came off his body. She shook and shuddered. He pushed her down on the bed and his hands began undressing her, his mouth still on hers and his body heavy on top of her.

She felt behind her, put her hand into the open handbag and pulled out the knife. Because she could feel his heart beating steadily against her right breast she knew where to stab and she stabbed again and again. The bright red heart's blood spurted over her clothes and the bed and the two peppermint creams on the tray.

JOYCE CAROL OATES

Joyce Carol Oates is the author of more than twenty novels, as well as numerous short story, essay and poetry collections. She has won several O. Henry Awards for her short fiction. In 1970, the year she won a National Book Award for her novel *them*, she began to experience a series of waking visions, and particularly vivid dreams, which seemed to her to come from another personality, not her own. She began to write stories unlike her usual work, set in an unknown land she identified as 'Portugal'. Unwilling to claim authorship of works she felt had been dictated by another, Oates credited herself, when the stories were first published, as the translator 'from the Portuguese' of works by Fernandes.

Literary cross-dressing – women writing in a male persona and vice versa – is too common to require any comment, yet it seems especially appropriate that the following story was written by a woman who felt herself to be, while writing it, possessed by the spirit of an

The Secret Mirror

You are alone in your rented room. You are alone before your full-length mirror, which is on a large, cumbersome mahogany

stand so that it can be tipped one way or another, according
unknown man.
to your desire. You adjust it with a touch of your fingers –
just so – exactly so. But when you let go, the mirror eases
back into its old position as if taunting you.

No matter. First, the copper-coloured curls, a gentle explosion of light. You fit the cap snugly onto your head, stretching
the elastic band around the perimeter of your scalp. It fits
perfectly. The coppery curls will move in the wind, they will
bounce and tickle your face. You stare at the curls in the
mirror and a cry escapes you – an exclamation of surprise and
pleasure.

The curls were put on too quickly, too eagerly, and now
they will get in the way of your other things. But you hesitate
to take them off when they fit so perfectly. The elastic band
might break, or lose its resiliency.

Now the undergarments, the secret garments. You dress
yourself slowly. All your things are white and with white you
must move slowly. You raise your arms as if in a ceremonial
gesture, in order to slide the white silk slip down over your
head. It glides down upon you gently. A faint odour of
perfume about it, though you have brought no perfume here.
The white of the slip is very white and seems to glow in the
mirror, a brightness disturbing to the eye.

A single strand of copper-coloured hair floats down, down
to the floor. You watch it fall, not breathing.

The stockings are a pale brown and they will hide the
terrible pallor of your legs. The ugliness of your legs! It is
difficult to resist the impulse to hurry now, drawing the

stockings up onto your legs. You release your breath slowly upon them, because they are made of such sheer, delicate material. How is such a miracle of fineness possible? You fear that even the gentlest touch might damage it.

Now the white shoes. No laces to tie, no buckles. You simply step into these shoes, twisting your feet a little so that they fit. The shoes are almost large enough. Your feet are pinched, but not badly; it does not matter. Straightening, you glance at yourself in the mirror and see that you are suddenly taller – you are pressed forward, a fraction of an inch forward, and your hips are oddly raised.

Now the dress: It is made of white linen, fine linen, white enough and fine enough for a wedding dress. In fact, this is your wedding dress. You lift it cautiously, reverently, over your head. Must be very careful with the curls . . . You make certain that the dress is unbuttoned, the pearl buttons undone all the way down, so that there will be plenty of room to pull the dress over your head. Slowly. Move slowly. You pause for an instant, thinking there is someone on the stairs – but you hear nothing – The door is locked and you are a stranger here in this secret room; there is nothing to fear. Anyway, there is no noise out on the stairs.

A rented room. A borrowed name.

The dress slides down over your head. Soft. Weightless. You open your eyes eagerly and find that you are staring at a young woman with an angular, bony, pale face, her eyes snatching at yours.

Hair flames about her head.

Her hands dart up to these curls, these coppery curls. They do not feel very soft – rather strawlike, artificial. But they look soft.

Now the buttons, which are very small. It takes several minutes to button them. You work painstakingly, without haste. It should be a pleasure to button this dress! Slowly, no hurry, no one is about to hammer upon the door and burst in upon you. You are absolutely alone.

And now the face . . . The face must be applied with love. You have a small case with the necessary items, bought in a theatrical supply store. First you apply a liquid make-up that is called 'Sunflower'; you smooth it carefully on your face and throat, using only upward strokes. Then you work on your eyes. This takes several minutes, because your hands are shaky and the mascara gets onto your lower eyelid. Then you outline your lips with a lipstick pencil and apply lipstick. The shade is 'True Red'. Finally you lift a box of loose powder and timidly pat a powder puff onto your skin. At first the effect is strange – too pale – ghostly – and then you even the powder out. Must work slowly, because a face is a work of art. Out on the street other people will glance at you, and your face must be a work of art.

Now.

You contemplate the young woman in the mirror.

The descent to the street – the bustle of the noontime street – you walk with small, mincing steps, because your shoes are a little tight – your heart pounds with apprehension – your hands little tight – your heart pounds with apprehension – your hands move up nervously to check the copper-coloured hair, ah, the headband is so tight! – and now you hesitate at a curb, watching the traffic officer's baton—

The god of the baton.

Around you people have begun to stare. A child snickers. A woman smiles angrily at you, then her smile fades. Several men approach you. You begin to walk fast, back the way you have come. A sound behind you of footsteps – you look around in terror and see huge animals in the shapes of people pursuing you. You must run – the white shoes are painful, torturous – you want to kick them off but there is no time – the god of the crowd is nearly upon you—

You are the eye of a catastrophe that plummets through the city at noon, attracting stares on all sides, slowing traffic, causing the very clocks to pause – Someone jumps out of a doorway ahead of you. He is a fat-bellied man whose face shows that he is good-hearted and can recognize evil. His arms open wide for an embrace. You try to duck around him but it is too late – the first of the crowd has caught up with you – you feel yourself being mauled, shoved from hand to hand, your copper-coloured hair torn from you in one instant with a laugh of derision, your clothes torn from you, the stockings and the garter belt flung up in the air—

If you were a woman, the world would rush at you now and penetrate you and deposit in you, in the pit of your belly, a seed that would flower into the world again, blossoming into the world and renewing it. But you are not a woman and the world cannot penetrate you. It can only pound upon you with its fists and kick at you and shout into your face with a hearty furious derision.

So you will not go down to the street after all.

It is noontime. There would be danger out on the street. You stand before your secret mirror for a long time – for fifteen, twenty minutes – hypnotized by that reflection. It is a woman who stares back at you with watery eyes. Her mouth quivers beneath its perfect red shape.

You remove the curls with your own hands, beginning to weep. At once the reflection in the mirror begins to weep. You are both weeping for your lost selves, whom no one can return to you, but who have slipped out of the mirror now, untouched, unpursued.

LISA TUTTLE

Lisa Tuttle was born and raised in Texas, but spent the 1980s in London and now lives in a remote part of Scotland. She's the author of six novels, including *The Pillow Friend*, and three short collections as well as works of non-fiction. She previously edited *Skin of the Soul: New Horror Stories by Women*.

'A Dress' is based on a fantasy which grew out of something that never happened and includes two real dresses cunningly stitched together with a thread of autobiography and the whole cloth of fiction.

A Dress

Sorting through my old clothes the other day, I came across a dress I hadn't worn since the early 1970s, although I'd kept it with me through many changes of home, lifestyle, even country, always packing it away safely, never seriously considering throwing it out or giving it away. It carried too powerful a charge.

I was barely twenty-one when I bought it, in 1972, from a big department store in Austin, Texas. I hadn't worn a dress

174

for nearly four years, but with graduation on the horizon I had to start planning for job interviews and needed to look grown-up and business-like. Bored with the idea already, I managed to find a couple of skirts – one with a matching jacket – that I knew my mother would have approved, and began to search for a complimentary blouse or two. Then, on a sale rack, I saw this dress.

It was maroon velour, with long sleeves and an ankle-length skirt, a scooped neckline and a laced bodice: anything less appropriate to wear to the sort of job interviews I was hoping for would be hard to imagine. But as soon as I touched it I wanted it. I've always loved velour even though there are very few days in the year when it can be worn with comfort in the climate of central Texas. I already had a brown velour trouser suit for the occasional evening out; I didn't need this dress.

But once I'd tried it on, felt the smooth slither and cling of it, I was hooked. Looking at myself full-length in the dressing-room mirror I realized that what I'd taken for an abstract design appliquéd on the sides was actually the outline of two hands, as if a man was standing behind me, holding me by the hips, getting ready to . . .

My mouth dried. I let my eyes go out of focus a little, staring at the mirror, at the hands, until I could almost see them move, imagining them rising to tug at the bodice strings, opening the front of the dress to free my breasts.

It was the perfect fucking dress. That's what it was for; that was the whole point of wearing it. *Fear of Flying* hadn't yet been published, but people fantasized about the joys of sex without zippers or other sartorial obstacles before Erica Jong invented the phrase 'zipless fuck'. I'd often thought that kilts and robes should be more widely accepted as menswear in my culture, at least for dating.

Stroking my body in the velour dress, wishing I'd come shopping with Peter, that I had him there in the changing room with me, all thoughts of a sensible working-woman's wardrobe flew out of my head.

I couldn't wait to get it home and try it out on Peter. I'd have worn it if the temperature had been less than 80 degrees, or if the air conditioner had worked in my car. But if this dress was going to be drenched in bodily fluids it should be *après* intercourse, not before.

Peter was at home, moodily tuning his guitar. It was a familiar posture, narrow shoulders hunched, head down, the long, red-gold hair veiling his handsome, sullen, brown-eyed face. Yet for all that he was so self-absorbed, he wasn't alone. My stomach tightened unhappily when I saw Allie curled up on the sofa opposite him. The Blond Bombshell. The first time I'd seen her, shortly after she'd moved into one of the apartments across the street, I'd felt she was the sort of effortlessly gorgeous creature who made me feel like a female impersonator. Loyal to my sex, I assumed she was intelligent – she was a college student, after all – but she had yet to reveal her intellect in my presence. Her basic conversational mode was breathless and brainless. She was fucking a married professor, and didn't seem to be doing much else towards her degree. At any rate, she was always hanging around. I reckoned she had her eye on Peter, and I knew Peter fancied her because he'd told me so. Sooner or later I was going to have to give my consent to their union.

This was the early seventies, remember. Naturally, Peter and I were opposed to bourgeois, patriarchal institutions like marriage, compulsory heterosexuality, and possessiveness. Our relationship was, in theory, 'open'. In practice, however, we'd had sex only with each other in the year and a half since we had become lovers. We'd agreed that the greatest thing would be to meet another couple whom we both fancied, and all go to bed together, breaking a whole load of outworn taboos in one go. So far this couple hadn't come along. But Allie had, and Peter was ready to test the theory of 'contingent affairs' (as my heroine, Simone de Beauvoir, dubbed the sanctioned holidays she and her main man took from each other). He'd kindly offered to wait until I found someone I liked as well. The pressure was on.

Allie's eyes fastened on my shopping bag, and she jumped up with a tiny squeal:

'Ooooh, what'd'ya get?'

'Just a dress.'

'Let's see, let's see!'

I hesitated. I'd been so intent on modelling the dress for Peter, and on what his response might be to it, that I could hardly bear to get it out of the bag with someone else in the room.

Allie must have picked up on something sexual in my hesitation, because her eyebrows arched as she said, 'I thought you said it was a dress?'

177

'Yes, it is.' Now I was embarrassed by my own embarrassment. I pulled the dress out with a rustling of tissue paper. 'I got it on sale.'

'Oh! It's *gorgeous*!' She rushed over to stroke the deep nap of the material. Then, with a quick glance to make sure I didn't object, she lifted it and let it fall, holding it out at arms' length, regarding it. 'Beautiful . . . *soooo* sexy,' she purred.

Peter had set aside his guitar and was watching us. 'Nice colour,' he said.

'You should *feel* it,' said Allie. Then she looked at me and smiled a complicitous smile. My heart jumped. I thought she was going to ask me to try it on. But instead what she said took me by surprise.

'Wouldn't you love to see Peter in this?'

Peter snorted.

I couldn't help smiling. 'I bought it for me.'

'That's what I *mean*,' she said with a knowing smirk. 'Think of the fun you could have with him in this.'

I giggled, and found myself liking Allie for the first time. 'Peter and I could take turns . . .'

'Playing the helpless maiden. Sure, why should just one of you have all the fun?'

'All the fun? Who thinks like that? You make sex sound one-sided, like rape,' Peter objected.

Allie shrugged. 'I only meant, why should the same person always have to be the girl. You should try it some time, Peter.'

He looked away from her, absently rubbing his chin. I sensed Allie's annoyance. 'Come on, Peter. Try it on.'

The coaxing sweetness in her voice made him look at her, but when he saw that she was holding the dress out to him, he stiffened a little. 'It wouldn't fit.'

'Of course it would!'

'I'm taller than Liz.'

'So am I, and I'll bet it would fit *me*.' Allie held the dress against herself, demonstrating. She was in fact exactly Peter's height, about two inches taller than me, but curvier than either of us. 'Feels like a very forgiving dress.'

'Peter, we've worn each other's clothes before,' I said. I wasn't sure what made me weigh in on Allie's side, but I didn't like him talking to her as if I wasn't there. And, anyway, it was true.

'That's different.' He scowled, not meeting my eyes. I realized he hadn't looked at me properly since I'd come in.

'It's not. I wear your jeans. Why shouldn't you wear my dress?'

'You know why not.'

'Look, it's not like I'm asking you to go out in it. Just try it on,' I said.

'No.'

'Why not?'

The breath hissed out between his teeth. 'Because I don't want to.'

'Pwease,' said Allie in a baby voice. 'Pwetty pwease wiff a cherry on top?'

'No!'

'Oh, come on,' said Allie. She lowered her voice. 'For me?'

My pulse quickened apprehensively, but Peter only shook his head. Suddenly it was important that I succeed where she had failed, that Peter should put on my dress because *I* asked him to.

'For me,' I said quietly. 'For me, then, Peter.'

'I said no!'

Why didn't he just say 'Later, when we're alone', give me a sexy smile, something to tell Allie he was mine? Why did he have to refuse so flatly, as if my asking meant no more than hers?

Then Allie said, 'Put the dress on, Peter, and we'll take you to bed. Both of us. Right now. And we'll show you what it's like, being a girl.'

The breath caught in my throat. It was like the moment when I looked at myself in the mirror, wearing the dress, only more intense. Scarier.

I couldn't imagine him refusing such an offer, the two of us together, but he scowled like it was a big, unfunny joke, and stomped out of the room.

I looked at Allie and she looked at me and shrugged. 'Enjoy yourself, honey,' she said. 'I guess I better go.'

Later Peter confessed that he and Allie were not long out of bed when I'd come home. 'I know we agreed I'd tell you first, but how could I? You weren't here. We didn't plan it or anything, it just sort of happened. You don't mind, do you? It doesn't make any difference to *us*. I'm attracted to Allie, but you're the one I want to *be* with.'

To prove it, he made me put on the dress. Some of

A DRESS

the shine had gone off it for me now, but as sales items
were unreturnable, I thought I might as well get some use out
of it.

Without discussion, we fell into a dominance–submission
thing, which was not at all our usual scene. I resisted when
he kissed me, but he persisted, and began to fondle my
breasts. I tried to push his hands away, and he caught hold of
me around the waist and pushed me down on the bed. He
pinned my wrists together with one hand above my head, and
with the other hand undid the bodice lace, exposing my
breasts. He kissed them, teasing the nipples with his tongue
before settling down to suck on one. I was cold and remote at
first – despite telling him I didn't, I *did* feel betrayed, and I
wanted to punish him for it.

But my body began to respond to the strong, steady pulling
of his mouth on my breast. There's some nerve that runs
directly between the nipple and the uterus (something which
was to shock me all over again, years later, when I nursed my
son) and I could no more resist the seductive pull than I
could have ignored an electrical charge. I began to arch my
back, and groan. While he went on worrying my nipple with
his lips, he reached down to snake his free hand underneath
my dress. My thighs parted at the stroking of his fingers. He
stood up then – my breast, soaked with his saliva, felt
suddenly cold and exposed – and I watched through slitted
eyes as he unfastened his jeans and pulled them off. He wasn't
wearing underpants.

He climbed on to the bed and knelt over me. 'Suck me,' he
said in his slightly hoarse voice.

181

I rose up on my elbows to take his penis into my mouth. The smell of another woman hit me like a slap in the face. I started to pull back but he caught my head and held me there. I tasted Allie's cunt on Peter's cock, and my excitement swelled unbearably as fantasy scenarios swirled in my brain. I was Peter, forcing Allie to become me, fucking her; I was Allie, seducing Peter. I sucked as hard as I could and rubbed my own breasts.

He pulled out of my mouth with a groan and moved off the bed again. I licked my lips. He lifted my skirt, bunching it in rich, soft folds around my waist, and I raised my knees. Then, as he was positioning himself between my legs, suddenly I sat up.

'Peter – wait—'

'What?'

'Do something for me.'

He grinned. 'I was about to.' He stroked my labia slowly with two fingers; slowly probed inside.

'Something else.'

'Name it.' He pulled his fingers out, then swiftly slid them in again, making me catch my breath.

'Put my dress on; let's fuck that way.'

Something – fear? desire? – flickered on his face a brief moment, and then his lips thinned like his eyes; his mouth hardened. 'Bitch,' he said. 'You think I don't *have* a cock, is that it?'

'No, Peter.' I was puzzled.

'I'll fuck you all right, you bitch; you think I can't? I'll show you.' He pushed me back onto the bed and pinned my wrists with one hand. 'I'll fuck you all right.'

'Peter, I don't want to play this game.'

'It isn't a fucking *game*.' He thrust into me so hard and suddenly that, wet as I was, it almost hurt. But there was more pleasure in it than pain, even though Peter's anger seemed incomprehensibly real. I moaned.

'What's the matter, is my cock too big for you?' He panted as he thrust in and out. 'But you like it, don't you? You like feeling my big cock in you. That's what you like. I know.'

I let my eyes go out of focus and gazed at him through flickering eyelashes. With the long red-gold hair, smooth skin, high cheekbones, and full lips, it could almost have been the face of a woman. As I came – almost too quickly, almost simultaneously with his furious, triumphant roar – I dreamed that I was being fucked by a woman, and that I was wearing her stolen dress.

Now I had to find another lover, to even the score. Vaughan, one of Peter's friends, volunteered, but although I did find him quite attractive, I didn't want my 'contingent affair' to be with anyone that easy and unthreatening. Why should Peter be let off so lightly? I had to prove that I was as free as he was, that I could find someone as sexy and scary as Allie for my own.

That weekend a norther swept down from the plains and the temperature dropped thirty degrees in an hour. I wore my new dress when we went out that night to the Armadillo World Headquarters. We went in a group: me and Peter, our housemates Marshall and Robin, Marshall's girlfriend Peggy, Vaughan and some stoned girl he'd picked up at the lake.

I don't remember what band was playing, but to remember Alex all I have to do is stroke the velvety nap of my old dress. Twenty-six years later I raise it to my nose and sniff, and it seems to me I can still catch hints of sandalwood, cigarette smoke, patchouli and sex clinging to the musty cloth.

Ironically, it was Peter who introduced us. We got to the 'Dillo, got our beers, and were looking around for somewhere to sit.

'Hey,' he said. 'There's Alex – isn't it, Vaughan? From the Department. He's a really, really good artist. Does some really, really different stuff. There's already a gallery in Manhattan interested in his work. Looks like he's by himself. Let's go say hello.'

I was on the prowl that night, so my sexual antennae were out, and as I came in range of Alex, they quivered.

Alex was like Peter, a skinny, long-haired, brown-eyed boy with a smooth, almost pretty face. But where Peter was fair, red-haired and freckled, Alex had an olive complexion and straight, jet-black hair.

We joined Alex or maybe Alex joined us; anyway, we all ended up crowded around a small table together, and I was soon pressed thigh to thigh with him. At some point our eyes met, and a spark flashed between us in the smoky, muggy air.

'I love your dress,' he said, stroking my arm. Beneath the velvety material, I tingled.

'Thanks, I do, too.' He gazed, smiling, at my cleavage. I

looked down and realized that the bodice lacing had loosened, and the way I was sitting pushed my breasts forward, nakedly revealing them. I sat back, my heart thumping, and shifted my shoulders until they were covered again.

'Awww,' said Alex softly. 'Such pretty nipples.'

I licked my lips and watched as his tongue mirrored the action with his own. Under the table, his hand was on my velour-skirted inner thigh, rubbing gently, moving higher, and I was possessed by the overwhelming urge to feel those fingers on my bare skin, on my inner lips, inside me.

He read the desire in my eyes and murmured, 'Let's go outside.'

I don't know if Peter saw us go. By that time, under the combined influence of a couple of beers, some grass, and Alex, I didn't care. Outside, in the parking lot, Alex pressed me against someone's car and began to kiss me.

He was a brilliant kisser. Peter was good, too, although I sometimes found him a little impatient: whereas I could happily have spent an hour or more just kissing in pre-orgasmic excitement, Peter's sexuality was more demanding; he didn't like to wait that long for satisfaction.

Alex, now, seemed to have desires more in synch with my own, yet, strangely, as he kissed me sensuously and slowly as if we had all the time in the world, I became feverish with impatience, desperate to get on to the main course.

I tried to get into his jeans but he stopped me. 'None of that!'

'But I'm so horny,' I said plaintively.

His smile was like the sun coming up. 'Ahhh, I see. When kissing alone is not enough . . . You're wanting some attention down here?' He pressed his hand against my crotch.

I sighed in anticipation, leaned back against the car behind me and spread my legs. Alex sank to his knees, lifted the bottom of my skirt, and then surprised me by disappearing beneath it. I felt his hands on my legs, and then his face. His lips and tongue found my clitoris, and I cried out and jerked away, startled by the sudden, intense intimacy.

I felt his laughter in my pubic bone. He began to touch me more gently, with lips, tongue and fingers, gently, gently until I relaxed. Then he fucked me with his tongue, then with his fingers; he stroked me and sucked me until I was moaning and clutching his head, trapping him between my thighs, urging him on, lost to everything else in the world but the one building, ravenous need.

After I came, he stayed under my dress for a while, his mouth still pressed to my cunt, his hands gently cupping my bare cheeks. I rested as much of my weight as I could on my back and shoulders against the car and hoped that no one would notice us and approach.

Finally, Alex emerged, grinning at me, his face wet and shiny with my juices. 'How was it?'

'If you have to ask, you can't afford it,' I slurred, and we both giggled helplessly. I felt a great wave of affection and gratitude sweep over me. I wanted to kiss him, and knew I could do more.

'Now you,' I said. 'Let me do you.'

I reached for his fly but he stepped aside, shivering. 'It's cold out here!'

His words came out as clouds, and for the first time, no longer wrapped in the heat of my desire, I realized just how cold it actually was.

'Do you have a car?' I asked.

He gave me a sideways look. 'Come back to my place?'

There was a fluttering in my rib-cage. 'I'll have to go get my purse and tell my . . . friends . . . I'm going.'

'OK. I'll meet you by the front door.' He lit a cigarette as I walked away.

Peter stared at me blankly when I told him I'd be making my own way home later.

'Why? What's up?'

I hesitated, uncertain about the proper etiquette. 'I'm uh, going, uh, with somebody else. You know.'

'Alex?' He looked astonished.

'Yes. He asked me to . . . uh, we want to spend a little time together.'

'Alex!'

His surprise seemed excessive, seemed to portend something, and made me defensive. 'What's wrong with that?'

'Nothing. I thought he was gay, that's all.'

'Well, he's not,' I said irritably. This struck me as a slur on my womanhood, and strange coming from Peter. 'He's just another long-haired hippie artist, like you.'

He caught my wrist before I could walk away.

'What?'

187

'Don't go.'

My heart jumped. 'Don't you want an open relationship?'

'I didn't mean that. You can fuck whoever you want. But why go to his place? Why not bring him home?'

'Oh, sure!'

'I mean it. I'd feel better about it.'

'Oh, really? You want to watch?'

His soft brown eyes were fixed unblinkingly on mine. 'If you want me to.'

Actually, the idea turned me on. He was aroused, too, I knew the signs, and suddenly I was furious with him for trying to steal my adventure and make it his.

'No, thank you, Peter! I don't need your permission anyway. You didn't ask me before you and Allie . . .'

'Uh-oh. You *are* mad at me. This is about revenge, not lust. You're not in touch with your feelings at all, are you, Liz?'

I felt like screaming, but made myself speak slowly and quietly. 'I know perfectly well what I want. Let go of my arm, Peter. Thank you. I'll see you in the morning.'

The effort of controlling myself meant that by the time I rejoined Alex in the parking lot I was feeling nothing at all.

'Where's your car?' I asked.

'We'll have to take the bus. I'm on one of the shuttle routes; it's no problem.'

He didn't take my hand or try to touch me as we walked to the bus stop. Our earlier passion in the parking lot might have been a dream. There were others waiting for the bus, so I didn't say anything, but after we were seated, with the noise of the engine for privacy, I told him that I lived with Peter 'in a non-monogamous relationship'.

Alex nodded, as if this was not news. Without intending to, I blurted, 'Peter thought you were gay!'

He smiled. 'Yeah, well . . . I came on to him one day after class. We were sharing a joint, there was definitely something in the air between us, I found him attractive and I could feel him responding to me, so – '

'Peter's not homosexual!'

Alex gave me a pained smile. 'Homosexual is a term which should be applied to acts, not people. I don't think it's a very useful category, anyway. After all, don't you find you're attracted to someone – or not – *before* you find out what sort of . . . equipment they've got hidden in their jeans?'

'So you'd say you're bisexual?'

He hesitated, staring out of the window, away from me. 'I think so. Yes. I was reading a book that said that, really, everybody is bisexual.'

'Well, in theory, maybe. But in practice?'

'Here, this is where we get off.'

'What about practice?' I pursued, as he led me across the street and around the side of a big house into an alleyway. 'Have you had any actual practice in bisexuality?'

'Here, up these stairs.'

I followed him through an outer door into a small, untidy kitchen.

'Don't look in the sink,' Alex cautioned. 'Just go through.' I entered the living room. Ahead was another door, into the bedroom. I hesitated, feeling an inward tingle, and looked at him.

'Sit down, I'll get us something to drink. There's two beers in the fridge, or I could make coffee with Kahlua.'

I perked up. 'Kahlua and cream?'

'It's Half-and-Half.'

'Even better. Forget the coffee. Kahlua and cream's my favourite.'

He smiled. 'I'll just be a minute.'

While he was gone I did the usual thing of examining his record collection. I put on Janis Joplin's 'Pearl', then wandered to the bookcase. Some big art books, a few textbooks, history and psychology paperbacks, science fiction, mysteries, and then, surprisingly, *The Female Eunuch* by Germaine Greer, and *The Dialectic of Sex* by Shulamith Firestone. I picked up the latter and opened it. His name, Alex DeBarr, was written in blue ink inside the front cover. A sheet of paper fell out: a flyer from the Ad Hoc Women Artists' Committee calling for a public protest against the Whitney Museum in New York, quoting statistics: at their annual survey of American art in 1970, only four and a half percent of the artists shown were women, etc. I remembered the action, which had received a fair amount of attention even way down in Texas. A long winter and spring of protests by AHWA had resulted in the Whitney's 1971 show including a lot more women artists – slightly over twenty per cent. Which was still not a lot, although the way some male critics talked, you'd have thought the Whitney had turned over its walls to murals drawn by Girl Scouts in defiance of artistic values. From what Peter told me, most of the female students in the University's Art Department were interested in teaching, illustration, or the decorative arts; none of them were 'serious' artists like Peter, Vaughan and Alex.

Alex came into the room carrying our drinks. I tucked the flyer into the book, and put it back on the shelf, but he'd seen what it was.

'You should read that,' he said, nodding approval. 'I'll lend it to you.'

'I've read it.'

'You have? What did you think of it? Pretty radical stuff, huh: the abolition of all sexual distinctions!'

He sounded eager to talk, but I didn't like discussing feminism with men. I got angry, and they took it personally. Which was maybe as it should have been, but it seemed a bad idea as a prelude to sex.

'You never answered my question,' I said as he handed me a glass.

'What question?' He gently clinked his glass against mine. 'To us.'

The look in his eyes, his smile, made me shiver with pleasure, remembering him beneath my dress. He'd known just what to do; he was obviously experienced with women. And since he'd said . . . I said, 'Have you ever had sex with a man?'

'Yes.' He met my eyes candidly. 'I'm not a virgin. I've had more than one lover. And I do like sex with men.'

'So—' I was astonished. 'So it's *women* you don't have experience with?'

191

'You're my first.' He gulped down his drink.

'Wow. I'm really flattered.' An unpleasant thought occurred to me. 'It wasn't because I'm Peter's girlfriend?'

'Oh no. It was the dress. That's why I noticed you. That's what caught my eye. I love that dress. The colour, the texture, the cut . . . I love the feel of it, and then, the way you filled it out made me want to feel *you*.'

Feeling warm and sexy again, I began to stroke myself suggestively through the dress. 'I hope you'll want me when I take it off.'

Eyes gleaming, he stepped forward. 'Why don't we find out?'

I thought he would undress me, unlace the bodice or pull the dress up, but he seemed content just to hold me and stroke the soft velour over my hips and back and bottom while his mouth moved soulfully against mine.

We kissed for a while, standing up pressed tightly together, really getting into it while Janis Joplin wailed in the background. But I was aware of another pressure which could not be denied, and finally I broke away.

'I need to go to the bathroom.'

'Go on, then. I'll meet you in bed.'

I took my time in the bathroom, dithering over whether to take off the dress or not. I peeked into Alex's medicine cabinet. Nothing very exotic; the contents weren't that different from mine at home: a pink bottle of Pepto-Bismal, some aspirin, a box of Band-aids, a tube of Clearasil, Vaseline Intensive Care hand lotion, a blue box of Tampax . . . I frowned. Whose? Did he have a girlfriend? Had he been lying to me?

I opened the door. Sitting on the bed was a woman in a dress just like mine.

'Surprise,' said Alex, standing up. It was still Alex, but he'd turned into a woman. Or had he always been she? 'See, we have the same taste in men *and* clothes. I knew I had to have it, the minute I saw it hanging on the rack. I thought this is the perfect fucking dress. You don't wear any underwear with it, and you're always so turned on just by the *feel* of it, that you'd let practically anybody do you anywhere, anytime. Standing up, bent over, leaning against a wall . . . I bought it as a Christmas present for myself. Until now, nobody but me's ever seen me in it. What do you think, does it suit me?'

I stared at the figure in front of me. The breasts were small, but undeniably real. I remembered that all the time we were kissing, standing pressed against each other, I hadn't felt the expected swelling in his jeans. And he hadn't let me touch him, when we'd been in the parking lot.

'What are you?' I asked, finally.

Alex arched an eyebrow, and smiled seductively. 'Come and find out.'

Michael, my son, came in and found me with the dress on my lap, still dreaming of my youth.

'What are you doing up here?'

'Just clearing out some old clothes – you'll need suitcases for this summer.'

'What about the clothes – anything I can have?'

'They're pretty old—'

'Seventies style is in,' he said, rummaging through the untouched pile still in the case. 'Flares, tie-dyes, psychedelia . . .' Then he swooped and before I could react snatched up my dress.

'Hey!'

'Oh, wow,' he said, touching it reverently. 'Can I have this?'

'Michael, it's a dress!'

'I can see that.'

'What do you want a dress for?'

'What do you think?' He held it up to himself and pranced. 'Does it suit me?'

'Not really.'

'I think I'd look brilliant in this. They'd all love me!'

'It wouldn't fit you.'

'Oh, I think it would. Very slinky. Very forgiving fabric.'

'You wouldn't really wear it – in public?'

We stared, each baffled by the other.

'Sure I would. I'd have to fight the chicks off.' He said 'chicks' with heavy irony, but he was serious.

'Really? They wouldn't think that you're gay?'

'Not the sort of clubs I go to. The girls love it. Don't you think it's a turn-on? A guy in a dress?'

I nodded slowly, amazed by how much time had passed, how much things had changed.

'So can I have it?'

'Sure, go on, take it. I can't wear it anymore.'

*

I had never worn it again after my night with Alex. I never saw Alex again, either. I never told anyone what had happened, never revealed Alex's secret.

Peter and I had an emotional, highly charged reconciliation the next afternoon, and spent the next two months cleaving only unto each other. I avoided Alex until it became obvious that Alex wasn't actually around to be avoided. After graduation, Peter and I went our separate ways. Alex went to New York and within two years had his first one-man show. For years I kept the yellowing clipping from *The Village Voice* which spoke of the 'mastery' and 'virility' of Alex's use of space and texture.

One day, at the end of the eighties, in London with a free afternoon, I was flipping through the listings in search of something to do. I scanned the galleries, and one name leaped out at me: 'DeBarr'.

Was it Alex? The work was on display with other artists at a gallery in the East End. I went out there.

I saw it as soon as I walked in. Unmissable. Alex's dress.

It was framed and hanging on the wall, the dress I remembered, the dress I'd embraced, and worn myself, although with a few alterations to make it a work of art. Sewn around the neckline was a necklace of tiny pink plastic babies. Pinned about where each breast would be were two cut-out photographs of wine glasses. The appliqued hands had been adorned with long, silvery nails. And at the crotch there was a rectangle of thick, maroon velour, richer and darker than the rest of the dress. On this was stuck a paper label which read 'Pull'.

I hesitated and looked around. The tall, heavily made-up girl in the strapless leather bustier who guarded the door was watching me, and she nodded. 'It's OK, it's meant to be touched.'

So I pulled. The flap came away with a tiny, ripping velcro sound, and out fell a set of male genitalia: a colour photograph screen-printed onto cotton.

I read the title of the piece: 'The Perfect Woman'.

MICHAEL BLUMLEIN

Michael Blumlein is a medical doctor and writer living in San Francisco. Since the publication of his first short story in 1984 he has had the reputation of a daring and original writer in the fields of science fiction and horror. His second novel, *X, Y*, features as one of its main characters a sexy young woman who suddenly becomes convinced that she is really a man trapped inside a female body. He has also written on the subject of sexual metamorphosis in several short stories. 'Hymenoptera' is a weird and subtle tale about desire, masquerade and an obsession with clothes which crosses the border not merely of gender, but of species.

Hymenoptera

The wasp appeared in the salon that morning. It was early spring and unusually cold. The windows were laced with ice, and there was frost on the grass outside. Linderstadt shifted uncomfortably on the sofa. In nothing but shirt and socks, he was fighting both chill and dream. He had quarrelled the night before with Camille, his favourite model, accusing her of petty treacheries for which she was blameless. After she left,

197

he drank himself into a stupor, stumbling from one workshop to another, knocking down mannequins, pulling dresses from their hangers, sweeping hats to the floor. He raged at his own astounding pettiness, the poverty of his newest collection, the bankruptcy of life in general. Had he been cinched up in one of his own tight-fitting corsets, he couldn't have felt more constricted. Pinched of breath, of vision, blind to the most obvious truths. And this the man who just the week before had yet again been dubbed King, whose attention to detail, to sleeve, waist, and line were legendary, whose transcendent gowns were slavishly praised, copied, stolen. Linderstadt the Genius. The Master. Linderstadt the drunkard, wrestling with his empire of taffeta, guipure and satin, flailing at success like a fly trapped behind glass.

Dawn came, and sunlight appeared along the edges of the heavily curtained windows, penetrating the salon with a wan, peach-coloured light. Linderstadt was on a couch at one end of the room, half-draped with the train of a bridal gown he had appropriated from one of the ateliers. The wasp was at the other, broadside and motionless. Its wings were folded back against its body, and its long belly was curled under itself like a comma. Its two antennae were curved delicately forward but otherwise as rigid as bamboo.

An hour passed and then another. When sleep became impossible, Linderstadt staggered off the couch to relieve himself. He returned to the salon with a glass of water, at which point he first noticed the wasp. From his father, who had been an amateur entomologist before dying of yellow fever, Linderstadt knew something of insects. This one he located somewhere in the family Sphecidae, which included wasps of primarily solitary habit. Most nested in burrows or natural cavities of hollow wood, and he was a little surprised to find the animal in his salon. Then again, he was surprised to have remembered anything at all. He had scarcely thought of insects since his entry forty years before into the world of fashion. He had scarcely thought of his father either, preferring the memory of his mother Anna, his mother the caregiver, the seamstress, for whom he had named his first shop and his most famous dress. But his mother was not here, and the wasp most unmistakably was. Linderstadt finished his glass of water and pulled the bridal train like a shawl over his shoulders. Then he walked over to have a look.

The wasp stood chest-high and about eight feet long. Linderstadt recognized the short hairs on its legs that used to remind him of the stubble on his father's chin, and he remembered, too, the forward palps by which the insect centred its jaws to tear off food. Its waist was pencil-thin, its wings translucent. Its exoskeleton, what Linderstadt thought of as its coat, was blacker than his blackest faille, blacker than coal. It seemed to absorb light, creating a small pocket of cold night right where it stood. *Nigricans.* He remembered the wasp's name. *Ammophila nigricans.* He was tempted to touch it, to feel the quality of its life. Instinctively, his eyes drifted down its belly to the pointed sting that extruded like a sword from its rear. He recalled that the sting was actually a hollow tube through which the female deposited eggs into its prey, where they would hatch into larvae and eat their way out. Males possessed the same tube but did not sting. As a boy he had always had trouble telling the sexes apart, and examining the creature now in the pale light, he wondered which it was. He felt a little feverish, which he attributed to the after-effects of the alcohol. His mouth remained parched, but he was reluctant to leave the salon for more water for fear the wasp would be gone when he returned. So he stayed, shivering and thirsty. The hours passed, and the room did not heat up. The wasp did not move. It was stiller than Martine, his stillest and most patient model. Stiller in the windless salon than the jewelled chandelier and the damask curtains that led to the dressing rooms. Linderstadt himself was the only moving object. He paced to stay warm. He swallowed his own saliva to slake his thirst, but ultimately the need for water drove him out. He returned as quickly as possible, wearing shoes and sweater, carrying pencils, a pad of paper and a large pitcher of water. The wasp was as he had left it. Had Linderstadt not known something of insect physiology, he might have thought the animal were carved in stone.

By the fading light he began to draw, quickly, deftly, using broad, determined strokes. He worked from different angles, sketching the wasp's neck, its shoulders and waist. He imagined the creature in flight, its wings stiff and finely veined. He drew it feeding, resting, poised to sting. He experimented with different designs, some stately and elegant, others pure whimsy. He found that he had already assumed the wasp was female. His subjects had never been otherwise. He remembered Anouk, his very first model, the scoliotic girl his mother had brought home to test her adolescent son's fledgling talent.

He felt as supple as he had then, his mind as inventive and free-spirited as ever.

He worked into the small hours of the morning, then rested briefly before being woken by church bells. In his youth he had been devout, and religious allusions were common in his early collections. But sanctimony had given way to secularity, and it had been thirty years since he had stepped foot in a church. What remained were the Sunday bells, which Linderstadt savoured for the sake of nostalgia and a lingering guilt. He was a man who held to habit.

The morning brought no visitors, and he had the store to himself. It was even colder than the day before. The wasp remained inert, and when the temperature hadn't climbed by noon, Linderstadt felt secure in leaving. His drawings were done, and his next task was to locate a suitable form on which to realize them. He owned hundreds of torsos of every conceivable shape, some bearing the name of a specific patron, others simply marked with a number. He had other shapes as well, baskets, cylinders, mushrooms, triangles, all of which had found their way at one point or another into a collection. As long as an object had dimension, Linderstadt could imagine it on a woman. Or rather, he could imagine the woman in the object, in residence, giving it her own distinctive form and substance, imbuing each tangent and intersect with female spirit. He was a pantheist at heart and expected to have no trouble finding something suitable to the wasp. Yet nothing caught his eye, not a single object in his vast collection seemed remotely to approach the creature in composition or character. It was enigmatic. He would have to work directly on the animal itself.

He returned to the salon and approached his subject. To a man so accustomed to the divine plasticity of flesh, the armour-like hardness and inflexibility of the wasp's exoskeleton presented challenges. Each cut would have to be perfect, each seam precise. There was no bosom to softly fill a swale of fabric, no hip to give shape to a gentle waist. It would be like working with bone itself, like clothing a skeleton. Linderstadt was intrigued. He stepped up and touched the wasp's body. It was cold and hard as metal. He ran a finger along one of its wings, half-expecting that his own nervous energy would bring it to life. Touch for him had always evoked the strongest emotions, which is why he used a pointing stick with his models. He might have done well to use the same stick with the wasp, for his skin tingled from the contact, momentarily clouding his senses. His hand fell to one of the wasp's legs. It was not so different from a human leg. The hairs were soft like human hairs, hairs that his models assiduously bleached, or waxed or shaved. The knee and ankle were similarly jointed, the claw as pointed and bony as a foot. His attention shifted to the animal's waist, in a human the pivot point between leg and torso. In the wasp it was lower and far narrower than anything human. It was as thin as a pipestem, a marvel of invention he was easily able to encircle between thumb and forefinger.

From a pocket he took out a tape and began to make his measurements, elbow to shoulder, shoulder to wing-tip, hip to claw, jotting each down in a notebook. From time to time he would pause, stepping back to imagine a detail, a particular look, a melon sleeve, a fringed collar, a flounce. Sometimes he would make a notation; other times, a quick sketch. When it came time to measure the chest, he had to lie on his back underneath the wasp. From that vantage he had a good view of its hairless and plated torso, as well as its sting, which was poised like a pike and pointed directly between his legs. After a moment's hesitation, he rolled over and took its measure too, wondering casually if this were one of those wasps that died after stinging, and if so, was there some way he could memorialize such a sacrifice in a dress. Then he crawled out and looked at his numbers.

The wasp was symmetrical, almost perfectly so. Throughout his long career Linderstadt had always sought to thwart such symmetry, focusing instead on the subtle variations in the human body, the natural differences between left and right. There was always something to emphasize, a hip that was higher, a shoulder, a breast. Even an eye, whose iris might be flecked a slightly different shade of blue than its neighbour, could trigger a report somewhere in the colour of the dress below. Linderstadt's success to a large degree rested on his uncanny ability to uncover such asymmetries, but the wasp presented difficulties. There was nothing that distinguished one side from the other, almost as if the animal were mocking the idea of asymmetry, of individuality, and by inference, the whole of Linderstadt's career. It occurred to him that he had been wrong, that perhaps the true search was not for singularity but for constancy of form, for repetition and preservation. Perhaps what abided was commonality; what endured, the very proportions he held in his hand.

Linderstadt took his notebook to the main atelier to begin work on the first dress. He had decided to start with something simple, a velvet sheath with narrow apertures for wing and leg and a white flounce of tulle at the bottom to hide the sting. With no time for a muslin fitting, he worked directly with the fabric itself. It was a job normally handled by assistants, but the master had not lost his skill with scissors and thread. The work went fast, and partway through the sewing, he remembered the name of the order to which his wasp belonged. *Hymenoptera*, after *ptera*, for wing, and *hymeno*, for the Greek god of marriage, referring to the union of the wasp's front and hind wings. He himself had never married, had never touched a woman outside his profession, certainly not intimately. Some suggested that he feared intimacy, but more likely what he feared was a test of the purity of his vision. His women were jewels, precious stones to be admired like anything beautiful and splendid. He clothed them to adore them. He clothed them to keep them in the palace of his dreams. Yet now, having touched the wasp's body, having been inspired by a creature as unlike himself as woman to man, he wondered if perhaps he had not missed something along the way. Flesh begged flesh. Could such a lifelong loss be rectified?

He finished the dress and hurried to the salon. The wasp offered no resistance as he lifted its claws and pulled the dark sheath into place. The image of his father came to mind, deftly unfolding a butterfly's wing and pinning it to his velvet display board. The Linderstadt men, it seemed, had a way with animals. He straightened the bodice and zipped up the back of the gown, then stepped back for a look. The waist, as he expected, needed taking in, and one of the shoulders needed to be re-aligned. The choice of colour and fabric, however, was excellent. Black on black, night against night. It was a good beginning.

Linderstadt did the alterations, then hung the gown in one of the dressing rooms and returned to the workshop. His next outfit was a broad cape of lemon guipure with a gold chain fastener, striking in its contrast to the wasp's jet black exterior. He made a matching toque to which he attached lacquered sticks to echo the wasp's antennae. The atelier was as cold as the salon, and he worked in overcoat, scarf and kid gloves whose fingertips he had snipped off with scissors. His face was bare, and the bracing chill against his cheek recalled the freezing winters of his childhood when he was forced to stand stock still for what seemed hours on end while his mother used him as a form for the clothes she was making. They had had no money for heat, and Linderstadt had developed a stoical attitude toward the elements. The cold reminded him of the value of discipline and self-control. But more than that, it reminded him how he had come to love the feel of the outfits being fitted and fastened against his skin. He loved it when his mother tightened a waist or took in a sleeve. The feeling of confinement evoked a certain wild power of imagination, as though he were being simultaneously nurtured and freed. What he remembered of the cold was not the numbness in his fingers, the misting of his breath, the goosebumps on his arms. It was the power, pure and simple, so that now, even though he had money aplenty to fire his boilers and make his rooms hot as jungles, Linderstadt kept the heat off. The cold was his pleasure. It was fire enough.

He worked through the night to finish the cape. When Monday morning arrived, he locked the doors of the salon, turning away the seamstresses, stockroom clerks, salesgirls and models who had come to work. He held the door against Camille and even Broussard, his lifelong friend and advisor. Hidden by the curtain that was strung across the door's glass panes, he announced that the collection was complete, the final alterations to be done in private by himself. He went to his strongbox and brought back bundles of cash, which he passed through the mailslot for Broussard to distribute to the employees. He assured everyone that the house of Linderstadt was intact and invited them all to return in a week for the opening of the collection. Then he left.

Back in the workshop he started on his next creation, an off-the-shoulder blue moiré gown with a voluminous skirt festooned with bows. He sewed what he could by machine, but the bows had to be done by hand. He sewed like his mother, one knee crossed over the other, head bent, pinkie finger crooked out as though he were sipping a cup of tea. The skirt took a full day, during which he broke only once, to relieve himself. Food did not enter his mind, and in that he seemed in tune with the wasp. The animal signalled neither hunger nor thirst. On occasion one of its antennae would twitch, but Linderstadt attributed this to subtle changes in the turgor of the insect's blood. He assumed the wasp remained gripped by the cold, though he couldn't help but wonder if its preternatural stillness sprang from some deeper design. He thought of his father, so ordinary on the surface, so unfathomable beneath. Given the chance, the man would spend days with his insects, meticulously arranging his boards, printing the tiny specimen labels, taking inventory. Linderstadt could never quite grasp his father's patience and devotion. His mother claimed her husband was in hiding, but what did a child know of that? By the time it occurred to him to ask for himself, his father had been dead for years.

The weather held, and on Wednesday Linderstadt wheeled one of the sewing machines from the atelier to the salon so that he could work without leaving the wasp's side. Voices drifted in from the street, curiosity-seekers making gossip, trying in vain to get a glimpse inside. The phone rang incessantly, message after message from concerned friends, clients, the press, M. Jesais, his personal psychic, called daily with increasingly dire prognostications. Linderstadt was unmoved. He heard but a single voice, and it kept him from distraction. He wondered why it had taken so long to hear.

He stitched a sleeve and then another. Forty years of success had brought him to this, needle, thread, tubes of fabric fashioned together like artifacts for a future archaeology. Barely a week before, he had felt on the verge of extinction. Ghosts had begun to visit, ghosts of past models, of deceased friends, of his parents. The more he had tried to capture his vision, the more it had eluded him. Juliet in satin, Eve in furs, the nameless queen, arrogant and imperious in stiff brocade.

MICHAEL BLUMLEIN

Sirens of impossible beauty, triumphs of yet another man's muddled desire. Success, it seemed, rested on vanity. Such was the sad lesson of his career. And after forty years he had tired of the pretence. He had seen too many Camilles, too many Martines and Anouks. Seen and not seen. He was better off with no one at all.

But now there was the wasp. The wasp was different. The wasp added a twist. Chitin was not flesh, six not the same as two, six legs and claws, six declinations of angle, line and force. And wings, wings that were stronger and finer than the angel Gabriel himself, a painting of whom Linderstadt had used to model his '84 collection. Eyes too, compound eyes, able to see God-knows-what. And antennae, to sample the world's invisible delight. Linderstadt tried to imagine Camille as an insect, crawling down the runway, striking a pose. Camille on four legs, on six, Camille on her belly, inching along like a caterpillar. From that vantage his gowns were no more than cocoons, pallid reflections of a more vivid reality. His life's vision had suffered from being too petty. It was flawed by arrogance. His adoration of women was an insult, his lofty ideals of grace and beauty, sophistry. The way of his heart was simpler and more direct. It was rooted inside, just as the wasp was rooted there in his room.

Linderstadt thought again of his father. He was dressing for work, buttoning up his navy blue postman's jacket with the yellow stripes around the cuff. He was talking about a moth he had found whose body looked exactly like a woman. Was he talking to Linderstadt's mother? Linderstadt couldn't remember. There was tension in the air, he remembered that. And something else. Rapture?

He finished the last seam and held up the dress. The shimmering moiré reminded him of a sea; the six-legged gown, of a creature delectably adrift. To a lesser talent the sleeves would have been a nightmare, but in Linderstadt's hands they flowed effortlessly into the bodice. Each one sported a ruffled cap and was zippered to aid in getting it on. Once the gown was in place, Linderstadt stepped back to have a look. The fit was uncanny, as though some hidden hand were guiding his own. It had been that way from the start. There were five gowns now. Five in five days. One more, he thought, one more to complete the collection. The bridal gown, his signature piece. For forty years he had ended every show with such a gown. Brides signified life. They signified love and the power of creation. What better way to signal his own rebirth?

The dress took two days, which Linderstadt knew only because he had paused at one point to listen to the Sunday bells. He was working on the veil at the time, a gorgeous bit of organza that looked like mist, sewing and thinking what a pity it would be to cover the wasp's extraordinary face. And so he had devised an ingenious interlocking panelled design that simultaneously hid the face and revealed it. After the veil he had started on the train, using ten feet of egg-white chiffon that he gathered in gentle waves to resemble foam. Where it attached to the skirt, he cut a hole for the sting and ringed it with flowers. The main body of the dress was made of brilliant satin with an Imperial collar and long sleeves of lace. Queen, Mother, Bride. The dress was a triumph of imagination, technique and will.

He finished Sunday night, hung the gown in the dressing room with the others, then wrapped himself in overcoat and scarf and fell asleep on the couch. Early Monday he would get up and make the final preparations to receive his public.

That night the cold spell broke. A warm front swept in from the south, brushing away the chill like a cobweb. In his sleep Linderstadt unbuttoned his coat and pulled off his scarf. He dreamed of summer, flying a kite with his father at the beach. When he woke, it was almost noon. The room was thick with heat. A crowd had gathered outside the store for the opening. The wasp was gone.

He searched the workshops, the stockroom, the offices. He climbed to the roof and looked in the basement. Finally, he returned to the salon, bemused and somewhat dazed. Near where the wasp had stood he noticed a paper sphere the size of a small chair. One side of it was open, and inside were many tiers of hexagonal cells, all composed of the same papery material as the envelope. Linderstadt had a glimmer of understanding, and when he discovered that his gowns too had vanished, he realized his mistake. The wasp was not a *Sphecida* at all, but a *Vespida*, a paper wasp. Its diet consisted of wood, leaves and other natural fibres. It had eaten its own gowns.

Linderstadt surveyed the remains of his work. The nest had a delicate beauty of its own, and briefly he considered showing it in lieu of the collection. Then he caught sight of a bit of undigested material peeking out from behind the papery sphere. It was the bridal veil, and he followed it around the nest, where it stood on the floor like a fountain of steam frozen in air, unattached to its gown but otherwise intact. Outside, the crowd clamoured to be let in. Linderstadt drew back the curtains and lifted the gossamer veil. The sun seemed to set it aflame. Like the smallest fragment of a memory, it recalled every memory. He placed it on his head. A smile played across his face, the first in months. His eyes shone. With everything gone there was nothing left to hide. A single thread would have sufficed. Drawing himself up, proud and erect, Linderstadt went to open the doors.

PATRICIA DUNCKER

James Miranda Barry was a real person, born around 1795, entering Edinburgh College at about fifteen years of age, apparently a 'frail-looking young man' and becoming, although few if any besides herself would have realized it, the first woman MD in the UK in 1812. Barry entered military service and served in South Africa, the West Indies, the Crimea and Canada. Patricia Duncker, born in the West Indies and now dividing her time between Wales and France, has recently completed a novel based on Barry's life. Her first novel, *Hallucinating Foucault*, won Dillons' First Fiction Award, and the McKitterick Prize for the best first novel published in 1996.

James Miranda Barry 1795–1865

The moths plunge towards the lamp. I sit here at my desk, smoking to keep off the mosquitoes, listening to the sharp, brilliant sounds of the tropics, the roar of the night, frogs, crickets, weird cries in the bush, the dogs howling against their chains. The hospital reports are neatly stacked, separate from the accounts. I look with satisfaction upon my own

212

unblotted, immaculate hand. I have a new steel pen. And I shall scratch my way across the official paper, sheet after sheet after sheet, perfected for the archives, posterity, history. I have always gone in for all the latest inventions. If it works, I will make use of it. Other men fear innovation, change crumbling their easy lives. I never have.

I lean back, breathless with heat, my tongue on fire from the chillis in my supper. I have a native cook. And we eat the same food. Sometimes served in a calabash. If we have no company I eat with my hands. Does that shock you? I am not surprised. So many of the other officers pretend that they are still in England and import their own men. They keep a fine wire netting between themselves and this humid island. Drenched in sweat, they struggle in stiff collars, evening dress, pickle their nights in alcohol, die young from yellow fever. White men will never do well here. They count the months of their postings, hide in the mountains all summer long, buy black women from the village men. If any man on my staff dares to touch my women who work in the hospital, he is sacked. I see to that personally. I investigate every complaint. And I believe what the women say. I have absolute standards.

Listen to the buzz of insects against the screen. My tobacco smoke hangs blue in the shadows. I watch a small patrol of cockroaches moving off the edge of the carpet. Beautiful things, hard black shapes, a marching mass of claws. This night, despite the smell, which is very disagreeable, I have not the heart to kill them. I am not always sentimental. We found a colony in the rotten wood beneath the verandah a week ago. I ordered them to be burned.

213

I have watched death daily here, in the hospitals, among the shacks in the villages, in the cool, polished white houses on the great estates. The smell of death never leaves my nostrils. I drench my uniform daily with rose water. The flowers mock my profession, hibiscus, bougainvillaea in torrents against the hospital steps, orange, white, pink sweet frangipani, daily at odds with putrefying flesh, pus oozing from raw sores, the smell of fresh blood. I travel a good deal, of course. An epidemic of one sort or another among the regiments can always be counted upon. Nights like this, peaceful, solitary; they seldom come to me.

I glance at the newspapers. We get them months late. Society events long past, scandals already forgotten, illnesses which have since done for the sufferer. Tonight I will not waste my solitude with stale news. Instead, I set aside the last reports and lower the wick on the lamp. Shadows lurch across the room. My servant appears at once in the doorway. He waits, waits, waits every night for his master.

'No, lad, go to bed now. Call me at the usual time in the morning. I will lock up the doors and fetch my own water. Leave me now. Goodnight.'

Loosen my cravat, cuffs, braces, remove my top studs. Light another cheroot. Tonight it will be my turn to watch. To remember. And now the shrieking night bides the hours with me.

I dream the frost. Frost sealed the studio windows; the bare panes, luminous and opaque passed on the cold into the huge, cobwebbed vault, into the wooden joists, leaping up into the dark. The iron stove, humming peacefully, made very little difference to the air outside its immediate reach. The dark rafters hung with cold, and the great canvases, leaning against the bare walls, stuck together by the creeping frost. The water had frozen over in the bucket by the empty copper. A man, shrunken inside a greatcoat, moved like a fly before a huge, unfinished painting dealing with an historical subject. The figures moving in the paint might have been Romans, their swords and cloaks flickered red in the shifting light of the tallow candles. A horse's nostril flared, then vanished. There was one candle stuck to the rim of the cracked slab of glass he was using as a palette. His hands, encased in fingerless mittens, occasionally hovered about it. The firelight was just visible through the grid at the bottom of the stove, making great shadows dance at the man's feet. He moved slowly, a lumbering distorted monster. Soft creaks, gentle scratchings and the odd, choked thud of the falling logs were the only sounds rimmed by frost. Then the door opened, disturbing the cold air and a small child stood at the top of a dark flight of stairs.

She had risen in the dark and now she paused like an apparition, the unsummoned ghost. The man stared for a second, then ignored her. Without turning round he said, 'Shut the door. There's a wind coming up the back staircase.'

'Won't make any difference here.' Her voice was like that of an adult. Suddenly, she took on the unexpected aspect of a dwarf.

'I said shut the door,' the man repeated tonelessly and went on working. She shut the door with unnecessary force and the frost shimmered on the inner panes with the vibrations. Then the silence closed round the two figures, one hardly moving before the still painting, the other silent on a dusty stool by the stove. The frost grew, stealthily, from the guttering, coating the roofs white in the darkness.

For a long time the child stared at the picture, mumbling the edge of the dress in her mouth. She stared and stared, until at last she saw the huge, fleshy thighs of the Sabine women looming out of the candlelight. Suddenly her high dwarf's voice rose in the frost. 'I shall never marry,' she said.

The painter ignored her completely, so she said it again.

This time he spoke to me, without turning round, working steadily at the red muscles of a ravishing Roman arm. 'Then, child, you must become a man. Learn to live in this world. Earn your own money. And stay out of debt.'

He laughed bitterly at the painting. He said nothing more. He went on working.

I have spent my life in exile, ferociously guarding my privacy, travelling my world, searching out hot climates, courting danger, discovery, court-martial, disease. I have never been wealthy. I have never been loved. On my desk I have a small old-fashioned miniature, a silhouette of a woman with her hair piled in curls. If anyone is so imprudent as to inquire after the original I tell them that it is my mother, in tones which indicate I will not welcome further inquiry. Often the questioner apologizes, or murmurs their deepest sympathy. But this woman is not my mother. I met her years ago, in some lost corner of the colonies. She was beautiful, angry and bored. I was a junior officer, reticent, morose and hard-

216

drinking. She asked me to dance, assuring me that in the wilderness where we found ourselves this was quite the done thing.

I corrected her upon this point. What she pleased to term a wilderness in fact possessed an indigenous culture of a nature so sophisticated that it in many ways surpassed our own. She bowed in acknowledgement as we took the floor and said, quite seriously, 'I see that we are both radical in our opinions. We shall get on very well together.'

And she looked straight into my face, unblushing, like a street girl. 'And am I also to assume, sir, that we are in all respects alike? Small, red-haired and bad-tempered?'

'Your stature and colouring, madam, only add to your charm. Your temper remains to be revealed.'

'Thank you for the compliment. It is only fair of me to inform you that your temper has a grand reputation and has preceded your arrival. Is it true that you fought a dozen duels in Africa and killed your man every time?'

This was not a promising beginning to our acquaintance. But it did not end there. She wrote to me, visited me once at the hospital during my rounds. I sent her packing, of course. She was like a fly in hot weather. I could not be rid of her.

After six months I relented. Her parents were away. She was alone with her sixteen-year-old brother and the servants. I joined them for dinner, in full regimentals. There were no other guests. The boy and I drank liquor at the table until he was almost unconscious with the heat. We laid him out like a gentleman. Then she raised her eyebrows at me, still unblushing. Yes, this was the woman who, after I had pleasured her so many times that the sheets were wet with her happiness, reached for the studs on my shirt. I held her at arm's length, away from my body, smiling in the candlelight. I felt her tense and uncomprehending – then came the moment of exhilaration, recognition, joy. Holding the candle to my face, her eyes gleamed like fireflies in wet guinea grass.

'What are you?' she said.

'You know,' I replied. And I covered her damp breasts in kisses, all of which she repaid in full.

There was talk, of course. I really did fight a duel on her behalf, killed the man and was posted elsewhere as a result.

Water. All the water I touch is polluted. My servants even boil the water they bring to me every morning. I see water muddied with antiseptic. Swabs awash with germs and disease, dressings piled in the iron buckets for burning. The only water I can endure, clean, sharp, the salt wind rising, is the sea. I spend this night walking the beach. The coconut palms lean out in the darkness, sand blown against the roots. I feel the breath of the undertaker's wind upon my cheek, the slow lift, slap and gurgle of the retreating tide. My boots' imprint vanishes at once in the soft sand. The earth renews itself. We leave no trace.

Then I see them, sitting in a circle. Big black women from the village, squatting like gods, smoking in darkness, or chewing the leaf. They are talking. They ignore my approach. One woman, her headscarf superb as an Egyptian crown, leans slightly towards me. 'Evenin', Doctor.'

I bow to the group. I do not speak.

'Is all right, man. Siddown.' Her teeth flashed in the dark. 'Siddown. We know what y'are.'

Damp sand clings to my buckles, to my face, to the roots of the coconut palms. We watch the surf break, glimmer and vanish. The women continue to speak – in a language I do not understand.

I sit among them, contented. Here, at last, I am no longer misunderstood.

MELANIE FLETCHER

In pursuit of sexual pleasure the ancient Greek gods didn't change merely their clothes, preferring more absolute transformations. Zeus, in particular, is remembered for his brief, lustful metamorphoses on earth in order to have his way with desirable and unsuspecting mortals. In the following story, Zeus discovers the most sexually arousing changes of all.

Melanie Fletcher is an American science fiction writer and graphic artist living in the Netherlands. Of this story she says, 'There's something about the ability to shift between sexes that's extremely sexy in itself; not androgynous but hermaphroditic, combining the best of both genders to create something new and exciting. Besides, I liked the idea of sticking it to Zeus.'

Hermaphrodite

'Damn that oafish, obsessive, fornicating IDIOT!'

Aphrodite glanced up, startled. 'My lady?'

Hera, queen of the gods, scowled at the goddess reclining across from her. 'My husband,' she spat. 'I tell you, Aphrodite, I have had it up to *here* with Zeus and his philandering!'

The goddess of love sighed. Hera's latest explosion had begun after she'd discovered that the king of the gods was missing from Mount Olympus. Again. Since this meant that Zeus was busy with his favourite hobby – seducing maidens – the queen had predictably gone into a rage. And since the arena of love and its casualties were Aphrodite's department, she had been nominated by the other gods to go into the lioness's den, as it were, and placate the queen.

Not that she was trying too hard. 'Believe me, my lady, I understand your position,' Aphrodite said wearily. 'I have every respect for Father Zeus, but he's gone through my priestesses like a sailor on shore leave. In most cases, I'd be willing to overlook it – I am the goddess of love, after all – but he doesn't even bother to apologize.'

'Of course not. He doesn't think he's done anything wrong,' Hera snorted. 'Whatever issues from Zeus's loins is absolutely perfect as far as he's concerned, including all the bastards he's sired. I don't even remember how many he has, anymore.'

Aphrodite frowned. 'Well, there's Apollo, Diana and Hermes, of course,' she said thoughtfully. 'And Athena, but she's more motherless than a bastard. Then there's Dionysus, Perseus, Helen,' she started counting on her fingers, 'Pollux, Minos, Rhadamanthus, Epaphus—'

The queen rolled her eyes. 'Aphrodite. Please.'

'Well, you did ask.'

'It was a rhetorical statement, dear,' Hera said, pained. 'What I meant was, I have a husband with the sex drive of a rabbit and the tact of an Etruscan goatherder. Have you *seen* some of the forms he's used with those idiot girls? A bull, a

221

swan, even that bizarre shower of golden rain with little what's-her-name—'

'Danaë,' Aphrodite said absently. 'Yes, it does seem that he'll go to any lengths for a seduction, particularly if the seductee is young, female and, um . . .' She trailed off.

'Large breasted?' Hera said pointedly.

Aphrodite knew better than to notice the queen's rather small chest. 'Er, yes.'

'Of course.' The queen snorted again. 'My husband, the god with the mammary fixation.'

Aphrodite shook her head. 'Actually, my queen, I don't really think it's about breasts at all,' she said thoughtfully. 'Of course, physical beauty plays a role, but I think Father Zeus gets his greatest pleasure out of something else entirely.'

'Such as?'

'Control.'

Hera arched one perfect eyebrow. 'Explain.'

'Well, with a few exceptions, Father Zeus usually restricts his – activities – to young, fairly naïve girls whom he can dazzle with shape changes and magic. And even the nymphs and demi-goddesses, who should know better, can't really refuse him – he is their king and god. So all Zeus knows about seduction is the pleasure he receives as the dominant partner, which can be rather intoxicating after a while.' The goddess smiled dryly. 'If he knew what it was like to be on the receiving end, maybe he wouldn't be quite so eager to add another notch to his lightning bolt.'

Hera pursed her lips. 'The receiving end,' she repeated.

Unexpectedly, she smiled, and the temperature in the room dropped ten degrees. 'My goodness. You amaze me at times, Aphrodite.'

The other goddess blinked. 'M-my lady?'

'Yes, you're quite a genius,' Hera purred, in a tone that made the goddess of love want to crawl under the furniture. 'It's all about power and control, isn't it? And poor, silly Zeus is intoxicated by it. But if you think about it, it's not really fair for my dear husband to experience only one end of the spectrum – he should experience all of it.' She tapped her lips with a fingertip. 'We'll simply have to help him, I think.'

'Um. You don't mean—'

'Why, yes, I suppose I do.' The queen beamed. 'But I'll need your help, seeing as you're an expert in this area. You will help me, won't you?'

Aphrodite was racking her brain for a good reason to refuse, when she felt the pain underneath the command in the other goddess's voice. This was the queen of the gods, by birth as well as marriage, and even she was reduced to a powerless spectator as her husband fucked his way through Olympus's collection of nymphs and demi-goddesses. And then there were the priestesses, the innocent maidens, the virtuous wives – all those poor mortal women, used and left behind as if they were nothing.

Aphrodite thought about Zeus, the mighty Zeus, stripped of his power. Struggling. *Helpless*.

It would be for his own good. She was the goddess of love, after all. And Love always finds a way.

Smiling, she reclined on the couch and picked up a grape. 'My lady,' she murmured, 'what would you like me to do?'

Zeus, ruler of the gods, king of heaven and earth, was having a marvellous time as an albatross. He soared over the Greek countryside, allowing Zephyr and his own large wingspan to carry him effortlessly through the spring-warm air. Olympus was a lovely place, he mused, but sometimes a jaunt around the earth was absolutely irresistible.

Of course, jaunting wasn't the only interest on earth. For a god such as himself, there was always the promise of a romp with some lovely young thing – *aha* – such as the one below him in a grove of laurel trees. Grinning to himself, Zeus swooped lower to get a better look, and almost fell out of the air. *Cronus and Rhea, she's lovely*, he chortled.

Unaware of the god hovering over her, the girl walked through the grove with a basket slung over one arm. She was tall and slender, with an olive complexion set off by sea-blue eyes and masses of chestnut hair held back from her face with a band. Best of all, Zeus mused, was the magnificent body – high, firm breasts, rounded hips and long, graceful legs – all covered by a short robe that could be easily removed.

The bird-god savoured the passion rushing through his veins as he soared closer to his target. He finally aimed for the ground in front of the girl, releasing his divinity at the last moment.

The girl was stunned when the huge seabird dropped in front of her, disappearing in an explosion of light. Just as abruptly, she was standing in front of a tall, handsomely bearded man. 'Tell me,' he said, giving her a predatory grin, 'what's a beautiful mortal like you doing in a grove like this?'

Eyes going wide, the girl clutched her basket to her chest. 'W-who are you?' she stammered.

The man's grin cocked up a notch. 'I am Zeus, king of the gods and ruler of heaven and earth,' he replied, adding a touch of subsonics on the last bit. The resultant echoes rolling through the grove were quite satisfying. 'You may have heard of me?'

Immediately, the girl sank to her knees. 'My lord,' she murmured, covering her face with her hands, 'what have I done to deserve this honour?'

Zeus was pleased with her piety. *And her position is an excellent one, too.* 'You have enslaved my heart with your beauty,' he said expansively, letting his eyes roam over the curve of her breasts. 'Tell me your name, lovely one, and I shall have it written in the heavens forever.'

The maiden dropped her hands, but kept her eyes shaded by the thickest, most luxurious lashes Zeus had ever seen. 'My name is Mentirea, lord,' she said, quickly taking the basket off her arm and uncovering a small amphora of wine. 'Please, divine one, the afternoon is warm and you must be tired from your flight. Allow me to serve you a cooling cup of wine.'

The god arched one bushy eyebrow. 'And hospitable, as well,' he said approvingly. 'I'll have to come back here more often. Yes, Mentirea, serve me some wine.'

Bowing her head, the girl uncorked the amphora. Deftly, she poured a measure of the blood-red wine into a beech cup, then handed it to a dubious Zeus.

Beech. Hmm, have to do something about that. The god flexed his powers, and the cup changed to oak, heavily worked with gold. Satisfied, he sipped the wine, revelling in the complex tastes of grape, sunshine and earth. 'This is a magnificent vintage,' he commented, licking his lips. 'Where did you get it?'

Mentirea blushed with pleasure. 'My family are vintners, lord. This wine is a special blend, reserved for kings and priests on feast days.'

'How appropriate,' Zeus said, drinking the rest of the wine. Refreshed, he handed the cup back to the mortal and opened up the next line of attack. 'You're a good girl, my dear, and a lovely one as well. I'm sure your father must be beating the suitors off by the chariot full.'

'Oh, no,' Mentirea said, shaking her head. 'I don't have time for boys. Father says they only want one thing, so he keeps me working as much as possible. I don't even get to attend the public feasts. He only let me go today because Melenpus was busy and the wine jar had to be delivered to the temple.' She pouted, her lower lip sticking out deliciously. 'I *would* like to have a bit of adventure now and then,' she said wistfully. 'Staying at home all the time is boring.'

And so it begins. 'Poor thing,' Zeus purred, moving closer. 'Perhaps I could show you what you've been missing, hmm?'

She brightened. 'You'd take me to a feast?'

'Well, not exactly,' Zeus chuckled, lifting her chin with a

fingertip. 'I was thinking more of showing you what you were missing with the boys. Unless you wish to displease your god by refusing his attentions.'

As his meaning sank in, Mentirea flushed, gazing at him from under those wondrous lashes. 'My lord,' she said hesitantly, 'I am a devout worshipper, and I would never turn down your advances. B-but, I mean, I've never—'

'I know, I know,' Zeus said soothingly. 'It's obvious you're a maiden, sweet. Your innocence shines from you like a glorious light. But spend the afternoon with me, and I'll temper that light to a warm, womanly glow through the power of my love.'

Her face went blank for a moment. If he hadn't known better, Zeus could've sworn she was trying not to laugh. *Must be my imagination – the girl is obviously entranced.*

As if on cue, the sweet expression returned. 'My lord, it would be an honour to lie with you here,' she said, twining a curl around one finger as she gave him an endearingly shy glance. 'My only request is that . . . well, you're quite handsome, of course, but . . . could you assume another form for our love?'

Zeus hesitated. He'd been looking forward to a bit of sex in his own form – but she would've heard the stories, he reminded himself, and a maiden likes that kind of attention. Besides, it was a chance to demonstrate his power and entice her even more. 'Of course, my petal,' he said, feeling generous. 'What would you prefer? A glorious albatross, perhaps, or the downy softness of fog? Or how about the tawny strength of—'

'Could you become a woman?'

'A wo—' The god blinked, then burst out laughing. 'My dear, are you serious?'

'Yes,' Mentirea said shyly. 'I'm sorry, Lord Zeus, but the male form, even one as magnificent as your own, doesn't really excite me. But a woman's body . . .' She lifted a hand to her throat, and her expression changed, became more knowing. 'My lord, have you ever rested in a hollow of sun-warmed grass, a sweet breeze playing overhead, with a maiden who was all giggles and velvet skin, willing to put everything completely at your disposal?' she asked, her eyes shining. 'To taste her lips, to hear her sigh as you caress her nipples and slide your fingertips between her thighs, teasing the moist hair there. Touching that silky flesh, and the tiny nub that makes her gasp and want you even more?'

Slightly dizzy, Zeus smiled at the now-excited maiden and her lustful words. 'Yes, I know what you mean,' he said, feeling the bloodrush in his groin.

Mentirea gave him a direct look. 'Ah, but can you imagine what it's like to *receive* those attentions, my lord?' she murmured. 'To wear a woman's body, and enjoy all of the pleasures that come from being loved by another woman?'

That stopped him. 'Er. Well . . . um, no, not really,' he admitted. But as Zeus thought about it, he warmed to the idea. It certainly couldn't be any worse than being a swan. 'Very well, my precious – if you wish to love a woman, then a woman it shall be.'

Stepping back, he imagined an idealized female form and channelled his divine power into it. A brilliant cloud of light surrounded him, obscuring his body as it changed form. When the glow faded away, the towering form of Zeus had been replaced by a large-breasted Amazon, with a wanton face and flowing red hair curling over her broad shoulders. 'What do you think?' s/he said, pleased.

Mentirea shook her head. 'Forgive me, my lord, but I don't like it,' she said gently. 'It's too overpowering – you could hurt me and never even know it. It'd be ever so much better if you were more like, um,' and she gestured towards her own body.

Zeus considered the request. 'Well . . . if you really want me to,' he said dubiously.

'Oh, yes, please!'

'All right. Let's see.' S/he concentrated again, and this time the light billowed and shimmered slightly longer before revealing the new figure. As the glow faded away, Mentirea saw that Zeus was now slightly under her own height, with shoulder-length auburn hair and huge green eyes in an elfin face. As requested, the god's new curves were definitely nymph-like, with slender hips and small, high breasts that bobbed slightly as s/he breathed. A tiny V of ginger curls covered the delicate pouting of nether lips and provided an attractive contrast to the porcelain of her skin. 'Does this please you?' Zeus asked, in a light contralto.

'Oh, yes,' Mentirea breathed, clapping her hands together. 'Dearest Zeus, you're the most beautiful creature in the world! But I can't call you Zeus anymore, can I? Perhaps . . . Zeia?'

'As long as Hermes doesn't find out,' Zeus/Zeia muttered. Mentirea chuckled and took the transmogrified god/dess by the hand, guiding her to the warm ground beneath a laurel tree.

Working from prior experience, Zeia expected the girl to play with her breasts a bit, then go straight for the prize between her legs. She was surprised when Mentirea simply brushed aside a lock of hair and kissed the tender area beneath her ear. 'Slowly, beautiful one,' she murmured. 'We have all afternoon.'

Confused, Zeia closed her eyes and allowed her head to fall back, giving Mentirea full access to her throat. The girl took advantage of this, tracing a line of fire down Zeia's neck and nuzzling at the sensitive hollow. One hand caressed the god/dess's shoulder, moving with infinite delicacy to the side of her breast. Zeia was amazed at the erotic force of this touch. She found herself holding her breath, waiting for Mentirea to stroke her nipple.

Instead, the mortal girl moved back up to feast on Zeia's mouth. *Earth and air!* Zeia moaned silently, losing herself in the kiss. Her own lips relaxed as the girl's tongue slipped nimbly between them, exploring the sweet interior and sending tingles of excitement through Zeia's body. An age seemed to pass before Mentirea pulled away with a slightly breathless smile.

'You never did this with any of your maidens, did you?' she said playfully, nipping at the god/dess's chin.

'No. There never seemed to be a reason – oh, *my*.' A hand had slipped over Zeia's breast, gently rolling her nipple between two fingers. 'That's wonderful,' she said, her eyes wide with delight.

'So you like that?'

'Oh, yes,' Zeia said dreamily. The tantalizing pressure, just this side of pain, seemed to go straight to the area between her legs. 'Mentirea, it's so *good*.'

'I told you it would be,' the girl murmured. 'There's more to sex than a bit of fondling and sticking it in, my lord.' And now Mentirea's mouth shifted, licking down Zeia's neck and chest to the peak of the other breast. Zeia arched her back under the delicious suction, unable to think beyond the circles of a velvet tongue on one nipple and the skilful pressure of fingers on the other. She moaned when Mentirea released the nipple with an audible pop, then moaned louder as the mouth continued its journey downwards, pausing to kiss the hot, juicy crevice beneath a breast before coming to rest at the border of curls above her *mons*.

Spreading Zeia's legs apart slightly, Mentirea moved between them and leaned over the dark pink core of flesh, inhaling its musk-salt scent. Pursing her lips, she blew gently over Zeia's exposed labia, manipulating the flow with her tongue until it became a vibrating stream of air. Zeia gasped, thrashing her head from side to side at the luscious assault on her clit. 'Oooooo, yes, please,' she breathed.

Smiling, Mentirea replaced the air with her tongue, gently flicking up and down the labia in quick butterfly strokes, then directly across the erect nub, still sheathed in its translucent hood. She was rewarded with a gurgled moan from Zeia. 'Does it hurt, lord?' she asked sweetly. 'Should I stop?'

Zeia couldn't reply for a moment, she was so entranced by the sensation of Mentirea's tongue on her clit. 'No – yes – ahhh, I don't—'

'No, you don't. So I will.' The girl bent her head back to the task, licking and sucking Zeia's cunny with exquisite skill. Introducing one finger, then two into the tight core, Mentirea began to fingerfuck her while keeping up the fluttering tongue strokes on the god/dess's clit, pausing occasionally to lap at the sweet-salt juices trickling onto her chin.

On the receiving end, Zeia's mind was almost short-circuiting from the intense stimulation – *Oh yes, I never knew uhhh yes, harder, no THERE, yes, suck it suck me lick me velvet it's like velvet and ohh I can't I can't no please ahhh yes yesyesyes ahhhhhh—*

'Gods, oh GODS!!' Zeia clutched at the grass and screamed as a burst of ecstasy rocketed through her body. Bucking, she locked her thighs around Mentirea's head and rode the girl's magical tongue to the finish. 'Ahhhhoohh*YESSSSS!*'

Zeia's cries were still echoing through the grove when she finally sagged back on to the ground, spent. Giving the heavens a totally silly smile, she giggled. 'I never knew it could be like that!' she whispered. 'Oh, Mentirea, you are a treasure. Would you,' she paused to take a breath, 'would you like to become a minor goddess? I'm sure I could arrange something on Olympus for you.'

Mentirea chuckled. 'Not necessary, my lord,' she replied, her voice slightly muffled.

'Oh, I think it is,' Zeia said smugly. She didn't notice that the girls' cheeks had become rougher as it slid up the inside of her thigh. 'You're definitely better than any of my other maidens.'

'Was that really their fault?' The voice was husky, somewhat lower than before. 'They didn't have much choice, did they?'

'Well, no,' Zeia sighed, her attention still on the sky. 'But that's the way the game is played, after all.'

'The seducer makes the rules?'

'Of course.' She glanced down. 'Why do you ask—?'

Zeia did a double take. The person grinning at her from between her thighs was definitely not female. 'Mentirea?' she squeaked.

'Mentirius,' the man corrected, continuing to stroke Zeia's cunny as he smiled up at the distracted god/dess. On second glance, Zeia could see the resemblance to the now-gone maiden – both of them were attractive, with the same colouring and hair type, but curves had been replaced by sleek muscles and a scattering of thick, straight hair on the now-masculine chest. The robe had changed, too, morphing into a short chiton that covered his hips. 'I thought I'd surprise you with a change of my own,' he said urbanely. 'And perhaps a new game, hmm?'

Before she could do anything, the man sprang to a crouch over her. Both wrists were captured and pinned down above her head. His other hand was busy caressing her breasts, pinching the nipples roughly and making them stand up. 'Now, about the seducer making the rules,' he purred, rubbing his cheek against hers, 'why don't we play for a while and see what you think then?'

Still a beat behind, Zeia struggled in a futile effort to avoid his hands. 'W-who are you? What are you doing?' she demanded.

'What do you think?'

The situation finally sank in, and stunned anger flooded

233

through her. 'You can't do this to me – I'm the king of the gods!'

'Prove it, then,' Mentirius said easily. 'Change into a bull. Strike me down with a thunderbolt. Stop me.' He trilled the last words in an insulting sing-song, tweaking her nipples.

'I will!' Furious, Zeia commanded her body to change back to its original form, complete with powerful muscles to pound this insignificant worm into a grease spot and a sizzling thunderbolt to set the grease spot on fire—

Nothing happened.

She tried again, with the same result.

Sudden horror dawned on her. 'The wine,' she whispered.

Mentirius chuckled. 'Correct, my little godlet. A magic spell in the wine, courtesy of a good friend of mine. It's temporary, of course – you should be just fine in a little while,' he added, nuzzling her neck. His hands continued to stroke and fondle her breasts, teasing the sensitive valley between them. 'But until then, you're in sexual thrall to me. Something of a change for you, I suspect.'

Trying to ignore the growing need inside her, Zeia did her best to bite the shapeshifter. 'Pig. Whale snot. *Bureaucrat.*'

'Such language,' Mentirius tsked, dropping his hand so that it swept in gentle circles around her belly. 'But at least it's a step up from "What's a maiden like you doing in a grove like this?" – really, Zeus, that line's older than the Pyramids.'

The god/dess fumed. And squirmed. And wriggled under Mentirius's expert touch. As he leaned down to tease her flesh with his teeth, Zeia could feel the moisture forming between her legs and fought against the urge to open them. A blazing miasma of anger, guilt and sexual heat churned in her – and unexpectedly, a thread of divinity as well. She seized it and hung on like a drowning man. 'You're . . . going to . . . regret this,' she said breathlessly, bending every ounce of will to enlarging the thread.

'Somehow, I doubt that,' Mentirius replied, moving his fingers between her thighs. Zeia groaned between clenched teeth, desperately channelling some of the raw lust his caresses unearthed into her divinity. *Just a little more, please. Please, yes—*

Now! Pushing as hard as she could, Zeia released the divinity and ordered it to change her form. Blinding light exploded from nowhere, surrounding them both; gloating, she felt the sexual heat disappear as her body began to shift.

When Zeus's ears formed again, the first thing he heard was a lazy laugh. 'Oh, that's marvellous,' Mentirius said, admiringly. Slightly woozy from the transformation, the god looked down at his new body.

Fortunately, it was a familiar one. Unfortunately, it wasn't his own. 'Earth and air, I look like *Ganymede*,' he moaned.

'Your page?' Mentirius inquired sweetly. His hand was still between the god's legs, stroking what was now an erect phallus. 'Yes, I always thought he was a lovely lad, and you wear his frame admirably. Now let's see if it's as flexible as the original.' Without a pause, Mentirius slid an arm underneath Zeus and flipped him onto his stomach.

'Mentirius, wha–ahhhh.' Zeus groaned as strong fingers pried apart his buttocks, and a hot tongue licked at the nether hole. The stimulation was intense, almost unbearable, and

Zeus could feel answering ripples through his balls and cock. 'Why are you doing this to me?' he pleaded.

'Because I can.' The unseen tongue snaked down the threaded flesh, to the underside of Zeus's sac. 'Because it's fun. Don't you think it's fun?'

'Nooo, dammit,' Zeus moaned. 'I don't like it.'

Mentirius chuckled. 'Of course you do, lord.' The tongue disappeared, and Zeus was appalled to find that he missed it. 'Your cock likes it. Your body does, too.'

Vainly, the god struggled against the truth in that statement. 'But my mind doesn't,' he groaned. 'It's not fair!'

Mentirius paused. 'Where does it say I have to be fair, lord?' he murmured. 'You said it yourself – the seducer makes the rules, and the seduced must follow them.'

Zeus opened and closed his mouth like a gaffed fish, choking on his own words. 'But I didn't mean it like this,' he finally spluttered. 'I seduce maidens – I don't rape them!'

'Don't you?'

Zeus's mouth stayed open as Mentirius's words sank into his mind, deep into memory. And an image came to him, of a girl in a cave. Crying. He'd heard the sobs as he was leaving, but his mind was already a million miles away, on the next battle, the next conquest. And she hadn't been the only one to cry.

'Oh,' he said, defeated. 'I . . . oh. But . . . I never meant—'

'I'm sure you didn't,' Mentirius agreed. 'Still, you've been quite the goat, lord. And the amazing thing is, it's not nearly as much fun this way. You're struggling too hard to enjoy it, and I have to work to hold you down. Wasn't it better when we were both willing and eager?'

'Well . . .'

Suddenly, Zeus's arms were free, and he was able to roll onto his back. Mentirius was looking down at him thoughtfully, reaching to brush a lock of hair from the god's eyes. 'It was, wasn't it?' he asked.

Zeus let out a shuddering sigh. 'It was,' he said slowly. And deep down, he realized it was true. This afternoon, as Zeia, he had felt more joy, more sheer pleasure, than he had in the last millennium. 'I never knew it could be like that.'

'Then you learned your lesson. I'm proud of you, lord,' Mentirius murmured, gazing at him with approval. Then the gaze changed, intensified, hanging in the silence until it seemed to fill the world.

The god found himself holding his breath, wishing that the beautiful man above him would touch him again. 'Mentirius,' he said, hesitant. 'Mentirius, do you care about me?'

The shapeshifter chuckled. 'Care about you? I love you. I've loved you all my life, you silly god.' His voice changed, thickening with need. 'And I want to love you. I want to fuck you until we're both mindless and drained. But you have to want me, or it's not worth the bother. Please, tell me you want me.'

Zeus trembled as he caught the heat from his lover's body. All that power and passion, focused on him alone. 'I want you,' he whispered.

'Tell me to fuck you.'

'Fuck me. Please.'

Savagely, Mentirius bent down and kissed him, ravaging his mouth with sweetness. Zeus groaned under the assault, and reached for the shapechanger's chiton. It was missing.

'It was getting in the way,' Mentirius whispered. He clutched at divine thighs, bending them up so that they were out of the way, and positioned the head of his already-slick cock against the warm, puckered opening. 'Like this?'

'Mmmmmmm, yes.' Zeus smiled, pushing back until the pressure was almost too much, almost painful. Then his body finally yielded, and both of them gasped at the sudden tightness. The mortal paused, waiting for Zeus's body to accept him. When it did, he began a careful stroke, allowing the god to revel in pure feeling.

Hot. Velvet. Thick, so damned thick. Like a key in a lock, as perfect a fit as any he'd ever felt with a maiden or even Ganymede, only now he was the receptacle. He began to moan, gently at first, then with growing abandon as the electric sensations tore down his last shreds of resistance. Grinning, Mentirius leaned closer between his widespread legs so that the god's growing erection could receive its own delicious friction between their bellies.

'Earth and air,' Zeus gasped, 'don't ever stop.'

'As you request, Lord.' The stroke became stronger, more powerful as the mortal pistoned in and out of Zeus's ass. Then Mentirius slid a knee between his thighs, changing the angle of entry until the god thought he could feel it in his throat. His inner muscles clamped, again, and then he was shouting as a blinding ecstasy rocketed through him. Sticky white come spurted up over his stomach, and Mentirius joined him a second later, plunging in to the hilt as he clamped his mouth on Zeus's and absorbed the god's cries in his own.

Finally, gasping, the mortal withdrew. Zeus let his legs drop to the ground and sighed happily as Mentirius wrapped around him in an exhausted embrace. They lay like that for what seemed like an eternity, basking in the warmth of the Greek afternoon.

Then Zeus glanced down at the head pillowed on his chest. 'Mentirius?' he murmured.

'Yes?'

'Who are you, really?' He nudged at the mortal's chin until they were face to face. 'You've managed to overcome the king of the gods, something that no one has ever done before. Even with help, that still takes divinity on your part. So just who on Olympus are you?'

Mentirius smiled. 'You might be surprised, lord.'

'I don't care. Surprise me.'

'If you insist.' The smile turned into a wicked grin, and Mentirius shimmered for a moment, his form melting into feminine curves and golden hair. And a familiar face.

Zeus's eyes went wide. 'HERA?'

'None other, husband.' The nude queen of the gods reached out to tweak his nipples. 'I was tired of being left behind while you worked your way through every maiden on earth, so I asked Aphrodite to help me catch you,' she said complacently. 'So what did you think?'

Zeus tried to feel angry, and found that it was impossible. 'It was very . . . educational.'

'And?'

'I see your point,' he admitted. 'Although you might've just told me, you know.'

'And miss all this fun? Don't be silly.' She gave him a coquettish look from underneath her lashes. 'It was fun, wasn't it?'

Much to her surprise, he took her hand and kissed it. 'Yes it was, my dear,' he murmured. 'I think I've been neglecting you for far too long – I wasn't aware of your genderflexing abilities. Perhaps,' and it was his turn to give her a sly look, 'perhaps we should explore those in more depth. If you would like to, that is?'

Hera looked startled, then laughed. 'Perhaps we should,' she dimpled.

NICHOLAS ROYLE

Sometimes an individual's enthusiasm for sex can hide
the fact that he has no interest in who his partner is,
because he feels no sexual desire as it is usually understood, being fixated on his own peculiar agenda, like the
narcissistic artist in this story by Nicholas Royle.

Born in 1963, Nicholas Royle is the author of nearly a
hundred short stories and three novels, *Counterparts*,
Saxophone Dreams and *The Matter of the Heart*. He has
also edited several anthologies, most recently *The Ex
Files* and *The Agony and the Ecstasy* (stories about the
World Cup), and works for *Time Out* in London.

Jack

The fundamental paradox of New York, Johnny Lucas
decided, and one of the reasons why he loved the place, was
that the possibilities were supposed to be endless, yet the city
was built on a finite grid. Everything – every bar you went in
for a beer, every movie theatre you visited to watch the latest
new release amid much catcalling and unrestrained chatter –
was anchored by a set of coordinates.

Right now, as he polished off a pepperoni pizza, mopping up the remaining tomato from around the plate with the last of the crust, he was at Second and Tenth.

Second and Tenth.

X and Y.

Abscissa and ordinate.

Only men could design cities on axes. Only men could be that coolly rational – and narcissistic – to create a city in their own image. Only men, after all, possessed both X and Y chromosomes.

He pushed the plate away and swallowed the remainder of his beer straight from the bottle. The waiter came for the plate. Five-eight, compact build, dark complexion. The sleeves on his white cotton T-shirt had been rolled up to show off the fruits of long hours spent at his uncle's gym at Broadway and 12th. Or Park and 118th. Johnny Lucas watched him lean forward at the waist to pick the plate up from the table, his legs six inches apart.

'You wanna see the dessert menu?'

'Just bring me a double espresso,' said Johnny, sitting right back in his chair, causing it to creak.

Johnny Lucas asked for the check, and the waiter handed back his Visa card when he'd done, saying, 'Thank you, Mr Lucas. Be sure and come again.'

'Call me Johnny. Actually this is already my third time here. Third or fourth. I like the pizzas. And I like the wood-fired oven.'

'I'm glad to hear that, Johnny. Say, maybe I recognize you from one of those times before.'

242

The waiter smiled. Would he still be smiling when Lucas had walked out the door? Johnny couldn't be sure. He never could these days – that was the problem. Or one of the problems.

Another problem sat waiting for him in the space he used as both studio and crash-pad, a fifth-floor walk-up on Avenue B between Third and Fourth. There were better neighbourhoods, but there were better-off people to rent apartments in them. There always had been and there always would be. Although he couldn't really blame Helen for that.

Helen was *not* the problem that was sat waiting for him in the fifth-floor walk-up on Avenue B.

Helen had stopped being a problem, as far as she was concerned, when she walked out of their supposedly rock-solid marriage four years previously in London.

'You've chiselled away until there's nothing left,' she'd said.

Johnny Lucas was a sculptor. It's possible you've heard of him, although unlikely. He was just beginning to get some attention when the hammer blow fell. Discreet little shows in one-room galleries in Spitalfields – write-ups in the glossy art mags, one or two gigs in the *Guardian*. Then there was going to be something in one of the Sundays. A Life In The Day or How We Met or some such palaver, featuring Johnny Lucas and a painter that the majority of readers *might* actually have heard of. Johnny's agent was excitedly planning all sorts of things to capitalize on the burst of publicity. It was going to be good.

'Don't fuck this one up, Johnny,' she'd said – the agent –

Cassandra, Clarissa, something with a C. As if he was in the habit of fucking things up.

'Don't worry about it,' he'd advised her. 'I'm even going to have the new piece finished in time.'

'Make sure you do.'

But he didn't, of course, and Helen chose the worst possible moment to drop her bombshell. Couldn't she see how inconvenient it was, quite apart from it tearing his life asunder?

'You're obsessed,' she said, gesturing angrily at row upon row of busts ranged higgledy-piggledy across the floor of the garage that he used as his workspace.

'I'm a sculptor,' he snapped back. 'I sculpt. OK? It's my job, you know? Like you compile crosswords and I make sculptures. I'm sorry if you think I'm obsessed, but it's part of the territory. It goes with the fucking job.' He stopped, looked at her – they failed to connect. Blindly, he continued: 'It's not as if you thought I was a bus driver when you married me. Jesus, you even liked the fact I was a sculptor. You know, there was even the tiniest chance I might hit the big time and you'd get to bask in the glory. Remember that?'

They glared at each other over a good fifty likenesses of Johnny's own features, some lifesize, others blown up, the odd one a shrunken head.

'Well, it's all about to come together, isn't it? The piece in the *Independent*. The show at Jago's. Buyers are queuing up, apparently. The press won't be far behind. That's where obsession gets you – *darling*.'

He looked around himself uselessly, searching for a prop –

something – anything to hold on to. Some new position to take up. Fresh pose to strike.

'It's not the fact you're a sculptor,' she said, restraining herself, biting back venom that would sting her as sharply as it would him, 'so much as what you choose to sculpt. You know what you are? Man with exceptional admiration for himself, ten letters. First letter N, last letter T.'

It wasn't as if she compiled crosswords for *The Times*. Just one of the women's magazines.

With which she turned around and left.

Johnny had thought he saw her stumble slightly as she hit the edge of the doorframe on her way out. If she'd fallen off her high heels he would have gone over to her and attempted to console her. They might even still be together. It was all a long time ago now.

The problem sitting in the Avenue B walk-up wasn't anything as banal as unpaid bills, disconnection notices – they'd made a packet on the house, buying and selling at just the right time. The problem wasn't money.

The problem was another bust. Strictly speaking, the raw material for another bust. The problem was he still didn't have enough of the raw material, and – narcissist or not – the raw material he used to get *at* his raw material was in short supply. In fact it had all gone. Drained away.

Before heading out for a pizza, he'd been sitting alone, as ever, in the Avenue B walk-up, nursing a beer and staring at the refrigerator door which concealed his raw material in its freezer compartment. For an hour, he'd barely moved.

*

Once Helen had announced that she was going – and managed to get through the door without toppling over – go she would, and you could be sure there wouldn't be much of a delay. Or any coming back. Not for nothing had her father taken Lucas aside at their wedding and drunkenly advised, 'You've got your work cut out there, y'know. Proudest woman in the whole fucking country. You make sure you look after her.' Nothing could have marred Johnny's enjoyment of that day, but his father-in-law's words rang in his ears, as at some distance he followed Helen into the house and watched her march from room to room sweeping anything that could be thought of as hers, rather than his, into a huge canvas hold-all.

He knew there was no point in saying anything, not now, and his impotence made him angrier.

As she clattered about downstairs and he skulked in their bedroom, he masturbated furiously. He heard the front door slam and hobbled to the window to watch her go. She slung her bags into the black BMW – a present from her father which he wouldn't be sorry to see the back of – and hit a metal dustbin reversing out of the drive. Still he pumped, oblivious to the pain, and as she squealed to a halt in the middle of her turning circle on the main road, he sensed the inevitability, the immediacy of his climax. She accelerated away. Like the pupil of an eye exposed to sudden daylight, the BMW shrank to a black dot in the grey of the suburban Tarmac. And Johnny's rush was upon him. Caught in an unfamiliar location, his free hand scrabbled on the window ledge for something in which to catch his mess. A small blue glass vase.

It would do.

It did.

Later that day. Sitting downstairs in the kitchen. Glass of single malt, uncapped bottle, Deanston.

Ashtray – he'd had to ransack the cupboards to find one. The cigarettes were stale; they'd been sitting in a guests' box for the past two years, opened but unsmoked. And the little blue glass vase, still with his lambent pearl nestling in the bottom.

The table in front of him was covered in cigarettes. He had tipped up the guests' box and been unable to bear leaving its contents lying in a heap on the table top. He positioned one at right angles to another, forming a corner; then added another to one side, and used three more cigarettes to complete a rectangle. He built a second oblong using one side of the first shape, and so on until the thirty or so slim paper tubes had formed a grid marching across the kitchen table.

He smoked one cigarette, then lit the next from its dying embers, plucking them one by one from the edges, rather than the centre, of his gridwork.

At some indeterminate point in that fathomless geometry of smoke he conceived of the Plan. The Great Plan. Marc Quinn, back then, had yet to invade the public consciousness with his blood head, 'Self', a bust fashioned out of nine pints of his own red corpuscles. Johnny Lucas had *his* idea independently, only he wouldn't use blood, and he wouldn't tell a soul about it until he'd saved up enough raw material. It would be his great secret work, conceived the night *she* left.

If she thought by leaving she could destroy his *raison d'être*, she was wrong. He could create another one, just like that. *This* would be the making of him. Not some poxy Sunday supplement article. A few chiselled profiles on the floor of some pissy gallery, hemmed in by suits holding glasses of warm wine and orange juice at the private-view-from-Hell. No thank you.

He got a sketch pad and a fountain pen. Tape measure. Frantic calculations spurted from his nib. When he was sure he'd correctly calculated the volume of his semen, he drained it into a plastic bag and lodged it in the freezer.

Two millilitres.

He already knew the volume of his head – he'd made enough moulds of it over the years, filling them with one substance after another. This would be just the latest in a long line, but it would take longer than usual and be worth waiting for. Meanwhile, his silence would generate interest. He would cancel the shows, the piece in the *Sindy*. Lose his agent. Go away. Yes, that was it: he would go away. Leave the country.

Four litres was the volume of his head and neck. Seven pints, more or less. But he would stick to litres, for accuracy. It mattered.

He would collect his raw material once a day and once a day only. He would never miss a day, nor would he do it twice in one day. If he increased the frequency, the volume would fall – he knew that much biology. Once a day from the very day she left. And in, what – two thousand days, five and a half years – he would have enough to make the head. And he knew what title to give it, even before his first sample had had time to freeze.

He'd call it 'Jack'.

Before heading back to Avenue B from the pizza joint, Johnny Lucas wandered the streets. Killing time. Delaying returning to the studio and the mocking refrigerator door. The problem within.

Back when he was still working with stone, a problem had been something which sat on his workshop floor for a few days before he figured out how to release his likeness from within. Helen had been right in that respect: his subject never really changed. But that was okay. When he'd started, he'd thrashed about wildly for a subject – and a medium – that would keep him entertained. One minute he was working with wire coat-hangers, back copies of the *Guardian* and wholesale tubs of wallpaper paste – but without an original idea in sight – the next he was taking a chisel to tropical hardwoods, fashioning the outline of a bird that might once have alighted on it. Look at any artist's early work, he reassured himself, and it's all over the place.

He patiently hacked his way through one unworkable proposition after another until one misty autumn evening when he sat motionless in his unlit workshop at the mercy of the dying day and watched shadows grow like mould on a lump of rock in the middle of the floor. A split second before looking away, he saw a rough image of his own face revealed in the lugubrious play of darkness and light.

He didn't dare look back in case he'd imagined it, but then he did and saw that it was still there, although already sliding back into the encroaching gloom. He grabbed a sketch pad and charcoal, his hand fluttering over the tablet as he captured this never-before-revealed aspect of his face.

The next morning he was in the workshop at first light, attacking the gritstone with determination. A week later he destroyed all his pre-existing work; he was putting in twelve hours a day on the self-sculpture.

Over the next couple of years, he would select various different lumps of stone: some because he saw instantly how to get at his image, others because he sensed its hidden presence but couldn't see a way to crack the stone's code – the more difficult stones became known as problems.

The problem he faced now, in New York, was of a different type entirely.

At Second and First he went into a bar and ordered a beer. It was a place he'd not noticed before. So small from the outside it was hardly noticeable; inside it was warm, dark and sleek as velvet. The guy behind the bar was heavily pierced. (Eyebrow rings that always made Johnny's eyes water just to look at.) The loudspeakers hanging from the ceiling bristled with the electronic nightmares of Cabaret Voltaire, which Johnny recognized from Camden dive bars he'd frequented in the early eighties – before Helen.

The clientele moved around the bar like sharks in an aquarium. They would loom out of the darkness, beady eyes checking out the new arrival, then flick their leathery tails and merge back into the shadows. But there was no threat. In fact, Johnny felt comfortable. Behind the bar was a long row of fridges with sliding glass doors. Bottle after bottle of Budweiser, Miller, Coors, Dixie Blackened Voodoo Lager. Bracketed to the wall, just like in any normal bar with a pool table and checkered cloths, was a TV set. Johnny watched CNN as he swigged his Dixie Blackened Voodoo Lager from the bottle. The sound was down, but it didn't take a lip-reader to figure out they were talking about the gay serial killer who had come to light in NYC over the summer months. Stalking bars and clubs, he was believed to have been behind the deaths of four gay men between June and August. At first, his trail had been confused with that of Andrew Cunanan – the narcissistic chameleon who was supposed to have taken out Gianni Versace. Johnny remembered the day after the Versace killing: although it had happened a thousand miles south of New York in Miami, people talked about nothing else on the streets of the East Village. All over Alphabet City, amateur sleuth canaries sang their own little favourite theories to whomever would stop to listen.

Then Cunanan turned his gun on himself, by which time only two of the four interconnected New York murders had been committed. The next followed closely after the Cunanan suicide, then there was a gap of a few weeks before the most recent slaying.

It hadn't stopped gay men from going out, Johnny observed as he signalled for another beer.

There had been no particular concentration of killings in one part of Manhattan, so that any part of the city was considered to be as safe – or as unsafe – as all the others.

A tall, vulpine man, teetering on the brink of his forties, leaned on the bar next to Johnny and offered him a cigarette, which the artist accepted.

'I don't recall seeing you in here before,' said the man, his face dancing from side to side behind the sudden flare of his lighter.

Johnny's only response was to look at the man as he lit his cigarette. The man took it as an invitation to lower his bottom on to the empty stool alongside.

'Kinda makes you wonder, doesn't it?' the man said, looking at the TV where the newsreader was still talking about the murders.

Johnny shrugged, then looked in the direction of the bartender.

'Get you a drink?' he asked the man.

'Beer.'

The bartender swung a bottle of Bud out of one of the fridges, uncapped it and snapped it down on the bar in one fluid movement.

'Not from around here?' the man asked.

'Not really. My name's Lucas. Johnny Lucas. I'm an artist – a sculptor.'

'Cool,' the man said, leaning into his beer. 'So what do you work with, like, lumps of rock or carve doodads out of wood, or what?'

'I used to use just about anything. These days I'm more selective. What I use is not that easy to get hold of right now. It's kind of in short supply.'

How could he tell this guy – this stranger – that he'd dried up? That he'd spent so many long years praying at his own temple that he'd passed through self-love to self-loathing. Whatever images he called desperately to mind now while trying to fantasize were blanked out by an overpowering sense of his own lack of self-worth.

Sex with someone you love, Woody Allen had called it.

But when it became an obsessive compulsion, you grew to hate that someone; the very act became meaningless – and, more to the point, without issue.

Generally he did it in the morning. First thing. It was how he started the day. The first time, as Helen was in the process of leaving, was not about fantasizing. It was an instinctive act, an internalization of his anger, pure friction, turning his cock to pulp – and it had set the pattern. Thereafter if he called an image to mind while masturbating, it was of the head he would one day create. When he had seen Marc Quinn's 'Self' in the Saatchi Gallery – by which time he was already a couple of years into the creation of his own similar piece, although of course it hadn't yet taken shape, not literally – he then inevitably 'saw' his own bust mounted in the same kind of refrigerated unit. Quinn's piece didn't make him angry, especially: the two men were perhaps on the same wavelength, having come up with their ideas independently, and while 'Self' had a certain poetry about it – Quinn had collected nine pints of his own blood over a period of several months, nine pints being the volume of blood in the body – Johnny Lucas was going to go further. His dedication to his art was more extreme. He would give up sex – with anyone other than himself – for the required period. He would adhere to a strict timetable and would work on no other projects in the mean-time. This ironic testament to self-love would be not only his greatest work and a masterpiece of modern art, but it would become the most talked-about sculpture since Damien Hirst first took a chainsaw to a farm animal – since Carl André's pile of bricks – since Michelangelo's 'David' – Johnny Lucas's 'Jack' would become the new touchstone.

Sections of the press, he knew – the red-tops, the intelligence-free tabloids – would call him a W***ER, but he would be the one who was laughing, all the way into the art history books.

Charles Saatchi would beg for the right to exhibit the piece.

But after five years, even as the image of the completed head slowly imprinted itself indelibly on his retina – despite its being for now no more than a hallucination, a shot in the dark – its power faded. It could be no more powerful than its creator, and as his self-sufficiency diminished, melted clean away by the steady, increasing drip-drip-drip of self-loathing, it lost its capacity to stimulate. Either it rendered him impotent, or he hand-jived until he was red raw and nothing happened. Suddenly he was down from once a day to a weekly collection, and so the months dragged on, until he found himself sat in a bar in downtown Manhattan, at Second and First, his collection of raw material just two mls short of completion.

Once more – that was all that was required.

So near and yet light-years away. He'd been stuck in this impasse almost three whole weeks now.

'Maybe this isn't your kind of place?' the man suggested, resting his hand on Johnny's leg. 'Maybe we should move on? Get a beer some place else? Whadda you say?'

Maybe it *wasn't* his kind of place. Maybe he didn't know what *was* any more.

'It was all so easy once,' Johnny said, swallowing mouthful after mouthful of Blackened Voodoo. 'I thought I knew what was what. I liked girls. Period. There was no question of it being any other way, you know? Then there was Giacomo.'

The man began squeezing Johnny's leg.

'Giacomo was the most beautiful boy I'd ever seen. He's *still* the most beautiful boy I've ever seen. We worked in this bar in London. This was fifteen years ago. I realized I was looking forward to getting in to work and I didn't know why. I even started getting in early. And it didn't take a genius to work out it was because I thought I might be on a shift with Giacomo. When I got in and discovered him already there I felt so good I realized that that was what it was all about, you know?'

The man's hand paused, halfway up Johnny's thigh.

'It's pretty strong, this stuff,' Johnny said, trying to read the label on the bottle of Blackened Voodoo. He swallowed a long draught and motioned to the bartender for another round.

'I thought I was just pleased to see him. Like he was a mate, or something, and we could have a laugh. Only we barely communicated. He didn't speak any English and I know about three words of Italian. Enough to talk three Italian girls into bed – although unfortunately not at the same time. Three *blind* Italian girls, a friend of mine used to joke. So we just sat there drinking coffee, the chairs still stacked on the tables all around us.'

Johnny wasn't aware of it, but the man had withdrawn his hand and was looking over Johnny's shoulder.

'The other guys all called him Jack, but I preferred the name he'd been given by his folks. I practised saying it on the bus on the way in to work. Giacomo. What a great name, I thought. He had this hair that stood up. Christ knows how he did it, how he found the energy to apply whatever it was he used every morning. His skin was so perfect. His eyes – what colour were they? Christ – blue, green? I don't know. They were beautiful and clear. I didn't want to fuck him or *be* fucked by him. I didn't even know if he was gay. You know? Like that wasn't the point. I didn't even consider the possibility that *I* was gay. All I knew was this kid made me feel good. He was a dream.

'So maybe I thought about lying next to him. Looking at him. Maybe running my finger down his hairless chest to his stomach. Maybe even looking at his dick, you know, watching him react . . . Seeing if there *was* a reaction . . . Watching it happen. Knowing I'd *caused* it to happen. Getting a hold of it. Wrapping my hands around it, both hands. And would he be looking at me? Touching me? I guess he would, but it didn't really matter. I'd be content for him to be passive. Not that I wanted to fuck him.' Johnny wagged his finger – although no one was watching. 'Wasn't about penetration. All that mess and pain and embarrassment. Who'm I trying to kid? It wasn't.'

Johnny was slumped over the bar now, all alone. The man had disappeared. But Johnny was aware only of his crystal-clear memories of Giacomo. Of the excitement he invariably felt as he walked the final hundred yards to work each morning. Would he be there? For some reason he never quite got his head around Giacomo's schedule. If he wasn't there when Johnny got in, he'd hope the kid might turn up late, and when he didn't, he just thought about seeing him the next morning. He even turned up on his own mornings off, sometimes.

In all the thoughts he had about himself and Giacomo, he never once dreamt up penetration. If he thought about it in a more detached way, about the idea of doing that, or having it done, it did nothing for him. Anal sex. He'd never fucked a woman that way, or been asked to. It was the last thing in the world it would occur to him to do, and yet he'd imagine taking Giacomo's cock in his right hand and guiding it to his mouth, flicking his tongue over its tip, closing his lips over it. Taking it into his mouth as far as he could. And if he was really lucky, if the world really did work the way he hoped it might, he'd feel the boy's hands taking hold of *his* cock and lightly massaging it.

But how often had things worked out the way he planned them?

Would he really be sitting in a gay joint at Second and First talking to anyone who'd listen – the clichéd drunk in bar – if things had turned out the way he'd planned?

Guess not.

Would the world really get put to rights if he managed to collect his final two mls of come, add it to the 3998 mls in his ice-box, let the whole lot melt, then pour it into his mould?

Would it make any difference if he used it as it was – technically two mls short? What possible difference could that make? No one would know and even if they did it wouldn't matter.

But he knew that *he* would always know.

It had always been four litres for a life-size head and so should it be this time, for his masterpiece. Possibly his ultimate work. It was a question of pride.

Whatever good it would or wouldn't do, he had to do it. His life was on hold until he did. And if he couldn't do it on his own, then maybe he should stop trying. His capitulation in that sense would enrich the work with extra meaning. Don't try to live alone, reach out for your fellow man – that sort of thing. But being a lonely drunk wasn't the best way to meet his fellow man.

Back on Avenue B, although drunk and tired, Johnny couldn't sleep. He twisted around in bed so many times he forgot which way was up. In the end, he switched the light on and grabbed something to read. A three-week-old copy of *Time Out New York*. The news pages had a big feature on the gay serial killer. He tried to figure out their angle – was it that the cops weren't trying because he was only killing gays? Probably. And why was he called a gay serial killer? Was it because he only killed gay men or because he himself was gay? How had he made that known if it was the case? Did he leave the bodies all neat and tidy? Who was to say he wasn't a straight serial killer preying on gay men? What did the cops know that they weren't telling?

Johnny turned to the visual arts section, wondering why he always found the reviews so annoying, before he realized it was because they never mentioned Johnny Lucas.

He flicked through the classifieds, lingering over the personal ads, and slowly an idea started to form.

Three weeks on from the episode with the tall, vulpine man, Johnny Lucas was back in the bar at Second and First. A bottle of Dixie Blackened Voodoo Lager before him on the bar, almost untouched. Johnny was glad that there'd been no sign of the tall man – he wouldn't have to ignore him.

Johnny had placed a personal ad in *Time Out*. English guy looking for a male companion to have a laugh with – something like that. A good time. No strings. No stress. He got enough replies to be able to weed out the obvious nutters and borderline psychos. After a couple of calls he narrowed it down to a guy who called himself Eddy. His accent was indeterminate and Johnny didn't ask where he was from, although the guy did volunteer that he was from out of town and found New York a little difficult to get a handle on. Tricky to negotiate. Too many streets, east and west; avenues, numbers and names. They arranged to meet in the bar at Second and First. Johnny would be sitting at the counter drinking Dixie Blackened Voodoo Lager. The other guy was medium height with short hair just beginning to go grey, was all he'd told him. Johnny decided that would be enough.

But the guy was already half an hour late. Johnny was on

to his second beer and still no trace, but he didn't get stressed. If the guy didn't show, he didn't show and that was that. He'd got cold feet, whatever – it wasn't important.

At 8.45 p.m., forty-five minutes after they had arranged to meet, a man of medium height with very close-cropped greying hair slipped on to the stool next to Johnny's, the angle of his body favouring Johnny rather than the bar. To be honest he was losing his hair and it looked as if it had been going grey for quite some time, but Johnny could forgive the man a little vanity.

'Hi there,' the man said.

'Hi yourself,' said Johnny, 'you want a beer?'

The man hesitated a moment, looking into Johnny's eyes, then, seeming to reach a decision, said, 'Sure. A beer would be good. A beer would be just fine.'

'Couple beers over here, please.'

If the bartender recognized Johnny from his previous visit, he was tactful enough not to show it.

'So how's it going?' Johnny asked, once they had a cold beer apiece.

'Real good,' the man said, nodding his head slowly. 'Real good.'

'I guess it can be difficult to meet people,' Johnny said, 'if you don't really know your way around.'

'I guess,' the man said, tipping back his beer.

While the man was hardly Quasimodo, he wasn't quite Johnny's idea of the perfect partner – even for an evening. But you couldn't expect a blind date necessarily to work out in that sense as neatly as you would like it to. Medium height was OK – Johnny was no giant – and he sort of liked the man's cropped hair. The plates of his skull could be seen to shift infinitesimally as he drank his beer. But, since that initial gaze, the man hadn't met his eyes once. In fact, he looked a little shifty. Although it would be fair enough to put that down to nerves.

'Do you do this often?'

'Meet a stranger in a bar?'

Johnny nodded.

'I guess we're all strangers, you know what I mean? And we're tryin' not to be.'

'Right.'

Then the man looked at him for the second time and there was a half-smile on his lips, enough to indicate he wasn't taking himself too seriously and neither should Johnny. Both men laughed and relaxed a little.

'So what do you do?' the man asked, finishing off his beer and catching the bartender's eye. 'Two more beers.'

Johnny couldn't remember how much he'd told the man over the phone. He knew he hadn't told him the *real* reason for wanting to meet someone.

'I'm an artist.'

'Uh-huh.'

Eddy had told him a little about what he did.

'You're in marketing or something?'

'You could say that. I buy and sell. Move things around. You wanna move on some place?'

Johnny was feeling confident, but then part of him also wanted to get this over and done with.

'I live just a few blocks away,' he said.

The half-smile reappeared on the man's lips.

In the Avenue B walk-up, Johnny fixed a couple of single malts.

'Straight, no ice,' said the man.

'How else?'

They were large ones.

Something – whether it was the unfamiliarity of the situation or the sight of the man's tightly packed crotch as he sat back on the sofa – had already got Johnny more turned on than he had been for some days. That afternoon he'd been out and bought some KY jelly and a packet of Trojans – the strongest they had. As Johnny walked past the end of the sofa with the drinks, the man grabbed him by the belt buckle, his fingers slipped inside the waistband of Johnny's jeans. With his free hand he took one of the two glasses of scotch and swallowed it in one. He threw his head back and made a strange noise in his throat. Johnny looked at the man's hand at his waist and thought what the hell, knocking back his own whisky as well.

The man pulled him down on to the sofa and placed his mouth over Johnny's, his hand unbuckling Johnny's belt. Johnny tried to picture Giacomo but found the contrast – between that innocent fresh-faced boy and this gruff stranger – too distracting. The further the man got into Johnny's pants, however, the less confident and practised his coordination appeared to become. Johnny had to push his own jeans down, raising his bottom from the sofa to do so. The man fell upon

Johnny's cock like a hungry guest at a feast and Johnny knew he would have to take the upper hand if he was going to get what he wanted out of this. In his clumsy eagerness, the man was catching Johnny with his teeth.

'Hey, relax,' Johnny said. 'Get up. Stand up.'

Meek now, the man did exactly as Johnny said, allowing Johnny to undo his jeans and push them down to his knees. The man rolled his own boxer shorts down after them and Johnny ordered him to kneel on the sofa, facing into the cushions. Johnny himself was not prepared to get fucked and the best way to ensure that didn't happen – and withdraw from the encounter with what he needed – was to fuck the guy himself.

The condoms and the jelly were on the table in front of the sofa. Johnny was good and hard by now. He unrolled a condom on to his cock and smeared a glob of jelly where it was about to go. Took a deep breath and—

He was amazed at how easily it went in. He guessed it was the jelly – he'd once used some to squeeze his wedding ring over a badly swollen knuckle after hitting himself with a hammer.

The man gasped, his hands gripping the edge of the sofa and his head turned to one side. Johnny thrust into him, working up a rhythm. Inevitably he was reminded of making love with Helen, and that, too, was a distraction he could do without. So maybe it was a little tighter, but that was no bad thing when all that was at stake here was filling his condom.

But it wasn't *quite* as clinical as that. Johnny couldn't deny he was getting off on this. He bent forward and reached around the man's hips to touch his cock. The size of it sent a shiver of a thrill through him. As he continued to glide smoothly in and out, he clasped his right hand tightly around the man's penis and moved it firmly up and down. White lights flickered at the edge of Johnny's vision. He closed his eyes and felt everything narrowing down to one point of sensation.

As far as he was concerned, the man was not important. He was an absence, a cipher, a stand-in. A stunt-cock for Johnny himself.

As Johnny held him, it was like holding himself, but with the touch of a stranger's hand. Just another way to wank.

Dimly aware of the man's indistinct vocalizations, he sensed the sudden inevitability of his own climax, and carried on shunting until they both came at the same time with a great concerted roar.

In the bathroom, Johnny worked the condom free, snapping a simple knot into it to conserve his prize. Once it was secure, he stuck it under the cold water tap before putting it safely in the cabinet above the sink. He washed his hands and returned to the main room.

The man was standing up, fastening his belt.

'I gotta go,' he said, that nascent smile teasing the lower half of his face again. 'I'll call you.'

Johnny paused. It couldn't do any harm. He could always say no.

'Sure, call me.'

The man waited.

'Your number?' he said eventually.

'You have it already.'

'How would I have your number?'

'You called me the other day.'

'Look feller, I don't know what this is, but I didn't call you. I never saw you or spoke with you before tonight.'

Johnny stood and stared at the man.

'I guess I better go,' the man said, picking up his leather jacket and heading for the door. He opened it and passed into the shadow of the stairway without looking back, closing the door behind him. Johnny stood in the centre of the room, his hands on his hips.

After a time he went to the refrigerator and brought out the frozen block of come in its polythene bag. He placed it on the table between the sofa and the TV, then took a look at the sofa and turned one of the cushions over. He collected the final specimen from the bathroom cabinet and added it to the rest. It formed a tiny pool in a little uneven depression on the top edge of the block.

He didn't feel anything.

He sat looking at it for a moment, then switched on the TV, which was tuned in to a news channel.

There had been another murder. The body of a man in his thirties had been found in an abandoned warehouse at Eleventh and Twenty-Fifth, but the reporter was speaking to camera outside a bar at First and Second which he described as being 'popular with homosexual men'.

First and Second.

The dead man was Eddy Jongehans, according to his passport, a Dutch tourist on a three-week holiday in New York.

The killer, as usual, had taken nothing from the body, leaving only his trademark clues, which the police of course would not reveal for fear of copycat killings. All the police had to go on, the reporter said, was a scrap of paper in the dead man's wallet. Part of a page removed from a magazine, with a personal ad ringed in red ballpoint.

Johnny Lucas stared aghast at the screen.

Eddy Jongehans had muddled up his X and Y coordinates. Put his street before his avenue. He should have gone to Second Avenue and First Street, but he'd gone to First Avenue and Second Street instead – First and Second, not Second and First – only he wasn't to know that. He was from out of town, as he'd told Johnny on the phone. He found New York tricky to negotiate. Johnny had been living in Manhattan too long and had assumed the man was familiar with the convention of putting the avenue before the street.

Forcing an entry into Johnny's empty apartment a few hours later, having traced the man who placed the personal ad, the cops would assume Johnny Lucas had fled because he'd made himself an easy target. They wouldn't know what to make of a slowly spreading pool of come, covering the table in front of the sofa and several square feet of carpet. They certainly wouldn't think it had anything to do with remorse.

SUE THOMAS

In virtuality (aka cyberspace) there is no fleshly reality, only words which construct, in William Gibson's phrase, a 'consensual hallucination'. The citizens of cyberspace are free to describe themselves in any way they like, which includes not only changing age, appearance and sex, but inventing new genders. Sue Thomas writes, 'In virtuality there is a consensus that nothing is real and yet everything can be believed. That the world around you is a deliberate lie and yet you admire its artifice. That the bodied are invented and yet you can touch them ... And despite the head games of unbodied cyberspace one thing is for sure – it is incredibly sensual.'

Sue Thomas, Artistic Director of the trAce International Online Writing Community based at Nottingham Trent University, is also the author of two published novels, *Correspondence* and *Water*. As research for her third novel, *The[+]Net[+]of Desire*, she created a virtual space by the same name, which can be visited on the Internet at LambdaMOO, virtual location #87887. The following story is a taster for the novel.

SUE THOMAS

The Talent for Virtuality
a configuration of *The[+]Net[+]of Desire*

Virtual Body Language

<<consider this>>

When we meet a person in the flesh for the first time, what do we do?

We look at them.

And in those initial first few seconds, often before any words have been exchanged, we make up our minds. Before we have even said 'hello', we have already completed a complex assessment based on the usual data – gender, age, race, looks and clothes – all salted with our own past experiences and prejudices. And as soon as they're in close enough proximity to activate our olfactory nerves, we smell them too. Often this last piece of data is powerful enough to override all our previous conclusions.

And when they do finally speak, we can add further items to our already extensive pool of data. We glean a more solid picture of their background, preferences and priorities. We can add what they say to how they say it, and almost always this corresponds to the data we have already accumulated.

But when the two (what they say and how they say it) don't quite match up, we're quickly alerted to the fact that there may be a problem, that perhaps there's some dysfunction or some attempt at deception going on. And so we may start to pay extra attention to their words. We might ask a few searching questions and if the answers don't satisfy us we will almost certainly review our opinion. But in most cases there's no mismatch. We have evaluated them with our eyes and nose and backed up the data with our ears and everything fits. Fine!

In text-based virtuality, however (otherwise known by the confusing names of MUDs and MOOs), instead of a conglomeration of data we get a narrowing of bandwidth, so that an entire physical body is condensed into just a paragraph of description. Where in Real Life we use words to double-check what our other sensory data has already told us, in this environment words are all we have. We make assessments about our companions based solely on the words they choose to type. It's like listening to a play on the radio, where your imagination fills in a large part of each scene.

What all this compression and encoding means is that you have to concentrate. You must focus **hard**.

And here in virtuality, where text equals body, the very powerful link between the way we breathe and the way we write comes into force with a vengeance in a way which is only possible during synchronous communication. Every line, every phrase, every paragraph gets its form and punctuation from the breathing pattern of its typist at the very moment of writing it down. It means that as a player reads the lines appearing on the screen, they are probably breathing in and out at precisely the same points as the typist did during the seconds it took to write them.

Sometimes lovers read each other's words aloud as they appear on the screen, breathing the rhythm of the punctuation and fitting tongues and lips around the syllables as if each were a cherished part of their beloved's body. They concentrate hard, pacing themselves carefully through each sentence, counting a beat for each syllable, a one-second pause for commas and semi-colons, two seconds for colons and three for full-stops. An onlooker might imagine that they are reading music, and so they are, but it is a concerto of words rather than notes which flows silently through their heads as they sit murmuring at their keyboards renewing every vowel, every consonant, every phrase.

So how can the meat be separate from virtuality when even the very act of reading allows the flesh and brain to interact?

It is this intense concentration which brings about the profound mind-meld that sometimes occurs between players. In other words, we add our own preferences to the mix to make out of it whatever we will. But the virtual player does not need to understand all this theory in order to appreciate the delicate manoeuvres between one identity and another, and different bodies are adopted almost instinctively as the player moves between one mind state and the next. And what are those bodies like? Anything you care to invent . . .

Liis. and Obsidian

Liis. Her cheeks are flushed, her lips moist. She is wearing a black silk evening gown, slightly torn in places, and beneath the gown her body is curved and full. Her feet are bare and slightly dirty, her toe-nails painted a deep red. Gazing at her, you breathe in the mingling perfumes of roses, honey and blood.

Liis is dozing on the sofa in the Lounge at PuppetMOO, when suddenly she comes awake, certain that someone has entered the room.

'Hello?' she says.

Then, 'Is anyone there?'

'Sorry, am I intruding?' The sound is deep and low, like the rumbling of a landslide, and at that moment she becomes acutely aware of Obsidian. He is not exactly standing beside her . . . it's more as if he is everywhere.

Such a pleasant voice, she thinks, and then is surprised to feel herself blushing.

'Intruding? No, not at all.'

Now he comes into view.

Obsidian. Born of a great heat but found the world toooo cold . . .

Deep black, sharp-edged.

Take care.

The Talent For Virtuality

Consider the virtual player sitting at the keyboard, eyes intent on the screen, fingers poised in thought, or rapidly typing. The only noises are those of breathing and of the CPU fan massaging the air.

Watch another, the lover of the first, as the body hardly moves, barely makes a sound, and yet inside that meaty shell blood courses through the veins, the heart races, the mind rushes on . . .

They are here and they are not here; they are in separate rooms but they are also together inside a binary labyrinth called PuppetMOO where their blood is changed into current, their arteries into wires, their brain activity into code.

Consider them as they concentrate, most of their major physical sensoria set to idle . . . their senses of taste, smell, hearing, touch all subdued and running in the background, whilst another set takes over, entering through the portal of their eyes and using only the medium of sight to trigger the pathways of the brain.

And what is this sensorium like? It is not new, although the technology it uses certainly is. In the Middle Ages it was as familiar as the more mundane physical realms of the well-known five. Today we are only accustomed to the type of data collected by the senses of touch, taste, hearing, sight and smell. Indeed, without these Cartesian quintuplets we would have no way of knowing what is going on out there beyond the prison of our own skins. But over the centuries philosophers have devoted a great deal of time to identifying and quantifying the sensorium and they have come up with an interesting variety of senses: heat, cold, pleasure, discomfort, desire, fear, hardness, wetness and speech, to name but a few.

Speech. Today we tend to think of our senses as mere passive receptors of data, but in the past they were perceived as proactive agents able, for example, to issue rays from the eyes which actively mingled with the object being looked at. Viewed in this light, the output of speech is just another of those sensory manifestations, but it is difficult for us to think in those terms because we are obsessed and enslaved by the elevation of meat above spirit.

There is also another, newer 'sense' which comes into play in cyberia, and that is our everyday engagement with an environment dominated by electricity. Already we are used to living inside a crude form of auditory cyberspace, surrounded as we are by the constant hum of domestic machines and urban noise. Our brains are finely tuned to select, comprehend and digest screenfuls of text, complex blends of fast editing, dialogue, music, sound effects and subliminal messaging. Our bodies are accustomed to the emissions of electrical equipment, to the noise, to the changing magnetic fields, to the perpetual bombardment of every type of radiation from high energy gamma rays to the subtlest of radio waves.

When entering the cybersensorium we must be prepared for our minds to jump and twist as they open up to different modes of perception.

At first, it might seem that the predominant sense in cyberia

273

is sight – after all, one needs to be able to 'see' the screen. But whilst our eyes are obviously very useful, our reliance upon them can often prevent us from taking the imaginative leap necessary in order to enter this unorthodox space. The act of looking implies distance, detachment, objectivity – and often control. It relies heavily upon a collective belief in only three dimensions. But one of the first lessons the novice cyberian traveller must learn is *not* to believe the evidence of their own eyes – there is always more to discover than that which is instantly revealed.

In the third century the philosopher Origen identified a set of spiritual senses which twinned the physical ones and enabled the perception of transcendental phenomena such as the sweetness of the Word of God. This doctrine of the five spiritual senses was given much credence during the medieval period and subsequently gave birth to the idea of the 'inward' sensorium, comprising memory, instinct, imagination, fantasy and common sense, which acted as a processor for the data gathered by the physical senses.

This sensorium could almost correspond to the CPU of your computer. There can be no doubt that both the spiritual and the inward sensoria will prove to be very useful inside cyberspace. It cannot be denied that it engages our most intimate intellectual imagination in a way never before encountered. Once accessed by sight, sound or touch, the computer bypasses the physical senses to hook us in directly and soon we are there

<<inside at last>>

finally released from the gridlock of meat and bone which has held us in thrall for so long.

Liis and Obsidian

Despite the fact that he has no proper description, Obsidian seems to be everywhere. Liis can almost hear him breathing.

Oliver is highly sensitive to the ebb and flow of the electrical impulses inside his computer. At this moment, as the ancient creature buzzes and whirrs and quivers, he knows he's in serious danger of losing his connection.

'I wonder . . .' she begins, unaware of the technical problems occurring in Real Life, '. . . might I ask you something?'

'Of course.'

'What *are* you exactly? Most people I've met here have humanoid bodies, but you don't seem to have any form at all . . .'

'Hmm . . .' Obsidian's colour deepens and his sharp edges gleam as an urgent desire for retreat surges through him. He has been in seclusion for a long time, although it was not always this way. But of late he has learned to prefer his own company to that of the group and has only emerged from his private rooms today after being driven by a sudden and unaccountable wish to seek out some companionable conversation.

He considers her question, and wonders if his answer will sound odd. Then he realizes he doesn't care too much – after all, if you can't be yourself in virtuality, where can you? He begins . . .

'All you see is simply what I am. It is just a different representation, displaying essence rather than ornament.'

Essence. Yes, he is pleased with that.

'But don't you find that rather intimate?' She is embarrassed, but presses on. 'Generally one begins with the outward person and works inwards, getting to know them gradually, but by doing it this way you make yourself so . . . exposed . . . so . . . vulnerable . . .'

'Of course you're right. Although I have to confess that this body was designed to do exactly the opposite. But perhaps it's easier to hide behind a simple representation than an abstract idea. Hmm. I'll think about that.'

He is intrigued but also embarrassed by her forthright manner. 'To be truthful, I have not entered society here for quite some time – in fact this is my first outing for a while.'

He pauses.

The screen is so dirty Oliver can barely read it – and he wants to read it. He wants to know who this person is. He runs the flat of his palm across the dusty glass and there's a loud POP! as it bites back in a tingling burst of static. Grimacing, he pulls back his hand and accidentally knocks the CPU so that the power cable slips out of its socket and everything goes suddenly dead.

'So why . . .?'

She stops, realizing that there is a sudden emptiness in the room.

Obsidian has gone. The only remaining sensations of

him are a faint tarry perfume and a slight glittering in the air.

Damn! A loose power connection – such a stupid thing! He must get some tape and fix it. Maybe he should buy a new lead. Maybe he will. He switches on the nearby transistor radio, tunes it to some soothing music, and pushes the plug back in. As he presses [-on-] there is a crackle, a hiss, and the starting whirr of the fan followed by the scream of the CPU booting up in tune to the radio, but then suddenly everything fades back and falls into silence once more, leaving only the tumbling tunefulness of a piano to smooth out the ruptured air.

Has he run away? Has his connection failed? Maybe he'll be back soon, or perhaps she'll never see him again.

Oh, this place can be so frustrating! Is she doomed to constantly meet interesting people and then lose them? Not this time, she thinks, I won't let this one go.

Cursing, he leans across and jiggles the wire at the back, repeating the operation several times as the machine hisses and sputters until finally everything connects and the screen blinks its way to life again. He starts to type. But now the

machine screeches and screams in time to the electric guitars
as the signals sing to each other from radio to computer and
back again. He grits his teeth. His nerves are jangling with the
noise, the bursts of static, the flickering light of the screen. He
hits the off-button on the radio and tries to concentrate.

Disappointed, and feeling acutely lonely, Liis returns to the
shady retreat of her own room when Obsidian reappears.

'Hello!' she says softly. 'I thought I'd lost you. . .'

'Oh no . . . just a small technical hitch.'

He smiles.

She laughs and kisses him lightly on the cheek.

'Good! I'm glad you're back!'

Silence.

Spasm.

So what happens here now?

A shift.

A flux.

A dive.

For just a moment he hesitates, but something is occurring
that he can't ignore no matter what the future holds. He
shudders, then pulls her to him.

'kiss me . . .'

'kiss me . . .'

'kiss me . . .'

> *Louise stares at her fingers on the keyboard*
> *and imagines their twins, somewhere halfway*

across the world, typing exactly the same words at the same time.

'kiss me . . .'
'kiss me . . .'
'kiss me . . .'

Oliver is frozen with emotion. Every nerve tingling, his penis thickening, his heart surging.

Here they sit, embracing, but speaking not a word.

Louise is locked to the screen. Her brain is racing, her blood pounding through her veins.

Suddenly he finds himself whispering into the dark:
'I want you.'

His words flicker their screens back to life.

'Yes,' she murmurs.
She leans her head on his shoulder.
In the space of just a few seconds, something has occurred here. There is a recognition, a patterning, a synchronicity which defies explanation and yet is almost tangible in the swirling air of cyberspace.

279

It is certainly tangible in Real Life, where Louise's fingers tremble against the keyboard, and Oliver's forehead shines with sweat.

Obsidian strokes her hair and breathes in the scent of deep crimson roses.

She sighs.

'What's happening to us?'

As Obl/iq, Oliver has performed virtual erotics many times, but Liis feels like his first-ever lover. With her he is Obsidian, he is a virgin once more.

He leans back in his chair, pulls the keyboard on to his knees, and proceeds to make love to her slowly, tentatively, soaking her in, his hands caressing first the keys, then every part of his body in turn. He strokes the tender skin of his belly, his throat, the tightness around his eyes. He finds himself running a finger along the inside of his lower lip, twitching at it with his tongue, as if it belongs not to him but to his lover.

And Louise begins to understand how hollow are the pleasures she has so far experienced compared with the joy of being so close to Obsidian, this consciousness so intimate with her own. She reaches out to touch the screen

*and traces the O of his name, longing to push
her fingers inside him as if his whole body is
an O, as if the only reason he exists is to
encompass Louise and her hunger. Then
patiently, gently, she finds in herself a strange
and delightful newness.*

It takes very little to fall in love in virtuality. But what
causes it? There are no physical interactions, no sights, smells,
or sounds, no pheromones, no body language. You cannot see
or smell or touch each other. You can't hear your lover's voice
or taste their lips.

There are only words, words and electrons. That is all.

'You have bewitched me,' she whispers.

'Perhaps,' he replies, 'but I am yours in return.'

'Are you a woman?' she asks. 'A man? I don't care. It makes
no difference to me. I love you.'

'I don't know who you are. Your name. Your job. Your age.
But does it really matter?'

'All I need to know is that everything else was a mirage.
You are the person I have been looking for.'

'This is new. *We* are something new.'

*Louise closes her eyes, opens them, and he is
still here, his sentences running horizontally
across the glass like a ribcage of desire contain-
ing only their two beating hearts.*

CAROL EMSHWILLER

Carol Emshwiller has published two novels, *Carmen Dog* and *Ledoyt*, and several collections of short stories. 'Sex and/or Mr Morrison' first appeared in Harlan Ellison's *Dangerous Visions* in 1967. In her afterword she quoted Blake's 'The head Sublime, the heart Pathos, the genitals Beauty, the hands & feet Proportion' and commented on the sickness of a society in which genitalia were considered 'dirty' and hidden away. The idea for this story had come to her while watching a production of Stravinsky's *The Rites of Spring* and thinking how ludicrous it was that the dancers should be wearing 'naked suits' instead of going naked. She remembered that as a small child she'd felt that people must be hiding their genitals so carefully because they really were each entirely different from one another: 'And if people didn't wear clothes, I thought, what peculiar and wondrous things we'd see.'

Sex and/or Mr Morrison

I can set my clock by Mr Morrison's step upon the stairs, not that he is that accurate, but accurate enough for me. Eight-thirty, thereabouts. (My clock runs fast, anyway.) Each day he comes clumping down and I set it back ten minutes, or eight minutes or seven. I suppose I could just as well do it without him but it seems a shame to waste all that heavy treading and those puffs and sighs of expanding energy on only getting downstairs, so I have timed my life to this morning beat. Funereal tempo, one might well call it, but it is funereal only because Mr Morrison is fat and therefore slow. Actually he's a very nice man as men go. He always smiles.

I wait downstairs, sometimes looking up and sometimes holding my alarm clock. I smile a smile I hope is not as wistful as his. Mr Morrison's moon face has something of the Mona Lisa to it. Certainly he must have secrets.

'I'm setting my clock by you, Mr M.'

'Hey, hey . . . my, my,' grunt, breath. 'Well,' heave the stomach to the right, 'I hope . . .'

'Oh, you're on time enough for *me*.'

'Heh, heh. Oh. Oh, yes.' The weight of the world is surely upon him or perhaps he's crushed and flattened by a hundred miles of air. How many pounds per square inch weighing him down? He hasn't the inner energy to push back. All his muscles spread like jelly under his skin.

'No time to talk,' he says. (He never has time.) Off he goes. I like him and his clipped little Boston accent, but I know he's too proud ever to be friendly. Proud is the wrong word (so is shy) but I'll leave it at that.

He turns back, pouting, and then winks at me as a kind of softening of it. Perhaps it's just a twitch. He thinks, if he thinks of me at all: what can she say and what can I say to her? What can she possibly know that I don't know already? And so he duck-walks, knock-kneed, out the door.

And now the day begins.

There are really quite a number of things that I can do. I often spend time in the park. Sometimes I rent a boat there and row myself about and feed the ducks. I love museums and there are all those free art galleries and there's window-shopping and if I'm very careful with my budget, now and then I can squeeze in a matinée. But I don't like to be out after Mr Morrison comes back. I wonder if he keeps his room locked while he's off at work.

His room is directly over mine and he's too big to be a quiet man. The house groans with him and settles when he steps out of bed. The floor creaks under his feet. Even the side walls rustle and the wallpaper clicks its dried paste. But don't think I'm complaining of the noise. I keep track of him this way. Sometimes, here underneath, I ape his movements, bed to dresser, step, clump, dresser to closet and back again. I imagine him there, flat-footed. Imagine him. Just imagine those great legs sliding into pants, their god-like width (for no mere man could have legs like that), those Thor legs into pants holes wide as caves. Imagine those two landscapes, sparsely fuzzed in a faint, wheat-coloured brush, finding their way blindly into the waist-wide skirt-things of brown wool that are still damp from yesterday. Ooo. Ugh. Up go the suspenders. I think I can hear him breathe from here.

I can comb my hair three times to his once and I can be out and waiting at the bottom step by the time he opens his door.

'I'm setting my clock by you, Mr M.'

'No time. No time. I'm off. Well . . .' and he shuts the front
door so gently one would think he is afraid of his own fat
hands.

And so, as I said, the day begins.

The question is (and perhaps it is the question for today):
who is he really, one of the Normals or one of the Others? It's
not going to be so easy to find out with someone so fat. I
wonder if I'm up to it. Still, I'm willing to go to certain lengths
and I'm nimble yet. All that rowing and all that walking up
and down and then, recently, I've spent all night huddled
under a bush in Central Park and twice I've crawled out on
the fire escape and climbed to the roof and back again (but I
haven't seen much and I can't be sure of the Others yet).

I don't think the closet will do because there's no keyhole,
though I could open the door a crack and maybe wedge my
shoe there. (It's double A.) He might not notice it. Or there's
the bed to get under. While it's true that I am thin and small,
almost child-sized, one might say, still it will not be so easy,
but then neither has it been easy to look for lovers on the
roof.

Sometimes I wish I were a little, fast-moving lizard, dull
green or a yellowish brown. I could scamper in under his
stomach when he opened the door and he'd never see me
though his eyes are as quick as his feet are clumsy. Still I
would be quicker. I would skitter off behind the bookcase or
back of his desk or maybe even just lie very still in a corner,
for surely he does not see the floor so much. His room is no
larger than mine and his presence must fill it, or rather his

285

stomach fills it and his giant legs. He sees the ceiling and the pictures on the wall, the surfaces of night table, desk and bureau, but the floor and the lower halves of everything would be safe for me. No, I won't even have to regret not being a lizard, except for getting in. But if he doesn't lock his room it will be no problem and I can spend all day scouting out my hiding places. I'd best take a snack with me, too, if I decide this is the night for it. No crackers and no nuts, but noiseless things like cheese and fig newtons.

It seems to me, now that I think about it, that I was rather saving Mr Morrison for last, as a child saves the frosting of the cake to eat after the cake part is finished. But I see that I have been foolish for, since he is really one of the most likely prospects, he should have been first.

And so today the day begins with a gathering of supplies and an exploratory trip upstairs.

The room is cluttered. There is no bookcase but there are books and magazines by the hundreds. I check behind the piles. I check the closet, full of drooping, giant suit coats I can easily hide in. Just see how the shoulders extend over the ordinary hangers. I check under the bed and the knee hole of the desk. I squat under the night table. I nestle among the dirty shirts and socks tossed in the corner. Oh, it's better than Central Park for hiding places. I decide to use them all.

There's something very nice about being here for I do like Mr Morrison. Even just his size is comforting for he's big enough to be everybody's father. His room reassures with all his father-sized things in it. I feel lazy and young here.

I eat a few fig newtons while I sit on his shoes in the closet, soft, wide shoes with their edges all collapsed and all of them shaped more like cushions than shoes. Then I take a nap in the dirty shirts. It looks like fifteen or so but there are only seven and some socks. After that I hunch down in the knee hole of the desk, hugging my knees, and I wait and I begin to have doubts. That pendulous stomach, I can already tell, will be larger than all my expectations. There will certainly be nothing it cannot overshadow or conceal, so why do I crouch here clicking my fingernails against the desk leg when I might be out feeding pigeons? 'Leave now,' I tell myself. 'Are you actually going to spend the whole day, and maybe night, too, cramped and confined in here?' Yet haven't I done it plenty of times lately and always for nothing, too? Why not one more try? For Mr Morrison is surely the most promising of all. His eyes, the way the fat pushes up his cheeks under them, look almost Chinese. His nose is Roman and in an ordinary face it would be overpowering, but here it is lost. Dwarfed. 'Save me,' cries the nose. 'I'm sinking.' I would try, but I will have other, more important duties, after Mr Morrison comes back, than to save his nose. Duty it is, too, for the good of all and I do mean all. Do not think that I am the least bit prejudiced in this.

You see, I *did* go to a matinée a few weeks ago. I saw the Royal Ballet dance *The Rite of Spring* and it occurred to me then . . . Well, what would *you* think if you saw them wearing their suits that were supposed to be bare skin? Naked suits, I called them. And all those well-dressed, cultured people clapping at them, accepting even though they knew perfectly well . . . like a sort of Emperor's New Clothes in reverse. Now just think, there are only two sexes and every one of us *is* one of those and certainly, presumably that is, knows something of the other. But then that may be where I have been making my mistake. You'd think ... why, just what I did start thinking, that there must be Others among us.

But it is not out of fear or disgust that I am looking for them. I am open and unprejudiced. You can see that I am when I say that I've never seen (and doesn't this seem strange?) the very organs of my own conception, neither my father's nor my mother's. Goodness knows what *they* were and what this might make me.

So I wait here, tapping my toes inside my slippers and chewing hangnails off my fingers. I contemplate the unvarnished underside of the desk top. I ridge it with my thumbnail. I eat more cookies and think whether I should make his bed for him or not but decide not to. I suck my arm until it is red in the soft crook opposite the elbow. Time jerks ahead as slowly as a school clock, and I crawl across the floor and stretch out behind the books and magazines. I read first paragraphs of dozens of them. What with the dust back here and lying in the shirts and socks before, I'm getting a certain smell and a sort of grey, animal fuzz that makes me feel safer, as though I really did belong in this room and could actually creep around and not be noticed by Mr Morrison at all except perhaps for a pat on the head as I pass him.

Thump ... pause. Clump ... pause. One can't miss his step. The house shouts his presence. The floors wake up squeaking and lean toward the stairway. The banister slides away from his slippery ham-hands. The wallpaper seems suddenly full of bugs. He thinks (if he thinks of me at all): well, this time she isn't peeking out of her doorway at me. A relief. I can concentrate completely on climbing up. Lift the legs against the pressure. Ooo. Ump. Pause and seem to be looking at the picture on the wall.

I skitter back under the desk.

It's strange that the first thing he does is to put his newspaper on the desk and sit down with his knees next to my nose, regular walls, furnaces of knees, exuding heat and dampness, throwing off a miasma, delicately scented, of wet wool and sweat. What a wide roundness they have to them, those knees. Mother's breasts pressing toward me. Probably as soft. Why can't I put my cheek against them? Observe how he can sit so still with no toe-tapping, no rhythmic tensing of the thigh. He's not like the rest of us, but could a man like this do *little* things?

How the circumstantial evidence piles up, but that is all I've had so far and it is time for something concrete. One thing, just one fact is all I need.

He reads and adjusts the clothing at his crotch and reads again. He breathes out winds of sausages and garlic and I remember that it's after supper and I take out my cheese and eat it as slowly as possible in little rabbit bites. I make a little piece last half an hour.

At last he goes down the hall to the bathroom and I shift back under the shirts and socks and stretch my legs. What if he undresses like my mother did, under a nightgown? Under, for him, some giant, double-bed-sized thing?

But he doesn't. He hangs his coat on the little hanger and

his tie on the closet doorknob. I receive his shirt and have to make myself another spy hole. Then off with the tortured shoes, then socks. Off come the huge pants with slow, unseeing effort (he stares out the window). He begins on his yellowed undershorts, scratching himself first behind and starting earthquakes across his buttocks.

Where could he have bought those elephantine undershorts? In what store were they once folded on the shelf? In what factory did women sit at sewing machines and put out one after another after another of those other-worldly items? Mars? Venus? Saturn more likely. Or perhaps, instead, a tiny place, some moon of Jupiter with less air per square inch upon the skin and less gravity, where Mr Morrison can take the stairs three at a time and jump the fences (for surely he's not particularly old) and dance all night with girls his own size.

He squints his Oriental eyes toward the ceiling light and takes off the shorts, lets them fall loosely to the floor. I see Alleghenies of thigh and buttock. How does a man like that stand naked before even a small-sized mirror? I lose myself, hypnotized. Impossible to tell the colour of his skin, just as it is with blue-grey eyes or the ocean. How tan, pink, olive and red and sometimes a bruised elephant-grey. His eyes must be used to multiplicities like this, and to plethoras, conglomerations, to an opulence of self, to an intemperate exuberance, to the universal, the astronomical.

I find myself completely tamed. I lie in my cocoon of shirts not even shivering. My eyes do not take in what they see. He is utterly beyond my comprehension. Can you imagine how

thin my wrists must seem to him? He is thinking (if he thinks
of me at all), he thinks: she might be from another world.
How alien her ankles and leg bones. How her eyes do stand
out. How green her complexion in the shadows at the edges
of her face (for I must admit that perhaps I may be as far
along the scale at my end of 'humanity' as he is at his).

Suddenly I feel like singing. My breath purrs in my throat
in hymns as slow as Mr Morrison himself would sing. Can
this be love? I wonder. My first *real* love? But haven't I always
been passionately interested in people? Or rather in those
who caught my fancy? But isn't this feeling entirely different?
Can love really have come to me this late in life? (La, la, lee
la, from whom all blessings flow . . .) I shut my eyes and
duck my head into the shirts. I grin into the dirty socks. Can
you imagine *him* making love to *me*!

Well below his abstracted, ceilingward gaze, I crawl on
elbows and knees back behind the old books. A safer place to
shake out the silliness. Why, I'm old enough for him to be
(had I ever married) my youngest son of all. Yet if he were a
son of mine, how he would have grown beyond me. I see that
I cannot ever follow him (as with all sons). I must love him
as a mouse might love the hand that cleans the cage, and as
uncomprehendingly, too, for surely I see only a part of him
here. I sense more. I sense deeper largenesses. I sense excesses
of bulk I cannot yet imagine. Rounded after-images linger on
my eyeballs. There seems to be a mysterious darkness in the
corners of the room and his shadow covers, at the same time,
the window on one wall and the mirror on the other. Certainly, he is like an iceberg, seven-eighths submerged.

But now he has turned toward me. I peep from the books, holding a magazine over my head as one does when it rains. I do so more to shield myself from too much of him all at once than to hide.

And there we are, confronting each other eye to eye. We stare and he cannot seem to comprehend me any more than I can comprehend him, and yet usually, it seems, his mind is ahead of mine, jumping away on unfinished phrases. His eyes are not even wistful and not yet surprised. But his belly button . . . here is the eye of God at last. It nestles in a vast, bland sky like a sun on the curve of the universe flashing me a wink of heat, a benign, fat wink. The stomach eye accepts and understands. The stomach eye recognizes me and looks at me as I've always wished to be looked at. (Yea, though I walk through the valley of the shadow of death.) I see you now.

But I see him now. The skin hangs in loose, plastic folds just there, and there is a little copper-coloured circle like a quarter made out of pennies. There's a hole in the centre and it is corroded green at the edges. This must be a kind of 'naked suit' and whatever the sex organs may be, they are hidden behind this hot, pocked and pitted imitation skin.

I look into those girlish eyes of his and there is a big nothing, as blank as though the eyeballs are all whites . . . as blank as having no sex at all . . . like being built like a boy doll with a round hole for the water to empty out (something to frighten little-boy three-year-olds).

God, I think. I am not religious but I think: my God, and then I stand up and somehow, in a limping run, I get out of there and down the stairs as though I fly. I slam the door of

my room and slide in under my bed. The most obvious of
hiding places, but after I am there I can't bear to move out. I
lie and listen for his thunder on the stairs, the roar of his feet
splintering the steps, his hand tossing away the banister as he
comes like an engulfing wave.

I know what I'll say. 'We accept. We accept,' I'll say. 'We
will love' (I love already) 'whatever you are.'

I lie listening, watching the hanging edges of my bedspread
in the absolute silence of the house. Can there be anyone here
at all in such a strange quietness? Must I doubt even my own
existence?

'Goodness knows,' I'll say, 'if I'm a Normal myself.' (How is
one to know such things when everything is hidden?) 'Tell all
of them that we accept. Tell them it's the naked suits that are
ugly. Tell them the truth is beautiful. Your dingles, your
dangles, wrinkles, ruts, bumps and humps, we accept. (We
will love.) Your loops, strings, worms, buttons, figs, cherries,
flower petals, your soft little toad shapes, warty and greenish,
your cat's tongues and rats' tails, your oysters, one-eyed
between your legs, garter snakes, snails, we accept. (Isn't the
truth always more lovable?)

But what a long silence this is. Where is he? For he must
(mustn't he?) come after me for what I saw. If there has been
all this hiding and if he must wear that cache sex thing across
his front, then he *must* silence me somehow, destroy me even.
But where is he? Perhaps he thinks I've locked my door. But I
haven't. I haven't.

Why doesn't he come?

YANN MARTEL

Yann Martel was born in 1963 and now lives in Montreal. He is the author of a short story collection, *The Facts Behind the Helsinki Roccamatios*, and the novel *Self*, a fictional autobiography published in 1996, from which the following extract is taken.

Self

My parents were early feminists and they did not use the word 'opposite' when speaking of the sexes. Indeed, why should they be considered opposite? The word is aggressive, defines by negation, says very little. The sexes are complementary, said my parents – a more complicated word which they explained to me by analogy. Male and female were like rain and soil. Except that whereas they were speaking of sex, of impersonal details of biology, I understood them to be speaking of love, elaborating on what I already knew. The universe struck me then as amazingly well engineered. Imagine: somewhere out there, totally separate, of independent origin, was a sexual organ tailored to suit mine, to suit me. I set out to find my complementary sexual organ, my true love.

There is no greater mystery than this, the mystery of cathexis. Why do some people make the fish crowd our eyes, and others leave them utterly fishless? Is love some unique food that will feed only our fish? Or is it whatever food happens to be nearby when our fish get hungry? I have no idea why I fell in love with Noah Rabinovitch. It was too long ago. Memory is sometimes a distant spectator which can name emotions but not convey them, and this is the case here. To be sure, in some way Noah was my complement. When I was alone I was happy and whole, but when we were together the whole was greater. There was an added brightness to things, a greater and deeper perspective. But I could say the same thing, to only a slightly lesser degree, of other people, even of animals and objects. There was more to it than that. Only I don't know what. I think I remember that I liked the way Noah walked. He walked, therefore I loved him.

One day, as my mother arrived at the kindergarten to pick me up, I informed her that I had found my future wife and I proudly pointed to Noah, who was new at Jiminy Cricket. His father was an Israeli diplomat and they had just arrived in Costa Rica, mid-year. Noah came up to my mother, extended his hand and said he was pleased to meet his future mother-in-law. (Noah was sickeningly polite.) But then he had the effrontery to add that I would be *his* wife, and the two of us started again on the same tiresome argument we had had all morning, which I thought was settled. For some reason, neither of us wanted to be the wife.

My mother interrupted us by asking me why I thought Noah would be my wife. There are some circumstances where one cannot blurt out, 'Parce que je l'aime!' 'Because I love him!' '¡Porque le amo!' I was more concrete: Noah had the sexual organ complementary to mine. Did he, she replied, an uncontrollable smile running across her face, my first clue that I had missed something. She took my hand, said goodbye to Noah in English and we headed for the car. I clearly remember turning as we were walking off and bleating, with infinite sadness in my voice, 'Bye, Noah,' for in a vague way I realized that I had just lost my husband. Before opening the car door for me, my mother bent down and gave me an unwanted hug and a kiss. On the way home she gave me the first facts of my sexual persona. Things were far more limited than my open mind had imagined. There were in fact only *two* sexes, not infinite numbers. And those little bums and little fingers that I had seen in the various I'll-show-you-mine-if-you-show-me-yours exercises I had conducted were the complementary sexual organs in question, all two of them, one little bum for one little finger. I was amazed. This question of complementarity referred merely to a vulgar point of *biology*, an anatomical whim? The menu for ocular fish had only two items on it? And it was decided in advance which they could select, either little bum or little finger, steak or chicken? What kind of a restaurant is that, Mother? I had indeed noticed only little bums and little fingers so far, but I thought this was simply a reflection of the small size of my sample. (In a similar vein, though most of my coevals at Jiminy Cricket were white, on the basis of the skin colour of a few of them, reinforced by things I had seen on television and in magazines, I was quite confident that there existed people who were black, brown, yellow, red, blue, orange, perhaps even striped.) But no, there were only two, my mother insisted. Even more astonishing, she said that little bums were to be found exclusively in girls and little fingers exclusively in boys. Girls, *by definition*, were females with little bums who could only be wives. Boys, *by definition*, were males with little fingers who could only be husbands. I should remember these permutations for there were no others. No, husbands could not be girls. No, a wife could not marry another wife. No, no, no.

In the time of a brief car ride I became an indubitable boy, I discovered one of my defining characteristics and the universe, up till then myriad, broke into two camps. I was grief-stricken.

'Est-ce que je peux toujours aimer Noah?' je demandai, éclatant en sanglots.

'Can I still love Noah?' I asked, bursting into tears.

'Bein sûr,' repondit ma mère doucement, me passant la main dans les cheveux. 'Aime-le autant que tu veux. Il est important d'avoir des amis.'

'Of course,' my mother replied soothingly, running her hand through my hair. 'Love him as much as you want. It's important to have friends.'

Friends? Oh, Mother. I was given permission to love, yet I could sense – I cannot quite explain how – that oceans were now trapped in aquariums. She must be mistaken, I thought. I kept at her, convinced that there had been a misunderstanding. But I was so immeasurably confused that I could only approach the matter from the small end, this niggling point of biology.

'Femelle et mâle? C'est tout? Même sur les autres planètes?'

'Nous sommes seulement sur cette planète-ci, mon amour, la planète Terre.'

'Pourquoi elle s'appelle Taire? Ça veut dire quoi, Taire?'

'Ça veut dire "ici" en grec et en latin.'

'Et nous sommes seulement sur cette planète-ci?' je dis, regardant par la fenêtre, comme si le bord de la planète était juste passé le champ.

'C'est très grand, tu verras.'

'Il n'y a personne sur aucune des étoiles?'

'Pas que nous sachions.'

'Et il n'y a personne sur la lune?'

'Non.'

'Seulement ici?'

'Seulement ici.'

'La Taire?'

'La Terre.'

'Femelle et mâle?'

'Mâle et femelle.'

'Alors elle est femelle ou mâle, cette voiture?'

'Female and male? Is that all? Even on other planets?'

'We're only on this planet, love. We're only on planet Earth.'

'Why is it called Erth? What does Erth mean?'

'It means "here" in Greek and Latin.'

'And we're only on this planet?' I said, looking out the window, as if the edge of the planet were just beyond the field.

'It's a big place, you'll see.'

'There's nobody on any of the stars?'

'Not that we know of.'

'And there's nobody on the moon?'

'No.'

'Just here?'

'Just here.'

'Erth?'

'Earth.'

'Female and male?'

'Male and female.'

'So this car, is it female or male?'

'Euh . . . façon de parler, elle – non, non. Mâle et femelle s'appliquent seulement aux êtres vivants. Cette voiture est une simple machine. Elle n'a pas de sexe.'

'Ahhh.'

Un moment de réflexion.

'Alors il est femelle ou mâle, cet arbre?'

'Non. Seulement les êtres vivants – et qui bougent.'

'Mais il bouge, l'arbre. Et tous les autres. Regarde.'

'Oui, mais c'est le vent ça. Ils doivent bouger d'eux-mêmes. Vivants, et qui bougent d'eux-mêmes.'

'Il est quoi, le vent? Femelle ou mâle?'

'Non, non, non. Le vent n'est pas un être vivant.'

'Mais il bouge!'

'Oui, je sais. Mais il est invisible. Pour être mâle ou femelle, une chose doit être vivante, bouger d'elle-même, et être visible.'

'Alors c'est pour ça, les

'Uh . . . well we say – no, no. Male and female apply only to living things. This car is just a machine. It has no sex.'

'Ohhh.'

A pregnant pause.

'So that tree, is it female or male?'

'No. Only things that are alive – and move.'

'But it is moving. And all the others, too. Look.'

'Yes, but that's the wind. They have to move on their own. Things that are alive, and move on their own.'

'What's the wind? Female or male?'

'No, no, no. The wind isn't a living thing.'

'But it moves!'

'Yes, I know. But it's invisible. To be male or female, a thing has to be alive, move on its own, and be visible.'

'So that's what microscopes

microscopes? Pour voir le sexe des petites choses?'

'Tiens, regarde, une vache.'

'Elle est femelle ou mâle, cette vache?'

Ma mère regarda. 'C'est une vache femelle.'

are for? To find out the sex of small things?'

'Oh look, a cow.'

'Is that cow female or male?'

My mother looked. 'It's a female cow.'

She smiled. She'd got it right, she thought.

Many biology classes later, when I learned that plants do in fact have a sexuality, when I fully understood the terms pistil, stamen and pollen, I discovered with pleasure the slow, charged sexuality of nature. No wonder spring was such a sensuous time. Trees were not hard, irritable things, but discreetly orgasmic beings moaning at a level too deep for our brutish ears. And flowers were quick explosive orgasms, like making love in the shower.

As for Noah Rabinovitch and the strange mutilatory practices of the Jews, it would be a while yet before I understood that his clipped foreskin complemented something other than my own penis.

The next day at recess we hid around the corner and I offered right away, happily, to be his wife.

'OK,' he said, as casually as if I had just offered him a marble rather than my life. 'Here, look what I've got,' he added, pulling out of his pocket a brand new Coca-Cola yo-yo. 'Let's go play with it.' And he walked off, his disappointed and disgruntled wife in tow.

My relationship with Noah was nonetheless deeply satisfying. On the outside we appeared and behaved like no more than the best of friends (her word), but on the inside I felt that wonderful, sizzling feeling, the basis of all love: complicity.

Noah disappeared from my life as suddenly as he had appeared. Prime Minister Levi Eshkol died of a heart attack on February 26, 1969. Golda Meir replaced him. In the long domino-chain of changes that this brought about, a distant, painful one was the recall in the summer of 1970, at the end of grade I, of diplomat Etan Rabinovitch to Jerusalem after barely a year and a half at his new posting.

I spent my last year in Costa Rica a widow. For company I had only the beast television, which I watched avidly, expressing my dislike of it by sitting far away, and the boy who had attacked me, this savage on the periphery of my playground.

Though I was interested in the sex of others, I don't recall as a child being very curious about my own penis. It was the organ with which I urinated, a casual part of my identity, *c'est tout*. By an imperceptible cultureal osmosis I gathered that it was a 'private' part, but this did not turn it into a source of interest, let alone of shame or embarrassment. It was private in much the same way that a bedroom is: guests are invited to sit and chat in the living room, and only once they have achieved a sufficient degree of intimacy may they be shown around the house and see the bedroom. At puberty my level of interest would change dramatically and my penis would become the object of dedicated attention, the source of a pleasure so powerful that I might call it extraterrestrial, but even then I never felt that this small member – for that is what it is – was an inspiration for architecture or organization charts or anything else.

I have a black and white photo of me when I was very young, perhaps three. I am outside on a hot sunny day, naked and standing at the top of some wooden steps. I am holding on to my adored, tattered towel. The photographer, my father, is below me and I am looking at him gravely. I am not yet inhibited by modesty – the way I stand then, every square inch of my skin is equally presentable. My sex seems very large for the size of me. Perhaps sexual organs have their own rate of growth, or get started earlier. Yet it's tiny: a scrotum like half a walnut shell and a penis attached to it that is no more than a stubby cylinder of skin. But what really surprises me is the way the two float on the surface of my body. Atop my layer of baby fat, they seem unconnected and unimportant. They are there, but they could be elsewhere, like a large mole – and could seemingly be excised like a large mole by a simple operation should they become malignant. There is no hint of how deeply rooted in me they are, how, in a way, they are half of me, and how the point at which they join my body is a fulcrum.

A short time after that momentous car ride with my mother, I showed her a thick, juicy worm I had captured in the garden.

'Il est femelle ou mâle, ce   'Is this earthworm female
ver de terre?'   or male?'

My mother, a cool woman, a woman who always displayed grace under pressure, hardly squirmed. She carefully gathered up the papers she was working on from beneath my dangling worm, and she looked at it and at me.

'En fait, les deux. Le ver de terre est à la fois mâle et femelle. C'est une exception à la règle.'

'Well, as a matter of fact it's both. The worm is both male and female. It's an exception to the rule.'

Both male and female! I looked closely at this supreme brown creature as it twisted limply in my fingers. Both! How extraordinary.

'Où sont ses organes sexuels?'

'Where are its sex organs?'

'Je ne suis pas sûre. Ils sont très petits. Tu ne peux pas les voir.'

'I'm not sure. They're very small. You can't see them.'

'Eh bien, son nom est Jésus-Christ et elle est ma meilleure amie!'

'Well, his name is Jesus Christ and she's my best friend.'

'Et aucun des deux ne reste dans la maison. Ils seront plus heureux dans le jardin.'

'And neither one of them is staying in the house. They'll be happier in the garden.'

I carried away this miracle of the universe. Every time the words occurred to me – 'Both male and female!' – I was amazed anew. Surely if God existed—? – He, She, It must have the wriggly blunt head of a worm. I looked up at the sky. I could see it very well: an enormous, beautiful worm circling the earth, gracefully moving around and through the white clouds. I played with Jesus Christ for a few minutes and then cut them up into very small pieces with a sharp knife, trying to find their sex organs. Both female and male. Incredible.

LUCY TAYLOR

Lucy Taylor is an American writer who's had four collections of her short stories published, the most recent being *Painted in Blood*. She lives with seven wonderful cats and a shepherd/rottweiler named Bear in the hills outside Boulder, Colorado. Commenting on her story here she says, 'I've always felt that everyone is fundamentally bisexual and that peace between the genders might be achievable if each of us were required to live for at least six months as a member of the opposite sex. Other than that, I can only add that, considering how pleasurable and effortless I generally find erotic *encounters* to be, it never ceases to amaze me how difficult I find it to *write* erotica.'

Hyena Winter

Our first morning in New Orleans, as I'm scrutinizing myself in the bathroom mirror, Cyn slinks out of the shower and wraps her wet, fragrant arms around my waist. Her hair is plastered to her skull in a sleek copper cap. She smells of soap and almond-scented shampoo and although there is no time for it, I *want* her.

Her hands slide slowly down to grasp my cock and tilt it up to rub against my belly. For some reason that I don't understand – shame, perhaps, or the fact that I'm afraid and hate admitting it to her or to myself – I extricate myself from her caress. In the mirror, her big, unblinking eyes are sultry still with sleep, but she *sees* it nonetheless – my fear – and gives it back to me reflected in her gaze.

'You're allowed to change your mind, Rene.'

An invitation to back out – how dear of Cyn and yet how treacherous. How can she understand my terror and my longing? Living with her, watching her make the transit from one sex to the other makes me feel like a traveller gazing out at a distant shore, lured there by inner tides that call and beckon, but bereft forever of a passport. Like it or not, it's she who's brought me to this point, who's made me wonder if a body whose only transformation is the decrepitude of old age isn't really a kind of cage and that the profoundest kind of self-expression must be the ability to recreate oneself in both male and female form.

'Look, I can't back out now. We've come all this way, booked the hotel room, made the appointment. I couldn't get my money back at this point if I wanted to.'

'Fuck the money. It's not important. You are.'

'I want to do this, Cyn. If I don't, I'll always wonder what I missed.'

I reach behind me to fondle her pussy. In the thicket of pubic curls, my fingers encounter what feels like either a large clitoris or a very small dick. Surprised, I draw back slightly.

'Did you know your next cycle would be starting on the day I saw the Hyena? Is that why you chose this date?'

She nods. 'I checked the calendar, yeah. This is such a big change for you. I guess I thought I'd feel left out if I weren't changing, too.'

I stare at her lovely woman-on-the-verge-of-becoming-man body in the mirror. Then back at my own adult male body, which frustrates and disappoints me, even though it is the only reality I've ever known. And back at hers, which, even now, when I'm about to become like her, still has the power to enthrall and terrify me.

I remember when we met, in a SoHo club that caters to that secret subculture of people whose genders wax and wane and transform with the shifting of hormonal seasons, like planets forever altering their orbits to revolve around a different sun. When they appeared among us at the end of the twentieth century, it was thought that something in the air, the water, some hormonal glitch had brought them into being, but Cyn and others of her kind believe themselves to be a preview of what is to come, the human race evolving towards a higher stage of being.

As a Uni-sex male, the Androgens had become both my intellectual and erotic obsession. I longed to satisfy my curiosity once and for all. It had taken weeks of delving, prying, slipping cash to the right people to even get the address of one of their clubs. Understandable. Such places have been burned and bombed. The Androgens, who are both feared and envied, have had their genitals and breasts hacked off, the photographs of their dead bodies plastered on the doors of places they are known to frequent.

No wonder then that the atmosphere seemed charged with an edgy combination of fear and pheromones.

I was sitting at a corner table, studying the restroom doors which bore, respectively, a generic landscape and seascape, trying to decide if these were meant to correspond to male and female or if the whole concept was ridiculous here and the paintings were merely decorative, when I spotted Cyn, a lithe and lynx-like creature whose neck was draped in a gold-printed black silk scarf.

Unfortunately, when I'm nervous, I sometimes revert to adolescent behaviour and try to cover it up by acting brash and boorish. Approaching Cyn, I boldly and presumptuously inquired if the person I was addressing were male or female.

To which Cyn haughtily replied that such an inquiry approximated in rudeness a stranger questioning a man about the length of his dick. Chastised, I retreated, but Cyn took off her scarf and wound it round my neck, holding on to one end as she led me on to the dance floor. I remember when we fucked that night, it was not unlike the sex I've had with other women. And yet, because of who Cyn was, it felt completely different. Like a trip through the sexual looking glass, which left me hungry to return.

At the time, I thought of Cyn as an experiment, a fling, the sexual equivalent of an exotic holiday in a country one has dreamed of visiting, but has not the slightest intention of ever dwelling in. I meant to leave her the next morning and then the morning after that. Until recently, in my own mind, I'd been 'leaving' for over a year, but how could I stay away – when Cyn was my connection to this alluring other world?

'At least let me go with you,' she says, nuzzling my neck, contriving flute-playing patterns on my cock. 'I want to be there with you when it's over.'

'You know we talked about that. I have to go alone.'

Cyn scrunches her plush mouth, gnaws her lower lip. Anxiety in every eyeblink.

'I think I'm more afraid of this than you are. I've only known you as a "normal" male. What if it isn't just your body that changes? What if it's more than that?'

'Then I guess that will be part of the adventure.'

'After you make the change, what if you don't want me anymore?'

My thoughts exactly with regard to her, but the chance I have to take.

I dress while Cyn sits on the bed. When I'm about to leave, I look through her suitcase and pull out the black and gold scarf she was wearing the night we met. Trying to appear jaunty, I wrap it around my neck.

'In case you don't recognize me,' I say, but she doesn't smile.

In summer there's no place hotter than New Orleans. In winter, the Arctic couldn't be as cold. It's January now. The cold doesn't sit politely atop my skin, but gnaws its way in with rat-teeth. I'm wearing two sweaters, a vest, and my winter coat and I'm still freezing as I flag down a cab.

I give the cab driver an address. Within ten minutes, she drops me off outside a pale peach house with wrought-iron fences and balconies at the end of one of the Quarter's lesser-known streets. No tourists here. No buggy rides or curio stores, no café au lait-coloured kids hawking tickets for shows that purport to offer everything from onstage sex to psychic spells cast by the ghost of the voodoo queens. Just pale, cracked walls crawled over with ivy and a pair of jade and turquoise parrots, visible through a window, in a wicker cage.

I wait in a tatami-covered lounge that somehow manages to feel ten degrees colder than it did outside, listening to an orchestrated babble that sounds like the musical equivalent of hieroglyphics. My testicles are drawn up hard and small, my asshole clenched and knotted like the mouth of an obstinate child with a spoonful of medicine in his face. Do I truly want to be here? Is life as a Uni-sex, which until recently was the lot of all humankind, really so deprived, so empty?

But I fantasize, too, about experiencing the lush eroticism of being female – the lusty exuberance that must come from possessing hips and belly that swell and curve, breasts that bob against the tender insides of the upper arms, and the amazing receptivity and willingness of a vagina that moistens to receive and stretches to accommodate.

How can I be truly male without being female, too? Or truly female without having been a male?

The creature I have come to meet is known as the Hyena, a name Cyn tells me derives from the medieval belief that the hyena changes its sex each year. For about the same price as a cruise to Bali, her services can be bought.

The shoji screen slides back. A person so slim and pale that I'm reminded of a wax museum figure peers in.

'Take off your clothes and leave them in the chair,' her low melodious voice instructs me. 'Then follow me.'

The Hyena's long, lupine face is powdered white – her mouth, a tiny scarlet stitch in an inhumanly flawless face, her eyes olive green slits whose dark gleam is accentuated by gold-eyeliner. She wears a gown of brocade and silk and tiny gold brocade slippers. After I remove my clothes and stack them in a neat pile, she guides me through a corridor to a mirrored room, where plumes of steam rise from a series of hot tubs. In the fragrant mist, I hear water dripping on to the tile floor. The hanging plants are so profuse I cannot see the ceiling.

'We're going to make love,' she says, 'but you will be the passive partner. You may enjoy it that way. Some do.'

She lets the robe slide off her shoulders, revealing large pale breasts that appear to be encased in what I first take to be an ornate undergarment of skin-tight lace. The illusion is only momentary. Then I realize that her skin is patterned with intricate black and white tattoos. Designs that look like spider webs connect the cocoa-coloured nipples of her large, low-swaying breasts and descend her belly into her pubic hair. Nothing that I can see is representational – instead the tattoos form a complex geometry that make me think of the ornate designs of the wrought-iron fences seen in the Quarter or the arabesques in an Afghani rug.

She reaches down and leads me by my cock into the water, giving me a view of the tattoos that swirl across her back and buttocks. They curve where she curves, patterns that repeat themselves with subtle variations, like the markings of an animal or plant.

'From this point on, you won't talk unless I give permission.'

I sink into the scented, sudsy water, steam rising in grey plumes. The water is up to our necks, our chins. All I can see of the Hyena are her great dark olive eyes, but even these are changing now – gleaming iridescent green and indigo and dove grey. Flittery mandala eyes reflected in the perfume-scented water.

The Hyena slides her slender body against mine. She moves behind me, sliding her lathered body up and down, her breasts and pubic hair sponging my back. She has me squat on a stone bench at one end of the pool. Then, straddling me, she lowers herself down.

Her interior is hothouse moist and silky. Her nipples press against my chest, her buttocks settle on my thighs. She makes tight circles with her hips, then sits in perfect equanimity, eyes half-closed, while her breathing slows and almost seems to stop.

We sit in suspended, motionless arousal.

To remain like this without moving requires all my self-control and concentration.

I study her closed face. The painted lips, the gold-lined eyes. Delicate lines mimic quotation marks around her mouth. Is that the faintest stubble of a beard beneath her make-up?

Each time I start to squirm or speak, she motions me to silence.

We sit.

The Hyena begins to massage me with her muscles – a rhythmic pulsing of her interior that approximates the wet suction of a fellating mouth. Tug and gentle t-u-u-u-u-g some more, come i-n-n-n-n-nto me, her cunt invites – what my cock feels must be the reverse of the sensation a baby gets as it is nudged along the birth canal and pushed between the unfurled lips of the vagina.

Her breasts mash and flatten against my chest. My penis is enclosed in her warm moistness, but that warm moistness also feels like my own flesh. Am I fucking the Hyena or is she fucking me? Are those her breasts or mine?

Her dark pupils swirl like water spiralling down a drain. With eyes and cunt, she draws me deeper into her, deeper than I want to go, past what feels like some psychic point of no return.

My awareness of my own perimeters begins to blur. My cock feels like it's starting to retract into my abdomen and, as it retreats, her flesh expands to fill me. The sensation is bizarre, unsettling.

Suddenly I'm angry. I want to buck and thrust and ram, to reassert my physical dominion. I want to fuck her, but the Hyena rests her hands on my shoulders and signals *be still*.

I try to withdraw, but find myself held fast. It is a moment of both awe and horror – memories of crude jokes I've heard about copulating dogs combine with the adrenalin rush of my own primitive terror.

'What's happening?' My voice sounds wet and husky, as if my throat is clogged with semen.

She says nothing, but her grip loosens for an instant – I start to pull out – then she grips me again until it feels I'm being held inside a fist. Her arms wrap around me, hands moulding themselves to my back. I think of long, slick, pliant plants, softly petalled and powerful as a garrotte. Ivy-dark creepers that twine around my throat, streamers of salty, green-black kelp and delicate, killing kudzu.

She is settling in, engulfing me. Panic nibbles at my skin. We are profoundly, irrevocably one, but this oneness feels like drowning.

Stay still, stay still, I tell myself, or is it the Hyena's voice, already having garnered access to my brain, for I feel her capable of penetrating me there as well, even as I play at penetrating her.

We sit.

In the tarnished amber light, I detect movement, but think at first it is the shadows of the ferns above, stirred by some invisible breeze, playing on the Hyena's skin. For she is moving at the same time that she sits perfectly, exquisitely still.

The heat of the water, the pressure of the Hyena's body, dizzies me until it seems it's not her body that's transforming, but her skin – her tattoos undulate and slink, furling and unfurling, swaying like long hair underwater when it billows and swirls with the tides. A trick of light and shadow, I think at first, but then realize that an inky labyrinth, some complex wedding of swastikas and crosses, is creeping over the Hyena's torso and seething across my own.

I think of hordes of insects massing, tiny stinging ants

313

moving in formation, trekking across her skin and on to mine.

My scream is swallowed down her long throat. Her sweet saliva fills my mouth. A perfumed tongue laps and strums across my teeth. When she pulls back, her lips are plumper than before, a much darker colour, almost black, and I realize that the tattoos have crawled across her feral face and fastened themselves to her mouth. Pure panic ices through me. I feel absorbed, obliterated, and it is not the sweet annihilation that mystics and lovers moon about, but death in tiny, stinging, incremental doses.

My mind cartwheels. Does the twitch I feel belong to her leg or to mine? Is it my cock that occupies her pussy or her cock now penetrating me? It terrifies me that I cannot tell, for not to know where her genitals end and mine begin is to be de-gendered, neither male nor female, but part of a single entity that's both.

My arms and legs are bound to hers by serpentines and swastikas, designs that might have come from Celtic crosses or the baroque patterning of a Turkish minaret. Her breasts are fitted so tight against my chest that the mounded flesh might be my own. The tattoos turn green and yellow there, like bizarre and insidious plant life on our hothouse skins.

I try to free my forearms, which rest alongside hers. At my first effort to pull loose, the tattoo-vines constrict and tighten in a barbed caress. I feel warmth running down my arms, but it's only the Hyena's sweat and mine mingling with the steam that rises from the swirling water.

And something else.

A dance of flesh. Hers advancing, overwhelming, mine yielding, giving in.

The Hyena's limbs are elongating, her features coarsening, breasts withering. In the dim light, her face appears elastic, cheekbones the high taut pins over which silky skin flows and reshapes itself. At the back of her vagina, a cock is being born, pushing me back into my own flesh, penetrating me, dissolving the illusion that I am separate in my skin, that in the act of fucking, I remain unchanged, untouched.

When I dare open my eyes again, the tattoos, like a horde of obedient bugs, have crawled back onto the Hyena's skin. A face that might be male or female stares into mine. A cock that might be mine or hers shrinks and slides away, leaving within me a sensation of jarring emptiness.

I hear the slap of water on the Hyena's thighs as she leaves the pool. I try to follow, but I am weary beyond words, my muscles feel like wine-soaked sponges, heavy, inert. The unfamiliar mounds of flesh upon my chest are full and aching.

Strong hands pick me up and lift me. I'm carried to a bed and bundled tightly. The swaddling is welcome in that it focuses me back inside my body, redefining the parameters of my skin.

My skin.

My new and profound separateness.

My femaleness.

Weariness descends like a heavy winter and I sink into a slumber so deep it feels like death.

*

315

Morning?

Midnight?

The room I'm in is small and dark, conspicuously lacking mirrors. I get up slowly, intentionally refraining from touching my new body, and go outside into the room full of hot tubs where the Hyena and I bathed.

The waters are full of bathers now, lounging, frolicking, some making love. A man coming up the ladder of one of the pools glances over at me.

Although, of course, I've seen Cyn as a male before, the transformation still astonishes me. Her chest is flat and muscular, her hips have narrowed, thighs and calves turned muscular and hard. The tiny cock that was emerging yesterday has now swelled to adult proportions.

Yet, for all this, what strikes me most is not Cyn's transformation, but the fact that somehow nothing really has changed. For, male or female, it is still, unmistakably, undeniably, Cyn. My partner, my lover.

And me?

There are mirrors all around the room. I want to look, but don't dare yet, even though I know that nothing I will see is really new, but only newly visible.

I realize I don't have Cyn's scarf. No matter, for she is smiling now and walking toward me. I don't know what she sees, only that she knows it's me.

The mirrors can wait. Right now, the only image of myself I want to see is the one reflected in Cyn's eyes.

A L KENNEDY

A L Kennedy was born in Dundee in 1965 and currently lives in Glasgow. Her collection of short stories, *Night Geometry and the Garscadden Trains*, won the Scottish Arts Council Book Award, the Saltire Award for Best First Book and the *Mail on Sunday*/John Llewellyn Rhys Prize. Her first novel, *Looking for the Possible Dance*, won a Somerset Maugham Award. She has also published another novel, *So I Am Glad,* and two other collections of short stories, *Bliss* and *Now That You're Back* from which 'Failing to Fall' is reprinted.

We're used to being able to identify people as male or female, quickly and easily. When this isn't possible, when there's uncertainty, most people are made uneasy. But sometimes, as in the following story, uncertainty can carry a powerful erotic charge.

Failing to Fall

This is the one thing I know from the minute I lift the receiver and slip that voice inside my ear – once it's there, it doesn't matter how this happens. It *will* happen.

*

'Come now.'

'What?'

'I need you. I need you to come right now.'

'I'm working.'

'And I'm not. I'm at home. Come on.'

'You don't—'

'I do. Tell them you're feeling ill. You've got to be somewhere. There's an emergency. This is an emergency.'

'I can't.'

'Will you come now. I want you to. I want you.'

'I can't.'

'I want you.'

'Really, it's impossible.'

But, really, it happens that way. I walk through the typing
or crashing or silent corridors and clean out of the building
without even noticing whether I've put on my coat. I'm on
the way to somewhere else.

It seems a kind of falling and anyone can fall. When I think
of it now, I wonder if we don't all wait from time to time,
ready to make a dive, to find that space where we can drop
unhindered. Like an internal suicide.

So I leave my work and start my fall. The door into the
outside air swings snug behind me and I'm somewhere I can't
go at other times. Here we all walk together; are together.
Watch for our feet, see our bodies; we all of us have the same
music romping inside our heads. We're moving through a big,
blue waltz without a collision or a slip and I have my very
own personal direction, smooth ahead of me. You could plant

318

a wall across that direction and I would simply walk it down. Today I can do that. Look for my heart and you'll see it beating, even through my coat.

This is the only time I have when to be nothing other than me is quite enough. I love this.

It may have been raining a fortnight, there may be salted snow and litter greasing together under my feet, dog shit and vomit – the usual pavements we have to use – but today I will neither notice, nor be touched. Angels have decided it; I will be clean today. The air will shine.

And if I glance to the side, the effect is disconcerting. Things are blurred, as though I were watching them from a moving car. Once I have my direction, I can get up a fair head of speed. The final corner spirals off to my right, the sun is blazing a banner in every window and there they are, the reason I came, the taxis.

Observing this from a distance, I can't be sure why the taxis were always involved. I only know I have always taken taxis when I've been falling. When I could afford them and when I could not and when I had to borrow money before I climbed in. It was almost as if they had some claim on me. Indescribable. Sometimes I would find myself clipping that phone call short, just to get moving, to get aboard.

'Come now.'

'Yes, I'll get a taxi, I'm on my way.'

That kind of thing.

Standing there with the taxis, I pause for a wonderful moment at the stance – I enjoy that – and then I reach my hand out for the door. Inside, in the air freshener and cigarette and boot sole-smelling cab, things change. Moving away, the fear comes in.

With my face beside the window, I become acutely visible. I fill out with the feeling of being on my way and grow. It seems to me that I turn into something cinematically swollen. Surely, someone I work with, someone I know, someone representative of God's wrath will take away this much pleasure before it arrives. Because this is far too big for only me to have; I should be at work, I should be doing some intermediate something for someone I do not know. I shouldn't be growing this noticeably.

I am afraid of eyes that will see me this way and then not understand. I myself have no understanding, because I am falling. There are meadows and opening seas of room between working and paying and shopping and cooking and eating and sleeping and general household maintenance in which I can be me, doing what I want. I no longer have to look out of the window and wonder who has my life, and if I miss it.

Seated in the expectancy of the taxi, I can love all the halts, the lights, the flaring pigeons. My journey will take forever and no time at all.

When I pay the driver I will only faintly notice how much, because money is irrelevant. It lies in my hand, defeated – just for today, we've changed places and I can pass it across with a big, careless smile before the door barks shut behind me.

There is an irregular instant when I leave the cab, a slight loss of rhythm which is no more than natural, before I push the steps away beneath me and make the slow walk to the lift. Almost there.

I plummet up the storeys in a stale little scrawled-over can with a pulse in my stomach which makes it all right. There is the flutter of arrival, of the door sliding back, the final steps, another door. Then I feel the pressure of movement between my face and another; the touch of hands, of air, of breath within breath.

And the fall is over. I know what will happen now.

I don't want to remember this. I would much rather let it be over and hope it won't come back again, but I know that I am not a strong person and that I very much miss those times when I was me and that was enough. Once every two or three months, I could change the world. I'm only human, I find that attractive, even now.

And yet on the days when I was not falling I couldn't think of it – the fall was somehow beyond my imagination. A particular sky, the movement of a breeze, a conjunction of word and feeling could give me a spasm of what I might call completeness, but for the most part I simply existed and made myself satisfied with that.

Then even that satisfaction changed, beginning at the taxi stance when I arrived one morning and found there were no cabs there, I would have to wait.

'We're out of luck.'

The voice was calm, soft, really very pleasant.

'I said we're out of luck. Odd for this time of day.'

'Yes.'

'I believe I've seen you here before.'

'That's possible.'

'I mean at this rank. I wait at this rank quite often because of what I do. It's my rank.'

'Well, I suppose it's mine, too. If it's anybody's.'

I am not normally this ill-tempered, but I was too far into my journey to focus on anything else and I never like speaking to people I don't know – it makes me feel stupid. I end up discussing the weather when the weather is all around us and both I and whoever the stranger might be must surely have noticed it. We would be better off asking each other if our faces are still there.

Against my nature and my better judgement and possibly because this was the only way that Fate could have arranged it, I turned to the stranger and asked, with a little ironic twist I was rather proud of, 'What is it that you do?'

'I beg your pardon?'

'You said you were here often because of what you do. I wondered what that was.'

'I see. What I do.' The smile was fully there now. 'I make love.'

'What?'

'That's what I do. I don't mean that's what I'm paid my wages for. I mean that's the most important thing I do. My vocation.'

I wanted to leave then – this was obviously not the kind of person I would usually speak to, not even the kind who was capable of small talk. I couldn't go, though. It was that word – vocation – I knew exactly what that meant. For a pulse or

two I was aware that both of us were falling together, passing
and repassing, nudging briefly as we soared down our particular trajectories. I had never before met somebody so like me.
There was no need for words, but my companion spoke in
any case.

'I've offended you.'

'No, no.'

'I've surprised you then. I only mentioned it because . . .
well, because I thought we have similar reasons for being
here. A fling, an affair, a fuck. I'm in the right area?'

This was all delivered with a beery smirk and of course, I
was alone again at once, spiralling off in a way that no one
seemed able to understand. No one knew. I wanted to explain
the way things were for me. What I did wasn't about sex,
wasn't about running amok and dangerous diseases, perver-
sion, sweat. At that time, I could only have said that my sole
way not to feel squeezed all the time, was to set off on my
little journeys to someone close whenever I needed to, no
matter what. I needed to be able to fall, to meet sometimes in
a way that other people didn't, to be outside the average shape
of the day. Now that sounds like a whim, an eccentricity, but
it was the heart of my life and a total stranger was quietly
stamping all over it – purposely misinterpreting everything I
was about.

I wish I had pointed that out, instead of just saying, 'No,
not the same area.'

'You can tell me, it's alright. We aren't the only ones, by
any means. I know the type.'

'Uh hu.'

'No, you don't see what I mean. We aren't the only ones who come here to catch taxis to do . . . things in that area. I know the look. You do, too, if you think about it. You know how it feels. You think that doesn't show?'

I didn't want to hear this. It was like watching my own reflection wink and walk away without me.

'I think something shows.'

'Naturally it shows. When I first realized – what we were all doing – when I looked at the taxis, smiling and creeping along . . . well, even now I can hardly keep from laughing.'

The people around me had stopped being together and the day looked the way it normally did. Nothing was special. There was a metallic feeling about where my liver would be and, more than anything, I felt angry.

'No, I don't understand. It's not like that.'

'Like what, exactly?'

'Like the way you make it sound – as if we all just ran about doing all that we liked. No one can do that. There are consequences, diseases, people are dying of that.'

'Pleasure isn't fatal. I've been in the same relationship for more than a decade now, we simply happen to be unconventional. I thought I'd made myself clear – this is a part of me and what I am and nobody else's hysteria will stop me from being who I am. We are careful because we care and we are happy. You have any objections to that?'

'No, no, I'm sorry.'

'Do you really not know what it's like when you want to make that call – to see him, to see her, whoever is important for you? Are you saying you'd just give it up if somebody told

you to?' There was an ugly little pause. 'Surely you do that?
You do call?'

'No.'

'Really?'

'I don't make calls, I just answer them.'

We didn't say anything else after that. There was a polite
silence; as if something about what I said had been obscene.
By the time my taxi came I didn't want it, but I took it
anyway. I was going to be late and in the wrong mood and I
couldn't help looking for other taxis to see who was inside
and if they were happy.

That afternoon, it wasn't very good. I couldn't say what was
wrong about it and we made no fuss at the time, but the
atmosphere was odd. I strained somewhere in my neck.

It took several weeks before whatever difference we had
developed was dispersed and for all of that time at the back
of my mind there was a little fleet of taxis full of people I
didn't know. They were all being special without me.

Perhaps it was that slight mental disturbance which made
me keep thinking it was strange that I never made the call. I
was always the one that got the taxi. Never the caller, always
the called. Yet, it seemed more than likely the process could
work in reverse. There was a pleasant logic in it. The only
component transferred would be the element of surprise. Who
would begrudge that? There would still be an expectant
journey, a tension, a reward for waiting. No problem. So I
made a call.

*

'Right now.'

'Who is this?'

'You know who it is. I have to see you. Come now.'

'I can't now.'

'I want you to.'

'I can't.'

I waited at home for three hours and nobody came. I stayed in all that evening and nobody came.

Some time later, a matter of months, I found I was waiting at the stance for a taxi. It was going to be an innocent taxi and I felt a little embarrassed at catching it there. In fact, the whole situation was uncomfortable because I hadn't caught a taxi in hot blood since that unfortunate call and I didn't want to be doing it now. Everything was reminding me that I didn't know how to fall any more. I couldn't do it on my own.

'Hello, I thought it was you.'

It was, unmistakably, that voice. That mouth. The steady eyes.

'Here we are again. Not speaking?'

'We're not here again. I'm catching a taxi because I'm late.'

'That's a shame. Trouble at work?'

'What do you mean?'

'Excessive absenteeism?'

I didn't have to look, I knew the mouth would be smiling.

'If it's any of your business, it was trouble at home. No more taxis. Full stop. Not needed.'

'Now that is a shame. That's terrible news. Look, I'll write this down. Call me, will you?'

'What?'

'Call me. On the telephone. That's my number.'

'Why the fuck would I do that?'

'Call me and see.'

I can only say I was shocked and, because my journey was less important than those I had been used to, I walked away without saying another word. I didn't need the stance; I could flag down a cab in the street; it didn't matter.

I don't know if you are familiar with the story of the guru who told his pupil that the meditative life was simple, as long as you never, ever, once thought of a monkey. Naturally, after this, the pupil's meditations were filled with monkeys of every colour and description, arranged in a series of faintly mocking tableaux.

I was reading to try and improve my condition of mind and I had come across this story. Every time I walked down the street I would think of the pupil, the guru, even the monkey and none of them would help me because my particular problem was the taxis. They were everywhere. I didn't want to wonder where they were going and why. I didn't want to lie on my back in the night and hope that the phone might ring and there would be a journey and hands I could hold with my hands. I didn't want to wish for dreams of falling. But I wondered and hoped and wished almost all the time. Everything I did was something that wasn't wanted.

You can guess what came next. What else could I do but another thing I'd never intended? Who else did I know who had even the slightest experience in this field? I found I had no choice.

I hadn't thrown the stranger's number away, I had hidden it right at the back of a drawer in the hope I'd forget where I put it or that it might spontaneously combust: just disappear and go away.

I took under a minute to find it – a corner of paper torn from something more important with seven numbers printed on one side. I had a coffee and called. Engaged. The next time there was no answer; an hour later, the same. I gave the number one final try on two or three other occasions, the last of them late on a Sunday afternoon.

'Hello.'

I couldn't think what to say.

'Hello?'

We had never introduced ourselves and, even if we had, I wasn't precisely certain of what I was calling for. Perhaps help.

'I beg your pardon?'

'Hm?'

'Look, I'm going to hang up now.'

'No. I mean I – Hello.'

'Well, well, well. We met at the taxi rank, isn't that right?'

'Yes, yes, I'm sorry, we did.'

'You're sorry we did?'

'No, I'm not sorry we did, at all. I didn't mean that.'

'So why are you calling? I gave you my number for a reason – not for a casual chat. Why are you calling?'

'I . . . because I . . . am afraid.'

'Of what?'

'Of what I might do.'

'To whom?'

'I don't know. Mainly to me. I can't get this out of my head, the taxis, the journeys . . . the whole thing. I seem to have nowhere to go now. I thought, because you knew about it . . . You gave me your number.'

'Alright, alright. Don't worry. Now . . .'

I could hear a small disturbance at the other end of the line. Imagine that, the same noise, far away in a stranger's room and inside my head. Telephones are wonderful.

'Yes, here we are. Are you listening? Are you there?'

'I am, I am.'

'I want you to catch a taxi at the stance. I want you to tell it to go to the Odeon cinema. When you get there buy a ticket for the next screening in Cinema Three. Go in and take a seat in the fourth row from the back. Is that clear?'

'Yes—'

Far away in that other room, the receiver was replaced and I couldn't even say thank you, or goodbye.

And outside, the half moon risen, people were moving together again, the music was back and we were special. I stepped inside the taxi, rested my hands in my lap and let the world dip away to leave me somewhere altogether better. Even in the half dark, I knew my fingers were jumping a little with every heart beat, and we were in hot blood again.

Cinema Three was almost empty, pleasantly cool, and I tipped back my head while the trailers reeled by, feeling my breath going all the way in and then all the way out again.

*

'Good film, wasn't it?'

I held the receiver in both hands to stop it from shaking.

'You never came.'

'I'd already seen it.'

'I thought you would be there.'

'You thought wrong. Did you enjoy the film?'

'I . . . Well, yes, I enjoyed the film, but I was waiting for you.'

'You shouldn't have been. I didn't say I would be there. You don't know what you're calling for, do you?'

'What?'

'That's alright, I do. Give me your number at home and your number at work. Are you still there?'

'Yes.'

'Then give me the numbers. You do want this to continue, don't you?'

And, even if I had no idea what we were doing, I did want it to go on, so I passed over the numbers and that was that.

I don't think I lack pride; do you think I lack pride? In my position, you might have fed those numbers down the line and not considered it humiliating. I hadn't known why I was going to the Odeon and, yes, I had expected company, but at least something was happening now. I felt so much better, so much more special again. That isn't something you come by every day. Perhaps a month or two in the Seychelles would do it for you: a fridge full of cocaine: a night-sighted rifle and two hundred rounds. These things would be of no interest to me, but I never would blame anybody for making the best of whatever they'd got. I had a voice on the telephone.

So I do believe I kept a little of my pride, while admitting that I waited for the next call with something less than dignity. When it came, I was invited to wait by the Sunlight Cottages in the park. Call three sent me to the sea front; call four, the necropolis and on every outing, I met no one, spoke to no one, saw no one I recognized.

'I'm sorry, but what's going on?'

'Two o'clock, the Abbey. Be there.'

'But you won't be.'

'I know.'

'So why am I going?'

'Because I'm telling you to. Or don't you want to do this any more?'

'Please, I don't want to stop. I don't want that. I just want to understand what the fuck I'm doing. Please.'

There was a sigh. It came slipping all the way down miles of wire to me, soft but unmistakable.

'You still don't understand?'

'No.'

'Then there's no point in our continuing.'

'No. Please.'

I winced against the clatter of the receiver going down, but nothing happened.

'Please, don't hang up. If you explained I would understand, I'm sure of it.'

'What do you enjoy?'

'I . . . how do you mean?'

'What do you enjoy? What makes you take the taxis? What

do they do to you? You must know, it's you it happens to. Your heart fists up and quivers, doesn't it? The call starts and your blood is suddenly pushed high round your ears. You can hear it sing. There are pulses setting up all over you, ones you can't stop, and your stomach is swinging and then convulsing and then turning into a hole punched through to your back. Right?'

'Ye—'

'Right. All your senses shine – it's as if someone pulled a carrier bag off your head and life is very good and you feel special. Yes?'

'Mmm hmm.'

'And now you can remind me – did you enjoy that film?'

'Yes, I did.'

'You were there because you chose to go there – no one but you. You were happy. You were there and nowhere else, not even in your mind.'

'I think—'

'Don't think, we haven't got the time, just do it. Be there.'

'At the cinema again?'

'Do you still have my number?'

'I think so.'

'You'll find that I've changed it and I won't be ringing you again. This has already gone on too long. Good-bye.'

'No!'

'Take care of yourself. Good-bye.'

I didn't find this a very helpful conversation. I remember it very clearly, because, of course, it was the last. I imagined I might be angry, but the anger never came; there was only a numbness which would sometimes wake me in the early dawn, or lose my concentration when I worked. For a long time I thought I would just keep on that way, but the numbness faded and then I felt sad.

Particularly, I was sad because I thought I had really caught the idea of the thing. I'm not really so terribly stupid. I know about self-awareness and caring for the child within, I've read books. I figured out that it didn't matter where I was going in the taxi, as long as I went. It didn't matter who made the call. It didn't matter if there was a call, I could catch a taxi anyway, decide where I was going and then take off. I need never feel confined by my own existence again.

I took myself back to the cinema and it didn't work. I went back to the park and it didn't work. I took a taxi to cruise past that particular block of flats I had been so used to visiting and it didn't work. I walked up and down the streets, very often in the night, looking for a way into life, a tiny space to fall through, and it didn't work.

The last thing I've done is to write this. It should be that laying out all of these words and recalling the way that it felt when I really was living will help me. I've been turning the problem around here. I have even had to put myself in the place of the stranger on the telephone and that must mean we are a little closer than we were when we knew each other. Perhaps we have knowledge in common now that we didn't have then.

I can say I feel more peaceful than I have in a while and quite tired. When I read this back, it may be that things will come clearer. I think what I hope is that the sum of all I have written will amount to a tiny piece more than I intended and that piece will be what I was looking for all this time. I think that's what I hope.

M M HALL

Although pornography may have to insist on the sexual characteristics of its players – 'Look, this is a woman. This is a man, here's proof of it' – in the hope of arousing its viewers or readers, in real life the most ecstatic sexual experiences may be those in which such obvious distinctions fall away; where even the nature of appetite is undefined, and the only thing that matters is that there was a hunger, and that hunger is being fed.

M M Hall is a writer, artist, editor and teacher from Texas. She's had many short stories published in various magazines and anthologies, and recently edited the anthology, *Wild Women* (1997).

The Sweet Reward

The Candy Girl

I am a woman of many nothings. That is why I am here, on my knees in front of the gas fire, praying to the warmth instead of the cross. I want to believe in something but how is that possible when my whole body is a collection of unanswered questions?

There are my hands with lines on the palms I don't know how to read. There are my feet complete with calloused toes from shoes that don't fit right. My long thin legs with the bony knees. My shoulders that clench too tightly and bunch up with worry. The pale skin, still smooth and ageless, except the small area above my breasts just beginning to shout – 'Hey I'm not a teen anymore, so sue me.' That patch of gently sun-damaged skin reminds me how foolish I was to love V-necked shirts, sunbathing, working in the yard without sunscreen. I touch that skin, marvelling. I want someone else's hand to be there.

Sometimes when I'm like at a store or anywhere out in public where there are a lot of people, I see people touching. All my life I have been touched so little that I can't imagine what it would be like to be touched on a regular basis. Seems to me you could faint from so much skin-to-skin contact. The pressure must be terrible. Not that I haven't been touched, because I have been. When I was a child, it wasn't touching. It was hitting or slapping. No hugs. I was hugged a little by my grandmother Ida. But she's been dead a long time.

The hope for redemption is dying. Or at least, my dating chances. I don't want to place a personal ad or run around to singles clubs, a pretend smile on my face, desperation clinging to me like cheap cologne.

Is it because I can't believe in God or myself anymore?

I stare into the fire. There's a crucifix in my bedroom but it's too cold in there to pray.

I should be gone.

All I have in my life is the candy store I own and operate. I am a sweet nothing. Loneliness has eaten me and burped.

The Gourmand

I don't like cheap caviar. The stuff you find in the pseudo-gourmet sections of middle-class grocery stores. I don't like cheap chocolate. I prefer European chocolate. But I will eat cheapish caviar and cheapish chocolate when nothing else is available. When you're hungry and you're running out of money, it's amazing how suddenly the tastebuds change.

'Greg, you want to learn to make do; sometimes it comes in handy,' as my mom Maureen used to say. Maureen was a secretary, an executive secretary, as she would be quick to point out, 'a professional person expert without a PhD'. She reared my sister Kate and me without the help of our father, Alec, an alcoholic bum who left us to pursue the gutter when I was around eight, Kate, four. He died, what, ten years ago? I never really knew him but I liked the funky World War II photo of him Mom worshipped. His hat was tilted at a devil-may-care angle and his gaze reminded me of some romantic movie star, a Paul Newman or a Steve McQueen, looking for trouble and laughing at all the fools unable to laugh at themselves. 'He wasn't always a loser,' she'd say, holding the portrait in its sometimes tarnished silver frame. Usually, she kept it shiny. 'We had our day; it was short, but it was something, all right.'

337

I used to hate Dad for that. Despite his multitude of short-comings, Mom still loved him. Even after the divorce. She still loved him. I don't know if I ever did. I guess I just didn't know him. I knew of him but I didn't know him. He always looked at me with the eyes of a tourist. Postcard love. Never a whole letter from the guy. To any of us. But when he still came around during the holidays he would make the best devil's food cake I've ever eaten. Pecan pies at Thanksgiving were a marvel. Dad made his living after the war as a short-order cook. Another thing I recall was his cheeseburgers. I have yet to find one that quite measures up. And fudge to die for. Isn't it odd I recall his cooking and not what he ever said to me? His voice is a ghostly scratch on the chalkboard of my childhood. Damn, he was a bastard, going off the way he did.

'He should've never left the Air Force, you know what I mean? And yet, that's what made him turn to the booze,' Mom would explain, over and over. Who cares?

I have never married. I am forty years old. I have become an old coot. I work for a large newspaper. I have a food column. I have written a cookbook about desserts, YOUR JUST REWARDS, which was a bestseller. I drive an Eclipse and have four credit cards. I shouldn't be in debt, but I am. I eat well; I live well. Upon occasion I attend society events with rich widows and brittle divorcées who would marry me if I allowed them to. I'm a little paunchy, but who wouldn't be, critiquing all that food? It's a dirty job but somebody's got to do it. You betcha.

I should cut my own grass but I pay kids to do it. I need to exercise more. Lately, I've begun walking a bit in the neighbourhood. It's not the nicest neighbourhood in the world but it's not bad for a kid who grew up in a really low-rent area my mom called the wrong side of the tracks.

Candy Girl Decides to Leave the House

Sometimes you get so caught up in being wrong you can't get right. Thoughts spin round and round in your head and the loneliness screams at you till you can't hear anything.

When I was growing up I wrote tons of stupid diary entries. I found a box of them during a spring-cleaning attack. I sat right down and read what a silly kid I was but realized, when I compared them to my current journal, that not much in essence has changed. I'm still a silly kid in an almost middle-aged body. My friend from high school, Kirsten, would say, 'Amy, you ARE middle-aged – you just refuse to admit it.' She didn't, thankfully, add – 'and act like it'. I guess I should be thankful about that. Kirsten, the school teacher, is married to Hans, an entrepreneur in the plumbing industry with a lucrative sideline in toilet seats. They have three children, a nice home and two dogs, a cat, rich in the kingdom of family which I've somehow escaped. They know what love is. I'm not sure I ever will. I've been thinking a lot about it, though. I need to be touched but I don't know how to touch. Seems like every guy I date I scare off because I want to touch a lot and somehow I attract guys that don't like to touch a lot. My last boyfriend, Sid, one time recoiled from my embrace and said 'Jesus, I feel like I'm being raped.' We separated after that incident. Nothing like shame to kill the fire. I was ashamed of my desire. I just wanted to be held.

Mother didn't like to be touched. My father would hug me only when he had to, but that didn't bother me; when he did hug me, I knew he meant it. Mom just didn't hug me a lot after I started walking. She said that was sissy, that I wasn't a baby, when I'd ask for a hug or a kiss. They died when I was thirteen, victims of a drunk driver on some rainy April night. My grandmother, Ida, took care of me. She allowed a little touching, but not much. You'd think I wouldn't like to touch.

I am rambling.

I am alone too much.

I have three cats, Cleveland, Otis and Jo Jo. Only Otis allows me to pet him.

I have begun to talk too much. I took off a few days from the candy store. Or rather, the coffee and candy and croissant etc. store.

Opened it on the outskirts of a hip, increasingly upscale neighbourhood on the outskirts of downtown. I make incredible fudge. But in this world fudge is not enough. My little candy shop SWEET NOTHINGS quickly turned into SWEET NOTHINGS AND JAVA TO GO, then THE SWEET SHOP GRILL. Finally SWEET NOTHINGS became a separate entity, a name I marketed my packaged fudge under. I employ ten people now. I can afford to take off once in a while.

See what happens, though? I remember my hunger. My loneliness knows no autumn, winter, spring and summer. It is seasonless, seldom going away. Staying busy, that's the key. My grandma always said 'Idle hands are the devil's playmates' or 'If your baseboards are clean, so is your heart.' She showed me how to make fudge.

My mother liked to cook. She taught me how to make pie crust from scratch when I was eight. I do remember that even when I can't remember her voice or her face, although when I dream sometimes, she returns to me. I remember she used to touch me a bit when I was little. I do recall her holding me in her arms once and rocking me when I was sick. It felt so good. I was so happy, I wanted that moment to last forever.

I just ache sometimes. Is that a crime? I like making pie crust, the ooey-gooey texture neither too sticky nor too dry, resulting in a perfect crust or the perfect fudge – I can make it on the stove or in the microwave. It doesn't really matter, although I prefer the old-fashioned way. When it's perfect, not too hard, not too soft, it makes me so happy.

I've got to get out of this house. The silence is killing me.

I should do something.

I shall go for a walk.

The Gourmand Meets the Candy Girl

I should get some new shoes. My breath is on the verge of a doggy pant. Soon I'll start slobbering. This is ridiculous. I am out of shape. It's almost July. It's too hot for a walk. True it is a fine evening. June bugs and fireflies out in force. I had been wondering if both were on the endangered species list.

Hardly a breath of air.

There's a girl walking towards me. She's breathing kind of

341

heavy, too, although she's not paunchy around the middle like me, but her hips are a little broad. Her legs are a little thin, but pretty. I bet I could put my hand around her ankle. Her shorts are tight. Her breasts are drooping a little. Maybe she's not a girl, exactly. She's a woman. And she's smiling at me. I'm a little dumb. Life is not always a restaurant review.

I am aware I'm sweating a lot.

'Hi,' she whispers as she attempts to pass me.

'Evening.'

She nods, grinning now with an impish gaze not unlike my father's smile, a tangle of hair at a rakish angle. 'Hot, isn't it?'

We pause, simultaneously, viewing each other with sudden and self-conscious interest.

'Too hot, guess I'm out of shape,' I say, stating the obvious with a snorting laugh.

'Oh, you're okay,' she says. 'Good night.' The woman goes on her way. I want to follow her, only that might appear too serial-killer-like. Instead I head safely back home to my messy but air-conditioned refuge.

It's a little disappointing, though. My instinct was to follow her but I'm afraid. Hate to say it, but I am.

Candy Girl Makes a Pan of Fudge for Herself

'I'm an idiot.' I slam the front door.

Otis miaows his hearty agreement and heads for his dish. I automatically give him his snack. Cute little fishy shaped cat treats.

I begin to make a batch of plain fudge. My nerves begin to calm down. I can do this. It's okay to talk to strangers. A big meaty, sweaty man out getting much-needed exercise.

'I was sweaty, too,' I mutter, sniffing one armpit worriedly. Not too bad. A trace of DUNE still lingers on my wrist.

The kitchen is hot. I have to get out of the kitchen.

'I'm so tired of cooking,' I tell Otis. Jo Jo comes around the refrigerator and whines for his snack. 'Get it yourself!' Cleveland sits next to Jo Jo. Otis licks his paws. 'It's just not fair!'

I stare at the abandoned fudge and then down at the small roll of fat over my waistband as I bend down to give the cats their treats.

'Am I just too old and too ugly, or what? Did you say "fat", Otis? Look who's talking, you blubbery fur ball!'

The Gourmand Goes to Bed

I switch back and forth between David Letterman and Jay Leno, trying to decide if either one is a new show and not a summer re-run. I hate talk show re-runs. You can always tell in the opening monologue. References to historic events from a year ago or more. It's very depressing. I watch *Nightline* instead. It's too intellectual on a night like this. I bite into a Milky Way and marvel what I've come down to. Moping at home, sitting on a bare mattress. I pull on the old quilt I sleep with between my legs and ponder the pointlessness of the universe. I could go surf the Internet but I'm behind on my bills. I'm on two different servers.

E-mail is getting to be a bore.

One time I drove all the way to Denver to meet a provocative pussy I met through the Internet and discovered she was a balding seventy-year-old siren who'd been married eight times, hair black as a raven's wing. Claimed to be part Cherokee and part Choctaw. Claimed we were soulmates. The joke of the whole rendezvous was her decision that I had too much meat on my bones and not enough in the area that counted. At least to her. Yes, she got me to drop my drawers. She was seventy but she was built. Authored her own bestselling fitness books and videos, *Smart Abs for Seniors*, *Smart Butts for Seniors*, etc.

'Where is it?' she cackled, her claws grabbing for you know what.

It was very insulting. Not as insulting as my own stupidity. I'm tired of talk shows and mean old women.

That girl, though. She seemed so sweet. Once I had a girl as sweet as pie, who stroked my chest and made me sigh. I used to write poetry in college. Didn't get any published outside of the university lit mag. Recipes can be like poetry. I can write them. I don't cook, though. My secret's out. A bestselling cookbook author who doesn't cook. I appreciate.

I pull out the latest *Playboy* and search for inspiration. I abandon it for *Martha Stewart's Living*. I search and search till I find a photo of a smiling cook from some foreign country displaying her fudge, her eyes smiling but her face kind of sad, proud, still sad. It looks as if she's a little damp and sweaty. Her shirt's a little tight across her breasts. It looks like one nipple is about to burst the shirt wide open. I become aroused by this and I begin to soothe my naked body, still damp from the shower. My eyes shut for a second as I begin to stroke my penis, then flash open as my fingers reach for the magazine. 'Oh my God—' I sit bolt upright and look at the article more closely. She's not from a foreign country, she's from around here.

'I'm not just a candy girl,' Amy Carlton explained. 'Yes, it began that way. They called me the candy girl in high school because I made all the fudge for our fundraisers and then I won this fudge competition held by well-known cho-colatier.' 'It's her, good Lord. Where—?' I scan the entire article.

At the Sweet Shop

He has the sweetest eyes I've ever seen. He keeps looking at me with a smile. He's holding the magazine in his hand. I'm so embarrassed. He wants an interview. I ask him if he would like to eat first. He does.

'This cake is incredible. I must have the recipe.'

'So you can steal it?'

'Of course not, but now that you mention it, I may have to consider it.'

His hands are large. Everything about him is large. In a good sense. I like feeling small in the arms of a man ... I want him to encompass me, make me whole in his strength. I think I am falling in love. Look at the way he savours my cooking. The way his voluptuous lips smack just the tiniest bit and almost drool. The way his sleepy eyelids droop in languid joy over the homemade fudge icing.

I stare at his hands. I wonder how they would feel caressing my breast the way he caresses his fork, thumb brushing the handle as if it were made of the finest silver. He takes a bite of the devil's food cake. 'How have I missed this place? I must've been falling down on the job.'

'Well, Mr Barstow, what can I say – obviously you and your whole newspaper has.'

'I shouldn't have identified myself. Now I'll have to send someone else to review you. It's not our paper's policy to identify ourselves as critics. Still, I would like the paper to do a story on you. I'm sorry we haven't done one. I'm sure we will. Only I don't want to do the interview unless it's a personal one, off the record, on the most intimate level and could never be published. No, I don't want to review you, Amy Carlton,' Greg Barstow swallows the last delicious morsel and washes it down with milk. 'But I would like to take you out some time, my treat. You have the most incredible eyes.'

I tell myself it's not just a line as his eyes melt into mine. I realize they are the exact shade of Nestle's Tollhouse chocolate chips. 'A date?' I scan The Sweet Shop for eavesdropping patrons or Betty, my best waitress, but also the most nosey, or Will, her assistant, our high school intern. 'Why, Mr Barstow, and you haven't even tasted my fudge yet.' I can't help but laugh as he licks the last crumb off his index finger.

'And I can't wait till I do, Amy. And I really wish you'd just call me Greg. Okay?'

I feel weightless. My body may float to the ceiling. He might hold me. He might rock me. He might touch me in all the secret places no one has ever gone. He might eat me, swallow me whole. Drink me down. I'm so hungry and so thirsty.

In the Kitchen

The fudge was wonderful.

She took me to her kitchen.

We made fudge. I say we, but actually she did most of the cooking while I watched, taking furtive notes.

It's my father's fudge.

I don't know how she knew.

She said it was her grandmother Ida's recipe. Maybe they knew each other. I shall have to do some investigative reporting.

She keeps touching me. Her fingers place one more creamy morsel on my tongue. I go for her mouth. We share the chocolate. I lick. She licks. She's putting it down my pants. I freeze up then shiver with anticipation and dread. What if I'm not enough?

In the Bedroom

'Are you like all the rest?' I burst out. Won't he let go? Won't he touch me? Please? I find it. Not so big, not like the rest of him. 'Hold me close, please, Greg, please?'

On the bed, thrashing about. He is suddenly tearing off my clothes.

I am smelling him.

Sweet smells. Fudge smells. And flowers. Rose oil? Lilac? Lavender.

Vanilla.

When the skin touches skin and slides. Meshing. Melting. I want to get so close we become lost.

Rocking. In my mother's arms. I feel her breasts against my skin. My father's breath in her face.

'Daddy,' she cries.

'Momma,' I answer.

What enters him is something grown large from much longing, much loneliness. By being other I might bring back what is lost. 'Eat me,' I say. 'Swallow me whole.' I am thrusting all that is pain into the other.

The Gourmand is Satisfied at Last

We become one or the other.

Rocking in the boat of yearning.

It is no longer there. He has it and it's inside me.

The orgasm explodes in the microwave like an overcooked egg. Or like a cobbler with too much fruit in the pan, overflowing sticky sweetness. It's all over me. On my stomach. In my stomach. He eats me. My hands are my mother's hands shivering over typewriter keys. She never knew the Internet. She never was that free. He eats me. He licks my soul. My breasts drip honey on his breasts.

I sigh, holding his penis for one more kiss.

I am not hungry. I can't take one more bite.

The Candy Girl Grows Up and Becomes a Man

The hands keep blessing. The lips keep kissing. Touching is okay. What is lost can be found in the most astonishing way.

Sharing is caring.

Touching is releasing.

Love is a changeling thing. Like fudge. It's in the ingredients.

Separate, a cherry tastes good. Dipped in chocolate it is another thing. There are rules and then there are no rules. Absence and presence. Cherry fudge. Banana fudge. Fudge with nuts. Fudge without nuts. Vanilla mocha fudge. Coconut surprise fudge. Walnut and blueberry fudge. What is fudge? The best is plain chocolate without nuts. Simplicity. That's the bestseller.

In the dark you can be whomever you wish to be. It's not the penetration or the organ that penetrates. It's in being held,

349

the touching, exchanging souls. The not being abandoned, putting aside the anger and finding the lost child.

I am his father. He is my mother.

We swallow and go to sleep, our stomachs at last full.

NEIL GAIMAN

Neil Gaiman is probably best known as the writer of graphic novels and fantastic comic books, particularly *The Sandman* sequence. He also wrote *Neverwhere*, which was both a BBC television series and a novel about life underground in a mythic London. Born in England in 1960, he currently lives in the American midwest with his wife and three children. The following story looks at connections between sickness and sexuality and comes up with a completely new dirty word . . .

Changes

1.

Later, they would point to his sister's death, the cancer that ate her twelve-year-old life, tumours the size of duck eggs in her brain, and him a boy of seven, snot-nosed and crew-cut, watching her die in the white hospital with his wide brown eyes, and they would say 'That was the start of it all', and perhaps it was.

NEIL GAIMAN

In *Reboot* (dir. Robert Zemeckis, 2018), the biopic, they jump-cut to his late teens, and he's watching his science teacher die of AIDS, and we are following their argument over the dissection of a large pale-stomached frog.

'Why should we take it apart?' says the young Rajit, as the music swells. 'Instead, should we not give it life?' His teacher, played by the late James Earl Jones, looks shamed, and then inspired, and he lifts his hand from his hospital bed to the boy's bony shoulder. 'Well, if anyone can do it, Rajit, you can,' he says in a deep bass rumble.

The boy nods and stares at us with a dedication in his eyes that borders upon fanaticism.

This never happened, but the moment is central to all that occurred after, as what does not happen is so often the key to what does.

2.

It is a grey November day, and Rajit is now a tall man in his forties, with dark-rimmed spectacles, which he is not currently wearing. The lack of spectacles emphasizes his nudity. He is sitting in the bath, as the water gets cold, practising the conclusion to his speech. He stoops, a little, in everyday life, although he is not stooping now, and he considers his words before he speaks. He is not a good public speaker.

The apartment in Brooklyn, which he shares with another research scientist and a librarian, is empty today. His penis is shrunken and nut-like in the tepid water. 'What this means,' he says, loudly and slowly, 'is that the war against cancer has been won.'

Then he pauses, takes a question from an imaginary reporter standing on the other side of the bathroom.

'Side effects?' he replies to himself in an echoing bathroom voice. 'Yes, there are some side effects. But, as far as we have been able to ascertain, nothing that will create any permanent changes.'

He climbs out of the battered porcelain bathtub, and walks naked to the toilet bowl, into which he throws up, violently, the stage fright coursing through him like a gutting-knife. When there is nothing more to throw up and the dry heaves have subsided, Rajit washes his mouth with Listerine, gets dressed, and takes the F-Train into central Manhattan.

3.

It is, as *Time* Magazine will point out, a discovery that would 'change the nature of medicine every bit as fundamentally and as importantly as the discovery of penicillin'.

'What if,' says Jeff Goldblum, playing the adult Rajit in the biopic, 'just – what if – you could reset the body's genetic code? So many ills come because the body has forgotten what it should be doing. The code has become scrambled. The programme has become corrupted. What if . . . what if you could fix it?'

'You're crazy,' retorts his lovely blond girlfriend, in the movie. In real life, he has no girlfriend; in real life Rajit's sex-life is a fitful series of commercial transactions between Rajit and the young men of the AAA-Ajax Escort Agency.

'Hey,' says Jeff Goldblum, putting it better than Rajit ever did, 'it's like a computer. Instead of trying to fix the glitches caused by a corrupted programme one by one, symptom by symptom, you can just reinstall the program. All the information's there all along. We just have to tell our bodies to go and recheck the RNA and the DNA – reread the programme if you will. And then reboot.'

The blond actress smiles, and stops his words with a kiss, amused and impressed and passionate.

4.

The woman has cancer of the spleen and of the lymph nodes and abdomen: non-Hodgkin's lymphoma. She also has pneumonia. She has agreed to Rajit's request to use an experimental treatment on her. She also knows that claiming to cure cancer is illegal in America. She was a fat woman until recently: now the weight has fallen from her, and she reminds Rajit of a snowman in the sun: each day she melts, each day she is, he feels, less defined.

'It is not a drug as you understand it,' he tells her. 'It is a set of chemical instructions.' She looks blank. He injects two ampules of clear liquid into her veins.

In minutes, she sleeps.

When she awakes she is free of cancer. The pneumonia kills her, soon after that.

Rajit has spent the two days before her death wondering how he will explain the fact that, as the autopsy demonstrates beyond a doubt, the patient now has a penis and is, in every respect, functionally and chromosomally male.

5.

It is twenty years later, in a tiny apartment in New Orleans (although it might as easily be in Moscow, or Manchester, or Paris, or Berlin). Tonight is going to be a big night, and Jo/e is going to stun.

The choice is between a Polonaise crinoline-style eighteenth-century French court dress (fibreglass bustle, underwired décolletage setting off lace-embroidered crimson bodice) and a reproduction of Sir Philip Sidney's court dress, in black velvet and silver thread, complete with ruff and codpiece. Eventually, and after weighing all the options, Jo/e plumps for cleavage over cock. Twelve hours to go: Jo/e opens the bottle with the red pills, each little red pill marked with an X, and pops two of them. It's 10 a.m. and Jo/e goes to bed, begins to masturbate, penis semi-hard, but falls asleep before coming.

The room is very small. Clothes hang from every surface. An empty pizza box sits on the floor. Normally Jo/e snores loudly, but when freebooting Jo/e makes no sound at all, and might as well be in some kind of coma.

Jo/e wakes at 10 p.m. feeling tender and new. Back when Jo/e first started on the party scene, each change would prompt a severe self-examination, peering at moles and nipples, foreskin or clit, finding out which scars had vanished and which ones had remained. But now Jo/e's an old hand at this, and puts on the bustle, the petticoat, the bodice and the gown, new breasts (high and conical) pushed together, petticoat trailing the floor, which means Jo/e can wear the forty-year-old pair of Doc Martens boots underneath (you never know when you'll need to run or to walk or to kick, and silk slippers do no one any favours).

High, powder-look wig completes the look. And a spray of cologne. Then Jo/e's hand fumbles at the petticoat, a finger pushes between the legs (Jo/e wears no knickers, claiming a desire for authenticity to which the Doc Martens give the lie) and then dabs it behind the ears, for luck, perhaps, or to help pull. The taxi rings the door at 11.05 and Jo/e heads downstairs. Jo/e goes to the ball.

Tomorrow night Jo/e will take another dose; Jo/e's job identity during the week is strictly male.

6.

Rajit never viewed the gender rewriting action of Reboot as anything more than a side effect. The Nobel Prize was for anti-cancer work (rebooting worked for most cancers, it was discovered, but by no means all of them).

For a clever man, Rajit was remarkably short-sighted. There were a few things he failed to foresee. For example:

That there would be people, who, dying of cancer, would rather die than experience a change in gender.

That the Catholic Church would come out against Rajit's chemical trigger, marketed by this point under the brand name Reboot, chiefly because the gender change caused a female body to reabsorb into itself the flesh of a foetus as it rebooted itself: males cannot be pregnant. A number of other religious sects would come out against Reboot, most of them citing Genesis I, 27, 'Male and female created He them', as their reason.

(Sects which came out against Reboot included: Islam; Christian Science; the Russian Orthodox Church; the Roman Catholic Church (with a number of dissenting voices); the Unification Church; Orthodox Trek Fandom; Orthodox Judaism; the Fundamentalist Alliance of the USA.

Sects which came out in favour of Reboot use where deemed the appropriate treatment by a qualified medical doctor included: most Buddhists; the Church of Jesus Christ of Latter-day Saints; the Greek Orthodox Church; the Church of Scientology; the Anglican Church (with a number of dissenting voices); New Trek Fandom; Liberal and Reform Judaism; The New Age Coalition of America.

Sects which initially came out in favour of using Reboot recreationally: none.)

While Rajit realized that Reboot would make gender reassignment surgery obsolete, it never occurred to him that anyone might wish to take it for reasons of desire or curiosity or escape. Thus, he never foresaw the black market in Reboot and similar chemical triggers; nor that, within fifteen years of Reboot's commercial release and FDA approval, illegal sales of the designer Reboot knock-offs (*bootlegs*, as they were soon known) would outsell heroin and cocaine, gram for gram, more than ten times over.

7.

In several of the New Communist States of Eastern Europe, possession of bootlegs carried a mandatory death sentence.

In Thailand and Mongolia it was reported that boys were being forcibly rebooted into girls, to increase their worth as prostitutes.

In China, newborn girls were rebooted to boys: families would save all they had for a single dose. The old people died of cancer as before. The subsequent birthrate crisis was not perceived as a problem until it was too late, the proposed drastic solutions proved difficult to implement and led, in their own way, to the last Chinese revolution.

Amnesty International reported that in several of the Pan-Arabic countries men who could not easily demonstrate that they had been born male and were not in fact women escaping the veil, were being imprisoned and, in many cases, raped and killed. Most Arab leaders denied that either phenomenon was occurring or had ever occurred.

8.

Rajit is in his sixties when he reads in the *New Yorker* that the word 'Change' is gathering to itself connotations of deep indecency and taboo.

Schoolchildren giggle embarrassedly when they encounter phrases like 'I needed a change' or 'Time for change' or *The Winds of Change* in their studies of pre-twenty-first-century literature. In an English class in Norwich horrified smutty sniggers greet a fourteen-year-old's discovery of 'a change is as good as a rest'.

A representative of the King's English Society writes a letter to *The Times*, deploring the loss of another perfectly good word to the English language.

Several years later a youth in Streatham is successfully prosecuted for publicly wearing a T-shirt with the slogan, 'I'm a Changed Man!' printed clearly upon it.

9.

Jackie works in Blossoms, a nightclub in West Hollywood. There are dozens, if not hundreds of Jackies in Los Angeles, thousands of them across the country, hundreds of thousands across the world.

Some of them work for the government, some for religious organizations, or for businesses. In New York, London and Los Angeles, people like Jackie are on the door at the places that the in-crowds go.

This is what Jackie does. Jackie watches the crowd coming in, and thinks, 'Born M now F, born F now M, born M now M, born M now F, born F now F . . .'

On 'Natural Nights' (crudely, *unchanged*) Jackie says 'I'm

NEIL GAIMAN

sorry. You can't come in tonight' a lot. People like Jackie have a ninety-seven per cent accuracy rate. An article in *Scientific American* suggests that birth gender recognition skills might be genetically inherited: an ability that always existed but had no strict survival values until now.

Jackie is ambushed in the small hours of the morning, walking out from Blossoms, in the parking lot out the back, and as each new boot crashes or thuds into Jackie's face and chest and head and groin, Jackie thinks, 'Born M now F, born F now F, Born F now M, born M now M . . .'

When Jackie gets out of the hospital, vision in one eye only, face and chest a single huge purple-green bruise, there is a message, sent with an enormous bunch of exotic flowers, to say that Jackie's job is still open.

However, Jackie takes the bullet train to Chicago, and from there takes a slow train to Kansas City, and stays there, working as a housepainter and electrician, professions for which Jackie had trained a long time before, and does not go back.

10.

Rajit is now in his seventies. He lives in Rio de Janeiro. He is rich enough to satisfy any whim; he will, however, no longer have sex with anyone. He eyes them all distrustfully, from his apartment's window, staring down at the bronzed bodies on the Copacabana, wondering.

The people on the beach think no more of him than a

teenager with chlamydia gives thanks to Alexander Fleming. Most of them imagine that Rajit must be dead by now. None of them cares either way.

It is suggested that certain cancers have evolved or mutated to survive rebooting. Many bacterial and viral diseases can survive rebooting. A handful even thrive upon rebooting, and one – a new strain of gonorrhoea – is hypothesized to use the process in its vectoring, initally remaining dormant in the host body and becoming infectious only when the genitalia have reorganized into that of the opposite gender.

Still, the average Western human lifespan is increasing.

Why some freebooters – recreational Reboot users – appear to age normally, while others give no indication of aging at all is something that puzzles scientists. Some claim that the latter group is actually aging, on a cellular level. Others maintain that it is too soon to tell, and that no one knows anything for certain.

Rebooting does not reverse the aging process; however, there is evidence that, for some, it may arrest it. Many of the older generation, who have until now been resistant to rebooting for pleasure, begin to take it regularly – freebooting – whether they have a medical condition that warrants it or no.

11.

Loose coins become known as *coinage* or, occasionally, *specie*.

The process of making different or altering is now usually known as *shifting*.

12.

Rajit is dying of prostate cancer in his Rio apartment. He is now in his early nineties. He has never taken Reboot; the idea terrifies him. The cancer has spread to the bones of his pelvis, and to his testes.

He rings the bell. There is a short wait, for the nurse's daily soap opera to be turned off, the cup of coffee put down. Eventually his nurse comes in.

'Take me out into the air,' he says to the nurse, his voice hoarse. At first the nurse affects not to understand him. He repeats it, in his rough Portuguese. A shake of the head from his nurse.

He pulls himself out of the bed – a shrunken figure, stooped so badly as to be almost hunchbacked, and so frail that it seems that a storm would blow him over – and begins to walk toward the door of the apartment.

His nurse tries, and fails, to dissuade him. And then the nurse walks with him to the apartment hall, and holds his arm as they wait for the elevator. He has not left the apartment in two years; even before the cancer Rajit did not leave the apartment. He is almost blind.

The nurse walks him out into the blazing sun, across the road, and down onto the sand of the Copacabana.

The people on the beach stare at the old man, bald and rotten, in his antique pyjamas, gazing about him with colourless once-brown eyes through bottle-thick dark-rimmed spectacles.

He stares back at them.

They are golden and beautiful. Some of them are asleep on the sand. Most of them are naked, or they wear the kind of bathing dress that emphasizes and punctuates their nakedness.

Rajit knows them, then.

Later, much later, they made another biopic. In the final sequence the old man falls to his knees on the beach, as he did in real life, and blood trickles from the open flap of his pyjama-bottoms, soaking the faded cotton and puddling darkly on to the soft white sand. He stares at them all, looking from one to another with awe upon his face, like a man who has finally learned how to stare at the sun.

He said one word only as he died, surrounded by the golden people, who were not men, who were not women.

He said, 'Angels.'

And the people watching the biopic, as golden, as beautiful, as *changed* as the people on the beach, knew that that was the end of it all.

And in any way that Rajit would have understood, it was.

GEOFF RYMAN

Sexuality, no matter how fluid, is usually perceived as an interaction between no more than two genders, male and female. More abundant possibilities have been invented in science fiction, may be played with in cyberspace, and may exist in some post- or trans-human future. In 'Omnisexual', originally published in *Alien Sex* edited by Ellen Datlow, sexual feelings embrace the universe. At the time, its author called it 'probably the most optimistic story I've written, and, I hope, the sexiest'.

Geoff Ryman lives in London. He is an award-winning author whose novels include *The Unconquered Country*, *The Child Garden* and *Was . . .* His *253: A Novel for the Internet in Seven Cars and a Crash* can be accessed at www.rymannovel.com. The 'print remix' was published by HarperCollins earlier this year.

Omnisexual

There were birds inside of her. Was she giving birth to them? One of them fluttered its wings against the walls of her uterus. He felt the wings flutter too. He felt what she felt in a paradise of reciprocity, but she was not real. This world had given birth to her, out of memory.

A dove shrugged its way out of her. Its round white face, its surprised black eyes made him smile. It blinked, coated with juices, and then, with a final series of convulsions, pulled itself free. The woman put it on her stomach to warm it, and it lay between them, cleaning itself. Very suddenly, it flew away.

He buried his face in her, loving the taste of her.

'Stay there,' she told him, holding his head, showing him where to put his tongue.

And he felt his own tongue, on a sensitive new gash that had seemed to open up along the middle of his scrotum.

She was delivered of fine milky substance that tasted of white chocolate. It sustained him through the days he spent with her.

She gave birth to a hummingbird. He knew then what was happening. DNA encodes both memory and genes. Here, in this other place and time, memory and genes were confused. She was giving birth to memories.

'Almost, almost,' she warned him, and held his head again. The hummingbird passed between them, working its way out of her and down his throat. Breathing very carefully, not daring to move in case he choked, he felt a wad of warm feathers clench and gather. He felt the current of his breath pass over its back, and he swallowed, to help it.

It made a nest in his stomach. Humming with its wings, it produced a sensation of continual excitement. He knew he would digest it. The walls of its cells would break down, giving up their burden of genes. He knew they would join with his own. Life here worked in different ways.

He became pregnant. All over his skin, huge pale blisters bubbled up, yearning to be lanced. He clawed at them until they burst, with a satisfying lunging outward of fluid and new life.

He gave birth to things that looked like raw liver. He squeezed them out from under the pale loose skin of the broken blisters, and on to the ground. They pulled themselves up into knots of muscle and stretched themselves out again. In this way, they drew themselves across the ground, dust sticking to each of them like a fine suede coat.

They could speak, with tiny voices. 'Home,' they cried. 'Home, home, home,' like birds. They wanted to go back to him. They were part of him, they remembered being him, they had no form. They needed his form to act. They clustered around him for warmth at night, mewling for reentry. In the end, he ate them, to restore them. He could not face doing anything else.

Their mother ate them too. 'They will be reborn as hummingbirds,' she told him. She gave birth instead to bouquets of roses and things that looked like small toy trains.

He did not trust her. He knew she was collecing his memories from them. She collected people's memories. She saw his doubt.

'I am like a book,' she said. 'Books are spirits in the world that take an outward form of paper and words. They are the work of everyone, a collection. I am like that. I am communal. So are you.'

Her directness embarrassed him. His doubts were not eased. He walked through the rustling tundra of intelligent grasses.

The hairs on the barley heads turned like antennae. The grass was communal too.

When he came back to the woman who was not real, she had grown larger. She lay entwined in the grass, and hugged him; she opened up and enveloped him. Warm flesh, salmon pink with blue veins, closed over him moist and sheltering, sizzling like steak and thumping like Beethoven. He lived inside her.

Prying ribbons explored him gently, opened him up. They nestled in his ears, or crept down his nose, insinuated their way past his anus, reached needle thin down the tip of his penis. They untied his belly button, to feed him. Flesh was a smaller sea in which, for a time, he surrendered his independent being.

What conjunction could be more complete than that? When he emerged after some months, he was a different person. He had a different face. It had grown out of him, out of his old one. He looked into her eyes and saw the reflection of his new face. It was a shock. This was the face of a conqueror, a hero, older, like a head on a Roman coin.

Her eyes looked back at him, amused and affectionate. 'You will go away now,' she told him. 'You have become bored. You should always listen to boredom or disgust. It is telling you that it is time to move.'

On the other world, the world he had come from, there had been a fluorescent sign outside his window.

BUILDING TOMORROW, the sign had read, WITH THE PEOPLE OF TODAY.

It did not seem to him that this was possible.

Rain would pimple the glass of the window, breaking up the red light from the sign, glowing red light drops of blood. And he would listen to the wind outside, or fight his way along the blustery streets under clouds that were the colour of pigeons.

Everything was covered over by concrete. There were no trees; the buildings had been cheaply made and were not kept clean. The people were the only things that were soft.

People lived where they worked, crawling out from under their desks in the morning, sleepy, embarrassed, polite, smelling of body processes, wearing faded robes to blanket the smells, shuffling off to the toilets to wash. Their breasts, their buttocks were wrapped and hidden. Disease was a miasma between them, like some kind of radiant ectoplasm. He would rove the blustery streets, dust in his eyes, looking at the young people. He could not believe the beauty of their faces and bodies, and he ached for them, to think that they would grow old, and he wanted to hold them and to touch them, so that the beauty would not go unacknowledged or hoarded by only one or two others. He ached to think of them losing their beauty here.

He saw them losing it. He saw what they would become. The people he worked with had tiny cookers under their desks, and they made tiny meals. Everything in the office smelled of cabbage. Their faces went lined and apologetic and pale, sagging eventually into permanent, pouchy frowns. Loss provoked a longing within him. He wanted the old. He wanted to reach out for and soothe the ghosts of their younger selves and make what was left of their bodies bloom. He wanted the young, who were doomed.

They didn't have to live this way. They could choose freedom. He did. He had a vocation, a vocation to love. To have a vocation, it is necessary to give up ambition and normality. He went to live in another place where love was allowed because life there worked differently, and disease, and procreation. Those who went there could love without risk and come back clean. He did not want to come back. He gave up his desk and the smells of cabbage. He was called a whore.

This is not a story of other planets. It is a story of being driven from within. He was driven to a different place and a different time. Visitors came there to be loved and he loved them. It was a paradise of politesse. There were the approaches, elegant, or shy; and the jokes; and the fond farewells; and the mild embarrassment of separation when it did not work, and the kindly stroking of the hair that meant – this has been nice and now it is at an end. Some of them never believed he was not doing it for money. They left, believing that.

The man began to see that he had set himself an unending task. You could not touch all human beauty, not unless you flung yourself in threads across the space between the worlds and stitched all the people and planets together in one sparkling cobweb. You could not do it, give or receive enough, unless you ceased to be human. A paradise of politesse was not quite enough.

His tastes began to change. He wanted to go in and not out,

to stay with one person. He met the woman who was not real. He realized that this world had given her birth. Why she had chosen him, he did not know. Could she read his mind from his semen? First his tastes, and then his body had changed, from love and viruses.

And now he was bored with that, too.

He left the woman who was not real and walked across the austere tundra. His body had gone crazy. A steady stream of new life poured out of him, small and wet and sluglike, vomiting out of his mouth or dropping from the tip of his penis. He grew a pouch on his belly, to keep them warm. They would crawl up his stomach on batwings or hooks that looked like a scorpion's sting. Others darted about him like hummingbirds. His nipples became hard and swollen, and they exuded a thick, salty, sweaty paste. His humming children bit them to force out food. The others hung on to the hair of his chest or on to each other, mouthing him.

Berries grew on bleak and blasted shrubbery. He ate them and the fleshy protuberances that popped, like mushrooms, out of the earth. As he ate them, he knew that genetic information was being passed on to him, and through his breasts, on to his strange children. His body grew crazier.

Then autumn came and all his children dropped from him like leaves.

After the first snow, he built himself a hollow in the snow drifts. He licked the walls and his spittle froze. He lived in the hollow, naked, warming it with his body heat. He would crawl up the warm and glassy tunnel and reach out of the entrance to gather the snow. It was alive. It tasted of muesli and semen. He was reminded then of people, real and unreal.

Why had he come here at all, if it were only to huddle alone in a room made of spit? He began to yearn for company. He began to yearn for the forest, but a forest untouched by fantasy. He was a contradiction. Without simplicity, it is difficult to move. He stayed where he was.

Until he began to see things moving on the other side of the spittle wall and tried to call to them. He could see them moving, within the ice. Then he realized that they were only reflections of himself. He threw on his clothes and left the burrow in the middle of winter.

The snow was alive and it loved him. It settled over his shoulders and merged into a solid blanket of living matter that kept him warm. As he walked he turned his mouth up open to feed. Again the taste of semen.

The world was ripe with pheromones. It was the world that drew him, with constant subliminal promises of sex or something like it, of circumstance, of change. What use was an instinct when its end had no distinct form or shape? It was form or shape that he was seeking.

The snow fertilized his tongue. It grew plump and heavy. It ruptured as he was walking, spilling blood over his chin and down his throat. He knelt over the ice to see his reflection, holding out his tongue. It was covered with frantically wiggling, burrowing white tails. He sat down and wept, covering his face. It seemed that there was no way forward, no way back.

He broke off a piece of the ice and used it like a blade to scrape his tongue. The white things squealed and came free with peeling, suction-cup sounds. He wiped them onto the snow. The snow melted, absorbing them, pulling them down into itself.

He ate the ice. The ice was made of sugar. It was neutral, not alive, secreted by life, like the nuggets of sugar that had gathered along the stems of his houseplants back home. He still thought of the other world as home. He spurned the snow and survived the winter on ice.

He trudged south. Even the rays of light were sexual. They came at him a solid yellow. They shot through him, piercing him, making his flesh ache. They sent a dull yearning along the bones of forearm and thighs. His bones shifted in place with independent desire. They began to work their way loose, like teeth.

His left thigh broke free first. It tore its way out of his leg, pulling the perfect, cartilage-coated ball out of its socket with a sound like a kiss. The bone fell and was accepted by the snow, escaping. As he tried to find it, the bone above his right elbow ripped through his shoulder and followed, slipping out into the living snow. It too was lost. He was lame.

He drank his own blood, to save his strength. He walked and slept and grew new children. They were new arms, new legs, any of them, but they would not do what he wanted. They had a will of their own. They pulled back the flesh of his face while he dozed, peeling back his lips so that he gave birth to his own naked skull. His bones wanted to become a coral reef. They did not let him move. The plates of his skull blossomed out in thin calcium petals, like a flower made of salt. He waited, wistful, patient, resting, hopeless.

The spring came. The snow grew into a fleshy forest, pink and veined. There were fat, leathery flowers, and wattle-trees that lowed like cattle. Pink asparagus ran on myriad roots, chattering. His bones grew into dungeons and turrets, brain-shaped swellings, spreading fans, encrusted shrubberies. His body lurked in hidden chambers and became carnivorous again. It would lunge out of its hiding like moray eels, to seize capering scraps of flesh, dragging them in, enfolding them in shells of bone with razor edges.

Finally he became bored. Bored and disgusted and able to move.

The coral reef stirred. With its first shifting, delicate towers crumbled and fell. They smashed the fantastic calcium spirals and bridges. They broke open the translucent domes of bone. The whole mass began to articulate, bend. He pulled himself free, slithering out of its many rooms.

He no longer resembled a human being. He lay on his back, unable to right himself. It was the first night of summer, warm and still. Lying on his back, he could see the stars. He tried to sing to himself, and his many mouths sang for him. The forest swayed slightly, asleep, in the wind.

He loved the world. He finally, finally came to it. Semen prised its way out from under his thousand eyelids, scorching his eyes. It flowed from his moray mouths, from his many anuses, and from his host of genitals, a leaping chorus the colour of moonlight. The scrota burst, one after another, like poppy pods. He was no longer male. He slept in a pool of his own blood and sweat and semen.

By morning it had seeped away, given to this living world. The soil around him rippled, radiating outward. Everything was alive. Rain began to fall, washing him clean. Where he had touched the coral, he was stung and erupted in large red weals.

One of his children came to its father. It was no particular shape or gender. It had a huge mouth and was covered in lumps like acne. It was still an adolescent.

It found his real arms and legs, found the ones that were lame, and mumbled them, warming them. Deftly, with the tip of its tongue, it flicked bones out of itself, and pushed them through the old wounds back into place. Then it pruned him, biting, cutting him free from his accretion of form, into an approximation of his old shape.

'Ride me,' his child whispered. Exhausted, he managed to crawl onto its back. Hedgehog spines transfixed his hands and feet, holding him on to the back of his child. The thorns fed him, pumping sugar into his veins. As he rested, growing fat, he was carried.

His desires hauled him across the world. Staring up at the changing sky, he had opportunity to reflect. He could fly apart and pull himself together. His DNA could carry memory and desire into other bodies. DNA could combine with him, to make his living flesh behave in different ways. Was it only power that pushed him? To make the world like himself? Or was it that the world was so beautiful that the impulse was to devour it and be in turn devoured?

His child set him down in a cornfield. Great thick corn leaves bent broken-backed from their stalks like giant blades of grass and moved slightly in a comfortable breeze. He had never seen a cornfield, only read about them. He and this world together had fathered one.

'You have grown too heavy,' said his child. Its speech was laboured, the phrases short and punctuated with gasps for air. 'How long do I live?'

'I don't know,' he said. It blinked at him with tiny blue eyes. He kissed it and stroked the tuft of coarse hair on the top of its head. 'Maybe I will grow wings,' it said. Then it heaved its great bulk around and with sighs and shifting began its journey back.

The cornfield went on to the horizon. He reached up and broke off an ear of corn. When he bit into the cob, it bled. There was a scarecrow in the field. It waved to him. He looked away. He did not want to know if it were alive.

He walked along the ordered rows, deeper and deeper into the field. The air was warm, heavy, smelling of corn. Finally he came to a neatly cultivated border on top of the bank of a river. The bank was high and steep, the river muddy and slow moving.

He heard a whinnying. Rocking its way back and forth up the steep slope came a palomino pony. Its blond, ragged mane hung almost down to the ground.

It stopped and stared at him. They looked at each other. 'Where are you from?' he asked it, gently. Wind stirred its mane. There was bracken in it, tangled. The bracken looked brown and rough and real. 'Where did you get that?' he asked it.

It snorted and waved its head up and down in the air, indicating the direction of the river.

'Are you hungry?' he asked. It went still. He worked an ear of corn loose from its stalk, peeled back its outer leaves, and held it out. The pony took it with soft and feeling lips, breaking it up in its mouth like an apple. The man pulled the bracken out of its mane.

It let him walk with it along the river. It was hardly waist-high and its back legs were so deformed by rickets that the knee joints almost rubbed together when it walked. He called it Lear, for its wild white hair and crown of herbs.

They walked beside the cornfield. It ended suddenly, one last orderly row, and then there was a disorder of plants in a dry grassland: bay trees smelling of his youth, small pines decorated with lights and glass balls, feathery fennel, and mole hills with tiny smoking chimneys. Were they all his children?

They came to a plain of giant shells, empty and marble patterned. Something he had wished to become and abandoned. The air rustled in their empty sworls, the sound of wind; the sound of the sea; the sound of voices on foreign radio late at night, wavering and urgent.

All the unheard voices. The river became smaller and clearer, slapping over polished rocks on its way from the moors. The clouds were low and fast moving. The sun seemed always to be just peeking out over their edge, as if in a race with them.

They came to bracken and small twisted trees on spongy, moorland soil. There, Lear seemed to say, this is where I said I would take you. This is where you wanted to be. It waved its head up and down, and trotted away on deformed legs.

The man knelt and ate the grass. He tore up mouthfuls of it, flat inert and tasting only of chlorophyll and cellulose. It seemed to him to be as delicious as mint.

He walked into the water. It was stingingly cold, alien, clean. He gasped for breath – he always was such a coward about going into the water. He half ran, half swam across the pond and came up in the woodland on the opposite shore. Small, old oaks had moss instead of orchids. Rays of sunlight radiated from behind scurrying small clouds. The land was swept with light and shadow. Everything smelled of loam and leaf mould and whiplash hazel in shadow.

He sat down in a small clearing. There was a beech tree. Its trunk was smooth and sinuous, almost polished. The wind sighed up and down its length, and the tree moved with it. The soil moved, and out of it came his children, shapeless, formless, brushing his hand to be petted. 'Home,' they mewed.

Everything moved. Everything was alive in a paradise of

reciprocity. The man who was real had fathered the garden that had fathered him.

The woman came and sat next to him. She was smaller, flabbier, with the beginnings of a double chin. 'I'm real now,' she said. They watched the trees dance until the four suns had set. All the stars began to sing.

Acknowledgements

'Enough Rope' by Poppy Z Brite. Copyright © Poppy Z Brite 1998. A portion of this piece was originally published in *Dick for a Day* edited by Fiona Giles (London: Victor Gollancz 1997) and is reprinted by permission of the author.

'Pinkland' by Graham Joyce. Copyright © Graham Joyce 1998.

'Reflections' by Angela Carter. Copyright © the Estate of Angela Carter 1995. Reproduced by permission of the Estate of Angela Carter c/o Rogers, Coleridge & White Ltd, 20 Powis Mews, London W11 IJN.

'Nude on the Moon' by Paul Magrs. Copyright © Paul Magrs 1998.

'Juno' by Cecilia Tan. Copyright © Cecilia Tan 1994. Originally published in *Paramour Magazine* (Cambridge, Mass) Vol. 2, Issue 1, October 1994. Reprinted by permission of the author.

ACKNOWLEDGEMENTS

'Down the Clinical Disco' by Fay Weldon. Copyright © Fay Weldon 1985. First published by the *New Statesman* in 1985 and reprinted in *Moon Over Minneapolis or Why She Couldn't Stay* (HarperCollins, 1991).

'What's Normal?' by Mary Flanagan. Copyright © Mary Flanagan 1998.

'The New Girlfriend' by Ruth Rendell. Copyright © Kingsmarkham Enterprises Ltd 1985. Reprinted by permission of the Peters Fraser & Dunlop Group Ltd.

'The Secret Mirror' by Fernandes/Joyce Carol Oates. Copyright © *The Ontario Review*, Inc 1997. Reprinted from *The Poisoned Kiss and other stories* (New York: Vanguard Press, 1975) by permission of the author.

'A Dress' by Lisa Tuttle. Copyright © Lisa Tuttle 1998.

'Hymenoptera' by Michael Blumlein. Copyright © Michael Blumlein 1995. First published in *Dark Love* edited by Nancy A. Collins. Reprinted by permission of the author.

'James Miranda Barry' by Patricia Duncker. Copyright © Patricia Duncker 1989. First published in *The Pied Piper*, edited by Anna Livia and Lilian Mohin (Onlywomen Press, 1989) and reprinted in *Monsieur Shoushana's Lemon Trees* (Serpent's Tail, 1997). Reprinted by permission of Serpent's Tail.

ACKNOWLEDGEMENTS

'The Sweet Reward' by M M Hall. Copyright © Melissa Mia Hall 1998.

'Changes' by Neil Gaiman. Copyright © Neil Gaiman 1998.

'Omnisexual' by Geoff Ryman. Copyright © Geoff Ryman 1990. First published in *Alien Sex* edited by Ellen Datlow (Dutton, 1990), reprinted by permission of the author.